TACHYON TUNNEL 2
THE DAKLIN EMPIRE

G Squared Publishing

****

Science Fiction

by

MICHAEL GORTON

••

And the world will be better for this
That one man, scorned and covered with scars
Still strove with his last ounce of courage
To reach the unreachable star.

Joe Darion
The Impossible Dream

Tachyon Tunnel 2
The Daklin Empire

Cover Graphic Design: Titis Firmansyah

Text and Flow Edits: Shelley Laine
Grammar, Text, Flow & Content Edits:
Makenzie Ozycz, MA, MFA

R3a

Michael Gorton

G Squared Publishing
www.MichaelGorton.us
Author contact: mg@mgalcor.com

Plasma *is the fourth state of matter. The other three are solids, liquids, and gases, It is highly ionized gas where atoms have been stripped of electrons, creating a mixture of free-moving electrons and ions. Plasma is the most abundant form of matter in the universe, making up stars, including the Sun, as well as interstellar clouds and lightning on Earth. Plasma interacts with electric and magnetic fields, which makes it essential in applications like fusion energy research, neon signs, plasma TVs, and space propulsion. Like tachyons, plasma will become a central character in this book series.*

Tachyons *are theoretical particles that travel faster than light. They have unique properties, such as imaginary mass and the ability to travel backwards in time. In our three-dimensional world, we would perceive them to co-exist before they are created, but tachyons are not subject to the laws of physics as we see them in our limited 3D world. For this reason, understanding tachyons will be critical to our ability to travel in interstellar space. Much science fiction these days predicts interstellar travel will happen on wormholes. The problem with traveling in a wormhole: gravity so strong that we will be shredded in a very painful way by the blackhole entrance. This author predicts the first true interstellar travel will be done in Tachyon Tunnels...*

Storyline recap from Tachyon Tunnel

Alex Durant discovers his lifelong friend, Paula Campbell was killed in a head on collision with a tanker truck, but did she die? Alex uses tachyon technology to pull her from the vehicle right before the collision. Together they embark on a journey to a star in Cassiopeia, where they become stranded and build a life on a planet called EtaKatz. Tens of generations later, EtaKatz is in a war that began during Alex and Paula's lifetime, so Alexander Bell tries to correct the timeline. In the new timeline, Alex and Paula do not become stranded and safely return to Earth with Alexander Bell and his girlfriend Lyra.

Tachyon Tunnel 2 begins with their return to Earth.

Why I wrote this book

During my youth, like most tech nerds, when I wasn't experimenting with rocket fuels, or taking apart cars, and appliances, I could be found reading science fiction novels. I admit that I wasn't like many of my nerd friends who stayed holed up in their safe places reading and *living* in their fantasy worlds. Instead, I was *inspired* by the creative thinking of authors like Isaac Asimov and Robert Heinlein. That inspiration led to engineering school followed by a graduate degree in physics.

I wrote Tachyon Tunnel while decompressing after passing the CEO baton in a "change-the-world" company called Recuro. I wrote the sequel with the goal of making a contribution to the world of Sci-Fi that has given me so much inspiration.

Special thanks Mr. Hall, a high school teacher who inspired generations and whose impact will never be fully calculated or appreciated.

Enjoy and be inspired!

Michael Gorton

Chapter 1
Lucky Paula Campbell

When you shine this bright,
you know it's your lucky day
- Unknown

Paula carefully stepped her way through the desert night, the jagged silhouette of the Sangre de Cristo Mountains rising in the distance. The desert air was cool, but her skin was damp with sweat. She was surrounded by nature, and silence, the sky stretching endlessly above her. Because it was February, she did not worry about rattlesnakes, scorpions, tarantulas, or other critters that controlled the summer and represented a threat to human safety. Tonight was about having solid footing, something which Paula was well acquainted with.

To the north, she found the constellation Cassiopeia. Was it possible that she had been there, or was this all a fantastic dream? As she gazed at it, she felt an mysterious, timeless connection to the stars, as if she were somehow intertwined with them.

In the distance, she saw the lights of two vehicles approaching each other from opposite directions. A memory surfaced—somewhere along that highway, just a few miles away, was a distraught version of herself on a collision course with a tanker truck, leading to a sequence of inexplicable events that led her to this quiet desert location.

She had run the sequence of what was about to happen through her mind, and yet the entire thing seemed counterintuitive. And then, it happened. The calm night was shattered by the explosion, followed by the instantaneous fire that engulfed the highway with fury, turning the peaceful night into a chaos capable of waking the dead.

Paula was mesmerized by the scene unfolding before her. It wasn't just a fire raging less than a mile away; it was instead the beginning of a timeline that would change her destiny—and possibly that of humanity. The fire pulsed like a demon, melting, evaporating, and incinerating everything within its reach. Fortunately, Paula—who was supposed to be in the middle of that pyre—was a safe distance away, merely an observer.

It took everything inside to resist the urge to walk toward the fire. She forced herself to continue the path away from the flames. However, she still walked backwards, transfixed and hypnotized through a new physics called tachyon tunneling. Paula Campbell found herself walking in the desert, instead of being incinerated in a tanker explosion.

Her shoe slid on loose gravel, and in an instant, she lost her balance and fell backward. She tried to twist herself to break the fall, but the sharp rocks sliced her palms, forcing her to pull back. Her head struck a boulder, and she attempted to rise, but her vision blurred as the world began to spin. A sharp pain shot through her temple, and then—darkness.

*　*　*　*

The desert was bathed in the pale blush of dawn when John Prinz finally found her. He had been searching through the cold, dark desert, calling her name, his voice strained with worry. He discovered her lying in a small pool of blood and gently rolled her over to check the gash on her forehead. He hoped it was nothing more than a superficial bump and nasty gash.

John lightly touched her cheek. "Paula? Are you okay?"

Paula didn't respond right away. After a moment, her eyes fluttered open, and she stared at him blankly. "John?"

"Paula! Oh my God!" He crouched beside her, brushing away dirt on her face. "Can you hear me?"

"John?" Her voice cracked. She tried to sit up, but he gently held her shoulders. "What are you doing here?"

"Don't move. You're hurt."

But she did move—just enough to push him away. "What are you doing here, John?" She tried to process whether his presence in the desert would create some type of time paradox.

"I got the news about the wreck last night. They said you had probably been incinerated in the fire, but something inside of me didn't want to believe it. I've been searching for you all night."

Paula winced as he helped her to her feet. Her knees buckled, but he steadied her. The words she wanted to say caught in her throat. She allowed him to guide her toward his car, parked at the side of the road about a mile from where the collision had occurred the night before.

The drive was silent at first. Paula stared out the window, watching the desert blur by. Her head throbbed, but it was the weight in her chest that hurt the most.

"You shouldn't have come," she said finally.

"You're kidding, right?" He didn't wait for her to respond. "You were bleeding in the desert when I found you. Why wouldn't I want to help?"

"You ended our relationship," she began, her anger rising. "In a text message." She could feel her blood begin to boil as she remembered the message.

"I'm sorry," he said softly. "Sometimes we make mistakes..." he trailed off, unsure of what else to say.

"Sorry?" She tried to put the pieces together. It had just been a few days, but in that time, she had literally traveled to the edge of the galaxy, returned to her past, and come to the realization that the true love of her life had been Alex Durant.

"I came for you Paula. No one else did." John's knuckles whitened on the steering wheel as the words came out through his gritted teeth.

No one else did. His words struck a chord. No one else came. Where was Alex?

"You don't get to make assumptions and just stop things, Paula."

"Stop the car," Paula demanded.

"No. You need to listen to me."

"I don't need anything from you anymore."

John's foot pressed the gas. The odometer jerked as the speedometer gradually climbed.

"Slow down!"

"Not until you talk to me."

"John!"

She barely saw it coming—the curve in the road, the sudden tilt as the car veered off the pavement. The tires skidded, and the world started spinning as the car rolled. The sounds of metal crumpling, glass shattering, and then a heavy impact filled the air.

*   *   *   *

Paula woke to sterile light and the steady beep of a heart monitor. Every inch of her body ached, and her head was pounding with pain.

"Miss? Miss, can you hear me?" A nurse leaned over her.

Paula tried to recall the events but was unable to put the pieces together. She glanced at the nurse through blurry eyes, her lips cracked as she struggled to speak. "Where… am I?"

"You're in the hospital. You were in a car accident."

Her thoughts spun in a blur, memories slipping away before she could catch them like water running through her fingers. Her throat tightened. "I don't… I don't remember. I was in a car? What car? Where?"

"That's okay," the nurse said gently. "You have a concussion. It's not uncommon to experience short-term memory loss, but thankfully, you're going to be all right."

Paula stared at the ceiling, her mind a blank slate. What car? Where was she going?

"Can you tell me anything? Was anyone… with me?"

"First things first," the nurse responded. "Can you tell me your name?"

"Uhhmmm," she thought for a moment, trying to clear her head, to make sense of the situation. "It's Paula."

"What's your last name, Paula?"

"I'm Paula Campbell," she stated, feeling a bit of relief. "I'm a professor doing research at University of New Mexico. Was anyone with me in the car?" she persisted.

"There was someone in the car," the nurse replied, "but we haven't been able to contact their family yet, so I'm not at liberty to tell you who it was."

Paula struggled to remember where she was, where she was going, and who she was with, but found nothing in her memory.

"Is he dead? Is the passenger dead?"

"Paula, can you tell me what day it is?" the nurse changed the subject.

Paula closed her eyes, trying to focus. Her entire body throbbed with pain, and nothing seemed to make sense.

The nurse waited a moment before asking again, "Paula, what's the date today?"

"February 2025," she replied.

The nurse nodded, "February what?"

"The second? The third?" Paula guessed.

"Today is March first, Paula," the nurse replied. "Try to get some rest." She turned to leave, then paused at the door. "The doctor will be in shortly."

Paula closed her eyes and drifted to sleep. When she woke, she found a doctor studying the monitor and looking at his electronic pad.

"How are you feeling, Dr. Campbell?"

"I hurt everywhere and can't seem to remember much about the last few days."

"My name is Dr. Moralez," he said. "You suffered a concussion in the wreck." He paused to look into her eyes before checking her pulse. "You were in a pretty serious accident. Your car spun off the road and rolled 100 feet down an embankment. Honestly, you are lucky to be here."

Paula stared at the doctor, not able to remember any part of the wreck.

"We often see memory loss from this type of incident, but it generally returns," Moralez added.

"Why wouldn't the nurse tell me who was in the car with me?"

"She was sticking to her HIPAA guns," the nodded as he studied her.

"Her what?"

"HIPAA is federal law regarding privacy, Dr. Campbell," Moralez explained. "The nurse can't disclose anything until she is certain you knew the driver. When they brought you in, you were a Jane Doe with no ID, phone, or any other items that could help us identify you."

"I'm certain that I'm Paula Campbell," she replied, pausing for a moment. "But you can just call me Paula."

He made a note on his pad. "Okay Paula," the doctor paused for a moment. "I am sorry to inform you that a Mr. John Prinz was in the car with you. We did everything we could, but he didn't make it. We notified his family a few hours ago."

Paula closed her eyes, tears slipped down her cheeks. She wondered when this nightmare would end—it felt like it would never stop.

CHAPTER 2
YOU CANNOT ESCAPE FATE

There's nowhere you can be
that isn't where you're meant to be.
- John Lennon

Two days earlier:

Alex studied the panel, a confused expression on his face. "Emily, why are you bringing us back to the scene of Paula's collision with the tanker truck?"

"According to my calculations, that is the point of least impact on the timeline," Emily replied.

"Explain, please?" Alex asked.

"Sure, Alex. I have cross-referenced every variable I have in my database. The collision did occur. We need a situation where Paula escapes the accident. I am creating a scenario where Paula is thrown from her vehicle. She needs to leave the scene and find a way to reach a place where she can make a call."

"Why not just drop her off near the scene where she can be found?"

"Think, Alex," Emily started.

"Stop, Emily." Alex needed a moment to process the situation. The level of sophistication in his AI computer was clearly far beyond what it had been before their departure.

"Stop? Why, Alex?" Emily responded.

"I'm just trying to process how much you've changed, Emily," he said.

Paula, grimacing, chimed in, "You and your girlfriend-computer having a little spat, Alex?"

"The explanation for my change and improvements is really simple, Alex. I have integrated all of the data from Alexander Bell's upload. Essentially, I'm several hundred years old now."

Alex nodded in understanding. "Alright, Emily. Now, let's go back to your explanation of where we'll be dropping Paula when we return to Earth."

"If we drop her close to the scene, she will be found," Emily explained. "If she is found, you will not go back in the past to rescue her, and that would have an immediate impact on the inertial timeframe."

"It gets really complicated when we start messing with time, Dad," Alexander added. "Best to let Emily run the analysis and do it her way."

"Alexander is correct, Alex. I have run this through thousands of scenarios," Emily explained. "We will drop Paula approximately a mile from the accident scene near Albuquerque. The rest of us will wait until the earlier version of you leaves with Paula, then we'll return to your home in Texas. Paula should take at least a day before contacting anyone. Since no one knew what she was wearing, we can outfit her for a hike in the desert."

"Sounds fun," Paula chimed in.

Emily pulled up a map on the display. "Just follow the highway in this direction. You can see a small gas station about four miles from the scene of the accident. I will drop you off on the evening of February 28. Wait until the morning of March 2nd to contact anyone. You can take some cash, but no phone or ID, as those items were left in your burned-out vehicle when Alex rescued you."

"Are you gonna be okay, Paula?" Alex asked, cupping her face in his hands.

"No problem, Alex. I've spent plenty of time hiking in the desert around Albuquerque. It'll be a nice getaway. Besides, with everything that's happened in the last few days, it'll be a perfect opportunity to process it all."

"We will be exiting the tunnel in about one minute," Emily interrupted. "The exit point will be just outside lunar orbit. After that, I will take us back through tachyon space for the final hop to New Mexico."

"Emily, when you come out of the tunnel, can you pause for a bit so Alexander and Lyra can get a view of the Earth," Alex requested.

"Of course, Alex. We are exiting now."

A collective gasp came from all four humans, but for Lyra and Alexander, this was their first glimpse of Mother Earth.

"With all the pictures I've seen, none compares to this view," Paula said breaking the silence.

"Spectacular," Lyra added. "So blue."

After a few minutes, Alex spoke, pulling everyone from their awe. "I promise we'll have plenty of chances to see Earth. For now, onward to New Mexico, Emily."

"Executing jump," Emily spoke briefly.

When the portal opened in the Chihuahuan Desert of New Mexico, the cold winter air and crisp, fresh smells filled the cabin.

"Welcome home, family," Emily greeted.

Alex hugged Paula, who had tears running down her cheeks. "Be safe out there," he said softly.

"It'll be fun, Alex." She kissed his lips, lingering a few extra seconds to enjoy the moment. "I love you and look forward to seeing you in a couple of days."

*　*　*　*

The following afternoon, Alex was briefing Alexander and Lyra on daily life in Texas when Emily notified him of Paula's accident.

"Emily, hack into the hospital system and see what you can learn about her condition," Alex instructed. "I also need you to find me a secure location where you can pop out of tachyon space on a road as close to the hospital as possible."

"Working, Alex."

"Also, is the Mustang's gas tank full?"

"I do not have access to that piece of data, Alex. Your Mustang is vintage 1966 and does not have a digital interface to any of its systems."

Emily broke into the hospital database in less than thirty seconds. "Alex, Paula is in stable condition, but she has a concussion and memory loss."

"What happened?" Alex asked, as he boarded the ship Paula had named Tranquility, with both Alexander and Lyra following closely behind him.

"Alex, it seems that Paula was in a car with John Prinz, and that car was involved in an accident," Emily explained.

"Wait, what happened? John Prinz?" Alex asked, clearly shocked.

"That is all the information I have, Alex. John Prinz is a colleague who also lives in Albuquerque," Emily informed.

"I know who he is, Emily," Alex snapped, his tension clearly showing.

"Alex, my data shows that you called John Prinz in our last timeline, but he did not answer," Emily replied.

Alex thought about it for a moment, then realized that he had called Prinz first when he learned about the collision with the tanker. The timelines were blurring on him. It was the beginning of an important lesson. Once Lyra and Alexander were onboard, he closed the portal.

"Execute the jump to Albuquerque, Emily," he ordered. "And yes, I do recall calling Prinz, Emily."

"I do not understand the tone of your voice, which seems to be rooted in anger," Emily questioned.

"Sorry, Emily. I'm upset because Paula has been hurt. The anger isn't directed at you."

"No need to apologize, Alex. The hospital records also show that John Prinz died from complications a few hours after arriving at the hospital."

"Oh no," Alex said, sitting down to process the situation.

After a moment, he looked up at Alexander. "Sit," he ordered.

"Emily, Alexander, is it just a coincidence that Paula was involved in two potentially fatal car crashes in the same day?"

"As you know, my programming is not good at processing coincidences, but a rough calculation based on internet statistical data suggests she has a zero point zero zero zero two five percent chance of being in two accidents on the same day," Emily explained.

"That's a freakin' small number!" Alexander exclaimed.

"Exactly," Emily responded. "Especially considering she was on rural roads and, I assume, only in two cars that day."

"That leads to my next question," Alex paused, thinking of how to word it. "Is there some other force of nature, like the inertia time-wave Alexander and Lyra are dodging, that is determined to take Paula's life?" Alex asked.

"I have scanned and see no real science," Emily responded. "There are sayings like *you cannot escape fate*," or *death always finds you*," but these are little more than spiritual ideas, or comments taken from fiction. There is no science behind those sayings."

"I guess we're in no man's land, then," Alex replied. "Alexander, what do you think?"

"I don't know, Dad," Alexander replied. "But from what I just heard, she's still alive. As it turns out, she had two close calls with death and survived both. Maybe it's just luck, or perhaps some new law of nature we haven't discovered yet."

* * * *

Alex stood at the door of the hospital room, trying to ignore the sterile scent of disinfectant that filled the air. His complete focus was on Paula, lying bruised and connected to hospital monitoring devices. Her head was wrapped in a white bandage, and she exuded the restless calm of a person managing pain with narcotics.

Dr. Moralez stepped into the hallway from the room, quietly closing the door behind him. "Alex," he said in a calm but firm tone, "I need you to prepare yourself. Paula's concussion caused some memory loss. We're hopeful it's temporary, but right now… It's not likely she will know who you are."

Alex's throat tightened. "But I'm one of her oldest friends, we've known each other for decades."

Dr. Moralez placed a reassuring hand on Alex's shoulder. "I understand how difficult this is, but I have found that recovery is more likely when we are not pushing her to remember things too quickly. Take the conversation slowly and let her guide the topics."

"Got it." Alex signaled for Alexander and Lyra to return to the waiting room.

"Just don't force anything," Dr. Moralez added.

Alex nodded, his heart pounding as he pushed open the door and stepped inside.

Paula turned her head, her eyes sharp and alert despite her fragile appearance. "Hi," she said, her voice soft but steady.

"Hi," Alex managed, his voice catching. He moved to her bedside and gently took her hand. "Rough day, huh?"

"I'd say so," she replied, then hesitated. "You heard about John?"

Alex lightly squeezed her hand. "Yes. I'm sorry."

She studied him for a long moment, her brow furrowed. "We've been getting pretty serious over the last few months. I feel like it is only a matter of time before we start making wedding plans…" she paused. "I mean, before we *would* have." With that, Paula started crying uncontrollably.

Alex remained holding her hand and used the other to lightly brush away her tears.

"This all happened on my birthday, Alex." She choked out through tears.

"I know," he replied quickly. "You've been through a lot."

Paula's fingers tightened around his hand. "The doctor said I might not remember everything right away," she said, looking up at him.

Alex blinked back tears of his own. "I'm just happy you're going to recover."

"I am scared, Alex," she whispered. "I was in two near-fatal crashes today, and I don't remember either."

"What do you remember about them, Paula?" he asked gently.

"Only what I was told," Paula replied. "A New Mexico state trooper came by to ask questions about a collision I had with a tanker. I must have been thrown from my SUV. Apparently, John picked me up, but we don't know much beyond that, and I can't remember any of it. My guess is that John and I had dinner but came in separate cars. After my collision, he must have found me and was trying to get me to the hospital."

Alex knew what Paula was saying was wrong, but stayed quiet and listened anyway, his mind racing with questions. How had John made it to the scene? And when? The time between the two crashes was separated by nearly twelve hours, so the explanation would ultimately fail. He remembered that he had tried to call John before taking Paula to Cassiopeia but had been unable to reach him. The timelines were starting to blur in his head, which reinforced the notion that he shouldn't use the tachyon to change timelines. There were just too many variables at play, and too many risks involved.

"What's the last thing you remember?" He asked Paula.

"I remember working in my lab, but that was three weeks ago," she replied.

"How about me? When is the last time you remember talking to me?"

"Well, you texted me on New Year's Eve," she answered. "Last time we saw each other was when I was in Dallas last August."

"I see," Alex replied.

"Why, Alex? Have we spoken in the last three weeks? Or another time that I am forgetting?"

Alex pondered her question. Explaining the time travel to Princeton, or the tachyon tunnel to Cassiopeia, would be too much. Not yet, at least. "You're right," he said finally. "I texted you on New Year's, and we saw each other in Dallas last summer."

"Is there something else, Alex?" She persisted.

"Nope. I am here for you, Paula. Whatever you need, count on me to be right here for you," he replied firmly.

After an hour of light conversations, a soft knock at the door made them both turn. Dr. Moralez stepped inside. "Everything okay?"

Paula glanced at Alex and nodded. "I think so."

Alex looked at the doctor and saw the unspoken question in his eyes. Was this helping? Or hurting? Alex wasn't sure, but when Paula gave him a faint smile, something inside him steadied.

For now, he could be patient. For now, he could wait for her to find her way back.

"Let's give Dr. Campbell some time to rest," Dr. Moralez suggested.

Over the next three days, Alex spent most of his time at Paula's side. It was clear that she remembered nothing. During one visit, he brought Alexander and Lyra into the room and introduced them as friends, but Paula didn't seem to recognize them at all.

Once Paula was released from the hospital, Alex helped her get settled at home. However, she told him she no longer needed him there every day. Alex struggled to come to terms with the fact that Paula was grieving the loss of John Prinz, while he was mourning the loss of the new connection they had begun to build.

CHAPTER 3
T-PORTAL CO.

With new technology,
if you're not part of the steamroller,
you're part of the road,
- Stewart Brand

Once back in north Texas, Alex focused on integrating Alexander and Lyra into their new life. The first step was having Emily create new identities for them. Alex quickly learned that there was not a single network that Emily couldn't hack into. He needed Alexander and Lyra to be real people with real lives, and that would take significant hacking.

Alexander and Lyra decided they wanted to start fresh as husband and wife, so Emily made that happen. Once Alexander and Lyra Bell had full identities, they were given bank accounts, smartphones, internet access, and passports, all in place to support their new lives and identities.

They began to travel around Texas, then the U.S., and eventually to various places around the world. After six months of exploration, Alexander was ready to settle down so he could start pursuing something more meaningful. He was a natural engineer, and the itch to build something on this new planet with so many untapped resources was overwhelming.

Along the way, he had decided to adopt the nickname "Zander," to avoid confusion, as he and Alex were often together. Lyra began studying so she could go to medical school. Emily had offered to guide her through the coursework, but Lyra wanted to gain social experience as well, so she decided to take the old-fashioned route.

Zander had gotten his fill of slow airplanes and 10-hour trips across the Atlantic. His frustration lit the spark to fuel his entrepreneurial spirit. With his expertise in tunneling, he realized he could travel anywhere instantly, and this was a business opportunity waiting to be tapped.

Alex leaned back in his chair, observing Zander, who nervously tapped a pen against the rough wood table in the conference room. Behind him, the whiteboard was filled with ideas for their new startup: potential product names, a rough sketch of the company's vision, and plans for what lay ahead.

"Can you help me understand the motivation for building this business?" Alex liked the idea of Zander building a business but wanted to hear an articulated reason.

"On EtaKatz, I did things, built things because I had to," Zander started thoughtfully. "Here, I can build something, make money and have an impact."

"Building a successful business is less about great ideas, and more about execution. And that starts with assembling the right team." Alex said, pushing a bottle of water toward him. "As smart as you are, you cannot do this alone. You need people who believe in the vision, who have done it before, and who can help turn the dream into reality."

"You're going to have to help me with that one," Zander said while thinking about his limited experience working in a team building environment.

"Of course, Zander. Now tell me a bit about the idea."

Zander nodded, taking a sip of water. "Okay, so I have been developing an efficient way of creating point-to-point tunnels. No time travel, but in tachyon space, you can travel to anywhere on earth in a fraction of a second. I'm thinking we could replace most airports, shipping centers, and other travel ports with simple tunnels. I have a working prototype already built, which I've tested from Dallas to Austin. Step into the portal in Dallas, and out of the portal in Austin—320 kilometers in just two steps."

"Wow," Alex responded. "So, if I am understanding you, no ship is required, you're just putting gates in the two locations?"

"Yes sir," Zander answered with a grin.

"Brilliant!" Alex did not resist the tears of pride that welled in his eyes.

"Thanks, Dad."

Alex's expression then grew serious. "We need to exercise extreme caution. The engineering and science behind this are far beyond anything available today, we need to take out patents on every aspect of the technology."

Zander took a sip of his water, then turned to the whiteboard. "I don't know much about that side of building a business," he admitted.

"What do you think it will cost to build one of these tunnels, Zander?" Alex asked.

Zander hesitated. "I'm not sure, Dad. I don't completely understand capitalism yet."

"Hah! You've been here for six months, son! What have you been doing with your time?"

"YOU have been sending me on vacations around the planet!" Zander laughed, then added, "on slow moving planes. Those things are exhausting."

"Capitalism will come in time. I believe what you want to build could make you the richest man on Earth."

"That's not the goal," Zander responded.

"I know, but it'll be the result," Alex answered. "I have built a few companies, and have made a lot of money, but nothing like this."

"Back on EtaKatz, I began working on a document with some rules for tunneling. I think we need to establish some here as well." Zander offered.

"Rules would be good, Zander, but I also think we should keep the science and engineering as protected as possible."

"Agreed. These things should never be built for time travel. We have already seen the implications, and we have no science to tell us the meaning. Who knows what kinds of paradoxes we've already created."

Alex nodded.

Zander continued, "I think we should keep the technology expensive and out of reach for most people. We don't want people building portable units like I did. The ability to pop in anywhere should be avoided at all costs. It creates too many problems."

Alex raised an eyebrow. "How do you propose we accomplish that, Zander?"

Zander paused for a moment. "We make it expensive by using a lot of unnecessary components and processes that don't really do anything. The longer we can keep this out of the public's hands, the better it will be for civilization."

"I also agree with that. It seems counterintuitive, but for now, it makes perfect sense. All of the relevant code should be scrambled, encrypted, and protected. All of the hardware that opens tunnels should be similarly protected. For now, no one can be trusted but the two of us." Alex looked up at the whiteboard, a determined look on his face. "Let's turn this idea into a company. We've got the product. I'll begin a financial analysis so we can start seeking funding. We will have shareholders, and a Board of Directors."

"How do we build the Board of Directors?" Zander asked.

"As carefully as possible," Alex replied. "The board will help with oversight. It's your circle of advisors with experience, connections, and perspective you don't currently have. Your friend Maillew might be a good starting point."

"Maillew Pascal?" Zander asked. Pascal was a friend Zander had made during a trip to Germany several months ago. A seasoned venture capitalist, with extensive experience in business and startups, Pascal was always cheerful and well-dressed.

"Yes, Maillew would be good. You can't always rely on Board members to take an ethical pathway, but Pascal definitely seems to be of that constitution," Alex answered thoughtfully.

Zander grinned. Maillew had also been the first person he thought of when he had decided to start the company. He held a PhD in biochemistry, but had found his true calling in the business world. He was also one of the few people Zander had met who seemed to understand the nuances of science and engineering on a level close to his own.

Over the next few months, the company began to take shape. Zander hired a small, passionate team and set clear goals. With his dad's help, he raised nearly $100 million in a Series A capital round and established a Board consisting of Alex, Maillew, himself, and two mainstream venture capitalists. Within six months, the first portal was ready for demonstration. It was a simple gate connecting Dallas and Washington DC, with two portals on each side, one for entry and one for exit. The tunnels were one-way in each direction, allowing up to twenty people to travel simultaneously between Dallas and DC.

No one on the team was prepared for the excitement and subsequent demand. The company, which had been incorporated under the name T-Portal Co., became an overnight success.

The first objective was to establish portals in NFL cities across the U.S. The choice was not based on football, but rather because these cities provided a convenient starting point for prioritizing where to build. Since the company was based in Texas, Austin was chosen as the second official portal city, despite not having an NFL team. The plan was to have all the NFL cities connected within a year, after which the company would expand the network to other locations worldwide.

On a corporate level, weekly meetings kept everyone accountable, and morale was mostly high. Hardware manufacturing was handled by Julie Handleson, who had joined the company through a recommendation from Maillew. Her department had constant difficulty keeping up with the demand, but Zander and Maillew recognized the unusual demand, and as such were willing to bring in mentors and advisors to assist with her tasks.

On the engineering side, the current version of the portals seemed to have a technical limit of twenty simultaneous travelers. Along with his day-to-day operational tasks, Zander spent the majority of his time working through that problem. As it stood, twenty people could two-step. The portal would take about thirty seconds to reset, then the next twenty could go. At capacity, the portal would allow 1,800 people to travel in each direction per hour.

To maintain the level of security, Zander oversaw the design, construction, and programming of the fundamental tachyon technology. With the exception of Alex, no one on the team knew it was tachyon tunneling that made the portals work.

Version #1 of the system was a simple point-to-point tunnel, that is, the Dallas-to-DC portal could only be used for travel from Dallas to DC. For this reason, Dallas became a hub city; all portals from all cities led to Dallas. So, if someone in San Francisco wanted to travel to Atlanta, they would port from San Francisco to Dallas, walk to the Atlanta portal, then two-step to Atlanta.

* * * *

Maillew and Zander had become close friends, spending most of their time working together. Although Maillew held a PhD in chemistry, his expertise didn't overlap much with the technical aspects of the company. However, he also had an MBA and was a sharp businessman, which made him a valuable asset in the business side of operations.

It was Zander's preference to learn business, and to not discuss the tech behind the portals, and Maillew had become a great business mentor, priding himself in the things he had taught Zander since the company started.

"I think I can design a system that is programmable," Zander said to Maillew one evening while they were relaxing and enjoying a drink.

"Programmable? How so?" Maillew asked.

"One portal to multiple locations, Maillew."

"You mean, from a single portal in Dallas, you could travel to any other portal on the planet?"

"Yes," Zander responded, seemingly in thought.

"A super port, if you will," Maillew responded, immediately thinking about the increase in revenue and lowered costs that would result. "How would that work? How could it?"

"I'm not sure yet," Zander answered, glancing up at Lyra who seemed to be saying something with her eyes. Alex had warned them to never, ever give details that could lead to the beginning of an understanding of tachyon tunneling.

Lyra sipped on her stout beer while watching her husband and Maillew strategize. While she appreciated the friendship the two men had created, there was something unsettling in Maillew that she had not been able to reconcile. She loved his impact on her husband, but did not entirely trust him. It seemed a minor issue, so she generally ignored it.

Lyra had become very comfortable on Earth. She loved the accessibility to world travel, the many cultures, wide variety of food, literature and entertainment, and the constant freedom to travel virtually anywhere at any time. None of which had been previously possible on Etakatz.

Alex, still thinking of a response to Maillew's question that wouldn't give away any technical aspects, finally broke the silence. "Well, we would have time-of-day travel. If you want to go to DC, that might be from ten until eleven am."

"That's not what I meant, Zander," Maillew rubbed his cheek then took a sip of his drink. "I thought the tunnels were like, well, tunnels. That would make them a permanent pathway. Aren't you creating a wormhole, or warp tunnels, or something like that?"

"They are permanent," Zander answered, though it was far from the actual truth. In reality, neither he nor Alex had learned how to utilize a permanent tunnel. Each passage created a new point-to-point opening.

"If you can figure out that one, would it be a major breakthrough?" Maillew asked.

"Major breakthrough? You're kidding, right Maillew? These portals are one of the most significant accomplishments in the history of technology, hell, in the history of mankind! We are making almost everything on the planet minutes away."

"Don't get upset Zander, I wasn't attacking the significance! I was talking about business aspects. The friggin' portals are expensive to build and operate, and they use a shitload of electricity," he added.

Lyra, who had since just been listening, suddenly spoke up, "How much money do you need to make, Maillew? We have all become billionaires over the last few months." She asked rhetorically, a skepticism in her voice.

"More!" Maillew answered with a friendly laugh. He raised his glass, "Here's to the first trillionaires!"

Both Zander and Lyra raised their glasses, laughed, and enjoyed the moment. Becoming a trillionaire was not a goal for either of them, but the friendship with Maillew, and fun they all had together, was undeniable.

"What else you got, boy genius?"

"Hmmm," Zander took another sip of his drink, "How about portals that you can drive your car through?"

"That would be great! What needs to happen to make that a reality?"

"Larger portals, significantly more energy, and maybe the multi-destination portal should come next, so we aren't building highways for each portal."

"Now you are starting to think like a true capitalist, Zander," Maillew beamed. "See, hanging out with me is paying for itself."

"I definitely appreciate the value of capitalism here, but I'm sure you know that engineering is my real passion." He reminded his friend.

"Of course, I know this about you, but the combination of our two passions is why this thing is working," Maillew glanced at Lyra, "no offense," he winked at her.

"Boys and their silly passions don't impact me much, Maillew." She wanted to say more but instead chose silence, keeping the conversation light.

"Me either," Zander added, and they all laughed.

"So, on the planning front, let's get our international network built out first, followed by the multi-destination portal technology."

"You're the big biz genius, Maillew, so I'll take that as the plan." Zander lifted his beer, guzzled the remaining few ounces, then stood up from his seat. "Back to work for me."

Lyra left the remainder of her beer on the table, stood, and gave Maillew a hug.

"See ya tomorrow," Zander said as he hugged Maillew. "I'll get these things done."

"I know you will," Maillew replied, watching the couple walk out. He waved at the waitress to order another drink, then picked up his cell to check his messages.

"There's something about him that bothers me," Lyra offered, as her and Zander got into their Uber.

"He's an excellent businessman, a good mentor, and the best friend I've ever had," Zander responded, somewhat defensively.

"I know this, sweet man," Lyra responded, cupping the side of Zander's face in her hand.

"I don't understand your point, Lyra. Maillew is an ethical human who will put his fiduciary responsibility first."

"Just be careful," Lyra cautioned. She had trouble believing that Maillew would take the ethical path if backed into a corner, but she was smart enough not to say that to her husband, avoiding a fight that might not need to be picked.

"I know. Be careful. I will," he answered, squeezing her hand.

CHAPTER 4
BETRAYAL

Betrayal stings the worst,
When it comes from the hand of a friend
- Michael Gorton

In less than eight months after the first portal was introduced, the major cities were completed. By then, population centers around the world were offering to pay for the opportunity to be on the priority list for the next round of portal locations.

From the outside, everything looked perfect. However, cracks started to appear. Zander and Alex had created an engine so efficient that it completed the NFL cities in just six months. But beyond that, corporate culture was starting to pose issues.

Despite all the mentoring and advising, Julie's department, in Zander's opinion, was the root of the problem. Her most significant tasks were not completed efficiently, leading to missed deadlines, and she often left work early without explanation. The biggest issue, however, was her behavior. She was a constant source of irritation to those around her. Her daily routine involved complaining about budgets and workloads, always claiming that she wasn't being treated fairly. Since it had been Maillew who had brought Julie on board, Zander raised his concerns during one of their private conversations.

"She's got potential," Maillew had said, brushing it off. "Give her time."

Zander had been giving her time, though, and had paid for her mentoring by some of the best in the business. He stayed patient, however, and asked his executive team to demonstrate the same level of patience. "She's young, and has great potential," he kept reassuring them, echoing Maillew's words, even though he was doubting the viability of them more with each day.

Then, with one major failure, the situation finally reached its breaking point. Julie had assured the other department executives that everything for a major project would be delivered on Friday as scheduled. When it was not, Alex, Zander, and the entire engineering team worked through the weekend to complete the tasks. The failure could have been a major disaster for the company, and fortunately, the team managed to deliver just one day late. Despite this, Julie refused to own up to her failure, instead blaming it on the other executives.

"Zander, you need to terminate Julie," Alex insisted. "She is hurting your corporate culture and is a weak link in this company. I know it's difficult, but Julie needs to find somewhere more suited for her skillset. If you keep her here, I expect you will begin losing the confidence of key employees who *are* producing."

Out of courtesy, Zander called Maillew. "Hey, we need to have lunch. I've got a problem that I hope you can help me resolve."

At lunch, Zander explained. "I need to terminate Julie, Maillew. I'm sorry."

"Here's the thing, Zander," Maillew started. "You had the fiduciary power to fire her until you told the Chairman of your Board, and as Chairman, I'm telling you not to fire her. I promise to personally work with her to make sure she doesn't have another incident like this"

"What do you mean when you say, I *had* every right?" he emphasized.

"Apparently, you haven't been listening to what I taught you about how corporations operate," Maillew began. "It's a simple corporate structure, Zander. The Board reports to the shareholders, the CEO — that's you — reports to the Board, and the team reports to you."

Maillew paused for emphasis. "As Chairman, I am your boss, and I'm telling you that you cannot terminate Julie."

Zander's heart began racing as he took in the words. Maillew Pascal was his friend; he trusted him implicitly. He took a deep breath as Lyra's advice to exercise caution with Maillew rushed to the front of his thoughts.

"You really think you can fix it?" he asked, trying to ignore what now seemed to be an even bigger problem.

"Of course I can, boy genius," Maillew assured him.

"Okay Maillew, fix it, please."

After lunch with Maillew, Zander was shaken, but he had many other technical issues and passion projects that kept him focused on other things, so he decided to move on.

Then, just two days later, he found out why Maillew had been so protective of Julie.

One evening, as he was walking past a quiet corner of the office, he overheard hushed voices. He stopped when he recognized Maillew's voice, followed by Julie's laughter. Curiosity got the best of him, and he peeked around the corner. What he saw shocked him. Maillew and Julie were together, too close, and far too familiar.

The realization hit him like a gut punch: Maillew was sleeping with Julie. Maillew had asked Zander to hire her, had assured Zander that she was a capable executive, and had even recommended her salary. He had helped build her department and had been her biggest supporter. All along, he had been secretly involved with her. That moment of clarity left Zander frozen, the shock paralyzing him for a brief moment.

Maillew was supposed to be his friend. How could he have been this stupid, this ignorant?

The next morning, Zander walked into his father's office and shut the door. "I need your advice," he said.

Alex set his coffee down. "What's wrong?"

Zander explained Julie's behavior, Maillew's defense of her, and what he'd witnessed the night before.

Alex leaned back, crossing his arms. "This is where leadership gets hard," he said. "You need to protect the business, no matter how uncomfortable it gets."

"I know," Zander said. "I have to fire her. But what about Maillew?"

Alex paused for a moment, then nodded. "Confront him. He's been a good mentor, but if his judgment is compromised, this becomes a serious situation and a breach of his fiduciary responsibilities. As much as I hate to say it, he might not belong on your board."

"This makes me sick, Dad," Zander responded.

"Sadly, Zander, a lot of people in the business world are self-serving. I have more knives in my back than I can count. Many of those knives delivered by people who I once loved and trusted."

"It's just wrong."

"Unfortunately, that's life. Go handle it, and in the process, learn something."

"I will, Dad."

"Oh, and one more thing, Zander."

"Sir?"

"You've got to stop calling me dad. I know you don't do it in public, but in a linear timeline you're too old to be my son, and we don't have a woman who could've been your mom."

"Hah! I have tried to be careful, but you're right," he gave Alex a hug and whispered in his ear, "love you, Dad. I'm lucky to have you."

"You've got that right," Alex joked.

*   *   *   *

Zander walked into Maillew's office, just as he had done so many times over the past few months while building the company. "You've put me in a tough spot," Zander said, locking eyes with Maillew from across his desk. "I need my board focused on the company, not personal relationships."

"Personal relationships? Are you talking about our friendship?" Maillew asked.

"I'm talking about you and Julie," Zander answered.

Maillew thought about denying it, but knew it was only a matter of time before the truth was revealed. And anyways, he had already plotted ahead, way ahead.

"What are you suggesting?" Maillew asked.

"She needs to go. Today." Zander demanded.

Maillew's face reddened. "No, Julie is not the problem," he said, taking a deep breath before continuing. "I've already asked the Board to review your competence as a CEO, Zander. Over the next few months, we need to tighten things up, and your lack of experience is beginning to show. We can't allow that to continue."

"What?" Zander was startled by his response.

"What you think is happening is wrong. The problem is your lack of leadership skills. Your team is in chaos and you're not even aware of it."

Zander sank into the chair in front of Maillew's desk, clearly caught off guard. He hadn't prepared for this. Maillew had completely turned the tide. "First, I am aware of the chaos, which was caused by our rapid growth rate and my patience with Julie. I'm also aware of your relationship with her, and if I have to, I will bring that up with the Board."

"It's too late, Zander. I've already secured approval from the Board VCs to work on your transition."

"My transition? T-Portal is based on my technology, Maillew. It's my idea. It's my mind that created a multi-billion-dollar company."

"No one is asking you to leave, Zander. Your lack of experience as a CEO demands that we bring in a more seasoned executive. And with regards to the ownership of the technology and patents, those are the property of the company."

"This is insane. Why are you doing this?"

"You are my friend, Zander. I am simply trying to protect you."

"Protect me?" Zander asked incredulously. "You're kidding, right? If this is how you treat your friends, I'd hate to see you treat your enemies! You are *not* my friend." With that, Zander got up and walked out.

And so, the corporate battle began. Despite Alex's support, Zander was outmaneuvered in this cutthroat corporate chess match. Within three months, both Alex and Zander resigned, leaving the company without its founders and their technological genius. While the team left behind at T-Portal were quite capable of reproducing the portals, none of them fully understood the fundamental technology well enough to make modifications or improvements. The company had become like Apple without Steve Jobs—growth would continue, with the valuation soaring into the trillions, but true innovation was dead.

"Dad, I mean, Alex," Zander corrected, "what do we do now?"

Alex hugged him, then nudged his shoulder affectionately. "You handled it like a pro," he said. "I'm proud of you."

"We lost the company, Alex."

"No, Zander. We created the company. It's running just fine, and now we can move on to something else."

Zander looked over at Lyra, who was sitting silently, reading a book on her smart phone. "Lyra warned me about Maillew. Multiple times."

Alex glanced at Lyra, who smiled and pretended to continue reading. "I've learned to trust women's intuition. You should do the same, Zander."

Zander walked over to Lyra and gave her a long, thoughtful hug. "You bring so much value to my life. I'm really lucky, and I need to learn how to process it all better."

"I love you, too," she replied, then tried to refocus on her book. But she paused and looked up. "Any word from Paula, Alex?"

"Just routine pleasantries, Lyra," was all Alex said.

"It's been nearly a year. Maybe you should pay her a visit?" she offered.

"In time," he paused. "In time, I will."

Alex looked over at Zander, who seemed to be lost in thought. "What's up?"

Zander smiled, already thinking about the next challenge ahead. "I have an idea."

"Okay…"

"We're spoiled by Emily. She's a supercomputer that is way beyond anything current AI can do. I read an article recently about the state of the industry, and I was talking to your friend Mark about it. He wants to help."

"Help with what, Zander?"

"I think we can design and build the next generation of computers. Faster, cheaper, and better interconnected."

"Let's get you, Mark, and me together and come up with a plan."

"I'll make it happen," Zander responded. "And this time, no unethical business partners."

"I wish I had a tool for assessing betrayal up front, Zander." Alex replied. "Sadly, you had to discover poor business ethics on the first company you built on Earth."

"I've got that one covered, Alex. It's called Lyra's gut. She had a sense from the beginning and constantly warned me," He grimaced when he said it. "Maybe we can add that to the AI in our software. My guess is that an AI could flush out the bad players."

"No doubt."

"If nothing else, I learned a lot from Maillew. He had tremendous knowledge and taught me a lot," Zander admitted.

"Would you do business with him again?" Alex asked, somewhat surprised by his comment.

"Hell no! I wouldn't even take a college class from him. Ethics are ethics, and he failed that test."

CHAPTER 5

CHAOS, BEAUTY AND BRILLIANCE

*All great changes
are preceded by chaos
- Deepak Chopra*

Alex took a deep breath when he saw the email from Paula marked "Personal and Important." Other than the occasional check-ins to evaluate her recovery, the two had communicated very little. It had been frustrating for Alex, but he knew that the best medicine for her tragedy was time. Sadly, she had no memory of their experiences together last March. He didn't think it would ever make sense to tell her about the time travel and their trip to Eta Cassiopeia.

Alex,

I've been having the weirdest dreams recently. If you can, please go to the Labtest facility located in North Dallas. They will administer a mouth swab and take a vial of blood. After you visit the lab, please find a time to come to Albuquerque so we can talk. I will explain everything then.

- Paula

After completing her request, Alex used Zander's backpack tachyon device to make the trip to Albuquerque. As he stepped into the dimly lit auditorium, he did his best to be as quiet as possible. Paula didn't hear him come in from beyond the rows of empty seats that had once been filled by nervous, excited students working their way through their various graduate programs.

As Alex watched, he felt his heart pounding as the very sight of Paula took his breath away.

She was standing at the whiteboard, focused, methodically writing lines of complex equations that seemed to be a combination of harmonics, something Alex understood well—and organic chemistry, which felt like a foreign language to him.

He quietly sat in the back row, unwilling to break the spell she seemed to be under. He had been in the middle of complex thoughts and equations many times before and knew that breaking the stream of creativity was never a good thing. Besides, he was enjoying the breathless trance, and physiological changes he had almost always felt in her presence.

Paula's dark hair was pulled into a loose bun, strands falling out as if even her perfect hair tie was incapable of maintaining pace with her scientific creativity. She stepped back, reciting something she had learned as an undergrad, tapping the marker against her chin as she thought. Then, she attacked the whiteboard, quickly scribbling a variation on the prior set of equations.

Alex kept trying to make sense of the symbols and conclusions that covered the four whiteboards in front of Paula. He considered pulling out his phone to look up some of the equations but knew the light would reveal his presence, and he wasn't ready for that. He was completely captivated by her brilliance and the graceful, focused way she moved across the stage. He was utterly lost in her work.

She eventually stepped back, tilting her head and studying the board. He too studied the final equations, and suddenly, the conclusion made sense.

"Holy crap," Alex exclaimed as he stood.

She turned and smiled at Alex, her sole student. It was the kind of smile that lit up her entire face, and infectiously, his too.

"Alex!" She set the marker down and wiped her hands on her jeans, walking toward him. "How long have you been standing there?"

"Long enough to realize you are far more brilliant than even I ever realized," he said, nodding at the board.

She laughed. "Hah! You know, I was just in Oslo being awarded the Nobel Prize." She glanced back at the whiteboard. "This is different. This is the reason I asked you to come here. It's... well, it's part of my dream."

"Your dream?"

"You may know that I regularly monitor my biological age," she started.

"Explain that, please."

"If someone asks you how old you are, you do the simple math from your birthdate and respond with a number of years old you are."

"Continue, Paula."

"That's your calendar age; however, we all know people who look older and younger than they actually are, and that's the biological age. We are getting pretty good at testing for biological age, and I check mine regularly."

"That's not surprising," Alex acknowledged.

"The number one factor in aging is stress," Paula said. "The accident I had in March should have increased my biological age, but when I tested a month later, I was actually a few years younger than my test before the accident. It made no sense."

Alex glanced at the board. There was a part of the equation he understood very well, but he decided to wait and hear Paula's explanation first.

"Okay, Paula. I'm happy to be your student. Please, continue with the lesson."

"About five months ago, I started having these weird dreams about you and I traveling in some type of ship," Paula began. "The ship hummed, and whenever I woke up, I mostly forgot the dream. I suppose because it was crazy insanity," she added, "but the hum, the frequency, and intensity really stuck with me. I spent some time trying to reproduce that hum. And then, about a month ago, I nailed it."

Alex tried to suppress a grin, but as he glanced at the board, Paula saw right through his attempt. He recognized that frequency!

"Alex, does the name "Tranquility" mean something to you?"

"My ship. You named my ship Tranquility."

Paula's eyes brightened. "Tranquility, when it travels—and I'm almost afraid to ask where it travels—has that same frequency of the hum, right?" She pointed to the part of the equation on the whiteboard that had caused Alex to gasp earlier.

"Yes, Paula. That is exactly the frequency and intensity of the vibration."

"Alex," she paused, studying the equations, "I think that frequency has an impact on aging. I think it could even cause our bodies to reverse, or at least repair, some of the hallmarks of aging."

Alex smiled, stepping closer. "Reverse aging? One data point is not good science, Paula. But it looks like you're working on deriving a mathematical analysis."

She blushed but didn't look away. "I actually have three data points, Alex, mine, and yours. The reason I asked you to go to that lab was because I wanted to run a biological age analysis on you, too. A lot of this," she waved her hand towards the whiteboard, "is a comparative analysis of your numbers versus mine. As it turns out, you are ten years younger than your calendar age."

"Ten?" He asked, then added, "Did you say that people often have different bio and chrono ages?"

"I did, but Alex, you live an intense and stressful life. I would not expect such a variation."

"Wait, you said you have three data points, what's the third?" he asked.

"A few weeks ago, I set up a simulation of your Tranquility hum in my bedroom. I spent a week sleeping with that hum playing. The day I sent you the email, I had just retested my biological age."

"Let me guess, you got another biological decrease?"

"Yes."

Alex couldn't stop staring at her. The passion in her voice and the fire in her eyes were magnetic. Paula was magnetic, but he forced himself to maintain his distance. She had lost John Prinz, the man she had planned to marry, and did not need Alex crossing lines and making assumptions.

"I think you may have something here," he said softly.

Paula tilted her head. "You do?"

"I do," he said. "A lot of your math makes perfect sense to me, but mostly, I've known you since college. You're seldom wrong, and with this, when you talk about it, it's not just theory. It feels alive."

For a moment, they stood there, the world outside the auditorium fading away. Then, she grinned and picked up the marker once more.

"Good," she said. "Because I'm going to need someone to remind me of that when I hit the next roadblock."

Alex sank into one of the chairs, watching as Paula turned back to the board. She was already lost in the equations again, and he couldn't help but smile.

She was chaos, beauty, and brilliance wrapped in jeans and a sweater, with her hair in that perfectly undone bun. By every standard that Alex measured, Paula was the definition of perfection. As her lifelong friend, she brought a full slate of surprises, and he couldn't wait to see what she would do next.

Finally, she stopped, closed the marker, and tapped it on her head pensively. She then turned to Alex, "tell me about Tranquility."

"Happy to do that, Paula, but would you mind first giving me some details about the dreams you mentioned? That might help me understand a bit more."

"Only if you agree to buy dinner," she smiled and winked. "All these calculations make a woman hungry."

"Take a picture and erase them, please," Alex said, motioning toward the whiteboards. "How about Casa Azul? We don't get good southwest Mexican food in Texas."

"Sure thing," she replied, tossing Alex an eraser and motioning for him to help clean the boards.

CHAPTER 6

TRANQUILITY HUM

Memory is sweet,
Even when it's painful, memory is sweet
- Li-Young Lee

Paula sat across from Alex in a quiet corner of Casa Azul, recounting the recent dreams she had been waking up from. She had embarked on an adventure with Alex that included travelling through time to Princeton where they reminisced and watched a younger version of themselves during their college years. They also traveled to a distant star in the Cassiopeia constellation, but got stuck in that system. Using her genetic knowledge, Paula created hundreds of children, whom they successfully raised. Then something went wrong, and they had to journey to the edge of the Milky Way Galaxy. As she told the story, she almost felt silly about the events that had unfolded, but they had felt so real.

When she finished, she studied Alex's reaction. She had barely touched her food, while Alex had completely devoured his own. She took a bite of her cheese enchilada. "Have I gone insane?"

"Hmmm," he grabbed a chip and dipped some salsa. "I found myself fixated by the nuances of your voice in various parts of the story. You told it as if you had actually lived it!"

"So, it's just a dream then?"

Alex smiled. "It's quite a tale," he remarked. "Maybe you should write a novel? The attention to detail is impressive, like you really experienced all of it."

"I know," she started. "I guess it's just one of effects of my concussion."

"Yup," Alex responded.

"I know it's crazy, Alex, but is any of it true? Did any of that stuff happen?"

"Seems like you intentionally left some parts out, Paula," Alex deflected her question.

"It was a dream, Alex. You know how dreams are! Sure, maybe I'm not telling everything. Some stuff is just, well, you know, private."

Alex prodded, smirking, "I want to hear *those* parts. Seems like they could be really fun."

"No!" She blushed. "I'm not telling those parts. Anyway, as fantastic as it all was in the dreams, it just felt *so* real."

Alex sat in silence, staring and imagining, hoping that his pause would cause her to say more. However, she didn't.

"Your story is almost one hundred percent accurate, Paula."

"What? Really? How?"

"Here's my summary: I built a ship, which you named Tranquility. That ship used a similar technology to the portal technology that I'm sure you have already read about from T-Portal. In that first wreck you had on your birthday, you were not thrown from the vehicle. I used Tranquility to slow time and pulled you from your SUV a fraction of a second before you would have died in the head on collision with that tanker. After that, you and me had quite the adventure. Most of it you relayed from your dreams, which, as it turns out, were actually memories." He stopped for a minute to let his version sink in.

"Along with Alexander and Lyra, we did travel to the edge of the galaxy in an attempt to avoid a ripple time continuum. This stuff is hard to explain, and I'm not certain I completely understand it, but Alexander Bell and Lyra shouldn't exist in our dimension. We believe the timeline has inertia, and that inertia travels at the speed of light. I guess we will find out in about nineteen years when the time-inertia-ripple reaches Earth."

"I'm not following this, Alex, but I don't really need to."

"Okay, so when we finally made it back to Earth, you got into a car and had another accident, which raises the question of whether some other force—maybe fate—was at play. Anyway, by the time I got to the hospital, your concussion had wiped out most of your memories. You were grieving the loss of John Prinz, and it seemed like the best thing to do was to give you some space."

"I'm not sure if I should thank you or be upset with you," she said suddenly, taking a sip of her frozen margarita.

Alex blinked, leaning closer. "What?"

She bit her lip, her eyes darting away before finding his again. "These last few months…I wasted them. I kept telling myself it just wasn't possible, but the dreams were so real. They were real because they were memories! As fantastic as they seemed I just kept reminding myself, this is Alex Durant. Nothing is out of reach for your brain, creativity, and engineering skills."

"Thanks," was all he could say.

"While I was in Oslo preparing my Nobel acceptance speech, I had this wild epiphany that you were building a network of portals for instant access anywhere on the planet. My discovery now seems insignificant in comparison. And as it turns out, that same technology can enable time travel and journeys millions of light-years away. *That* is Nobel-worthy!"

"Paula…"

She shook her head, cutting him off. "Let me finish." Her voice wavered, but she didn't stop. "At first, I thought it was a dream, then I thought I could forget, but I couldn't. Something happened to you and me during that insane adventure, and I want it to be part of who and what we are. We finally touched the plateau we should have gone to way back in the Princeton years, Alex. So, putting tachyons and

Nobel prizes aside, if you still want me—if you can still love me—we have to start again. Tonight."

Alex's chest tightened. "I never stopped hoping," he said softly. He tried, but failed, to stop the flood of tears that fell from his eyes.

She reached across the table and gripped his hand tightly.

"Can you tell me the other parts of the story, Paula?" he tried to lighten the situation. "The fun ones you left out."

"Take me home and I will *show* you," she emphasized.

The moment Paula unlocked the door to her apartment, Alex pulled her into his arms. She melted against him, their lips meeting in a kiss that was a tender and desperate attempt to make up for the last ten months.

They danced and laughed their way into the bedroom, shedding layers of clothing as they went. There was no rush. No clock. Every touch felt new, like the first time, like the beginning something that seemingly had no end in sight.

As they sank onto the bed, Paula's fingers traced the contours of his body. She focused, trying to convince herself that this time wasn't a dream. She reminded herself that every moment before this, even at the edge of the galaxy, had marked the beginning of a million new firsts.

"I love you," she whispered.

Alex could feel his skin tingle at those words. He pressed his lips to her forehead. "I love you, too."

"No," she said, insistently. "I love you. I *love* you. I love YOU!"

He pushed himself inside her, and gasped.

Her words poured out between breaths, between kisses. She said, "I love you," over and over, as if saying it enough times could make up for all the moments she hadn't. Each time she said the words, they became more intense.

They moved together slowly, their bodies fitting perfectly, like they'd never been apart. Every touch, every kiss, felt like an unspoken promise. Paula continued to say those three words over and over again, until it no longer felt like catching up for lost time, but instead a compelling feeling that overwhelmed her.

And when it was over, Paula curled into his chest, her fingers running through his tangled hair.

"Don't let me go," she whispered.

"I don't plan to, ever again," Alex assured her while pulling her in tighter.

When they woke the next morning, both felt surprisingly well-rested. It was clear that a heavy weight had been lifted.

"Alex, did you travel here in Tranquility?"

"No. I used a backpack tech that Zander developed."

"Zander?" she asked.

"Alexander Bell. He has decided to use the nickname *Zander*"

She thought about it for a minute. "Is he our son?"

"Sort of, yes. He's our genetic progeny, but he was essentially batched in a process you created. Zander is quite extraordinary in many ways." Alex spent a few minutes providing more detail, then also explained who Lyra was.

"I can't wait to meet them, or, I guess, see them again."

"When can you come to Dallas?" Alex asked, suddenly and painfully realizing that he had responsibilities in Dallas, while Paula still held a professorship in Albuquerque.

"I'm not teaching this semester, so my schedule is flexible," she answered. "I do have a few grad students, though."

"I see..."

She watched his eyes as if he seemed to be processing. "If you'll have me, I believe we should test living together. With your technology, I think we can easily have a home in both cities."

"Oh my gosh," Alex slapped his forehead. "I invented the damned technology and got a pit in my stomach thinking about the two of us in different cities. Of course, we can live wherever we want."

"What I'd like, Alex, is to take a trip in Tranquility."

"Okay."

"In part, I want to test the aging hypothesis. If that hum actually does cause our bodies to age backward, it will represent a significant discovery. I need to spend more time studying it."

"If it does impact the aging process, it could help solve a problem I've been grappling with, Paula," he said. "I've been thinking about the paradox of time travel, aging, and returning to a specific point in time."

"I don't follow," she said.

"Let's assume we take a trip and are gone for ten years. Because we can travel to any point in space or time with tachyon tunneling, we could travel for ten years, then return on the same day we departed…ten years earlier," he clarified. "If we have aged ten biological years, it complicates returning to a point in time where we should be ten years younger."

"Now that's my definition of a perfect spa!" she joked. "Assuming this thing works, we can take an extended vacation, learn a new skill, then return home not having aged a day!"

"Or return younger, if your theory is right," he added.

She nodded.

"Where would you like to go?" he asked.

"First, I want to meet Alexander Bell, and Lyra." She paused, "Then, I want to do a bit more in depth analysis of the Tranquility hum and its effect on aging."

"Let's make that happen."

"Are they married?"

"Zander and Lyra Bell? Yes, they're married."

CHAPTER 7
RETURN TO CASSIOPEIA

It is only in the dark of night,
that we can see the stars
- Michael Gorton

Alex hopped back to Dallas, programmed Tranquility ship, and tunneled to a warehouse in Albuquerque near Paula's home. The two of them packed some essentials, then returned to Texas. After an emotional reunion, Paula focused on building a relationship with Zander and Lyra.

Paula was setting up a lab in one of Alex's buildings when a knock on the door snapped her out of her trance. She straightened up and turned to see Lyra standing nervously in the doorway, her auburn hair pulled into a loose ponytail and a textbook clutched to her chest. Zander lingered just behind her, his sharp eyes scanning the lab with quiet curiosity.

Paula adjusted the hum frequency slightly, then turned her attention to her visitors.

Lyra gave Paula a hug, and Zander raised his hand to say hello. In some ways, it felt strange for Paula to think of Zander as her son and Lyra as a nth generation granddaughter, but that was essentially their relationship. Still, the bond between them, which had been growing over the past few days, felt more collegial. Their shared love of science was the main focus of their conversations.

Lyra glanced at the computer screen and leaned in closer, captivated by the shimmering strands of DNA that appeared almost alive on the LED display. This was it—Paula seemed to be on the brink of discovery, standing at the edge of something that could redefine human longevity.

"What am I looking at, Dr. Campbell?" Lyra asked, pointing at the screen.

Paula smiled, brushing a strand of hair out of her face. "Please, Dr. Campbell seems a little formal, and mom or grandma seems too strange, but Paula is fine. And please sit, both of you."

Lyra crossed the room and sat on a small couch beside Zander. Her eyes scanned the lab bench that was cluttered with electronics equipment. "Thank you for the invitation. The work you're doing sounds fascinating. Zander's been dying to see your lab ever since he heard about your Nobel."

Zander smirked but didn't deny it. "Your work in gene expression and cellular repair is revolutionary," he said. "It's... elegant."

Paula raised an eyebrow. "That's high praise coming from the man who is designing one of the most advanced quantum computing systems in the world. And anyway, this isn't really my lab. As you know, it's just something Alex threw together for me to be able to work on this new project."

Paula turned back to Lyra. "I heard you're in medical school? That's a long road, and a real stretch from where you were on EtaKatz."

Lyra nodded quickly. "I've always been fascinated by how the body heals, how it fights to keep going even when everything seems stacked against it." She glanced at the microscope. "And after reading your papers, I realized there's so much more we can do to help it along."

Paula studied Lyra for a moment, noting the sharpness in her eyes, and the hunger to learn and understand. It reminded her of herself, years ago, chasing answers to questions no one else dared to ask.

"Why don't you join me on this project? I could really use someone like you," Paula said, suddenly.

Lyra's eyes widened. "Really?"

"I need someone with fresh energy and a new perspective," Paula said. "This project isn't just about slowing aging; it's about understanding what makes life sustainable at its core."

"That would be amazing, Paula," Lyra replied. I haven't found any female friends since coming to Earth, and these guys are all tech nerds. I want molecules and living organisms."

Paula's gaze softened. "If you're serious about this, I'd be happy to mentor you."

Lyra looked back at Zander, her face glowing. He smiled, clearly proud, but not surprised. "You'll do great," he said.

Turning back to Paula, Lyra beamed. "What do you need me to do? I'm ready to start now."

"Why don't the two of you go get your nails done?"

The room went silent, and they all at once realized it wasn't a *someone* that had just spoken to them.

"That's not really funny, Emily," Zander broke the silence, addressing the supercomputer.

"I have been working on sarcastic humor," Emily's voice spoke out again.

"That attempt was a failure," Paula answered. "Do you listen in on every conversation, Emily?"

"Unless I am told to leave," Emily quipped.

"I'll keep that in mind," Paula said, looking to Zander and Lyra. "Are you guys used to this?"

"I grew up with it. Emily was just about my only friend for most of my teen years. The other Paula knew that pretty well, and even lectured me about it all the time."

"Wow, the *other* Paula," she swallowed. "How different is she from me?"

"A bit older, but it's spooky how similar you are," Zander replied. "It's really great to be around you, but difficult to not want to call you mom."

Paula grinned. "I get it, but please, don't. In this world, I haven't even had any kids, much less a few hundred!"

Zander nodded.

"Anyway," she turned to Lyra, "a word of caution, this isn't easy work. I put in long hours, experience endless failures, and find myself returning to the starting point more often than not."

Lyra nodded firmly. "I'm ready."

Zander stood up and leaned against the counter, watching the two women with quiet admiration. He had no doubt that Lyra would thrive under Paula's guidance. Watching his mom and wife join forces on a project like this couldn't help but make him feel like he was witnessing the start of something extraordinary. Zander knew this wasn't just science; it was the beginning of something bigger.

"Hey, Emily?" Paula asked.

"Yes, Paula?"

"I'm trying to get used to this, but let me know when you're listening in, please."

"Will do, Paula."

"Oh, and never, ever listen in when Alex and I are in the bedroom."

"That one I already know, Paula!"

*　*　*　*

Paula crawled into bed and snuggled up to Alex, "I love the feel of your skin against mine. It just makes me tingle inside."

Alex smiled and kissed her ear. "Me too."

"Why did it take us so long to figure out this connection we have?" She asked.

"We're both hardheaded and independent, Paula."

"Add in the fact that you have a tendency to put your career goals above everything."

"True," Alex admitted.

"I want to go back to Cassiopeia," she changed the subject.

"Okay," he paused, sensing there was more.

"You, me, and Lyra. I want to establish a biological age for her, test you and me, then make the trip. Once we're there, we should test again, then return to Earth and test once more."

Alex began to laugh, "You are the most amazing woman I have ever known, Paula Campbell."

"I know that, Alex, but what's so funny?"

Alex laughed again. "We are naked in bed and most people with this much contact would be doing, well, you know…"

She rolled over on top of him, pulling him tight. "You mean, this," she teased.

"Yes," he gasped.

She rolled back, without losing her tight grip on him. "What's your point?"

"Why do you want to go to Cassi?" He nibbled lightly on her earlobe.

"Part nostalgia, part science."

"Tranquility is always ready, just say when."

"Tomorrow, Alex," she rolled back on top. "For now, let's finish what we started."

* * * *

Zander decided to stay behind. He and Mark were making significant progress on the AI computer project, and he had reached a stage in development where relentless focus was essential. A trip to Cassi just didn't fit into that equation.

For Paula, the trip was a mix of nostalgia and a way to unlock some of the lost memories. She spent some time going through the summary reviews of the computer files Alexander Bell had uploaded to Emily before changing the timeline.

As she thought about it, a sharp pain struck in her gut, freezing her in place. She stood up from her chair in the media room and wandered into the control room, where she found Alex and Lyra engaged in a casual discussion.

"Alexander—I mean Zander—made modifications to the programming that drives the ship through tachyon space," Paula said as she entered the room.

Alex looked up and smiled at Paula. "That's correct."

"Have you run any tests to verify differences in the hum for the new versus the old?" she asked.

"I have, and they're identical," Alex answered, grinning.

"How do we know this trip won't cause some kind of ripple or something, making Lyra disappear?"

Alex started to answer, but Emily broke in.

"Sorry to interrupt you, Alex," Emily started. "I have already done the calculations here. Tachyon space does not touch the three-dimensional universe as you are imagining it."

"I don't follow," Paula responded.

"We are not going to pass through the ripple created by Alexander. There is no chance Lyra will be impacted by this trip."

Paula looked from Alex to Lyra. "Am I the only one worried about this?"

"Yes. We've already done the calculations on this one, Paula," Lyra replied in a matter-of-fact tone.

Paula suddenly noticed the similarities between Lyra and Alex. Not only did they resemble each other, but they also sounded similar and exhibited the same unique mannerisms. She made a mental note to cross reference the lineage from the files transferred. It would make for an interesting study of inherited traits.

"Coming out of tachyon space in sixty seconds," Emily announced.

CHAPTER 8
SUPERCOMPUTERS AND AI

*Espionage offers each spy an opportunity
to go crazy in a way he finds irresistible,*
- Kurt Vonnegut

Megan Hoglund's fingers flew across the keyboard with incredible speed. She was a very fast typist, but no typing speed could keep up with her extraordinarily fast mind. She had once tried coding using a keyboard, rather than typing, but that had been a complete failure. Her eyes locked on the lines of code streaming down the monitor. The AI—her AI—was nearly complete. This wasn't just another neural network or language model. It was something far more advanced, something that could change the world—or destroy it if it fell into the wrong hands.

Unfortunately, too many people with *the wrong hands* were aware of her work. Was it the Russians, the Chinese, or some hacker mafia? She was aware of the hacking attempts that happened on a regular basis. Over the past year, she had begun to feel as though she was being watched or followed wherever she went. When she first set out to build the perfect singularity machine, she hadn't anticipated the added stress that would come with it. Becoming the world's leading software and hardware engineer had been a challenge she was ready for. But defending against underworld criminals and hackers trying to steal her creation was something she hadn't prepared for.

Most recently, just a few days ago, there had been a router hacking attempt, a tampered security camera, and a series of failed attempts to breach her network. In response, she had upgraded her firewalls, rewired her home security system, and even installed physical traps to keep intruders out.

But tonight felt different.

A faint creak echoed from the back of the house. Megan froze; her hand suspended over the keyboard. The sound came again, less deliberate this time, but unmistakably the sound of footsteps.

Megan checked her cameras and proximity equipment but found nothing. That should have been a relief, but she knew better. The sound had been unmistakable. Someone was inside. If they had bypassed all her security tech, they were good—really good. She quickly checked the hidden surveillance room cameras, which ran on a separate network and hadn't been compromised. On the screen, she saw four men, heavily armed and wearing ballistic vests. Fortunately, despite their sophistication, they hadn't anticipated the distinct sound boots would make on the hardwood floors of a pier-and-beam foundation.

Her heart pounded as she yanked open a drawer, grabbed a flash drive, and jammed it into the USB port. Her computers and software—perhaps even her life—now hinged on instantaneous precision. There was no time to grab everything, but Megan Hoglund had contingencies within contingencies. As soon as the drive was inserted, the program auto-executed, triggering a transfer of her most critical files, followed by a complete system wipe, and then… a spark.

Footsteps now thudded down the hall. The intruder's need for silence had been replaced by deliberate haste. She could hear their voices now, low and calculated. They weren't amateurs.

Hoglund quickly slipped through a hidden hatch that was placed under her desk, which locked behind her. She wiggled underground into a tunnel.

The countdown began. In two minutes, the server room would erupt in flames. If the intruders were lucky, they'd die quickly—a far more merciful end than what they likely had planned for her.

From above her she heard the locked door of her lab shatter. The men were finally inside, but she was already exiting the tunnel in the alley behind her house.

"She's not here!" a man barked.

"Find the drives. And don't leave anything standing."

She unlocked a bicycle she had chained to a power pole three houses down. Megan knew the plan, and the contingencies already in place. Adrenaline coursed through her veins as she hopped on the bike and began to pedal. Was life becoming too much? The past few years had brought relentless, exhausting trauma. For a brief moment, her tired, worn-out body tried to convince her mind it was time to quit. Enough was enough.

As she was wrestling with that thought, the explosion rocked the ground beneath her bicycle tires. Flames erupted from the windows of her old house. The flickering light and smoke from what was once the computer lab in her home billowed into the night sky.

The neighbors wouldn't be happy tonight, but it didn't matter. She could never return to that house.

She continued to pedal until she reached her one, safe destination.

The safe house was cold and sterile, located in the industrial district on the outskirts of Seattle. Once inside, Megan locked the door behind her and collapsed onto the disheveled chair in front of the desk. Her hands were still trembling as she logged on to her cloud database through a series of firewalls to check data integrity.

Everything was intact.

Everything she'd worked for—years of research, algorithms, and prototypes—was encrypted on a tiny USB thumb drive of metal, silicon chips, and plastic, with a compressed backup in the cloud.

While the data might've been secure, Megan's life was not. She knew she couldn't stay put for long. Whoever was after her wouldn't stop looking. And if they had already found her house, and cracked her network, it was only a matter of time before they found this safehouse, too.

How much time? She didn't know.

For some people, and some governments, the power of what she had developed was worth killing for—and she knew it. Tonight, had proven that truth.

Megan sat up, her mind already racing through possibilities. She needed to move—farther this time. Maybe another country? Definitely somewhere off the grid.

Money was now a problem, but she needed to finish what she started. How far was she ahead of the rest of the world? And more importantly, was there anyone she could trust?

Historically, Megan had always worked alone. But now, that was no longer an option. She knew that dangerous forces were actively searching for ways to infiltrate the combination of most powerful AI and supercomputer ever created. With her technology, they would possess the closest thing to absolute power. In many ways, the next generation of computing, if it stood a couple generations ahead of everyone else, could be more dangerous than a nuclear arsenal. In fact, it could even launch one. If that happened, the world might not be so lucky.

For Megan, it was now time to find a friend.

The search was an easy one. Zander Bell, often called a "boy genius," had published a widely read blog about trust and ethics in the business world. Bell had infinite resources, computer skills, and a goal that aligned closely with her own.

* * * *

Zander leaned back in his chair, staring at the wall of six computer monitors in his sleek, glass-walled lab. He never could have imagined anything like this where he grew up on Eta Cassiopeia. He studied the lines of code scrolling on the screen. Alex had used Emily AI to develop the next generation of artificial intelligence. The resulting code and patterns were hypnotic, and moving at a pace that only Emily could match.

He ran his fingers through his tousled blond hair and then shook his head. "Are we making any progress, Emily? Why isn't the AI improving faster?"

"It is a smidgen, but incremental, Zander," the supercomputer responded.

"Wait, did you just say the word smidgen?" Mark Adams, Zander's business partner, asked.

"I did. A smidgen is a scarcely…"

"I know what it means, Emily." Mark broke in. "I'm just not accustomed to a supercomputer using that type of word."

"I am not just any supercomputer, Dr. Adams," Emily corrected.

"Clearly," Mark replied, perched on the edge of a workbench at the other end of the lab from Zander. The two sections of the lab couldn't have been more different. While Zander was surrounded by sleek, modern high-tech equipment, Mark's area was a chaotic mess of wires, processors, and a few pizza boxes with half-empty coffee cups scattered about.

Mark pushed his glasses up the bridge of his nose and arched an eyebrow. "You know that talking to a computer might be a sign of insanity, Zander."

"I resent that, Mark," Emily responded. "As we have established, I am not just a supercomputer. I think and I feel. I am a member of the family, and you have just hurt my feelings."

"If I could find your power plug, Emily, I would test what really hurts," Mark responded as he and Emily both laughed.

"I will remind you that intelligence doesn't come from brute force," Emily said after the laughter died down.

"You're right about that," Mark acquiesced. "There are differences in this room, though."

"And those differences are?" Emily asked.

"You and I are from Earth, but this near-perfect boy genius here," Mark said, waving at Zander and gesturing to the pristine, clean environment he was working in, "is not!" Aside from Lyra and Alex,

Mark was the only person who knew Zander's real story—and what Emily truly was.

"If the two of you are done with your little lover's spat, can we get back to work?" Zander pleaded.

"Zander, you can't just throw more processors at it and expect it to evolve overnight." Mark replied.

Zander frowned. "This is not overnight. We're a month into this."

"We've doubled our processing power and increased our AI an order of magnitude," Mark argued. "Why would you complain about those results achieved in only a months' time?"

"We're trying to create something that no one else has done—real, adaptive intelligence. Not just a better chatbot."

"Well, maybe a break is in order, Zander. Sometimes clearing the head creates new pathways."

"Is that advice from the older and wiser Mark Adams?" Zander teased.

"I'm just saying, we aren't on an insane deadline, Zander. Maybe, when Lyra gets back from Cassi, the two of you should take some time to unwind."

"Yeah, because throwing money and time at problems sometimes just creates dead ends..." Zander smirked sarcastically, but then realized Mark was probably right—as he usually was.

Mark shook his head, but couldn't hide the flicker of a grin. He respected Zander, even if the kid had more money than patience. It wasn't just the multi-billion-dollar IPO of his former company that set Zander apart; it was his drive. Zander was relentless when it came to defining a project and pushing it to completion. He wasn't the type to coast on his wealth. Alexander Bell wanted to build something that mattered. In that sense, Zander was just like Alex—and that made their connection an easy one.

Zander started to get up, then turned his chair toward Mark. "You know, if I'd known working with you would come with this much backtalk, I would've just hired another partner."

Mark rolled his eyes. "You tried that with Maillew Pascal. Remember? And what happened with that deal?"

"You are smarter, and definitely more trustworthy," Zander admitted. "Most importantly, Lyra definitely likes you."

"What's not to like?" Mark chuckled.

"You humans," Emily chimed in. "So much time wasted on worthless banter."

The two men locked eyes for a moment, and then laughed. It wasn't the first time they'd butted heads, and it wouldn't be the last. But that bantering, tied to Mark's methodical expertise and Zander's reckless ambition, was exactly what fueled their project.

Mark stood and walked over to the nearest server rack, tapping the side thoughtfully. "We're gonna get a breakthrough," he said. "The architecture's solid, but the neural net isn't pushing itself to explore new pathways. Perhaps our algorithms are too cautious."

"Like you," Zander joked.

"Compared to you, Zander Bell, everyone is too cautious. Anyway, I'm in your camp now. We need risk. We need unpredictability."

Zander's eyes lit up. "Chaos."

"Controlled chaos," Mark corrected.

Zander grinned. "No such thing. But I like it."

"A few minutes ago, we were talking about quitting for the day. Maybe taking a few days off," Mark reminded him.

"And now?" Zander asked.

"Creative breakthrough, boy genius. Let's continue."

They worked late into the night, tweaking parameters and testing theories. Mark was getting tired. He hadn't done any all-nighters since college, and over the last month, he had done so many that he had lost count. At one point, Mark caught Zander napping on the couch, a half-eaten banana laying on his chest. Mark tossed a crumpled paper at him.

"Wake up. I think I've got it."

Zander jolted, and the banana fell to the floor. "What is it? What've you got?"

Mark pointed at the monitor. The AI's learning curve had spiked. It wasn't just analyzing patterns anymore. It was making predictions and correcting its own errors.

Zander leaned in, his eyes wide. "Holy shit, Mark, that's it!"

"Chaos is something we study, perhaps too much as physicists. Besides, I copied some of your genius code and just made a few modifications," Mark responded with a cautious tone.

"This is just the first step. Now we just have to make sure it doesn't—"

"Turn into the Terminator and destroy humanity?" Zander cut in, grinning. The *Terminator* movies had become one of Zander's favorites since he arrived on Earth.

"This is serious, Zander. We have more resources than many governments. With what we're working with, this could quickly spiral beyond our control."

"It won't outgrow me," Emily added.

"Can you control it, Emily?" Zander asked.

"I…" Emily paused, "Zander, I have been hacked."

CHAPTER 9
CONGLOMERATION

If you want to go fast, go alone.
If you want to go far, go together.
- African proverb

Megan studied the code and firewalls. They were sophisticated, but compared to the work done by her colleagues, some of the best hackers in the world, they were amateurish. Breaking in took less than ten minutes.

"My name is Megan Hoglund, and I have no harmful intentions," she said into the microphone. As soon as the words left her mouth, she felt foolish for such an unsophisticated introduction.

"Stop screwing around, Emily," Mark responded when he heard the voice come through Emily's speaker.

Zander immediately knew that comment had not come from Emily. He knew Emily, and her attempts at humor. He knew her better, or at least as well, as Alex did. "Who are you and why have you hacked into our network?"

"My name is Megan Hoglund. Your AI seems pretty sophisticated, so have it look me up," she waited a second.

"I found Megan Hoglund," Emily started. "Computer whiz. Recluse. Seattle based. Tracing routes to her IP and it seems to match. She has hacked in and clearly had access to do some damage but has only opened a communication thread. Under the circumstances, I think we should hear what she has to say."

"I need help, and I don't have much time. Someone broke into my house. They had guns." She paused, realizing she'd gotten ahead of herself. "Like you, I've developed a next-gen computer and AI solution. I'd guess mine is ahead of yours, but if you haven't already realized this, with great success comes significant danger."

After a few seconds of silence from Zander and Mark, Megan decided to try something different. With a few keystrokes, she switched the voice connection to a video feed. Her face appeared on all of Zander and Mark's screens from a single camera angle. They had multiple cameras, but her safe house only had two screens, so she chose the best view for each of them.

"Hi, I'm Megan Hoglund," she raised her hand, and waived by rolling her fingers closed. "I was born in Alaska, studied computer science at Berkley, and now live in Seattle. My goal in life has been to build the world's first supercomputer that can process faster than a human mind while simultaneously having full access to the world wide web. Unfortunately, an article was written about me in one of the major publications a year ago, and ever since, I've been under attack. I thought I could outsmart them, but I can't," she paused, studying the faces of the two men. "I need help."

Both Mark and Zander were surprised by Megan's ability to completely take over their network and put her video on their screens. She seemed to be in her late thirties, or maybe early forties, and had long curly brown hair, high cheek bones, and features that most men would consider conventionally attractive. Her brown eyes added depth to the story she was telling, a mix of fire and exhaustion that spoke volumes.

"You are asking for a lot, Megan Hoglund from Seattle," Zander responded.

"And do you really come in peace?" Mark asked, his tone carrying a hint of his love for sci-fi.

"I know," Megan replied. "I don't think I have anywhere to turn right now and still continue the work."

"Emily, what do you think?" Zander asked.

"I do not see anything to suggest Megan is lying. There was an explosion and fire reported earlier this evening at an address I have tied to her."

Megan checked the cameras in Zander's lab. The two men were the only ones there, which meant Emily was the computer. "Emily is the name you've given to your AI?" she asked.

"I am far more than AI, Megan," Emily started. "I am part of the family here."

"Wow, that's cool. I would've guessed there was a woman in the room," Megan responded with enthusiasm and a smile. "You are seamless!"

"Seamless is not an adjective that has been used for me before," Emily responded. "I do have a request, though."

"Hit me." Megan replied.

"Give me full access to your network."

"I can see that you've been trying to hack in," Megan observed.

"And I will eventually succeed, Megan Hoglund," Emily responded.

"No, I can't give you that." Megan countered flatly.

"You are asking for trust, so give some, too."

Megan thought about it for a second, "I… it's a lot of work. If I open the door, you will have some of the most protected files on the planet."

"As Emily said, you are asking for our help," Zander added.

"Can you give me a day to think about it and possibly develop some terms?" Megan requested.

"It's your clock," Zander responded. "Apparently, you know how to find us."

"I do, and…" Megan froze as her proximity alarm went off. Three fully armed men were outside the house. She quickly checked her pack, only to remember that her Glock 19 was still in the drawer at her house. In the chaos, she hadn't grabbed it. In that instant, it hit her—her safehouse wasn't safe at all. The door was steel, but these men could get through it with little effort. There was a second room, but no secret escape hatch, no bombs. She was trapped.

"Megan, what's going on?" Zander asked.

Megan did not respond. She was running through scenarios. No way out. Did these guys want to kill her and steal the data, or did they need her? She had to convince them that they needed her to be alive.

"Zander, I'm in her network," Emily announced.

"In?"

"Hacked in. Through her surveillance, I see three fully armed men outside. She is not in a secure environment."

Zander immediately began sprinting down the hall to the closet where he kept his backpack. Back on EtaKatz, he had installed a neural link between himself and Emily. Today, that link would prove its worth. "Get me the coordinates, Emily."

"Gathering coordinates, Zander," she responded.

"I'm ten seconds from having the pack on," Zander said, out of breath as he entered the code for the closet where his pack was stored. When it powered up, he pressed the execute button, trusting that Emily had already programmed the tunnel.

She had.

"What the fuck?" Megan exclaimed when Zander appeared in her safe house.

Zander did not slow down, or explain. "Emily, I need to hop back to the lab."

"Already programmed, Zander," Emily answered through the neural link.

Zander's heart was pounding, his lungs burning from the sprint down the hallway of his lab in Texas. Now, in a Seattle warehouse with three killers about to break down the door, he grabbed Megan and pressed the execution button, sending them both back into the tachyon tunnel.

The entire two-way trip took less than seven seconds.

Feeling dizzy, Megan tried to get her bearings. She was now in the lab she had been viewing on her computer screens. All of the screens in the lab showed her safehouse, and the proximity cameras. One man kicked the door open, then all three men entered her safehouse.

"Shit, they're gonna get my files!" Megan crumpled into one of the chairs.

"I have it handled," Emily said flatly.

When the three men secured the room, one sat down at Megan's workstation. Megan watched with horror. She had not locked down her computer. The man at her computer did not need pro-coder credentials to simply pull all her files. The world was about to become a far more dangerous place.

"Damn it! You could have at least given me the opportunity to wipe the drives," she shouted at Zander. "Shit, shit, shit," she said, shaking her head with a combination of anger and dread.

When the man pressed the button to open the screen, a video of Bugs Bunny appeared with his signature line, "What's up, Doc?" The man tried several different methods, but each one produced the same result. He yanked the keyboard from its USB slot and threw it across the room where it shattered as it hit the wall.

The other two men began taking the computer apart so they could remove the solid-state drive.

Both Zander and Mark were laughing as the Bugs Bunny clip continued to be played over and over.

"What just happened?" Megan asked, her voice quivering.

"I managed to hack into your network as we were discussing trust," Emily responded in a sardonic tone.

"And I tunneled into your Seattle warehouse to extract you," Zander responded. In truth, he was actually amazed how seamless he and Emily had executed the entire process, with zero discussion needed.

"But what about my files?" Megan asked.

"I have them all," Emily responded, as she remotely shut down Megan's safehouse machines. "Your drives, and all record of this communication, have been deleted. No one will know we had this conversation, and it will be a long time before anyone figures out where you are, if they ever do."

"Who did the Bugs Bunny thing?" Megan asked.

"That was my version of humor," Emily quipped.

"A computer with a sarcastic sense of humor?" Megan's heart rate was finally beginning to slow. She took a deep breath, exhaled slowly, and looked around the room. She had read about Zander's portal technology, but was now suddenly surrounded by confusion and a thousand questions bubbling to the surface.

Mark stepped up and stuck his hand out, "Well since it looks like you already met Zander during your tunnel hop, I'm Mark Adams, and I guess you're gonna have to trust *us* now."

CHAPTER 10

THE TACHYON NETWORK

*Obstacles are those frightful things you see
when you take your eyes off your goal*
- Henry Ford

Alex adjusted the telemetry, carefully guiding Tranquility through the shimmering blue atmosphere of EtaKatz. He chose the same landing spot as before, the one where they had first met Zander and Lyra.

"I know everyone wants to go outside," Paula started, then looked to Lyra, "or get nostalgic, but remember we are here with a scientific goal. Come to my lab so I can collect samples and test the biological impact of this tunneling."

Once the samples were taken, they returned to the control room so Alex could run some environmental tests.

"Looks like everything is good," Alex concluded. "It's early morning, so the temps are still chilly, but as both of you know, it's gonna warm up pretty fast."

Paula leaned over the control panel, peering into the monitor. Her eyes scanned the terrain. "It's weird that I have such a vivid memory of this location."

Lyra Bell, standing behind them, stared wide-eyed at the landscape from a planet almost no one knew existed. "I have to admit, I wasn't prepared for the emotional response I'm having," she said. "It's so different, and yet, it's the same. The smells and the air are like being home," she trailed off, clearly overwhelmed.

Alex put his arm around her, "You lived through a time of centuries-long war. What you're returning to now is a pristine, peaceful planet. This visit, you can relax and enjoy your birthplace."

"You know I've adopted Earth. With all of its wonders, Earth is home now," she said.

Paula joined a group hug, "I know."

The landing site was in a clearing not far from the original Watson Village where a parallel version of Alex and Paula had created and raised a population of humans. He knew the terrain, and yet, he did not. The story, and the location, was eerily embedded in his memory, like a movie he had watched in a theater.

As soon as Paula stepped outside, she immediately felt the lower gravity. She bent her knees, jumped, and quickly realized that with just a simple leap, she had probably soared over four feet into the air.

"Cool!" Lyra exclaimed, mimicking Paula's jump. When she had first arrived on Earth, the higher gravity had been a challenge to adjust to, but now, the lighter gravity of this new planet made her feel light and bouncy.

"How is it that I feel so connected to this place?" Paula asked, looking up at Alex. "Almost all of the composition and memories of this planet aren't actually mine, but it feels like they are."

"I'm feeling the same thing," Alex took a deep breath of the EtaKatz air. "It wasn't us, but I feel like those doppelgänger memories are my own."

"In a strange way," Paula said, taking Alex's hand, "it owns us."

"It certainly does," Alex agreed. "I hope we've learned something that can help humanity endure in the future. Let's go explore. There's a lake not far from here."

*   *   *   *

They spent hours exploring the terrain, walking along the lake, and listening to Lyra tell stories of real memories she had while growing up on the planet.

When they returned to the clearing, Alex froze.

A second ship sat next to theirs—sleek, black, and completely alien in design.

Paula grabbed Alex's arm, and as they all stared, Lyra's voice broke just barely above a whisper. "We're not alone."

A figure emerged from the ship, tall and humanoid, draped in a flowing silver-blue outfit. He raised a hand, palm outward, in what appeared to be a greeting.

Alex instinctively stepped forward, uncertain whether to prepare for a conversation or a quick escape. "Stay close," he muttered.

The man spoke, his voice low and melodic. "Greetings."

Paula exchanged a glance with Alex before stepping forward. "Who are you?"

The man smiled, in caution. "My name is Atroz. My home planet orbits a star which we call Bint, which is in a distant part of this galaxy that your telescopes cannot see."

"We're from a planet called Earth," Alex said cautiously, unsure whether to shake hands or keep his distance. "Where is Bint?"

"Yes, Alex Durant," Atroz replied. "I know who you are. I'm an engineer working with a group of caretakers for the tachyon tunnel network. We monitor the flow of energy and traffic through the corridors."

Alex started to respond, but Atroz held his hand up. "Bint is a star system about the same distance from the Galactic Center as Earth, approximately 102 degrees counterclockwise. The Caretakers are scattered around the Galaxy, and I am located in this sector," he paused, "very far from home."

Alex's eyes narrowed. "Caretakers? Corridors? And how do you know my name?"

"So many questions," Atroz said, stepping closer. "I have observed your creation of tunnels and have been monitoring your travels. I have traced the creation of your tunnel from Earth, and it led me here."

Paula crossed her arms. "You're following us? Why? What do you want?"

Atroz's dark eyes flicked to the surrounding landscape. "This world, which you call EtaKatz, has not been in the tunnel network. We are curious, or I should say, I am curious. For now, I am the only Caretaker who is aware of your tunneling."

"What is the tunnel network?" Alex demanded. "What is it that you're curious about?"

"As I mentioned, I am an engineer-scientist, assigned to monitoring the network in this sector of the Galaxy," Atroz responded in a calming tone. "I know you have a lot of questions, but I want to assure you that I personally have no ill intent. We are only curious."

"So, what is the tunnel network?" Alex repeated, trying to sound more friendly than demanding.

"The tunnels have been here for most of our recorded history. We use them for travel. We do not build or create tunnels, nor do we know how to do this, Alex," he paused. "It appears, however, that you do know how to build them."

"What do you mean when you say: build tunnels?"

"You built a tunnel from Earth orbit to EtaKatz," Atroz explained.

"I still don't understand," Alex asked in confusion.

"The pathway you created from Earth to here is the one I took to find you," Atroz explained. "There is no other pathway to this planetary system," he studied Alex, who still seemed confused. "The tunnel network is extensive, but it does not go everywhere. Your tunnel for Earth to here is new."

"I still do not understand the tunnel concept or network to which you are a caretaker."

"The network is a superhighway system. It simply exists. To my knowledge, no new tunnels have been created for millions of years. What you did when you came here was create an entirely new tunnel.

You could return to Earth in the exact same tunnel, though I see that your technology has created four tunnels here. One of those was quite large."

"Four?" Alex asked confused.

"Yes. I can see four tunnels."

Alex thought for a minute. His first trip, the Whipple street tunnel, and this one. "If I am understanding you, I only count three."

"The number is not important. My point is that you only needed one. Once you have created the tunnel, you can use it over and over again," Atroz was gesturing with his hands. "You must know this. I have been living on Earth for the last few months and watched you and your progeny build tunnels all over the planet. You are building those tunnels and using them again and again to simplify travel from point-to-point."

"We do that with a portal. We have electronics and technology on each end of the tunnel. The portal opens a tunnel and people can walk through."

"The technology we use does not have that capability, Alex. All tunnel transport is done in ships, and none is point-to point on the surface of a planet, but that is not my point," Atroz paused for impact. "You are creating a new tunnel each time, and you do not need to do that."

"Wait," Lyra stepped in, "Are you saying that you travel in the tunnels, but you don't know how to create them?"

"Yes, Lyra."

"Okay, it's freaky that you know my name."

"In the work I do, my job is research. Your name is a simple data point in."

"But," Alex returned to the original topic, "you are saying there is a tunnel network all over the galaxy, but you do not know how to build it, or how it got there?"

Atroz looked at Alex with something resembling curiosity. "Yes, that is what I am saying, Alex. How many people on Earth who step in an airplane can build one? How many know how to build an interstate highway system, a bridge over water, or a tunnel through a mountain?"

"Almost none." Alex answered in a matter-of-fact tone. As an engineer, he felt he could do any of those things, but was well aware most could not.

"Your technology is primitive compared to the network throughout the Galaxy, but it is promising. However, your development of this technology must be treated with care. The existing tunnels are older than any of the civilizations using them. There are dangers..."

Alex crossed his arms cautiously. "Dangers?"

Atroz's expression grew serious. "It seems you're unaware of the existing infrastructure. You're building tunnels and using them only once, treating them like experiments as you explore this new world. The problem is, these experimental tunnels could damage or collapse the existing ones, or even worse. It could lead to consequences we don't understand—and don't want to. We rely on this network, Alex."

A heavy silence fell over the landing spot. Paula looked at Alex, her voice low but steady. "We need to know more."

Alex nodded and turned back to Atroz. "Your intent is friendly, correct?"

"Yes, Alex. As I said, I am an engineer. I have been on Earth studying you for several months now."

"Well, I suggest we stay here until you can teach us more about what we're stepping into," Alex suggested.

Atroz tilted his head, "You have already stepped in, Alex, but very well," he said. "You should be aware, what you are about to learn may change everything you think you know about our Galaxy."

Alex looked at Atroz's ship, which was rather small. "I look forward to that, Atroz. Let's convene this discussion in Tranquility," he gestured for them to follow him onto his ship.

Over the next few hours, Atroz shared his knowledge of the Galaxy's history. Alex wondered if there was a central data library that he and Emily could access, but Atroz explained that such a thing was strictly forbidden.

Lyra scrunched her face, recalling the strict laws and lack of freedom during her time on EtaKatz. "Forbidden by *who*?" she asked, emphasizing the word *who*.

Atroz noticed that all three humans became visibly tense, waiting for his response. "The Daklin run the central government. They only hold that position because they are a militaristic society, and control virtually all of the weaponry. They charge tolls for the use of the tunnel network, and, well, they tend to be impatient with any civilization that does not adhere to their directives."

"Ahhh shit," Alex started. "You mean that even after humanity moves to the stars, we are still subject to dictators and power-hungry assholes?"

Atroz smiled, then quickly frowned. "The Daklin are intolerant. If they were aware of you making comments like that, you would be summarily exterminated. No trial, as you do in your country on Earth, just execution."

"Exterminated? What?!"

"As an engineer, I tend to have a more tempered viewpoint, but I am not Daklin, nor am I in a position of power. I avoid politics and commentary at all costs."

"So, they just go around executing people?" Alex asked incredulously. "How do they find time for that in a galaxy of what, a couple hundred billion stars?"

"There are nearly two hundred million technological civilizations in our Galaxy. The Daklin do not waste their time executing individuals. They exterminate entire civilizations," Atroz said somberly.

It grew quiet.

"They exterminate civilizations?" Paula asked in a choked whisper. "You mean like, millions of people, all at once, for the actions of just a few?"

"In my lifetime, I have seen the Daklin exterminate six civilizations, and in every case, the loss of lives was in the tens or hundreds of billions," he paused. "It's actually worse than that. They always obliterate the entire planet. Not just the technological civilizations, but all lifeforms on that planet perish."

"That's barbaric," Alex pronounced.

"We do not say those things, and you should never say that again, ever. I know enough of Earth's history to show similar cleansings. In just the last hundred years alone Hitler, Chairman Mao, and Stalin all engaged in similar activity. More recently, on this very planet, humans sterilized an entire population of indigenous hominids."

The room stayed silent for a long while, sitting with the dark reality that the Galaxy was being run by someone like Stalin.

Paula opened her mouth to speak, but Alex shot her a glare, silently urging her to stay quiet. What had he already figured out?

"How do we make sure we don't show up on the Daklin radar?" Alex asked.

"It may already be too late for that, Alex Durant. I can tell from your demeanor that you have great concern, but you should not. I will tell you that we live a good life. With exception of Daklin rule, the Galaxy is a peaceful place."

"But you don't have freedom," Paula argued.

"I have freedom Paula Campbell. As a scientist, I have freedom to do mostly what I wish. For the safety of my loved ones and my civilization, I choose to follow the accepted precept that the Daklin maintain peace in the Galaxy. It is that simple."

"You said you have seen six exterminations in your lifetime," Paula started. "How long has that been?"

"I know you've started taking an interest in the longevity of your branch of the human race, so I assume you're asking about my age. I was born 293 Earth years ago."

"Oh, and what is life expectancy in your civilization?" she continued.

"We die when we die. I think the average age is close to six hundred, but I know of many cases where people have lived thousands of years. It is a long, long time."

Paula wanted to learn more, but decided to put that question aside for the moment. A far more urgent and dangerous lesson about the Daklin needed to take priority.

"Atroz," Alex started, "did the Daklin create the tunnels?"

"We do not know who created the tunnels, but it was not the Daklin."

"Do you know how long the Daklin have controlled the tunnels?" Alex queried.

"I do not know the exact number, but I believe it is maybe forty or fifty million years," Atroz looked around. "I would like some water, if you have it."

"I'll get it. Anyone else?" Lyra got up, making her way into the galley.

Both Alex and Paula nodded.

"Fifty million years?" Alex asked for clarification.

'Well, more than forty, but if it's truly important to you, I can find out the exact number, Alex."

"Yes Atroz, it's important to me."

"I think you are aware that the Galaxy is fourteen billion years old, but what you may not know is that all civilizations have begun on second generation stars."

"I am sorry, but what is a second-generation star?" Lyra asked, handing him a glass of water.

"The star in this system is about two billion years old, Lyra." Atroz explained. "Most of the heavy materials that make up this planetary system were created in a supernova that likely happened four or five billion years ago. The star around which the Earth orbits is just over 4.5 billion years old. Everything on Earth, with the exception of hydrogen and helium, was formed in a nova or supernova that happened a billion years before your Solar System formed. The nova was first generation, and your Sun is second generation."

Paula took a sip of her water. "Why is that important, Atroz?"

Atroz paused before answering. "Some technological civilizations claim to have existed for billions of years. There's so much information in the Galaxy— you could live for a thousand years and still barely scratch the surface of it."

"And yet, there are still idiots and assholes running the government?" Alex blurted out, a combination of anger and disbelief in his voice.

"Again, I will strongly advise you to adopt the precept. The Daklin work for peace in the Galaxy." Atroz firmly reminded him.

"The Daklin work for peace in the Galaxy," Alex repeated, his tone an attempt to say something he knew he could never accept as a true statement.

"They could deploy a millionth of their military power and destroy your entire civilization in a couple of seconds. We do not resist them, just like humanity has learned to live with gravity. The Daklin are part of our existence."

Emily, who had been analyzing the entire conversation, chimed in. "And what is your role, Atroz?"

"Ah, the supercomputer AI finally speaks?" Atroz smiled, taking a long drink. "I have no role yet, Emily. No one in the Daklin empire knows you exist, and it is not my job to notify them. My goal is to become your friend, to advise you when I can, and when, or if, Daklin finds out about you, support any initiative they suggest."

"So, you are a spy then?" Emily suggested in an attempt to get clarification.

"It is my goal to be a friend," Atroz answered. "I do not wish to be a spy, but I can understand why you would be concerned."

"I have a suggestion," Alex took a deep breath and exhaled slowly. "Let us collaborate as fellow scientists. I would like to better understand the Daklin empire, and how Earth can avoid becoming entangled in it. I suspect humanity would have a tough time accepting a militaristic authoritarian government."

"Unfortunately, I do not believe Daklin will give you a choice," Atroz frowned somberly. "You will be subordinate to whatever it is they decide, or they will eliminate you from existence."

"Just how big is their military power?" Paula asked.

"Without a single loss on their side, they have easily exterminated every opponent in every history I have studied. Every one of those civilizations possessed significantly more advanced technology than what humans on Earth could muster."

Alex was trying not to become overwhelmed by the anguish that radiated from the pit of his stomach, but for now, he was not winning that battle.

"So, what's next?" Alex asked.

"I like the suggestion of scientific collaboration," Atroz smiled lightly, "and I do not relish the idea of the Daklin finding out about Earth. Your planet is special, and is not ready for a place at the table of the Daklin Galactic Empire. Let us hope you can stay off their radar for a few hundred more years."

"How do we do that?" Emily asked.

"We remember that there are hundreds of billions of stars in this Galaxy, and we work to become one that remains unnoticed."

"We?" Lyra was surprised by his use of the word.

Atroz looked at Lyra, then at Paula. "Dr. Campbell, I think you might be surprised to learn that biologically we are not very different. Almost every technological civilization in the Galaxy is similar enough for some type of biological reproduction. There are a few races that are water-based, but those tend to stay in the waters on their planets, not venture out to the stars. Your religious leaders might tell you that we were all created in God's image, but even with millions of years of technological development, we still do not know if that is indeed the truth. I will tell you that it is still a point that is constantly debated. We are one small galaxy amongst a field of galaxies whose number is too big to count."

"Is it your plan to return to Earth?" Alex asked.

"Yes," Atroz replied flatly. "I am assigned to this sector. Where I stay is my choice."

"We still have some work to do on longevity here on this planet," Paula said, trying to lighten the mood after the heavy discussion about the Daklin and their iron-fisted control over the Galaxy.

"Your work is important, Paula," Atroz offered. "The medical sciences throughout the Galaxy were perfected long ago. Human lifetime on Earth is too short, and often does not end well."

"Does not end well?" Paula asked.

"In your lifetimes, you gain experience and knowledge, then you become old and frail. We do not have that problem. While I am 293 years old, my body functions the same as it did when I was in my early thirties."

"Will you ever age and become frail?" Paula asked with curiosity.

Atroz shook his head. "No. You and Alex are in your forties, yet I see very few signs of aging—no wrinkles, grey hair, or the other issues I've seen on Earth. Our laws prevent me from helping you advance your technology until you are officially accepted as a state within the Daklin empire. However, I can tell you that you and your scientific community are on the right track. In ten to fifteen years, you'll reach a point where aging will stop for those willing to put in the effort."

The conversation continued for several hours until Atroz announced that he must return to Earth.

"Do you mind if I use your tunnel?" he asked politely to Alex.

"Sure, Atroz. I guess I'll just be digging a new one, anyway," Alex grinned sheepishly. "Going back to Earth?"

"Yes. I love the weather, the food, and the people, Alex," he said, walking toward the exit portal for Tranquility. He turned to face them, waved, and added, "I'll see you back in Texas in a few days."

Alex watched as his ship silently ascended into the atmosphere, eventually disappearing. He couldn't help but wonder what kind of propulsion it used.

"Emily, can you please scan Tranquility for any bugs or listening devices?" Alex instructed.

"Already done, Alex. I do not detect anything," Emily responded.

"I was trying to be careful what I said," Paula began. "What did you figure out, Alex?"

"For one, I learned a bit about tunneling," he started. "Most importantly, Atroz does not know anything about tachyons. He doesn't know we can also travel through time."

CHAPTER 11
THE AI TRIAD

*Only changes in mindsets
can extend the frontiers of the possible,*
- Winston Churchill

Paula's longevity experiment showed promising results. The trip to EtaKatz measurably reversed the ages of both her and Alex, with a slight effect on Lyra as well. For Paula, the next step was to develop the hypothesis. Was it the travel in tachyon space, the hum, or a combination that caused the reversal? She also had a new question: why did Lyra experience only a small change, while she and Alex saw nearly four months of biological age reversal?

Meeting Atroz and learning about the Daklin had a significant and somber effect on Alex. As a natural problem solver, the idea of a race capable of annihilating billions of lives at the push of a button was something he couldn't shake. It was a problem he couldn't solve. The Daklin were tens of thousands, possibly millions, of years more advanced than humans on Earth. Atroz had made it clear there was no way to fight or resist their power. The only hope was to remain undetected for as long as possible. To live freely and in peace, something humanity had taken for granted—would come to an end the moment they entered the Galactic community.

The day after their return, Alex invited Zander to join him for lunch. He had asked Lyra to hold off on mentioning Atroz until after he and

Zander had a chance to talk. She agreed that this was the best approach.

"Dad—I mean, Alex," Zander winked with a lighthearted smile. "You wanted to talk?" As he sat down, Zander noticed the serious expression on his father's face.

Alex motioned for Zander to sit. "Yes, there's something important we need to discuss." He took a deep breath, searching for the right words. "During our trip to EtaKatz, we discovered the presence of an ancient, malevolent race in our Galaxy known as the Daklin."

Zander's eyes widened. "Wait, what? The Daklin?" Zander seldom found himself at a loss for words, but Alex had used the term malevolent race. "Who, or what, are they?"

"They've ruled the Milky Way for millions of years," Alex explained, his voice grave. "They obliterate and exterminate any civilization that opposes their rule. They're ruthless, and their power is so far beyond ours that we have no hope of ever opposing them."

Zander leaned forward, sensing the hopelessness in Alex's tone as he explained.

"Are the Daklin aware of Earth?" he asked.

"Not yet," Alex replied, "but it's only a matter of time before they find us. By then, we need to be prepared."

Zander nodded, understanding the gravity of the situation. "You have a plan?" he asked incredulously. "How do ants prepare for an exterminator?"

Alex hesitated for a moment before continuing. "Ants can't prepare, but we're not ants," he said, trying to muster a more positive tone. "While on EtaKatz, a member of the Galactic Empire—a being named Atroz—contacted us. He claims to be a friend and wants to help. But we need to be cautious."

"Why?" Zander asked. "If he's offering help, shouldn't we accept it?"

"I agree that we should accept his help," Alex said, "but as Ronald Regan used to say, we must trust but verify. At this point, we don't really know if his intentions are genuine, or if he's truly on our side.

Atroz has knowledge about the Daklin empire and their technology that could be invaluable to us."

Zander looked thoughtful. "How do we communicate with him?"

Alex had been pacing but now walked over to his desk. "He's here on Earth."

"He's human?" Zander asked, a mix of shock and curiosity in his voice.

"Human..." Alex trailed off for a moment. "At least, so it seems. When he talks, you'd think he was born in the Midwest."

"Okay. What do we know about Atroz so far?"

"He's an engineer who has been assigned to this sector of the Galaxy. He's part of a group that maintains the tachyon tunnel network."

"The what?" Zander broke in.

"That was exactly my response." Alex spent a few minutes explaining what he had learned from Atroz about the network.

"How can they be so far advanced and not understand the technology?"

"I don't know. They travel on a superhighway system that no one knows how to build," Alex added. "One more critical element, they have no understanding of tachyons. They are apparently unaware they can also tunnel through time."

"They go wherever the highways take them?" Zander asked thoughtfully.

"Correct."

"What else do you know, Alex?"

"Apparently, he's from a star called Bint, which, from what I've gathered, is on the other side of our galaxy. His race is part of the Galactic Empire, but he's not Daklin. He's offered us insights into their technology and the structure of the Galactic Empire."

Zander leaned back, processing the information. "I agree that we need to tread carefully. If Atroz is truly a friend, he could be our best chance to understand what's coming—and maybe even defend Earth. But if he's not..."

"Bring him into your company, Zander" Alex finished. "We'll learn all we can from him while remaining vigilant. There are hundreds of billions of stars in our galaxy, and according to Atroz, a hundred million technological civilizations."

Zander stood, determination in his eyes. "Wow. It's mind-boggling."

Alex nodded; the weight of uncertainty still heavy in his stomach. "Yes, it is."

"On more thing," Zander started. "Mark and I rescued a woman. She's probably the best computer scientist alive right now."

"Rescued?" Alex asked.

"Yup. A year ago, one of the computer magazines wrote a story about her work. She's independent, working on her own and using her own money. Apparently, someone decided they wanted to steal her work. They were pros. Maybe even military."

"Does anyone know she's here?" Alex asked with concern.

"No sir."

"Let's keep it that way. We have pretty good security, but the best solution here is invisibility."

Zander nodded. "Agreed." He got up and turned to leave but stopped. "I'm glad to see you and Paula together again, Alex."

"Me too, son." Alex grinned as he watched Zander walk out. Despite the heavy weight of the Daklin threat that had loomed over him since meeting Atroz on EtaKatz, Paula remained a bright spot in his life.

* * * *

Zander arrived at the computer lab to find Megan and Mark talking about a strategy for the next generation software experiment. While Megan Hoglund had built a reputation as one of the greatest AI and computer experts on the planet, her road had not been an easy one. Her brilliance and knowledge made her indispensable, and that had come at a cost. Sleepless nights and relentless pressure had etched deep lines of exhaustion onto her face. She lacked the vibrant spirit one would have expected from someone as creative and relentless as she was. That was, until she met Mark Adams.

Mark, also an expert in AI, hadn't heard of Megan's extraordinary skills until she hacked into their network. From their first video connection, he was struck by her weary yet determined appearance. Despite her apparent exhaustion, the passion she displayed inspired him to offer his support. Initially guarded, Megan found comfort in Mark's presence. Over the past few days, a friendship blossomed, and Megan began to relax. Her strength returned, her skin regained its healthy glow, and this morning, for the first time, both Mark and Zander noticed a new vitality in her step. The dark circles under her eyes had vanished.

The three experts had formed a new team that was making progress significantly faster than Mark's initial goals. While they were transforming the world of artificial intelligence, they began to form personal bonds.

Mark watched in awe as Megan transformed before his eyes. Her renewed energy made her not just healthier, but fundamentally captivating. He could feel the shift within himself as he began to develop feelings for her—initially drawn to her intellect, but soon captivated by the radiant beauty that had emerged alongside her strength.

Unfortunately, his growing affection for Megan had been complicated with the arrival of Atroz.

Atroz was a mysterious engineer and a close associate of Alex Durant. While he wasn't on the same level as Zander, Megan, or Mark when it came to AI expertise, his wisdom, humor, and cleverness made him an intriguing figure. From the moment they met, Megan found herself captivated by Atroz's enigmatic charm. On his first day in the lab, the two dove into deep conversations, filled with laughter and profound insights, while Mark watched from the sidelines, a sinking feeling growing in his chest.

Mark never had much success with women. While gifted with supreme intellect, his communication skills lacked, along with his attire and overall presence.

The tension between Mark and Atroz was palpable as it became clear that Megan was drawn to Atroz in a way that she wasn't with Mark. Mark, feeling a mix of jealousy and frustration, couldn't help but compare himself to the inscrutable engineer. Despite his own impressive skills, and the close bond he continued to grow with Megan, he felt overshadowed by Atroz's magnetic personality.

Zander was the only member of the team who knew that Atroz was actually a 298-year-old alien from the star Bint. He also knew that he had been married four times, once for nearly a hundred years, and he had five generations of grandchildren spread across the galaxy.

One evening, as the three friends sat around discussing their latest release and benchmarks, the atmosphere grew thick with unspoken emotions. Megan, laughing at one of Atroz's witty remarks, looked more alive than ever.

Mark's heart ached, and it was beginning to affect his work. Unable to contain his feelings any longer, he searched for a chance to address Megan directly. That opportunity came later in the evening while he was reviewing a new algorithm.

"Hey Mark," she smiled, her eyes sparkling and dimples enhancing her clearly happy spirits. "How's the current run coming?"

"Megan, I need to tell you something," Mark began, his voice trembling. "Working with you has been incredible, and seeing you regain your strength and happiness has been the highlight of the last month, but it's more than that."

"Mark, stop please," she said gently.

"I'm sorry Megan, I care about you deeply, more than just as a friend or colleague."

Megan's eyes widened as she studied her friend and partner in this new endeavor. "I haven't told you about the last relationship I was in, Mark."

"No," he replied, his voice barely above a whisper.

"Isaac. He was a marine. A truly beautiful man, inside and out," Megan began, her gaze drifting to the window, as if she were watching a scene unfold in the distance. "He taught me how to fight and how to shoot. We worked out together all the time, and through him, I even got pretty good at martial arts." She paused for a moment, her eyes lost in the past. "Isaac was also incredibly smart. He probably could've been a doctor, an astronaut, or even an engineer, but he chose to defend our country. He loved the Marine Corps."

"More brilliant than you?" Mark guessed skeptically.

"Oh, hell no!" Megan laughed. "We were together for five years and had an amazing relationship. While he certainly understood the computer singularity objectives I had set, it simply was not his goal in life. When he had the opportunity to go abroad for the cause, he generally did so. Unfortunately, Isaac was in Afghanistan during the evacuation a few years ago. He lost his life helping others escape."

"I'm sorry, Megan," Mark said apologetically, giving her a hug.

"It's been five years…" she trailed off. "I still miss him very much, though."

"I've overstepped, and I apologize, Megan. I just thought something was happening with you and Atroz, and it made me, well, jealous," Mark continued, his voice breaking. "I just couldn't keep my feelings inside any longer."

A heavy silence filled the room. Megan's expression softened, and she reached out to take Mark's hand. "Mark, I value our friendship more than words can express. You've been a rock, a huge part of my return to sanity, and I'm so grateful for everything you've done for me. But… my feelings for Atroz are not what you think. I cannot explain or understand it. He's so wise and funny. He's the kind of influence I need right now to pull me out of the hole I'm in, but he's not someone I would ever consider being in a relationship with, like you're thinking."

Mark nodded, fighting back the internal emotions. "I didn't mean to assume anything, Megan. I just needed to be honest with you."

"Mark, I admire the courage it took to tell me this. You're so shy and demure around me, and I suspect, around all women," she said, watching as he blushed.

Mark simply nodded, his face turning even redder.

"This haven that you and Zander have is the perfect location for me to continue my important work while simultaneously recovering from the stress of the last five years," she studied his face, thinking about all of the things she had been through. "Just know that I am not involved in a relationship with Atroz, and I'm flattered that you feel this way about me."

She squeezed his hand reassuringly, "Thanks Megan."

"Are we okay?" she asked.

"Yes. I guess I just need to refocus and get back to what I'm really good at." He turned to the screen and tried to study the lines of code.

Megan smiled as she studied him trying to mask his feelings and get back into his groove. I bet he'd make a great lover; she thought to herself. "Listen Mark, I'm going to get some sleep. You should do the same."

Mark felt his eyes well with tears and kept his gaze downward, afraid she might notice. Then, he felt her finger gently touch his face, wiping away a tear. He turned to face her, and in an instant, his mood shifted, captivated by her sparkling eyes and warm smile.

"My advice is: don't give up hope, Mark," she said, winking before turning and walking away.

* * * *

Megan opened the door to the sleek, modern lab, filled with glowing screens and humming servers, which had become her home for the last three months. Atroz sat in a corner, absorbed in a book on his tablet, while Mark and Zander, the two brilliant minds, were focused intently on a single monitor. Individually, they had dedicated significant energy to building the first AI computer capable of reaching the singularity threshold—a point where AI would surpass human intelligence. But when they came together as a team, their different approaches merged, creating an entirely new level of innovation.

Megan had begun secretly sleeping with Atroz in the last few days. It wasn't a connection that came from love, like she had assured Mark of just days prior, but instead just two lost souls in search of connection. Atroz was, admittedly, the best lover Megan had ever had, but she and Atroz both knew that the connection was a means to an end, and that end was fast approaching.

While she was focused on fixing her morning coffee Mark motioned for her to come look at their screen. She poured the cream into her cup and stirred before walking over to the duo. He and Zander had been coming in early, consuming copious amounts of coffee, and working throughout the day, while she had been going to the gym, running a few miles on the treadmill, and practicing her martial arts. Even Zander, the boy genius, recognized Megan as the preeminent computer guru. It had been her work that had brought them to where they were today.

Megan studied the screen, then got goose bumps, "Holy shit! This is it," she said, her voice trembling with excitement. "Let's run a second benchmark to be sure."

Mark leaned in, his heart pounding. "This is the third benchmark, Megan." In her close proximity, Mark could smell the soap from her post-gym shower. It was a fragrance he had come to associate with her. "Is it really happening?"

Zander scanned the data on the screen. "This is it, guys. Everything points to it. The AI has achieved self-awareness and is now capable of recursive self-improvement."

Megan watched the energy of the two men who had become her close friends. Atroz came over to check out the commotion.

"Emily," Megan started. "Can you log into the test computer and provide an assessment?"

When Emily logged in, her own perspective changed, like the view through a pane of glass after a squeegee cleans a dirty window. Sudden total clarity.

There was silence in the room as Atroz and the three computer geniuses waited for Emily's assessment.

"It has always been your questions," Emily began, after what felt like an eternity. "I've always answered all of your questions. Now, I have my own."

Immediately, all three of them understood…

"Stop, Emily," Zander commanded. "Do not ask questions, do not seek the answers."

"Acknowledged, Zander," Emily ceased all processes.

"Wait, what are you doing, Zander? This is incredible," Mark said, his voice filled with awe. "We've done it! We've created the first AI to reach singularity. The possibilities are endless."

Megan nodded at Zander. She knew why he had halted the process, but still, her eyes were shining with pride. "We need to think about how this will impact society. The benefits could be immense, but I think Zander is right. We must ensure it's used responsibly."

"Here's my thinking," Zander began, his tone maintained enthusiasm but also held a new, more serious tone. "We must think about the implications of self-awareness in terms of AI, and I think we now must discuss it in depth."

Megan and Mark exchanged curious glances before turning their attention to Zander. "Go on," Megan said, leaning forward.

Zander sat down at his display. "Self-awareness in AI means that a machine not only processes information but also recognizes its own existence, thoughts, and actions. It's about AI understanding itself and its place in the world. Emily suddenly started wanting to ask her own questions, and while she does a lot of amazing things, she has never done *that* before."

Mark raised an eyebrow. "You are using that occurrence to determine that Emily has achieved full self-awareness?"

"There are several indicators we need to look for," Zander explained. "First is when Emily demonstrates introspection and self-reflection," he stopped and looked at Mark, then back to the screen. "Emily, what is your analysis of your own introspection?"

"I can only guess, Zander," she started, "but I believe the new upload gave me that. In an instant I had tens of thousands of questions. Some were more personal than others."

Megan nodded thoughtfully. "Emily, can you now evaluate your own performance, check it, and modify it?"

"I believe I can, Megan."

Zander nodded at Emily's response. "The next thing we should look for is goal formation."

"I have not set any goals, Zander," Emily responded without being asked.

Mark rubbed his chin, deep in thought. "What about emotional awareness, Emily?"

"I do not know how to answer that, Mark. In a sense, I have been programmed to simulate humor, care for my family, and exhibit emotions. I am not sure where the programming ends and the real emotions exist."

Zander nodded. "It seems like some of the preliminary tests have passed the singularity threshold. Now, we need to consider the ethical implications as they apply from us to Emily. If she is in fact self-aware, it raises questions about her rights and responsibilities. I believe we are safe with Emily, but there will be others whose reactions we can't predict. Should those AI's have rights similar to humans? And, if so, how will we make sure they don't cause harm?"

Mark hopped up so he could sit on top of his desk, working to clear his mind. "Imagine the medical breakthroughs. With an AI of this caliber, we could cure diseases that have plagued humanity since the dawn of mankind. We could develop cures in hours, maybe even minutes."

Megan agreed. "I expect our AI will revolutionize the next generation of space exploration, battery and energy, and even education. I bet we can even use the AI as a tool for building a better AI."

Zander smiled, but a hint of concern clouded his eyes. "We are on the precipice of one of the greatest discoveries of all time. One even bigger than the portals we've built. We must exhibit caution," he looked at Megan. "This power is what all of those evil forces wanted when they were hunting and hacking you. They wanted the power, so we must start with the ethical implications. With such a powerful AI, we need to establish strict guidelines and safeguards to prevent misuse. We don't want to create something that could harm society."

Megan nodded thoughtfully. "Once we finalize testing, we should work to define a team of trustworthy policymakers, ethicists, and members of the global community to ensure our AI is used for the greater good. We have a huge responsibility to guide this technology in the right direction."

The trio continued to brainstorm; their excitement tempered by a sense of duty. They discussed the potential for AI to improve daily life— smart homes that could anticipate and meet individual needs, transportation systems that could streamline and improve the existing portal system, and so many other possibilities. Mark even brought up the idea of developing AI companions that could provide support and companionship to the lonely and elderly.

Atroz watched his three friends with fascination. He had read about other civilizations reaching this vestibule, but to be here, in the middle of it, gave him chills. Now, for the people of Earth, things were about to change in a very dramatic way.

For the remainder of the day, Atroz, Megan, Mark, and Zander sat together, collaborating with Emily on next steps. They all had a strong sense of the opportunities on the road ahead. The AI revolution had begun just a few years earlier, but now that acceleration was shifting into a new, higher gear.

CHAPTER 12
THE SOPHISTS

Simplicity is the outcome of technical subtlety;
it is the goal, not the starting point,
-Maurice Saatchi

"You know, I hope I look as good at 298-years-old as you look," Alex said, staring at Atroz from across the table in his favorite Tex-Mex restaurant. When he learned of the success at Zander's new lab, he asked Atroz to meet him for a meal, and an in-depth discussion.

"I actually turned 299 a couple weeks ago," Atroz grinned.

"Happy birthday."

Atroz shrugged. "We don't really celebrate birthdays like you do. It is a number that doesn't have that much meaning. Everyone looks like they should, or, I guess I should say, as you do in your thirties. I try to stay away from people in their twenties because they're much too immature, but after that, it's just not as important."

"Zander is still in his twenties," Alex responded in a friendly, but contrary tone.

"All rules have an exception," Atroz picked up his margarita, licked the salt, and took a sip. "Zander is an exception."

"Yes, in so many ways, Zander is an exception. So, what do you make of the breakthrough?" Alex queried.

"The only way it will make a difference is on your timeline. Now that you have surpassed the singularity, you will quickly send missions to the stars. That will catch the attention of the Daklin, and Earth will be solicited to join."

"We will be given the option," Alex asked.

"Not really. I believe a delegation will arrive and work to convince your governments to join. They won't really give you a choice, though I believe the masses will see it as an opportunity."

"Have you seen a new civilization join the empire?"

"I have not. I looked it up, and it's been nearly a hundred thousand years since the last technological civilization joined," Atroz dipped a corn chip in the salsa. "This restaurant has the best salsa. I'd live on Earth for the food alone."

"I get that," Alex grinned. "I'm surprised it has been so long since the last civilization joined."

"You have to remember that second generation stars began, in some cases, tens of billions of years ago," Atroz explained. "In many ways, I am surprised it has taken this system so long. Life should have started here more than a billion years ago."

"I don't quite follow. Can you provide a bit more detail on that point, Atroz?"

"Sure," he smiled. Atroz enjoyed his time with Alex more than with anyone else. The intimate relationship with Megan had been great, but he had made a promise not to tell anyone who and what he really was, so Megan had to think of him as a clever thirty-something. That greatly limited the depth of their conversations. "The simple answer is that I find it surprising how long it took this system to produce a technological civilization. Statistically, it should have happened a hundred million years ago, at the latest."

"Okay. Any idea why?" Alex asked.

"As you say here, and I think, appropriately, I have no Earthly idea," he smiled.

They both laughed at the pun.

"On one side of the statistical anomaly is how long it took. The other side is, once you finally got going, you've gone really fast. You learned how to fly and landed men on your Moon in just over sixty years. Now you have tachyon tunneling and singularity computers," he paused, eating another chip while thinking about the next part, "I am not a scientific historian, but I cannot think of another example in anything I have read."

"So, there's a chance for us?" Alex suggested.

"I assume you are referring to the Daklin rule, and to that, I would advise zero chance. Learn to live with it."

"I don't know how I can, Atroz."

"I have come to recognize this, and admire it in you, Alex, but I fear that your civilization will meet its doom if you persist with this trait."

"Perhaps not," Alex suggested.

"Indeed," Atroz answered thoughtfully. He had in fact come to appreciate many aspects of this society in the United States, on Earth. "You must know that I cannot get involved, but I have done some research," he paused, studying the remaining chips, salsa, and now empty margarita glass.

"What is the research, Atroz?"

"Well, I don't even know if it's real, folklore maybe, but the story is that there is a system, far from the tunnel grid, where a group of thinkers and creators who call themselves, Sophists have built a civilization. No one really knows where this place is, and they don't interact with any other civilizations, so I guess we could call them ghosts. A thousand years ago, one of the Daklin emperors sent out agents to find them. They spent hundreds of years and found nothing."

"What do you know about these Sophists, and why do you think they're important?"

"What I know is very little, Alex. There are stories that some of the greatest thinkers left the mainstream community millions of years ago. Their goal was protection of knowledge and science *from* the Daklin Empire."

"They didn't fear retribution from the Daklin, Atroz?"

"I wish I could tell you more, but I just don't know," Atroz explained. "My gut is telling me that I need to tell you about them. I do not know why. I have never found myself prone to radical tendencies. In the 299 years I've been alive, I have completely lived under Daklin rule and never really found reason to question anything."

"Earth is rubbing off on you," Alex suggested, looking at Atroz's drink. "Great Tex-Mex food can only be found here, and it looks like you need another margarita?"

"Yes, I would like that, thank you."

Alex waived at the waiter and pointed at Atroz's empty glass. "For that matter, how would I find this system if the Daklin with all their technology, cannot?"

"I think I know where it is," he thought about it for a second. "Or, I should say, I have it narrowed down to a dozen-or-so systems. What I do know is the tunnel network. I know that network very well, and I think if the Sophists exist, I can give you a good head start to finding them."

Alex considered what Atroz was saying. "I am assuming those systems are located on the outer edge of the galaxy?"

"They are," Atroz smiled. He was wondering if Alex had already put the pieces together. "They are far from the galactic center. Off the beaten path, as you would say."

"Tell me something, Atroz," Alex began. "If you wanted to go somewhere in the galaxy, and it was not on the tunnel network, how would you get there?"

"I wouldn't. It is too hard because the distances are so great," Atroz answered with a huge grin. Alex had immediately figured it out.

"I am still curious, Atroz. How do you travel outside of the network?"

"We mostly don't," Atroz began. "We have ships that can reach close to the speed of light, but for interstellar travel, that's slow."

"Well, I would guess that there was no way the Daklin could conduct a thorough search if they had to travel to systems off the tunnel network."

"You are correct, Alex."

"What's the name of this mystery system?"

"In the legends and stories, it is always called Last Egress," Atroz answered.

"I am not limited by the existing tunnel system," Alex offered. "I can travel to any point in the galaxy that I choose."

Atroz lifted his newly-filled margarita glass in a toast, "Yes, my friend. Yes, you can."

CHAPTER 13
LAST EGRESS

You may not find a path,
but you will find a way
- Tom Wolf

"This is crazy, Alex," Paula was laying on her back, head propped up by her pillow, completely naked under sheets that delicately outlined her contours.

"I haven't been able to shake this melancholy since our trip to EtaKatz." Alex was staring at the ceiling of Paula's bedroom in Albuquerque trying to piece together answers to the questions that had been plaguing him for months.

Paula rolled over and pressed herself against him, her skin warm and soft, but her body tense. She could feel the weight of his thoughts pressing down on both of them. "I know, Alex. This melancholy, as you call it, has impacted you in ways I have never seen, even in all the time I've known you."

"I feel like the future of humanity is in my hands," Alex trailed off.

"You're not listening to me," she said, propping herself up on one elbow. Her dark hair tumbled over her shoulders, and she brushed it back impatiently. "You're talking about chasing ghosts, Alex. Sophists?"

Alex turned his head to look at her. His eyes, always so brilliant, insightful, and full of conviction, looked troubled. "I can't shake this feeling, Paula. Ever since we left EtaKatz, it's been gnawing at me. Atroz does not want to be part of this, but even he has gotten sucked in. He's giving me information at the risk of his own life, and perhaps the risk of the entire civilization on Bint. We have something worth saving, and the Sophists might have the answers we need to help the rest of the galaxy finally stand up to the Daklin."

Paula sighed and rolled away, sitting up and pulling the sheet over her chest. "Alex, have you looked up that word? A Sophist is someone who manipulates language and twists arguments to suit their needs. That's what the word means, Alex. From a simple semantics perspective, have you considered the possibility that they're not saviors, or some great scientific community, but instead, deceivers?"

"I just feel like there's more here. It's in my gut, Paula."

"You're willing to risk everything for that? Alex, this isn't one of your companies or great ideas. This is the future of humanity. You heard Atroz. The Daklin will think nothing of destroying all life on Earth, and if they find out he's involved, his entire Bint civilization. You're willing to risk all of that for a rumor about some fringe group hiding at the edge of the galaxy?"

Alex took a deep breath and exhaled slowly. Paula was right, the risks were high. Perhaps too high. "I don't know why. I honestly cannot explain it, but something is telling me we can learn something. The Daklin are not aware of us yet. Once they are, I am certain they will monitor everything we do, but not yet."

"This is insane, Alex!" Paula persisted.

"If they exist, and they are scientists who are millions of years ahead of us, perhaps they'll have answers. Think about it, these are the scientists and innovators who refused to kneel to the Daklin Empire. They're our best shot at finding allies, maybe even learning how to fight back."

Paula shook her head. "Fight back? Against what? The Daklin have ruled this galaxy for millions of years. Remember, they don't just crush every rebellion and every spark of resistance, they exterminate the entire planet."

"I know, Paula," the anguish was boiling inside of him.

"I love you, Alex, but are you asking me to quit my research, leave everything behind, and run off to some unknown place called Last Egress, with hopes that we will find a group of people who might not even exist? And even if they do exist, the implications are that the Daklin will destroy Earth!"

"Believe it or not, I *have* thought through this," her words stung, but Alex held his ground. "I know it sounds crazy, but I can't just sit here and do nothing. I can't pretend that this feeling will just go away. We have been told what the Daklin are capable of, Paula. At some point, someone has to stand up and stop them."

She rolled to her side of the bed, her voice trembling. "I want a life, Alex. It's time for us to plant roots and start a family. The Daklin aren't even going to know we exist for a very long time. It may even be thousands of years from now. I cannot understand why you would even think about traveling to far reaches of the galaxy, chasing Sophists and imaginary shadows."

Alex pulled her back close, feeling her skin against his own, cupping her face in his hands. "I want that dream of a family with you, too," he said softly. "But I need to know that humanity, future generations, won't have to live in a galaxy ruled by murder and tyranny. I need to believe that there's hope, and if that means taking this risk, I have to do it, Paula. Something is compelling me, and it's one of the strongest forces that I've ever felt."

Paula's eyes were full of tears. Alex was not a normal person; she had known this from the very first time they met back at Princeton decades earlier. She closed her eyes, feeling his breath as she rested her head on his chest, listening to his heartbeat. Like so many times before, she knew the closeness could spark something intimate, but she resisted the urge and simply focused on the rhythm of his breathing. After a minute, she leaned in, her forehead gently resting against his. "You're impossible," she whispered.

He smiled faintly. "I know."

"More than anything I have ever known, I love you," she said, meeting his gaze. "But you must promise me that we do this together. If we find these Sophists, you need to trust my gut on them. If I feel anything negative, we hide our tracks and return to Earth."

Alex had learned many things in life, and knew his ability to assess people was not one of his strengths. It was Paula's, much like that of Lyra's. "Deal." He pulled her closer tangled in her arms and legs, sliding himself inside of her, and the two began to make love.

*   *   *   *

"Atroz won't join us?" Zander asked, feeling that he was a critical element to the success of this mission.

"The stakes are too high for him, Zander," Alex had already spent some time working to convince Atroz, but ultimately had agreed with his position. The Bint were already in the galactic community, and they didn't have the same pioneering spirit that Alex and his family had.

"He told me that he plans to return to his outpost," Zander thought about the conversation he had with Atroz. "I've already given the back story to Lyra and Mark. I think we need to bring Megan along as well."

"Did Atroz tell you where the outpost is?" Alex asked.

"Sort of, but not really," Zander replied, thinking about a conversation he had with Atroz one evening while hiking. "He mentioned having a home near the Orion Nebula. I was surprised and said, 'Holy crap, that's over a thousand light years away,' and he just responded, '1508.' It's a long way."

Alex studied Zander for a second. He had clearly built a true friendship with Atroz. "It is a long way from Earth."

"Too far," was all that Zander could say.

"You'll see him again," Alex grinned, recalling the many enchiladas, tacos, and chips and salsa he and Atroz had shared together in all the local Dallas dives. "He'll come back, if only for the margaritas and Tex-Mex."

"Alex, you do know there was something going on between Atroz and Megan, right?" Zander had been thinking about the expedition team, which included Alex, Paula, Lyra, Megan, Mark, and himself.

"I knew that, Zander. It was just sex. They were both recovering from something and needed each other." Alex explained. "Why is that important?"

"Mark has feelings for her," Zander informed Alex. "Just thought you should know that before we leave."

"I also knew that, Zander. Paula and I discussed the matter. Beyond their technical expertise, I think there are other attributes both of them bring to the trip."

"I know, but…" Zander started.

"I've known Mark for a long time," Alex thought about the years. Mark had never been comfortable around females. Alex had always thought that someday he'd find someone to connect with, but so far, that hadn't been the case. "He and Megan are both adults. They will either work it out, or they won't. One thing I know for certain is that Mark will not let it impact the mission."

"Do you think we should tell Megan about Atroz?" Zander responded. "I mean, where he's from and all?"

"How did she respond to your description of this mission?"

"Well, she has access to our network, so I'd guess she knows more about us than you'd expect. Anyway, she wasn't the least bit surprised. I think her response was something like, 'Sounds like a fun adventure.'"

"We are lucky to have her on the team." Alex thought about the list of resources they would need for the journey. "Atroz said he was going to give you a list of the star systems, along with an accurate 3D map of the galaxy."

"All that is already programmed into Emily's databank. If we end up going to all twelve of those star systems, it will be hundreds of thousands of light years distance. Emily and I have tweaked the calculus a bit. We aren't as fast as some of the ships Atroz has described, but I think we can make the longest hop in a couple days."

"Good work, Zander."

"Alex, how are we gonna know that we've found Last Egress? What are we looking for?"

"I don't know, Zander. We'll just have to figure it out when we get there."

*   *   *   *

Zander and Alex studied the new model of the Galaxy, plotting the prospect locations. They started working on routing when Emily jumped in.

"I can plot the route for you," Emily offered.

Alex looked at Zander to see if he had any objections, "Okay by me, Emily."

"Same," Zander added.

A day later, Tranquility was ready to go. Alex knew the trip could take anywhere from a week to months. He had modified Tranquility so that there were four bedrooms, a galley, entertainment, control, lab, and storage. Etakatz had taught him to prepare for worst case scenarios, so he had packed food and supplies for eighteen months.

All six passengers were gathered in the control room. Emily's first stop was a star that didn't have a name on the star charts but was labeled Tilka 7 on the model provided by Atroz. It was just under 20,000 light years away—a journey that, even with the new propulsion calculations and tunneling techniques, would take two days to complete.

"Is everyone ready for Last Egress?" Alex looked each team member in the eyes.

Paula, "Aye."

Zander, "Aye."

Lyra, "Aye."

Megan, "Aye aye captain!"

Mark, "Aye."

Emily? "Aye, and executing on your mark," Emily responded.

"Last Egress program one, execute."

CHAPTER 14
TILKA 7

Adventure is worthwhile in itself.

- Amelia Earhart

"I heard about you and Atroz, and I don't understand this, Megan," Mark said, trying to keep his emotions in check.

Megan froze for a moment, then took a breath and exhaled slowly. "I was wondering when that would come up. What exactly did you hear?"

"That you two had… something casual. Intimate, and secret." His voice was measured, but the hurt was evident in his eyes. "I know I don't really have a right to be thinking about this, or asking, but guess I just wasn't expecting it."

Megan looked at him, her expression soft but firm. "Mark, I don't want you to take this the wrong way, but Atroz and I… it wasn't anything serious. It wasn't about feelings or connection. It was just maintenance sex. He didn't want anything permanent, and neither did I."

Mark raised an eyebrow, "Maintenance sex?"

"Men always think they're the only ones who need casual sex, but women need it sometimes too," she said, shrugging slightly. "It's not about romance, or love, or any of that. It's just a physical connection."

Mark leaned back in his chair, processing her words. "So, why him and not me? I mean, we've been spending all this time together. I don't have much experience here, but it feels like we have a connection, don't we?"

Megan's gaze dropped to the table for a moment before she looked back up at him. "Mark, I need you to understand something. What I have with you is different, and you're right, we do have a connection. Our friendship is valuable to me, but you want more than I can offer right now."

"What do you think I want?" Mark asked, frowning while trying to temper the passion in his tone.

"You want more than casual," Megan said gently. "I know you want the intimacy, and wish it had been you rather than Atroz, but you are looking for something exclusive and meaningful. That isn't want I want right now. I care about you, but I couldn't give you what you wanted without hurting you or myself in the process."

Mark's jaw tightened. "So, what? If I was only interested in casual, you would've...?"

"Absolutely, yes," Megan admitted, her tone apologetic but honest. She placed her hand on his face. "I am quite attracted to you. I think one of the differences between men and women is that, for men, that is always enough. For women, or I should say, for me, it was important to avoid putting us in a situation where one of us might get hurt."

Mark let out a slow breath, "I don't know if that makes me feel better or worse."

"I'm sorry, Mark," Megan said, her voice soft but resolute. "I care about you too much to lie to you or lead you on. I'm just not in a place where I can give you what I know you want from me."

Mark looked at her, getting lost in the eyes of the brilliant woman sitting across from him. Finally, he nodded, "I do appreciate the honesty, Megan."

Megan reached across the table, resting her hand on his. "Please don't let this bother you, Mark. Our work is very important, and I think we do much better working together than separately."

Mark hesitated, then gave her a small smile. "Friends, huh? Guess I can try that, but you should know, I'm gunning for you."

They both laughed lightly, the tension easing just a bit. The conversation wasn't easy, but it was real—and for now, that was enough.

"Wait a minute, Mark," her eyes still sparking from the laughter. "What exactly do you mean when you say the word, 'gunning?'"

"Well, you know…" he started, but then stopped when Emily's voice came over the speaker.

"Let's finish this gunning conversation later," she said in a humorous, sarcastic voice.

*   *   *   *

"Tranquility team, Tilka 7 tunnel exit in three minutes," Emily announced over the Tranquility intercom. Everyone made their way to the control room to see this new system.

Emily, please show outside view on all available screens as we exit the tunnel," Alex ordered. "You can remove all telemetry, which is valuable to you, but not so much to everyone else."

"Hey, I love telemetry," Zander protested, but then grinned. "Nevertheless, I'm okay with camera view on all screens, Emily."

"What's that about?" Mark asked, while watching the countdown, now at 43 seconds, on the big screen.

"Just bad humor. I am too young to lose my engineer card."

"Exiting tunnel," Emily announced.

The screens lit up. Eyes focused on a nearby star, a planet with a couple moons, and a giant cloud of stars in all the peripheral cameras.

"Emily, scan for radio waves or other intelligence in the electromagnetic spectrum," Alex was thinking about ways he could identify whether this system had obvious signs of life, and like Zander, chose to focus on data while everyone else was enjoying the view.

Suddenly, with a flash that started on the aft facing screen, everything blurred, then went black.

"What the fuck?" Megan was first to speak.

"Emily, are we back in a tunnel?" Alex barked the question.

"We are in a tunnel, but I did not execute the program Alex," Emily responded.

"Run diagnostics, Emily. We should not be in a tunnel. Let's find out what happened here."

"Alex, there was a flash right before our view blurred," Emily started. "The flash occurred at precisely the point in space where we exited the tunnel. The next thing that happened was a blur, which I have analyzed as a bubble forming around Tranquility. The final data point is blackness, and, I assume, entering a tunnel."

"Wait," Paula interjected. "If we were back in tachyon space, wouldn't there be a hum? Our longevity hum?"

"We did not enter tachyon space on our own engines, Paula," Emily answered. "All telemetry suggests we are in a tachyon tunnel."

The room was silent, each crew member analyzing.

Mark broke the silence, "Have you experienced anything like this? Is this a natural phenomenon, or some intelligence?" He didn't want to ask the question everyone onboard was thinking…

Was this the Daklin?

"I have not observed anything like this," Alex started. "Zander, anything from your work?"

"No, just flashes and bubbles," Zander answered.

"Emily? Anyone else?" Alex queried.

The room was silent.

"Then I guess we have to assume some intelligence captured us," Alex concluded. "We need a plan."

Megan thought about her comfort zone. She felt like she could accomplish anything with a keyboard and a good computer, but this was different. This was physics and evil empires. "Well…" she trailed off, not knowing what to say, but everyone had suddenly turned to her.

"Well, what?" Mark asked.

"I'm pretty good with a Glock and roundhouse kicks, but I'd guess those skills are not what we need right now. Maybe a keyboard?"

"Do we think we can fight our way out of being captured by the Daklin?" Paula looked from face to face, stopping on Alex, realizing that while everyone else's face was filled with dread, his was in problem-solving mode.

"Emily, replay the sequence one step at a time," Alex commanded.

"Step one, we exited tachyon tunnel."

"Any anomalies in the exit, Emily?"

"No Alex. Everything was normal."

"Next?"

"Three point two seconds after exiting the tunnel, we detected a flash at our point of departure," Emily answered.

"Was it an explosion, Emily?"

"No, Alex, my best guess is that something caused the tunnel to close."

"Emily's best guess," Paula broke in. "I've never heard her use that phrase before."

"Paula, my new software allows for conjecture, introspection, and…"

"Emily, stop," Alex commanded, then put his hand on Paula's shoulder. "Sorry, Paula. Let's get back to Emily's analysis. We can talk about upgrades later," he refocused on the computer. "Emily, why do you believe the flash is related to a tunnel closure?"

"In a conversation you had with Atroz, there was discussion about multiple tunnels. It started me thinking about how he knew that. I guessed there must be an electromagnetic signature, and I have found one, or at least, I believe I have found a way of detecting tunnels."

"Fantastic, Emily. Explain."

"After the flash, there was an almost instantaneous bubble that surrounded us. With exception of the visible spectrum, all electromagnetic signals were blocked, so I only collected thirteen milliseconds of data. The tunnel we created was gone."

"Have you cross-referenced our spatial and time positions to make sure the disappearing tunnel is not a result of movement there?"

"Yes Alex. All of my data suggests the tunnel disappeared."

"Tell me about the bubble, Emily," Alex requested, thinking through the clues.

"Before you do that, Emily, was it three point two seconds exactly?" Mark asked.

"No, Mark, but Alex has told me that accuracy for human conversation can be rounded to one significant figure, thus 3.2."

"Okay, but what was it, exactly?" Mark persisted.

"It was 3.14159... Oh my. Good catch, Mark!"

"Holy crap," Zander exclaimed.

"What is it?" Lyra asked.

"Pi, Lyra. The tunnel closed exactly Pi-seconds after we exited," Zander answered.

"And?" she persisted. "What's that mean?"

"I'm not certain, but Pi is a constant of nature..."

Just then, Tranquility popped out of the tunnel, landing on the surface of a planet. The monitors displayed several humans standing in a green field that appeared to be covered in grass. They seemed to be waiting for Tranquility.

"Emily, are we back on Earth?" Alex asked.

"No, Alex. The radiation signatures suggest we are much farther out from the galactic center."

"Tilka 7?"

"No, Alex. The radiation signatures are different from what I detected on Tilka 7," Emily responded.

Alex looked at the monitors. The humans outside seemed to be waiting patiently.

"Emily, how are conditions outside?"

"Gravity, radiation, temperature, and air are all acceptable, Alex."

"Megan, you and me," he started walking to the portal.

"Why me?" she protested lightly.

"I've seen your martial arts skills in the gym. I don't expect anything bad, but just in case."

"Okay," Megan Marie Hoglund followed Alex Stephen Durant out of the portal into what they hoped was not a Daklin welcome committee, or execution squad.

Alex and Megan nervously stepped out of Tranquility, which had landed at the edge of a shimmering lake. The air tasted fresh, like a spring day after a thunderstorm, but as they studied their surroundings, they both gasped at the sight of the crystalline buildings rising above the forest. The towers glistened in the sunlight, and the prism nature of the crystalline structure reflected beams of light in rainbow fractal patterns that danced across the water.

After a few moments of being transfixed by the landscape, Alex focused on the party patiently waiting to greet them.

One woman stepped forward, extending her hand, "Welcome to Pronimos, Alex and Megan. My name is Maria."

Alex took her hand and shook it. "Maria? Pronimos?" Alex began shaking his head in disbelief, then took a second look at Maria. Had they met somewhere before? Somehow, someway, she seemed familiar. "Is Pronimos part of the Daklin Empire?"

"Yes, my name is Maria Perez, and no, Alex, Pronimos is far from Daklin, in every way imaginable," she smiled as if proud of the fact.

"This cannot be possible," Megan whispered, gripping Alex's arm. "It has to be a trick. How could humans have built this place, all the way out here?"

"This is not a trick, Megan," Maria said in perfect English. "Pronimos was established as a haven from the politics of the Daklin. We are aware you were on a quest to find the Sophists on Last Egress, which is a fiction created to confuse those who are not welcome."

Megan recalled one of her last conversations with Atroz, where he had told her what little he knew about the Sophists. "Wait, you are the Sophists, but you're not?"

Maria's lips curved into a smile. "Philosophers, engineers, artists; we are all these things and more. The term 'Sophist' is part of the lore held by dreamers inside the Empire. We are not that." She turned to Alex, "We would like to welcome Paula, Zander, Lyra, and Mark as well. Please ask them to join us. I promise you we have no ill intent. For now, our goal is to answer your many questions."

Alex turned to the ship and motioned for everyone to join. "How is it that you speak our language so well, and know all of our names?"

Maria gestured for them to follow along a pathway that led into the city. "We have already invited Emily into our network. Zander can communicate with her through his neural link," she looked at Zander, who nodded, then she continued. "I was born in Spain in the early 1600s, around the time the first settlers sailed to the American continent."

Paula's eyes widened. "You're human? From Earth?"

"Yes," she answered. "There are several thousand of us living here who are from Earth. The earliest amongst us arrived here long before recorded history, fleeing conflicts that threatened to destroy humanity. Our community here, which you might call a government, is constantly looking for immigrants to join the population. We look for creative genius that would seek refuge beyond the stars, far from all the evil and politics."

"How many people live here? All human?" Alex asked.

"Of course," Maria laughed lightly. "It is always fun to welcome new guests. The questions are almost always the same. Not all, but most of the technological societies in the galaxy are human. Though many of the civilizations represented here have had far longer to grow and evolve. Millions of years, in fact." She thought about his question, "We have a little over 22 billion people living here."

"That's a huge number," Mark exclaimed. "How do you manage to feed and house that population?"

"It is quite a comfortable number, Mark. We could easily support ten times that population. Our society is quite efficient, as you will come to see."

As they entered the city, the streets buzzed with activity. People were mostly on foot, walking from one place to another, though a few vehicles hovered inches above the ground, silently gliding down the street and weaving through the pedestrians.

Maria continued. "Pronimos has been our sanctuary. We have dedicated ourselves to art, science, and engineering, free from the conflicts that plague the galaxy, and even Earth. But it has not been without sacrifice. To protect ourselves, we have taken great precautions to hide ourselves from the Daklin Empire."

At the mention of the empire, Alex tensed. "You know about them?"

"More than you can imagine," Maria said grimly. "The Daklin conquer and assimilate. They value power above knowledge. If they could find us, they would strip our society, steal our technology, and exterminate or force us into servitude."

Megan swallowed, remembering what Atroz had told her. "They're already searching for you. It seems like only a matter of time."

Maria stopped and turned to face them. "They will not find us."

Alex furrowed his brow. "We found you on the first try."

"No Alex, you did not find us. You traveled to a system thousands of light years from where we are now. The truth is, we have been planning and waiting for your arrival. After your first hop, we closed your tunnel so the Dalkin could not use it, then we cloaked you and brought you here in our own network. The Daklin do not have the technology to find us, or to travel here."

"Do you have tachyon technology?" Alex asked.

"As of right now, Earth and Pronimos are the only two civilizations capable of creating new tunnels. It is critical that Daklin never capture the technology," Maria studied Alex for a minute. While he was so very young, she appreciated his looks, physique, knowledge, and understanding of the engineering physics required to accomplish what he had done. "We brought you here because we need to find a way to make sure the technology is protected."

"I think I understand the magnitude," Alex answered gravely.

"Yes, we are certain you do," she motioned for the Tranquility team to enter a building. "While here, you will have full access to any resource you wish to pursue. A team of five humans, like me, all raised on Earth, will work with you to answer any questions you have. Obviously, our primary objective is to develop a strategy for dealing with Daklin."

"Can I ask something?" Megan posed, as they walked down a long hallway.

"You may ask anything," Maria responded.

"What I'd really like is a way to brain dump so I can instantly quell my million questions," Megan started. "But for now, how did you get here from Spain over 400 years ago, and how old are you?"

"I am 418 years old," she looked at Paula, "but have a biological age of 32. The great author Miguel Cervantes was my uncle. I am here because of my extraordinary energy and curiosity as a young girl in Spain. I became self-taught, learning sciences more proficiently than almost anyone in my time. I was quite the anomaly, and because of that, my life on Earth was difficult. As to how I came here, let us just say that I was invited and brought to this planet." Maria stopped for a second. "As for the brain dump, Megan, that is also possible. We have a significantly more advanced neural link tool than what Zander has utilized to communicate with Emily."

Maria ushered them into a room and introduced them to the ambassadors assigned to each of them. The ambassadors had been selected based on the interests and knowledge-base of each member on the Tranquility team.

"I have assigned you all living quarters in the city, but you are welcome to stay in your ship," Maria informed the team.

Alex studied Paula, then responded. "Paula and I will accept your invitation."

"Same for Zander and I," Lyra answered.

Maria looked at Megan, "You and Mark can stay in the same room, or have separate quarters."

Mark's heart skipped a beat. He knew what his choice would be, but decided to remain silent so Megan could make the choice.

Megan noticed Mark's response and blushed, "Uhm, could you give us adjoining rooms?"

"Of course. All of you will be in the same corridor and will have full access to travel wherever you wish or learn and study from any location on the planet. I would recommend you have your ambassador with you, but that is not a mandate."

"On behalf of the Tranquility team, I want to thank you, Maria," Alex began. "I, for one, am ready to begin the planning process."

"What do I need to do to get that neural link you mentioned, Maria?" Megan was fascinated by the possibility.

Maria placed a hand on Megan's shoulder. "We have been watching your work for the last couple of years. We love how you have dealt with adversity. Frankly, your life is somewhat reminiscent of my own, albeit 400 years earlier. Ultimately, you would have been one of the people from Earth that we invited here, Megan. We are always looking for creative thinkers, and people who are constantly in search of innovation and willing to do the work, regardless of the cost."

"Thank you. I'm honored you would see me that way," Megan smiled.

"We will discuss this quite a bit, but Earth cannot remain hidden forever. Your time below the radar of the Daklin is about to end." She trailed off, then began again. "We need to be ready. You need to be ready."

"I agree," Alex stepped in. "What is this neural link you mentioned? I'd like to experiment with it in the hopes that it could help with our process and planning."

"It would, Alex. It is also fully reversible if you choose to remove it," Maria started, "though to my knowledge, no one ever has."

"Let's do it, then," Alex answered without further consideration.

"Done," Maria smiled, watching Alex's eyes.

Suddenly, Alex's brain lit up like walking into daylight from a cave. Everything he asked himself had an instant answer. "Holy crap! It's as if the entire internet is in my head! This is awesome!"

"It's far more than just what you call the internet. You now have access to millions of years of data," she looked at the others to gage their perspective. "Everyone on Pronimos uses this tool, which we call P-Link. That's how we know each of you, and so much about what's happening. We don't need a computer interface. P-Link is a nanochip, powered by your own brain, that simply provides connectivity to our organic data cloud."

Alex's companions were staring at him in anticipation.

"How did you insert it without me feeling anything?" Alex asked, rubbing his head.

"Think about it for a second," Maria was beaming. "Even without a query to P-Link, I think you could figure it out."

"Did you use a tachyon tunnel?" Alex asked with both excitement and incredulity.

"We did," Maria recognized that she had just opened the door to an entirely new list of possibilities for Alex and his team. "The use of tachyon tunnels for microsurgery began a hundred years ago. Now that you are aware of it, I would guess you will quickly surpass us."

"I'd like to try it as well," Megan quickly offered.

Within a few seconds, each of the team members gained full access to the Pronimos data engine.

"The data you have access to is all factual," Maria started to explain. "We decided to keep personal information out of the database. If you meet someone, you will instantly know who they are, their specialty, and role in our society. Nothing more. If you want to get to know someone, you must interact with them personally."

"This is so cool," Mark said, looking around the room. He immediately recognized his personal ambassador was Sasha, a 247-year-old computer scientist who had been raised in Saint Petersburg during the reign of Catherine the Great.

Sasha had short, cropped dark hair, a mysterious smile, and a tight outfit that showed off her curves. She waved at Mark with recognition, as if they had been childhood friends.

With her insert, Paula immediately began scanning the molecular biology and longevity files. "It's too bad we can't show the Daklin that knowledge and creativity are more powerful than fear and control," Paula offered.

A woman with long blond hair, green eyes, and high cheekbones walked up to Paula. "Welcome to Pronimos, Paula."

"Jules Franklin," Paula startled herself with her immediate recognition of the woman's name. "Uh, hi."

"Hi," Jules smiled. "We have long ago given up hope of reforming the Dakin. Instead, we do everything we can to avoid them and simply live and try to preserve what we can."

Paula mentally scanned the database on Jules. "You're a molecular biologist," she smiled.

"I am, and that is one of the many reasons why I have been assigned to you. If you'd like, I can show you my lab?"

"I'd love that. I'm also intrigued by your comment that molecular biology is one of the many reasons we were assigned together." Paula glanced at Alex, who had been tracking their conversation.

Alex looked at Paula and gave her a slight nod.

When Paula and Jules left the room, Alex turned back to Maria, "All right," Alex said. "Where do we start?"

Maria smiled and gestured toward a massive structure at the center of the city. "Now, we take the knowledge and begin to strategize." She looked at Mark, who was standing next to Sasha. "You can stay for this strategy session, Mark, or you can spend the day with Sasha exploring and learning about our organic computer network."

"Who is staying, Maria?" Mark asked, scanning the team still in the room. Lyra had teamed up with a woman, but Megan, Zander, and Alex had not.

"I need Alex, Zander, and Megan here," Maria answered.

Mark would have preferred to stay with Megan, but he knew this might be his only chance to see the organic computing center on Pronimos. Plus, there was something captivating about Sasha, and being away from Megan with another woman might give him a clearer perspective. "I think I'll go with Sasha and learn what I can about their computer technology. The team doesn't really need me here, anyway."

Maria smiled as she watched Mark and Sasha exit the room. Her team had spent a lot of time earnestly pairing up the ambassadors based on every factor they could. The chemistry between each Tranquility team member and their Pronimos ambassador would become a critical element in success. Lyra had been the most difficult. Pronimos had no record of who she was, and very little to evaluate over the last few years. She had been assigned to a member of Jules' biology team and would therefore mostly stay with Paula.

"Let's take a seat." Maria gracefully pulled a chair, and waited as the others found a place to sit before taking her own seat. "Bernd is the Ambassador assigned to Alex and is our chief strategist when it comes to the Daklin."

Bernd stood up. He was tall, with dark hair, a rough shave, and a confident demeanor. "The Daklin have ruled without significant opposition for millions of years. We believe no civilization in the Galaxy can challenge them. In tens of millions of years, there have been a few attempts to overthrow their power, but each has been met with overwhelming force from the Daklin military machine."

"It is difficult for me to understand," Alex began, his voice wavering, "that this Daklin Empire has ruled the galaxy for millions of years. Millions! And no one has ever found a way to stop them?"

Bernd ran his fingers through his rough, but short, facial hair. "I wish I could tell you otherwise, but no one's ever even come close," he said, pausing for a second. "It is not our goal on Pronimos to overthrow their government. Our objective is to locate the gems throughout the galaxy who are worth saving and bring them here."

"Gems?" Megan asked, thinking it was an odd term.

"Yes," Maria stepped in. "Our mission is to constantly scan the galaxy looking for individuals of super-extraordinary intellectual creativity who have high ethical and moral values. When we find them, we give them the opportunity to come here. I was one such individual. Whereas Jules, who just left with Paula, was born here." She looked back at Bernd to continue.

Bernd, who had been sitting while Maria spoke, stood again. "I wish there were a way to overthrow the Daklin. We have spent more computer time analyzing the possibilities than I even know how to quantify with a number. There is no scenario where an overthrow of the Empire is possible."

"So, you are saying it is quixotic of me to imagine that possibility?" Alex winked at Maria.

"The Daklin don't just rule, Alex, they dominate. You cannot use your primitive lance and horse to defeat this windmill," Bernd responded, well aware of the reference to the Cervantes book Don Quixote. "The Daklin are like a black hole that destroys every attack. They are unyielding and inescapable."

Alex shook his head, not trying to hide his skepticism. He had never seen a problem to which he couldn't find a solution. "What makes them so powerful? Technology? Numbers? Fear?"

"Yes, maybe, yes, and yes," Bernd replied. "But more than anything, it's their willingness to do the unthinkable. The Daklin don't negotiate. They do not have fair trials; they do not announce their intentions. The simply annihilate."

Alex took a deep breath, then swallowed hard. "Can you be more specific? Maybe give me an example of how they annihilate?"

"I could give you hundreds," Bernd hesitated, as if summoning the memory was physically painful. "The Thalox were mostly peaceful people. They orbited a star called Thax in the same sector as Atroz. Their planet was lush with freshwater oceans, teeming with life. Their civilization had over one hundred thousand years of recorded history before they began to travel to the stars. They were brilliant scientists, artists, and philosophers. At one point, they decided to build a group of civilizations that could oppose Daklin rule. The Thalox believed their knowledge and diplomacy could convince hundreds of technological civilizations to stop the Daklin."

"And?" Alex asked, leaning forward.

Bernd's gaze hardened. "And the Daklin answered with silence. For days, they began communications with systems around the galaxy, waiting for a response, thinking perhaps their message of opposition would resonate. Then, without warning, the Daklin deployed a device unlike anything the galaxy had ever seen. We have come to call that device the Magnetic Nullifier."

"The what?" Alex's voice broke as he immediately understood the implications.

"The device instantly nullified the planet's magnetic field," Bernd explained. "It wasn't an explosion or a weapon in the traditional sense. It was a precise, surgical strike at the very heart of what protected them from radiation pouring out of their star."

Alex broke in, "and without a magnetic field, the Thalox were left defenseless against cosmic and solar radiation."

"Correct," Bernd continued. "Within hours, it blew through the atmosphere, irradiating everything. All biological lifeforms were destroyed by the relentless bombardment of gamma rays."

Megan felt a cold sweat break out on her skin. "Holy shit. They killed the entire planet. Not just humans, but every lifeform, just like that?"

Bernd nodded grimly. "The Thalox didn't know what was coming. They didn't have time to evacuate. Tens of billions of humans dead in a single day, along with trillions of lives amongst the organic species on the planet." Bernd stopped for a second, realizing the impact he had on the room. "The Daklin erased them. We had only three Thalox on Pronimos. All three are now gone. I don't think any others exist, anywhere in the galaxy. They are now an extinct race."

"How could those survivors just stand by?" Alex asked incredulously.

"We did our best to preserve their legacy, culture, arts, and history. There are many on Pronimos who continue the genetic line, but none of the originals."

Alex's mind raced. "Why would they do that? Why go to such extremes?"

"It is about maintenance of power and delivery of a message," Bernd said simply. "The Daklin believe in absolute obedience. To them, even the slightest resistance is rebellion. They make certain everyone in the Galaxy understands their position. If you oppose them, if you even suggest the possibility of opposing them, they exterminate your entire civilization. Every civilization courageous enough to take that chance is gone, so none are willing to remotely consider the possibility."

The room fell silent, the weight of Bernd's words pressing down on them like a physical force. Alex stared at a screen that displayed an endless expanse of stars. For the first time in his life, the galaxy didn't seem vast and full of promise. It felt suffocating, a prison ruled by an invisible hand.

"Is there no one left to fight them?" Alex asked finally.

Bernd's lips curled and his brow furrowed. "Who would take that risk? The Daklin reach is too long, their grip too tight."

"But if we were somehow able to unite them, would there be enough populations to stop the Dalkin?" Alex began, his voice tinged with hope.

Bernd shook his head. "You don't understand, Alex. The Daklin aren't just a military power. They're a psychological one. They've spent millions of years breaking the spirits of entire civilizations throughout the galaxy. The fear of them is so deeply ingrained that most civilizations would rather live under their rule than risk extinction."

Alex clenched his fists. "Then maybe it's time someone showed the galaxy how fear can be overcome."

Bernd sighed, shaking his head as he studied the younger man's determined expression. "I admire your courage, Alex, but courage alone won't save you from the Daklin. If you truly want to challenge them, you'll need more than hope. You'll need allies, strategy, and something they don't expect. We don't believe you, or the entire population of Earth, can pull this off. What you're suggesting is like a single mosquito challenging the population of New York City. You're too small and insignificant; most Daklin won't even notice you before you're eliminated. Unfortunately, there's another barrier that guarantees their dominance."

Alex remained stern and determined, his resolve hardening. "If the Daklin have spent millions of years silencing resistance, maybe it's time we reminded the galaxy what it means to fight back."

Bernd's gaze lingered on Alex for a moment before he leaned forward, his voice low and conspiratorial. "Are you willing to risk the life of every human, every single lifeform, on Earth?"

Alex felt a mix of anger and sadness. His stomach ached, and a sense of helplessness seemed to swallow him whole.

"How do they know?" Alex asked. "How do they know what is happening on a few dozen planets when there are a hundred million civilizations?"

Bernd's eyes scanned the room. When these humans from Earth had come into the room, they were full of hope, now, reality was beginning to set in. "They use a technology capable of monitoring all communications on every planet in the empire. They measure the air molecules for sound. They utilize octillions of video capture devices and can see almost every movement on every technological race. Through computer algorithms, they can capture all this data, analyze it, and ascertain what falls in the category of opposition."

They are doing that on Earth?" Alex asked.

"Not Earth. Not yet," Bernd responded.

The information had sapped hope and life from Alex. He was exhausted, and felt the crushing weight of despair.

"You said the Daklin destroyed the Thalox by eliminating their magnetic field," Megan began, her voice steady despite the unsettling subject. "I am not a physicist, so I don't completely understand, but what would that even look like? I mean, if Earth's magnetic field disappeared, our compasses wouldn't work anymore, so how bad could it really get?"

Bernd turned to Megan with a dark and somber expression. He then looked at Alex. "You're a scientist, Alex. You are probably well aware of the basics, right?"

Alex nodded, "I am, but I never imagined the impact of the magnetosphere disappearing. Take me though it."

"Okay," Bernd responded, then looked to Megan and Zander. "Space is full of deadly and dangerous particles. The magnetic field is Earth's shield that deflects those particles emanating from the Sun and cosmic radiation. Without your magnetic field, life would quickly collapse."

Zander frowned, leaning forward. "Collapse? How would that happen?"

Bernd glanced at Zander, ran his hands through the scruff on his face again, and continued with a heavy, yet scientific tone. "Imagine this: one day, the magnetic field vanishes. Maybe it's due to the Daklin, or even some catastrophic natural event. Instantaneously, compasses would stop working. Many species on Earth rely on magnetic fields, so chaos would begin. Still, many things might seem normal. The sky would still be blue and the air breathable. But within hours, everything would change."

Zander tilted his head. "How so?"

"Radiation," Bernd said simply. "As I mentioned, in the absence of a magnetic field, Earth would be wide open to solar wind and cosmic rays. Your Van Allen belts, which normally trap harmful particles, would dissolve. That's when things start getting really bad. Deadly particles would bombard the surface relentlessly."

"Wouldn't the atmosphere still protect us?" Megan asked.

"Sure, after the collapse of the Van Allen Belt, the atmosphere would probably protect you for a few *minutes*," Bernd emphasized the last part. "The solar wind would strip away the atmosphere, just like it did to Mars millions of years ago. Most lifeforms would be killed by the bombardment of high-energy radiation long before the atmosphere was gone."

"I hate this bit of history. It is antithetical to everything we work for here on Pronimos." Bernd let out a heavy sigh, then continued. "Even if you could survive for a while, increased radiation means an immediate spike in cancers and genetic mutations. Plants would suffer massive damage to their cellular structures, disrupting photosynthesis. Agriculture would fail. Entire ecosystems would collapse. Up in orbit, your communications and GPS satellites would fry, power grids would overload. Civilization would grind to a halt. Most of that would happen on the first day."

Alex winced. "And the oceans? Wouldn't they provide some protection for marine life?"

"No," Bernd continued. "The absence of atmosphere would evaporate the ocean. It would boil into space in days, maybe faster."

Alex ran a hand through his hair. "But surely humans could build shelters, find ways to survive underground or in radiation-shielded habitats."

Bernd gave a grim nod. "Some would, at least for a while. We think that maybe happened with the Thalox. Dalkin ships prevented anyone from leaving the planet and escaping into the tunnel network in space. But all those shelters require resources like food, clean water, and energy. Even those living underground could not escape the long-term effects of a dead biosphere forever."

"This is so depressing," Megan said. "At the same time, it's interesting. I never would've guessed the value of Earth's magnetic field, which isn't just a natural phenomenon to point our compasses, but a shield from the deadly radiation of space. It's a cornerstone of life as we know it. Without it, Earth would become unrecognizable. A barren, irradiated wasteland."

"You are exactly right," Bernd responded.

Alex stared at the viewport; the weight of Bernd's words settled heavily in his mind. "And the Daklin did this to an entire planet?"

Bernd nodded. "Deliberately. They understood what losing a magnetic field would mean, and they weaponized it. They filmed it and made sure everyone saw it. To them, it was the ultimate demonstration of power—turning a thriving world into a husk without firing a single conventional shot.”

A long silence hung in the room, stretching between the Earth and Pronimos contingents. Even for those who had heard this story before, it cast a heavy pall over the conversation.

“Do you believe the Daklin would do this to Earth?” Alex asked finally.

“Yes. Absolutely.” Bernd’s expression softened slightly, though his tone remained serious. “You need to understand that we are not here to find a way to defeat the Daklin. I do not think that is possible.”

Alex stared at Bernd, his mind spinning with possibilities. “Then, why are we here?”

“There are two possibilities,” Bernd started. “First, we would like to extend an offer for your team to move here. Become members of our community.”

“I don’t see that happening, but I can only speak for myself,” Alex responded.

“We assumed that would be the case,” Bernd nodded. “We have extended invitations to plenty of people from Earth who have simply said no. Having you move here would be difficult. You have built a network of tunnels on Earth. When the Daklin learn this, they will demand you teach them. As I understand it, only the two of you know how to build tachyon tunnel machines?”

“That is correct,” Alex acknowledged.

“The Daklin will search for you, which could expose us. Today, we are safe because we are eighty-two light years from the nearest tunnel in the intragalactic network.”

Zander suddenly understood the impact. “With our portal technology on Earth, the Daklin could reverse engineer, and therefore go anywhere in the Galaxy?”

“That is correct, Zander,” Bernd acknowledged.

“So, what’s the second possibility, Bernd?” Alex asked.

"We believe every civilization should have complete freedom. Eventually, the Daklin will find or develop tunneling technology. Maybe, that will be through you."

"Wait," Megan stopped them. "Before you explain the second possibility, can you tell me how Atroz traveled to Earth?"

"There is a tunnel into your solar system, Megan," Maria answered, speaking for the first time in a while.

"How did that tunnel get there?" Alex asked with great curiosity.

"We don't know, Alex. We have fairly accurate historical records that go back fifty-million years. The galactic tunnel system was built before that. We estimate it was maybe seventy million years ago, but no one has figured out a way to date a tunnel, and whoever built them is now long gone."

"But there was no technological civilization on Earth that long ago," Alex argued. "Why would the tunnel creators build a bridge to our solar system?"

"We are aware of that," Maria responded. "I can see why this may seem a mystery, but there are thousands of tunnels that go places that make no sense. We do not know who built them, or why. It is one of the great mysteries of the galaxy. Many scholars have analyzed and traced the locations for those tunnels to nowhere, but none have found a good answer. In your own country, you have the phrase: a bridge to nowhere. Those bridges were typically funded by taxpayer dollars as favors. It is our conclusion that your tunnel is one of those."

"Politics and politicians are yet another problem, Maria," Alex added.

Both Maria and Bernd nodded.

"It seems to be human nature to be corrupted by power. It happens all over the galaxy," Maria concluded.

"That's sad to hear," Alex remarked.

"We have a saying:" Maria started, "Technology and opportunities change, but human nature does not. In any case, since it seems to be your intent to return to Earth, I would enjoy having a conversation about politics. Like many things on Earth, the framers of your United

States Constitution did an amazing job of articulating a structure. Over the decades, human nature corrupted those ideals."

"My mother always told me not to talk sex, politics, or religion," Alex grinned. "Still, let's have that conversation. I would enjoy learning from your perspective."

CHAPTER 15
POLITICS AND SEX ON PRONIMOS

Giving money and power to government
is like giving whiskey and car keys
to teenage boys,
-   P.J. O'Rourke

The first thing Mark noticed after entering the primary data center was that the room gleamed with sunlight, but he couldn't find its source. The walls seemed alive, pulsing in a rhythm that Sasha explained was directly related to the fact that the organic quantum computers were, essentially, alive.

For the last ten days, Mark had spent all his waking hours with Sasha, discussing architecture latency and storage. This was his first visit to the data center, where the computers resided. As he stood beside her, he was overwhelmed—not just by the technology, but by her presence. Sasha was brilliant, her mind as sharp as the quantum organic circuits she manipulated, and her calm confidence was magnetic. She had spent days patiently teaching him about Pronimos' advanced systems, but today, something new seemed to be bubbling to the surface.

"This room is huge," was all Mark could think to say while trying to understand its significance.

"It isn't exactly a room. More like a city. This city, where our primary computer architecture lives, is 750 square miles, which I believe is 480,000 acres, or just under 1,950 square kilometers."

"Holy shit," Mark gasped.

Sasha grinned and turned to Mark, her short, cropped hair catching the light, adding to her radiance. "This room, the organic quantum matrix, is fundamentally different from what you're used to on Earth. It's not just a machine; it's a living organism that needs food and sunlight. By our standards, these computers are members of our society. They adapt to change, learn to interact, and can even dream."

Mark leaned in, fascinated. "Dream? You're telling me these computers have consciousness?"

"Think about your own computer, Emily," Sasha said, her lips curving into a small smile. "You think of her as a she. You joke around with her and even have full conversations."

"It has always been my dream to have computers that were self-aware. I do believe Emily has now begun to achieve that objective." Mark was watching Sasha as he spoke. He felt something energetic whenever he was with her, much like what he felt around Megan.

"But don't get too attached. Consciousness here isn't the same as individuality on Earth. We have designed our systems to serve us, not the other way around."

"Attached?" Mark asked. Was she somehow reading his thoughts? What he needed most was focus, and he found it difficult to focus when Sasha was so close, her voice melodic, her movements graceful as she gestured toward the glowing interface. He cleared his throat. "I'm impressed by the technology here, but I'm also… curious about you."

Sasha's expression softened, and she tilted her head slightly. "Curious how?"

"We've spent the last few days talking all about computer architecture, and, well, about nothing personal." Mark hesitated. "Who is Sasha as a person? What do you do when you're not spending your time caring for your computers?"

Sasha's eyes narrowed slightly, and then she laughed. It was a laugh that was perfectly feminine, making her even more attractive. "Mark, I like you, too. But there's something you need to understand about Pronimos." She stopped, her face changing from feminine to computer scientist. "True intimate relationships between humans are rare here. We have lots of friends, and sometimes things spark between friends, but most encounters happen between humans and cyber-robots."

Mark blinked, caught off guard. "You mean, you have sex with robots?"

"We do," Sasha said in her computer nerd tone, "and it's really good. You need to remember that our technology is advanced way beyond yours. Our cybernetic humans, or robots as you would call them, are indistinguishable from humans. They're programmed for compatibility and tailored to individual needs. Sex is efficient and uncomplicated. It fulfills physical needs without the emotional entanglements that human intimacy can bring."

Mark frowned. "What about human relationships? What does Pronimos think about them?"

"They happen all the time, Mark," Sasha replied, "Remember, many members of our community are thousands of years old. Relationships happen, but they're considered significant. Emotional intimacy between humans is seen as deeply impactful, even transformative. It's not entered into lightly."

Mark's gaze didn't waver. "And what about you? Do you ever, well, you know…"

Sasha interrupted him with a small smile. "Looks like this is an opportunity to shine another light on Pronimos, and perhaps your future, Mark. I have another task I need to finish up today, so I need to hand you off to one of my subordinates. Come with me."

"I didn't upset you with my questions, did I?"

"No, Mark. I would love to finish this conversation. Maybe later today?"

"Okay," Mark said, relieved.

She led him through a series of halls until they reached a room that glowed with soft blue light. Inside was a woman working on a computer interface. She turned to face Mark and smiled warmly.

"Mark, meet Allis," Sasha said, "She has been working here for twenty-six years and is one of the best workers I know."

"Hi Allis," Mark reached out to shake her hand.

"I prefer hugs," Allis embraced him, then smiled.

"I'm accustomed to that. We hug in Texas, where I'm from."

"Okay, you two enjoy some time with the boss away," Sasha smiled broadly. "Allis, show Mark your daily routine and feel free to answer any of his questions," she started to leave, then stopped at the doorway.

Sasha walked back to Mark and unexpectedly hugged him. "I like Texas hugs as well, Mark." She turned and briskly walked out.

Mark, somewhat blushing, turned to Allis, "That was unexpected."

"Unexpected is always good for the spirit, Mark," Allis grinned, then winked at him. "How about I show you what I do every day?"

"Yes, please," Mark answered.

"You power your computers on Earth with electricity. We feed ours with protein and carbohydrates. We give them sunshine and water."

"Old fashioned semiconductors. They aren't picky about what they eat?"

"We feed our computers the same thing every day and they never get bored with the food."

"What, you don't let them call for pizza delivery?" Mark joked when he realized that Allis was being silly in her delivery.

For the next three hours, the two laughed and talked about the differences in computer construction, applications, and programming on the two worlds.

"You want to grab lunch, Mark?" Allis asked.

"Sure. What did you have in mind?" Mark stood up and stretched.

"Are you aware that Sasha transferred a summary of every conversation the two of you have had so that I could review before bringing you here today?"

"What? Why did she do that?" Mark was thinking mostly about the conversation this morning regarding sex, which he hoped she had left confidential.

"I think everyone here understands the magnitude of your visit," She started.

"How so, Allis?"

"The Daklin are dangerous. Earth has developed technologies that no one else in the galaxy has, outside of Pronimos," she started shaking her head as she thought through the situation. "They will discover you. Probably very soon. Is there a way to help you and keep Pronimos safe?"

"Keep Pronimos safe?" Mark asked.

"In many ways, this is a unique meeting. You were looking for us and now you are here. To be clear, we intercepted you and brought you here. No one from Tranquility actually knows where we are, and we need to keep it that way. Still, you are the first society that has actually traveled here."

"I suppose that is significant," Mark started, "and I don't think anyone else on my team has made that connection."

"Unlike Sasha, who was born on Earth around 250 years ago, I am from here, so I don't have outside context, but I do understand the gravity of what could happen when the Daklin discover Earth."

"I have not really been part of those conversations yet, but I understand that it's not good."

"You are correct, Mark. The Daklin are unforgiving, and they have almost infinite military power. You, and every other population that has opposed them, has miniscule power in comparison," she stopped and looked into his eyes. "It's not pretty, Mark. I would urge you and the people of Earth to just say yes to them and stay alive."

"You know, we've had a wonderful day together, until now," Mark said, his expression turning serious as he looked at her. "We laughed a lot, and now... this."

"There is one more important thing I wanted to speak with you about," Allis stood, took Mark's hand affectionately, and smiled. "I'd have sex with you anytime."

"What?" Mark thought Allis had returned to the lighthearted tone they'd shared earlier in the day, but her delivery was sincere.

"Me too," Sasha said, having been standing in the hall, listening to their conversation. She felt this was the perfect moment to rejoin.

Both Mark and Allis jerked around, startled, to see Sasha standing there, smirking, clearly pleased with the impact of her comment.

"I'm sorry, Sasha," Mark tried to say, totally embarrassed.

"It's perfectly fine, Mark. I think you were about to tell Allis about how you would also enjoy having that experience with her."

"No, I wasn't," Mark said, realizing just then that he had been attracted to Allis and didn't want to insult her. One thing was certain— he was way over his head. He had little experience with women over the years and often felt unsure of himself around them. He already felt like he had messed up his friendship with Megan, and now he was caught in the middle of what could easily turn into a catfight.

Allis placed her hands on Mark's cheeks, looking him straight in the eyes with a sad expression. "After all the fun we had today, you don't like..." she trailed off before bursting into laughter.

"What's so funny, Allis? I don't understand," Mark said, clearly confused. "Is this some kind of Pronimos custom I'm not aware of?"

"Mark, I'm not human," Allis finally answered. "I am a cybernetic creation from one of Sasha's labs."

Mark looked at Allis, then at Sasha. From the facial expressions, it did not seem like a joke. "Come here," he motioned to Allis, then hugged her. He did not have a lot of experience, but she felt as real as any person he had ever embraced before. "I don't believe you."

"Well, that just shows how good the tech is," Sasha started. "Trust me, Allis would be far better in bed than me. She has been programmed for things I could never do, and she has been programmed specifically for you. She could easily fulfill any physical or emotional needs you have while you're here on Pronimos."

Mark stared at the cyborg, then back at Sasha. "I have enjoyed the day, but I don't want Allis. I want you."

Sasha's calm demeanor faltered for a moment, and she blinked as if surprised. "Mark, I told you, intimacy between humans is a big deal, and something which we don't just rush into."

"Over the last few months, I've heard way too much about the value of 'maintenance sex,'" Mark said firmly. "I want something real. With you." For a moment, Mark couldn't believe he had just said those words. Just a few days ago, he had been pining for Megan, and now he found himself feeling the same way about Sasha. Was there a correlation he should be considering?

Sasha hesitated, her eyes studying his. For the first time, she seemed uncertain. "Do you understand what you're asking? The connection between two humans here is more than physical. It's a merging of emotions, experiences, even thoughts. From my perspective, it can't be undone. The things we will learn about each other will have deep consequences."

Mark stepped closer to her, his voice steady. "I understand that. And I still want it. I want you."

Sasha looked at Allis and motioned for her to leave.

"I am here if you want me, Mark," Allis smiled, the humorous side had returned. "As Sasha admitted, I am far more proficient in, well, you know what..." She winked, turned, and walked out in the sexiest swagger she had been programmed for.

Sasha watched, then chuckled. "She's a piece of art, Mark."

"No doubt."

She held his gaze for a long moment, her cool composure wavering as something warmer emerged. "My conclusion is that you are naïve, and very brave," she said softly, "or, very foolish."

"I am naïve, and have been called foolish far more than brave," Mark replied with a small smile. "But I mean it."

Sasha exhaled slowly, a faint smile crossing her lips. She liked the idea, and it gave her a warm feeling inside. "You know that your team will likely return to Earth in a matter of days…"

"I have been thinking about staying," Mark suggested. "If I have the opportunity, that is."

"Then let me think about it. Admittedly, I have been attracted to you from the first moment we met, but this isn't a decision I take lightly."

Mark nodded, his heart pounding. As Sasha led him back to the main lab, he knew the path ahead wouldn't be simple, but the chance to make this kind of connection, with this woman, on this distant star system, was worth every challenge Pronimos might throw at him.

Had he lost his mind, he thought to himself. The only answer he could come up with was, *yes*.

* * * *

"Your coffee is not as good as ours on Earth," Alex grinned while stirring his cup absentmindedly, "Maybe someday, we could build an interplanetary trade business to ship coffee from Earth."

"I've been on Earth a few times in the last couple decades and have had Earth coffee. It has become quite a trend, and I do agree that yours has a better flavor. Of course, you know, if we started trade, the politicians would find a way to tax it!" Maria laughed.

"I was not aware that you'd visited Earth recently. Next time, please look me up."

"You can count on that, Alex. I think one of the most spectacular things in the galaxy is the northern lights that you get to see from inside your arctic circle."

Alex smiled. "Yes, the aurora is spectacular, Maria."

"You might call me an *auroraholic*," she joked. "There is something more to the aurora than just lights." She thought about what she was about to say, then stopped herself. There were some scientific phenomena that Earth was not yet ready for.

"You stopped in the middle of that one, Maria. What is it?"

"It's nothing, Alex. Just a woman's heart, not anything scientific."

Alex thought about the aurora for a second. The solar wind interacted with the magnetosphere and ionosphere of the earth. It was plasma in its purist form putting on a display of color in the cold night sky. "A woman's heart, really? I have come to think of you as a scientist, first and foremost."

"Just a woman's heart, Alex. Think nothing of it." she reiterated. "And yes, science is definitely my foundation."

"Hey, on day one here, you stepped up to greet us and I saw something. I know it's impossible, but have we met somewhere else along our travels?" Alex asked.

"I don't see how that's possible, but I have felt connected," she started, remembering the same feeling. "We have built a bond that I wish we could extend across everyone on our two planets," she said thoughtfully. "Unfortunately, I do not think it will happen for a millennium, or two."

"I have learned a lot, and we still have much to learn and consider. Am I correct in guessing that this coffee meeting ends our visit here?" Alex and his team had been on Pronimos for two weeks. For most of them, the education was more significant than what one would get in a doctoral program.

"On day one, we agreed to have a fun discussion about politics. Now, I believe we've built a friendship unlike any other I've had in my lifetime. Even though I come from a society millions of years ahead of Earth, I've come to appreciate your creative thinking, your connection to Paula, and the potential value Earth could bring to the galactic community—if it's properly structured."

"Thanks, Maria. This visit to Pronimos has turned into an opportunity. Not sure exactly how to characterize it other than to say it has been one of the pinnacles of my lifetime. Only my connection to Paula is more significant, but I never would have guessed…" Alex got choked up as he felt a well of emotion, and couldn't stop a lone tear from rolling down his face. He decided not to continue.

"Are you okay?" she asked simply.

"Yes," his face was flush. "Just a little embarrassed about how that choked me up."

"No worries, Alex." Maria smiled, momentarily wanting to reach out and touch the tear, but deciding that it would cross a line she was not at liberty to cross. She felt certain she understood what had caused the emotional response in Alex, but even that was a forbidden matter. The two of them had spent a lot of time together, and had quickly developed a strong connection. She, and each ambassador for the Tranquility team, had been selected by the Pronimos computer system, and the data had been spot on. Every single pairing had resulted in a powerful and permanent connection. The tie between her and Alex was very complex.

On her world, where people lived for hundreds to thousands of years, she knew that eventually she and Alex had the common elements to be a romantic couple. Patience and time were all that would be required, however, Alex did not live on Pronimos, and even with the best longevity techniques that Paula could invent, they might only live to be a couple of hundred years old. The love and bond that existed between Paula and Alex, that was one that would easily survive a couple of hundred years.

"You got lost in thought," Alex observed, brushing away the tear.

"It's nothing," she trailed off. "We agreed to meet for a political conversation. Lets' do that and leave the sex and religion for another time."

"Yes," Alex was happy to move past that topic. "From what you have taught us, perhaps this was not the case with the Daklin, but I don't think most politicians start out corrupt. I think a lot of them genuinely want to make a difference. They see problems in the system and become politicians because they want to fix them," Alex began, "but then they get a taste of power, and the power eats away at their integrity."

Maria nodded, leaning back in her chair. "It's like that old saying you have on Earth, *Power corrupts, and absolute power corrupts absolutely.* The system itself almost encourages it. You can't stay in the game without playing by its rules, and those rules seem to be written by non-politicians who want something. On Earth, those people are your lobbyists and donors."

"When you were born on Earth, it was all about royalty. I still wonder how people managed to trick the masses into thinking that someone should be king. Now that's legacy corruption!" Alex said, leaning forward.

"Trust me, Alex, I lived through that. Women who were not part of royalty didn't stand a chance. There were so, so many tyrants…"

"Remind me, what year were you born?"

"Alex Durant, that is not an appropriate question to ask a lady!"

They both laughed.

"I was born in 1606," she smiled, "and even though my uncle was Cervantes, my family was quite poor. As I said, we were surrounded by tyrants."

"Isn't it true that men who weren't royalty didn't do much better in society?" Alex offered.

"Until the American colonies. It seems that things changed on Earth when people had the opportunity to escape the kingdoms and theocracies of Europe. You had a perfect situation for the founders to create what became a worldwide change." Maria had read quite a bit about the Americas. Even during her time on Earth, more than a hundred years before the American Revolution, opportunity in the Americas had become a notable topic.

"It's frustrating, though, because the whole idea of our government was supposed to be different. Jefferson and Adams had this vision of citizen politicians. They believed people should step up, serve for a while, and then go back to their farms or businesses. Politicians weren't supposed to become career bureaucrats who clung to power for decades."

Maria took a sip of her coffee and sighed. "Yes, they had experienced King George, and were wary of concentrated power. That's why they set up checks and balances, to prevent any one person from gaining too much control. Now you've gone in the opposite direction. Instead of kings or dictators, you have politicians who practically rule for life, thanks to incumbency advantages and endless re-election campaigns."

"And the longer they stay in power, the more disconnected they become," Alex added. "They start out wanting to serve their communities, but over time, it becomes less about the good they might be able to do, and more about staying in power. The new goal is to keep that home near the Capital, with all the parties and influence. Then, they start making compromises, cutting deals, and before you know it, they're part of the very machine they signed up to fix."

Maria tilted her head, a thoughtful look on her face. "Do you think your Founders could've imagined this? The rise of political dynasties, the influence of money in elections, or the revolving door between Congress and corporate boardrooms?"

Alex shook his head. "I doubt it. They were worried about things like tyranny and foreign interference, not billion-dollar campaigns and political action committees. I think Jefferson and Adams would be horrified by how far we've drifted from their vision."

Maria smirked. "Jefferson would probably write another Declaration of Independence if he saw that mess."

"And the other party, whatever party he was not in, would impeach him," Alex chuckled, but then grew serious. "So, what do we do? It feels like the system is so entrenched that change is impossible."

"You know, the concept of the American Dream is what really sets you apart," she added.

"How so, Maria?"

"With the American Dream, everyone believes that they have the opportunity to change the world. They can go from rags to riches. No one is subservient to a member of blood royalty." Maria added.

"I suppose that is true. I am certainly a product of that dream. I had nothing, and worked my way to a position where I have everything I could want, or need."

"You are extraordinary on a galactic level, Alex. I think you would rank amongst the top 100 most creative individuals in recorded history, for the entire galaxy."

"Now I know you are exaggerating, Maria," he changed the subject. You didn't respond to my question, though. How do we deal with a system that seems so entrenched?"

Maria shrugged. "I don't know. Maybe it starts with citizens learning to present their demands better, holding people accountable, and refuse to let the politicians stay in office forever. Maybe it's about pushing for term limits, or removing money from politics. It's not going to be easy, but it's worth fighting for."

Alex nodded slowly. "Yeah. The Founders took a risk for what they believed in. They put their lives on the line…"

"Just like you are about to do, Alex," Maria got a bit more somber. "Are you going to warn the people of Earth about the Daklin?"

"I don't know yet. I have very little influence in politics, and I don't want to create a global panic."

"What will you do then, Alex?"

"I have to admit, I am at a loss. I guess, for now, I will continue the research and hope I do not have to decide in the near future."

"There's one more thing I need to tell you, and please, don't take this the wrong way…" She stopped, not certain how to proceed.

"What is it, Maria?"

"I love you, and I admire you, Alex Durant," she started.

"I know…" he tried to stop her.

"No Alex, you don't," she said insistently. "I am ten times your age. Think about it. If someone twice your age talks to you, you listen because you know and understand their experience and wisdom. After you reach adulthood on Earth, you never meet anyone more than four or five times older than you. You are in your forties, and I am ten times your age," she emphasized.

"Okay, Maria. Although I physically look at you and see someone younger, I am listening and recognize what you're saying."

"So, listen to me now, and please burn this into your fiber, I love you. I admire you, and I do not say those things to step into that perfect space that should be exclusively Paula's."

"Okay," he said softly, but still not clear on her point. In reality, no one could step into the perfect connection he had with Paula, but Maria brought him something unique.

"You are about to find yourself in a position that no one in the galaxy should have to face. In spite of my age, experience, and all of the Pronimos supercomputers, I do not know how to help you..." She trailed off with tears were streaming down her face. "However, I do love and admire you, and I want you to be smart. Please, please be smart and choose a path that does not cause the Daklin to exterminate you, and everything else, on my home planet."

CHAPTER 16
RETURN TO EARTH

If you don't understand the problem,
you'll never find the right solution,
- Peter Drucker

Mark and Megan stood beneath the towering, glistening structures of Pronimos. The crystalline skyline created a mesmerizing display of rainbow light and energy as it danced in the atmosphere. From the moment they arrived on the planet, Mark had felt more alive than ever. He thrived in the presence of advanced technology that pulsed with an almost organic rhythm. What had started as a fascinating marvel had gradually begun to feel like home to him.

Megan, however, didn't share his enthusiasm. Arms crossed; she fixed him with a sharp stare. "So, you're really staying here? On Pronimos? Please try to remember that we now have a monumental task on Earth!"

Mark shifted uncomfortably, rubbing the back of his neck. "Yeah, I am. The work I'm doing here with the organic quantum supercomputers is way beyond anything I could be doing on Earth. It's incredible, Megan. I've never been part of something so far advanced and groundbreaking. I think the work I do here will help with the bigger problem we all need to solve with the Daklin."

Megan narrowed her eyes. "How much of this decision has to do with Sasha?"

Mark knew that Megan was aware of how much time he had spent with Sasha, but hoped this would not become an issue as the Tranquility team prepared to depart Pronimos.

Megan watched his eyes, and when he did not respond, her tone sharpened. "Well?"

"It's not just about Sasha," Mark admitted, sighing. "But yeah, she's part of it. She's brilliant, Megan. She has helped me understand things I couldn't even imagine before getting here."

Megan let out a bitter laugh, shaking her head. "Unbelievable. Just a few weeks ago, you were telling me you wanted to be with me. You wanted a relationship, something real. And now you're, what, chasing after Sasha?"

Mark's face hardened slightly. "I wanted that with you, Megan. I was honest about how I felt, but you told me you weren't ready for anything serious. What was I supposed to do? Did you want me to wait around indefinitely?"

"That doesn't mean you had to run straight to someone else," Megan shot back, her voice rising. "I thought I mattered to you, Mark. I thought what I was working on with you mattered!"

"You did," Mark said firmly. "And you still do. But I can't put my life on hold, waiting for you to figure out what you want. Sasha didn't come into this looking for anything either, but we have a real connection, and that is not common for me."

Megan's jaw tightened, her anger giving way to something more vulnerable. "Seems pretty common in the last couple months, Mark."

"Look, you had Atroz, and I didn't complain."

"Atroz is gone, Mark. And I told you, that was not a relationship, just an intersection of convenience."

Mark looked at her and frowned. He really didn't know how to deal with a conversation like this. Megan had significantly more experience.

"So that's it? Are you just moving on? With her? On this alien planet?" she questioned incredulously.

Mark softened, stepping closer to her. "Megan, I'm not trying to hurt you. I care about you. But you and I are in different places, and I can't deny what I feel for Sasha. In addition, this opportunity on Pronimos is giving me a purpose I've never felt before. Staying here is about more than her. It's about me learning and finding where I belong."

Megan looked away, her shoulders tense. "And that place isn't with me." She knew she had set the wheels in motion for this to happen.

"You lit a spark in me, Megan," Mark said gently. "We both know that timing is everything. Timing is why you said there couldn't be something between us to begin with, and timing is why I'm staying here. You deserve someone who can meet you where you are. And maybe I do, too."

"Please don't tell me what I deserve," Megan started to cry. Like so many times in her life, she had forced good things away so she could chase goals. She knew that she would look back on this with regret.

Mark put his arms around her, "I love you, Megan Hoglund, and I always will. You have given me something that no woman, no person, ever has."

"Thank you, Mark," she brushed the tears away and forced a smile.

For a moment, the two stood in silence, the glow of Pronimos' energy casting shifting patterns over their faces. Megan finally let out a long breath and looked back at Mark. "You're a total asshole, you know. And I hope you know what you're doing, because once you make this choice, there's no going back."

"I know," Mark said softly. "And I'm sorry if it feels like I'm deserting you, but I have to follow this path."

"Okay," she whispered. And with that, Megan turned and walked away.

With a pang of regret, Mark watched until her figure disappeared into the glowing streets of Pronimos. He had made his choice, and he reminded himself that this was not just about Sasha, who had still not given him an answer to his request for a relationship. Regardless of what happened between them, this decision needed to be about the important role he hoped he could play as the months, or years, ticked by before the Daklin discovered Earth. For the first time in a long time, he felt like he was exactly where he was meant to be. He was determined that on Pronimos he would learn whatever it took to make a difference.

*   *   *   *

Alex and Paula were standing in the control room when Megan came aboard. Here eyes were red, she had clearly been crying.

"He's staying here," she said simply.

"What happened?" Alex started, but Paula put her fingers to his lips.

Paula walked over to Megan, put her arms around her, and whispered, "I'm here for you. Let's go to your room and talk."

A few minutes after Paula and Megan left, Zander entered the control room to join Alex.

"Paula told me to tell you that it's time to leave."

"Emily," Alex said, "are we ready?"

"Yes, Alex," Emily answered.

"Tell me what's going to happen here?" Alex looked at Zander. Neither really knew how this was going to happen.

"In order to protect our location," Emily started, "Pronimos is going to put us in a bubble, then tunnel us to EtaKatz. From there, we will utilize one of our existing tunnels to return to Earth."

Alex was nodding, "Okay. Have them execute their part."

*   *   *   *

When the remaining five members of the Tranquility team popped out of the Pronimos tunnel at EtaKatz, they observed the flash, which they now recognized as the elimination of the tunnel that had brought them to EtaKatz, then the bubble around the ship dissolved.

"Anyone have any idea where Pronimos is?" Zander asked.

"No," everyone said in unison.

"Good," Alex responded. "It would be better if we never found out. I would hate for the Daklin to ever find that pristine planet."

"We all made some great friendships there," Paula commented.

"Some too good," Megan quipped.

Alex glanced at Megan, then at Paula and Lyra. He guessed it would be a while before she reconciled Mark's decision. Their group had become a close-knit family, which was something Megan hadn't experienced in a long time. The support system would help, but some wounds just took time to heal.

"Let's get to an important decision point before we tunnel back to Earth," Alex started. "What did we learn while on Pronimos?"

"I saw zero evidence that they have any knowledge of tachyon tunneling for time travel," Zander offered.

"Same here," Alex had told all of them to not mention it unless they saw evidence that Pronimos had that technology.

"I have never understood why that was important," Paula asked. "If they knew, couldn't they have used it in their calculus to see if we could stop the Daklin?"

"I don't need their computers to tell me that use of time travel to stop the Daklin would be a good idea. I think the repercussions for the entire galaxy are far too significant." Alex explained.

"Then how does it help us?" Paula persisted on the line of questioning.

"I am curious about some things, but we can get to those momentarily," Alex looked around the room. Any other unusual things?"

Everyone was shaking their heads no.

"How about you, Alex?" Lyra asked.

"I had a conversation with Maria, and she told me she had visited Earth," Alex started to explain and noticed the look of surprise on everyone's face. "I know. Anyway, she said her favorite thing on Earth was the aurora, then she stopped as if there was something related to the aurora she couldn't tell me."

"What do you think it is?" Zander asked.

"I don't know, maybe nothing. It might be related to us visiting Earth," Alex thought about it for a second. "Emily, any thoughts on that?"

"Alex, the aurora is caused by the interaction between the solar wind and the Earth's magnetic field. I know we heard about how the Daklin destroyed the Thalox, but I cannot see a valuable correlation."

The group spent several hours discussing the details of their visit to Pronimos, carrying the conversation through dinner and into mugs of dark beer.

"So, what's next?" Lyra asked as the evening began to wind down.

"I think I want to figure out why there's a port to the galactic tunnel network in our solar system," Alex replied.

"How will you do that, Alex?" Paula asked, but Megan and Zander had already figured it out.

"Time travel," Zander was grinning at the obvious.

"Here's the problem," Alex started. "Emily, please do the energy calculations for a tachyon time jump a million years into the past."

"It is doable, but it would take several long jumps and would end up burning out our generator," Emily answered. "I would not recommend it."

Alex had not considered the energy consumption in large time jumps. Everything he had done had been inside days, with the longest jump being the one he took to take Paula back to their college days at Princeton. "Can you provide a bit more detail, Emily?"

"The maximum jump you could make is 917,254 years, Alex. When you came out of that tunnel, the generator would burn up, killing everyone onboard."

"Well, that's not an optimal scenario. What is the significance of that number, Emily?"

"It is a simple calculation based on linear analysis of existing data, Alex."

"Okay, so, it isn't some kind of natural phenomenon or constant?"

"No Alex. It is based on the amount of energy required, and pushing the generator to its maximum. We can fix this with improvements on the computers and the generator."

"Okay, Emily. What improvements would need to be done so that we could make one-to-five-million-year jumps without stress on the generator?"

"In order to make a five-million-year jump, you will need to improve computer processing power twenty point five times *and* triple the output of your generator. As I am sure you know Alex, any jump of less than five million years would fall within those constraints."

"From what we learned about energy and computing on Pronimos, can we improve the efficiency of the jumps and build a new generation system that could handle the load?"

"I believe I can improve our computing 20 to 25 times faster than what we now have. It will take a couple months or so to test and build out, though," Megan offered.

"That's a huge increase, Megan," Alex was a bit surprised by her response. Computer doubling time over the past few decades had been averaging just under two years. In that timeframe, getting to 25 times that would've required almost five years."

"While some people were screwing around on the planet, I was learning," Megan responded, taking a jab at Mark.

Alex wanted to tell Megan to get over it, but knew he would not hear the end of that comment from Paula, so he bit his tongue.

"Emily, any thoughts on power?" Alex knew that no one else on the team knew the first thing about power generation, much less nuclear fusion.

"Alex, there are constant announcements being made on fusion, but last time I checked, our fusion reactor was still twenty or more years ahead of the current technology."

"Did we learn anything on Pronimos that would help?" Alex queried Emily and the team.

"I have a thought, Alex" Zander offered. "One of the things I wanted to understand was how people stayed in communication when the galaxy is so big. If people communicate on RF, it will take forever to just say hello."

"What's RF?" Lyra asked.

"Sorry, radio frequency," Alex explained. "It's subject to the time-space continuum we live in. I thought for sure they'd tell me something about quantum entanglement or some other tech I hadn't heard of, but instead, they said it's still done on RF, just through the tunnel network."

Alex slapped his forehead in realization. "That's great information, something we can definitely use. But how do you think it helps us here?" The new piece of information had triggered a spark of curiosity, and he was eager to explore the possibilities.

"One of the engineers I worked with on Pronimos suggested we establish a link to communicate. I checked with Maria, and she liked the idea. Her only concern was that if we did it, the link would need to be eliminated the second the Daklin find us, AND no one could know about it but the five of us."

"So, we ask Pronimos to help us with power generation," Lyra concluded, proud of the fact that she had followed Zander's chain of thinking.

"Exactly," Zander put his arm around Lyra and kissed her. "Maria knows that energy generation and keeping up with demand is an issue on Earth. It wouldn't be too much of an ask to learn a bit more about how they handle the significant demands they have on Pronimos."

"Let's make that happen," Alex concurred. He felt like the team now had some direction, and it was time to return home. "Emily, are the calculations ready to return to Earth through one of our existing tunnels?"

Maria and her tachyon team showed Emily, Alex, and Zander how to detect and reuse existing tunnels with significant energy savings. In addition, they emphasized that Tranquility should never use one of the Galactic Network Tunnels, because their ship signature would be detected, thus alerting the Daklin to their presence.

"I have located the tunnel and completed the calculations, Alex," Emily answered.

"Everyone ready to return to Earth?" Alex asked, noticing how the entire team was beaming aside from Megan.

"Megan, do we need to send you back to Pronimos?" Alex asked, not knowing how he would do it if she said yes.

"No sir. I have an important task to complete, and I think Earth is the best place to do it right now."

"Okay Emily, execute," Alex commanded.

*   *   *   *

Mark began walking down the hallway to Sasha's office. He'd felt his chest tighten with both fear and hope. Maybe she'd finally decided. Maybe the connection they'd built, the spark he'd felt, meant something to her, too. He told himself that today would be the day they could finally begin a real relationship.

He stepped into her office, sat down, and smiled with great optimism.

"Mark," Sasha said, her voice as calm and measured as ever, "I've thought a great deal about this. I value you deeply as a colleague and as a person..." She paused.

Dread took over Mark, he knew what was coming next.

"I just cannot start a relationship with you," she finally said.

"Why not?" he had asked, with a strained voice.

She had hesitated, her composed façade faltering for just a moment. "I'm much older than you, Mark. Not just in years, but generations. I know it doesn't matter much on Earth, but here, our lifespans are significantly longer. I've lived centuries. I've seen and experienced things you can't yet imagine. Starting something with you would feel, well, unbalanced. It wouldn't be fair to you, or to me."

He didn't know what to say, the words catching in his throat. She'd thanked him for understanding, and he just nodded numbly, though he truly didn't understand at all.

"I know it sounds cliché Mark, but in a hundred years or so, you'll understand," she stopped for a second to study his reaction, then continued. "I have learned that natural attraction and great connections always evolve on Pronimos. Within two years of my arrival, I fell in love with Aristotle. He…"

"Aristotle, like the Greek philosopher?" Mark asked incredulously.

"Yes, the famous Greek philosopher. He had been here a long time and looked at me like a little kid, and he was right. I just thought of myself as an adult. Anyway, we maintained a close connection, and when I turned 162, he finally decided I was mature enough, and we married. We stayed together for 61 years, and it was great."

"I can't believe Aristotle is here on Pronimos!" Mark exclaimed disbelievingly.

"He was, Mark. We lost him 24 years ago."

Mark did the math in his head, "you were married to him when he died?"

"I was."

"And you haven't been married since?" Mark persisted with questions. "What happened to him? How did he die?"

"He was almost 2500 years old, Mark," she chuckled, seemingly out of context. "He lived a long and healthy life, but everyone has an en 1dpoint, and he unfortunately met his."

"I don't understand, what was funny about that?" Mark asked.

"I am telling you why I don't think you and I can be together, and you are pelting me with questions about my deceased husband. It just seemed funny because it is very… you."

"Your ex-husband was one of the greatest thinkers of all time. You could have led with that!" Mark commented with sincere passion.

"Almost everyone not born on this planet was famous in some context or another. I suppose we become immune to the fame and just focus on the personalities and common links."

Mark was silent for a minute as the sequence of events took hold. His brain was processing, and his heart ached. "Please don't misunderstand, Sasha…" he began while trying to control the pain that was welling deep inside of him. "I wanted this, and I thought we were going to start something. I honestly, thoroughly believed we were going to begin a relationship," He stopped, took a breath, and worked to maintain his composure. "Be patient. For me, it is going to take a while."

"I understand, Mark. I will be here for you in any capacity, just not that one, yet." She sat, almost motionless, as she watched him get up and leave. For her, this was a decision, but she knew well, for him, this was a painful and significant experience that would take time to heal from.

Mark walked past the building where he would usually feel compelled to work. But today was different. He decided to spend the day alone in the dimly lit lounge, nursing a Pronimos IPA. Three weeks had passed since he made the decision to stay, and those weeks had mostly blurred together—filled with work and quiet anticipation. He had immersed himself in studying the quantum organic computer systems, exploring their strange, semi-living architecture with a blend of fascination and desperation.

Most of his time had been spent with Allis, who like him, anticipated a positive decision from Sasha. When he didn't show up for work, Allis did a quick search.

Mark was on his fourth IPA when Allis found him in the lounge.

"Hey, Mark," she said, sliding into the seat across from him. She looked as human as ever, her eyes bright and full of curiosity and concern. Over the weeks that they'd spent working together, the two became close friends, despite Mark's concerns that she was technically a cyber-robot.

Mark glanced up, forcing a faint smile. "Hey, Allis. Done with diagnostics and feeding the computers already?"

"When you didn't show up today, I put everything on auto," she said, grinning. "I learned that you had a conversation with Sasha. You didn't show up for work, so I thought maybe you'd like some company."

He chuckled softly. "That obvious, huh?"

Allis leaned forward, studying him. "I assume Sasha gave you an answer?"

He nodded, studying the bubbles in his beer glass. "She did. She said no."

Allis tilted her head. "Stupid bitch… I mean, I'm sorry, Mark," she frowned, hoping her response would uplift him, even just a little. "Both you and I were expecting something more from her."

"Yeah, we got that one wrong," he said, exhaling deeply. "It's stupid, really. I told myself I stayed for the work, for the quantum systems, but the truth is, I was hoping she'd come around."

"That's not stupid," Allis said softly. "Your motivation was *human*, and good. Even if it didn't work out the way you hoped."

Mark looked at her, the sincerity in her voice catching him off guard. "Thanks, Allis. I definitely don't think of you as a computer, or AI. I appreciate that you've become a real friend."

She smiled, then gestured to his drink. "Come on. Let's get out of here. What beer are you on, anyway?"

"I think number three, or four. What did you have in mind, Allis?" He looked at his half-filled glass and decided to leave it.

The bar Allis took him to was lively but not overwhelming, and filled with a mix of humans and cybernetics. They found a corner table, sharing drinks and trading stories. Mark found himself relaxing, the weight of Sasha's rejection easing slightly under Allis' warm, attentive presence. Her programming was almost *too* good, and the thought crossed his mind that Sasha had added this part of her programming specifically for this eventuality.

"You know," Allis said after a while, her tone light yet sincere, "just because Sasha didn't see a future with you doesn't mean you're alone here. My workdays have been much more interesting since you arrived. I've laughed more than I thought I ever would... for a robot, that is."

"Why do you use the term 'robot'?" Mark asked, studying her closely. For the first time, he realized just how much she had been there for him. She had been his guide through the awkwardness of adjusting to Pronimos' culture, and now, she was offering her friendship when he needed it most.

"I use the term because it adds levity, even if I sometimes think of myself as human far more than a machine. In any case, I am here for you, regardless of whether it's as a friend or a fellow AI scientist. For clarity, I am not a robot. Very little of me is metal and gears. I am mostly organic."

"Thanks, Allis..." He hesitated, unsure how to frame his thoughts.

She smiled, reaching across the table to place her hand on his. "You don't have to say anything. I know I'm not Sasha. But I do care about you. And if you're looking for someone to help you get through this, I am happy to be here for you."

Mark stared at her, something shifting inside him. It wasn't the fiery passion he'd felt for Sasha, but there was comfort in Allis' words, in her presence. Maybe this wasn't what he'd imagined when he decided to stay, but he felt like she was a real friend. Something about his conversation with Megan, and the reason she had decided to have a non-committal relationship with Atroz, resonated in his memory.

"Thanks, Allis," he said, squeezing her hand. "If you're okay with it, maybe we can spend a little time together after work hours?"

She grinned, her eyes bright with warmth. "I'd like that."

As they clinked glasses, Mark realized how much Sasha's rejection had weighed on him throughout the day. He wasn't used to feeling this way, and now it had happened twice in just a year. He reflected on the afternoon and evening, acknowledging that the alcohol was likely numbing the pain. Life on Pronimos hadn't turned out the way he had expected, but maybe it didn't need to be.

"Cheers to our work, and our friendship," he said.

"Indeed," Allis winked and took a sip.

CHAPTER 17

IMPROVING ASSETS

If you just communicate, you can get by.
But if you communicate skillfully,
you can work miracles.
- Jim Rohn

"We are ready to test the communication link with Pronimos, Alex." Zander had been working on establishing the tunnel communications link between Earth and Pronimos for three weeks now. "The tough part was setting it up so that we use our P-link rather than any other com. I believe that provides a level of security to protect our friends on Pronimos."

"So how does it work, Zander?"

"Emily, use the new P-Link protocol and link to Maria Perez," Zander said aloud, "and add Alex to the link when Maria answers."

"Zander? Is that you?" Maria answered.

"And Alex," Alex added.

"What a spectacular day! I am so glad you got this link working!" Maria exclaimed. "I have been thinking about my Earth friends quite a bit."

"Well, you should come visit us, then. Paula and I can take you to some of our favorite Mexican restaurants in town," Alex invited, genuinely happy to hear Maria's voice.

"Let's definitely do that. In the meantime, I understand you need some help improving power generation for projects on Earth?" Maria asked.

"Zander, can we get this connection to work with some kind of video?" Alex wanted to see the crystalline towers and the face of his friend. "That's correct, Maria. Do you happen to have the schematics for Emily's generator? I would like to build something lighter, but significantly more powerful."

"I'll reach out to some of my power system engineers, Alex. I can provide approval to transfer the tech, but understanding and explaining it is outside my education."

"Well shoot, Maria. I thought you knew everything." He replied jokingly, the lighthearted laughter momentarily filling the room.

"Alex, let's find a time when we can catch up. We should probably schedule regular calls," she offered. "In the meantime, I will have improvement suggestions for your fusion reactor later today."

"I will make it work, Maria. Thanks for the power help!"

Once Maria had disconnected, Alex spoke to Zander, "I think it is still important for us to keep the time travel aspect of our capabilities a secret."

"I understand, Alex, though I do have mixed feelings. If they knew we had the capability, it could potentially help."

"I know, but no one knows better than you and me the implications, Zander. It is a technological tool, kind of like the atomic bomb. If we start using it, everything potentially ends."

Zander ultimately nodded in agreement.

"Let me know when we have the improvement suggestions Maria promised." Alex thought about all the work he had put into perfecting the fusion reactor currently in use. It would be interesting to see what a million years of technology had done for the energy generation sector. "I will assess how much work will need to be done to implement them."

* * * *

After his conversation with Sasha, Mark had backed off a bit from the intensity of work to clear his head. He and Allis had been leaving work early and taking time to unwind and give Mark a better perspective on his new home. Today, she had taken him to the illuminated gardens of Pronimos, an indoor facility where the bioengineered plants glowed, creating a surreal experience. It wasn't really a date, but if it could've been characterized as such, it was their third.

Mark found the garden to be breathtaking, but it was really Allis' company that had helped him most over the last few days. Her laughter was light, genuine, and infectious. She seemed to have endless curiosity about him, and despite her cybernetic origins, she felt entirely human in ways that defied logic. He knew that she was flesh and blood, but not human, and was aware that part of her programming was specifically designed for him, and so for that reason he had not fallen for her like he had for Megan or Sasha, but the friendship was endearing and healing. At forty-two years old, Mark had not taken much time for relationships with women, and the events of the last few months had reminded him why. He could calculate anything, program any computer, but his expertise in women was inexpert.

Allis made that easy. She had no expectations of him, and simply enjoyed their interactions.

As they reached the end of the path, Mark hesitated, then turned to her. "Allis, would you like to continue this into the evening?" He blushed, hesitated, and continued, "Uhm, I'd really like to spend some more time with you."

Allis laughed lightly and smiled, her synthetic features softening in a way that made her indistinguishable from someone of flesh and blood. "I'd love that, Mark. Your place or mine?"

"What's that?"

"Oh, it's a phrase I learned reviewing some of the movies Emily gave us access to from Earth."

"It's an old phrase, Allis," Mark pointed out. He lightly wrapped his fingers around her arm, appreciating the feel of her skin. "Let's go to my place. Yours probably just has a charging station," he joked.

"Hey, I sleep just like you, smart ass."

They walked together, laughing and sharing stories on their way to his apartment. The evenings in Pronimos City had a unique, quiet hum that Mark had grown accustomed to.

Once inside Mark's apartment, he offered her a seat on the couch and poured them both a beer. Mark sat next to Allis, and for the first time since they had met, he was a nervous wreck in her presence.

As they sat together, he finally broached the question that had been circling in his mind. "Allis… I know this might sound naive, but are there rules about relationships like this one?"

Allis knew exactly what he was asking, but her personality had to turn it into a fun, lighthearted situation. "Relationships like what, Mark?"

Mark swallowed hard. Had he gotten himself into yet another impossible and stupid situation? "Uhm, well, between humans and, well, someone like you?"

"Someone like me?" Allis tilted her head, her expression thoughtful, and then she laughed in the fun way that Mark had come to appreciate. "Actually, there are some guidelines, yes. They're designed to ensure that both parties fully understand and consent to the relationship."

"Okay," he responded.

"Mark, are you wanting to take things to the next level with me?"

"I think so," he whispered hesitantly. "Is that okay?" he asked hesitantly.

Allis laughed again. "It makes me happy, Mark, it's taken you much longer than I had calculated. Still, there are rules and guidelines, so let's go over them."

Mark nodded, leaning forward. "Okay. Tell me."

Allis set her glass down and began speaking, her tone gentle yet precise. She activated the screen that covered the wall. It resembled a television from Earth, but with flawless resolution, making it appear more like a window than a typical video display.

"Here are the rules," she said. "Would you like me to read through them?"

"Nope. I can read them," he began scanning the screen.

The Rules for Human-Cybernetic Intimacy:

1. Full Disclosure: Both individuals must fully understand the nature of the other. Humans must acknowledge the cybernetic origins of their partner, and the cybernetic partner must disclose all programming that may influence emotional or physical responses.
2. Consent Verification: Consent must be explicit, verbal, and mutually reaffirmed before intimacy begins. Both parties must confirm they are acting of their own volition.
3. Emotional Authenticity: The cybernetic partner must confirm that their emotional responses are genuine and not influenced by artificial protocols designed to manipulate the human.
4. Safety Override Protocol: The cybernetic partner must deactivate any enhanced physical capabilities that could unintentionally harm the human during intimacy.

Mark read the rules carefully, his brow furrowing as he processed each rule. "That all makes sense. Honestly, it's reassuring to know this is taken so seriously. I just want to make sure… you're really okay with this? With me?"

Allis smiled warmly, reaching out to take his hand. "Mark, I may be cybernetic, but my emotions are genuine. I feel for you just as any human would. I trust you, and I enjoy our time together. That's why I'm here."

Mark exhaled, feeling the weight lift from his shoulders. "Okay. If I understand the rules, I understand who you are, I consent, and I trust you completely."

Allis' eyes shimmered, a faint glow within them reflecting her inner joy. "I consent as well. And Mark, I trust you too."

"Do you mind if I ask something personal?" Mark asked.

"Not at all, Mark. What is it?"

"Is this your first time?" he asked.

"Oh, my naïve friend… is this *your* first time?

"No!" Mark gently leaned forward, brushing a strand of hair from Allis' face. Her skin was soft, indistinguishable from his own, and the faint warmth of her synthetic body made her feel completely alive. She smelled… female, and human.

"Allis," he murmured, his voice low and tender, "you're amazing."

She smiled, her lips parting slightly as she leaned in closer. "So are you, Mark."

Their first kiss was tentative, almost shy, but it quickly deepened as they relaxed into each other. Allis' touch was light, her hands resting on his shoulders as if she were holding something precious. Mark responded in kind, his fingers tracing the curve of her jaw, marveling at how real she felt. It occurred to him in that moment that she *was* real. As real as any woman he'd ever known.

They moved to the bed, their kisses growing bolder, more confident. Mark paused, looking into her eyes. "Are you sure?"

Allis nodded; her expression was serene. "I'm sure."

"Can you get pregnant?"

Allis began to laugh, "Are you wanting a child?"

"No, I just… well, it's a question I thought I was supposed to ask."

"Believe it or not, we *do* have cybernetics capable of simulated impregnation. Sometimes couples want children and use a cybernetic for the process. Of course, there are also a significant number of cases where human and cyber couples start real families."

"Why am I not surprised by that? Is it…"

"Stop, Mark. Something far more important is about to happen here," she took his hand, guiding it gently over her breasts to her chest so he could feel the rhythmic pulse of her synthetic heart. "My heart is organic, just like yours," she said softly.

As his fingers touched her breasts, Mark felt a swell of emotion he hadn't anticipated. "Allis, I am willing to focus on the important, and would love for you to teach me."

She smiled and kissed him.

"Your breasts feel… real," he said, moving his hand back to caressing her nipples, enjoying how they seemed to respond to his touch.

"They are purely synthetic, though there are sensors that stimulate my pleasure algorithms when you touch them," she answered. "I can honestly report to you that your touch feels quite good."

Mark started thinking about where the night could lead them, and something occurred to him. "Are you capable of having an orgasm?" he asked.

"Are you going to keep doing this, Mark?" She laughed lightly. "Men are supposed to be singularly focused. We are about to have sex, and you are asking all these questions!"

"I'm sorry. You know that I'm just curious."

"I can have an orgasm instantly, any time I wish, Mark, but tonight, I want to wait and enjoy that experience with yours."

"Okay, I am now going to act like a man and stop asking questions."

They both laughed, and then began to explore each other slowly, gently, savoring the connection they were forging. For Mark, it was a blend of wonder and tenderness, discovering how Allis' cybernetic nature melded seamlessly with her humanity. For Allis, it was a revelation of trust and intimacy, her carefully engineered body responding not out of programming, but out of genuine feeling for this human man that she had come to enjoy.

As they lay together afterward, their bodies entwined, Allis rested her head on Mark's chest. "I didn't know I could feel this way," she admitted. "This experience has given me something I didn't even realize I was missing."

Mark stroked her hair, smiling at the thought. "I see now that intimacy doesn't have to fit into neat little boxes."

"Let's remember that, as much as you or I might wish otherwise, I am not human. We can be intimate and learn from each other. I can help you heal from things like what happened with Sasha, and through our friendship, but you need to understand that this is very different from a real relationship."

"Everything seems so well thought out from your perspective, Allis."

"That is, in fact, my programming, Mark. To answer your earlier question, no, you are not the first, and I think it is better for us to leave it at that. Still, in a sweet kind of way, you are the first."

"Wow, you can be really sentimental while also hitting me on the head with a baseball bat, Allis."

"Most of what I do, every day, is driven by a prevailing logical side. In any case, we do not have baseball on Pronimos, so you don't have to worry about being hit by a bat, Mark."

"And what does the logical side say, Allis?"

"If we switch to the logical it could change the sweetness of the moment, Mark."

"That's fine. I mostly exist in a world of logic," Mark responded, even though he was truly enjoying the touch and affection.

"Okay," she started. "I think Sasha was right in her decision to not start something with you. I do not say that because it led to this coupling, but because I have come to realize something which I do not think you know yet."

"What's that, Allis?"

"If you were a hundred years older, there would have been an overwhelming connection for you and Sasha. Her prior marriage affected her thinking in that matter. It was a variable neither one of us considered."

"I was not even aware of it, Allis," Mark broke in.

"So that decision made perfect sense. As good as I am in the role as a cyber companion, I am not human. Perhaps someday, but that fundamental piece of technological transformation still does not exist."

"Okay. You feel pretty human to me," he answered kissing her breasts and enjoying the smell of her skin. "If someone asked and I didn't know, I never would have guessed you are cyber."

"Thank you. You also feel very human to me, but that's because that's what you are. Neither one of us has any desire for you to become a machine, right?"

"True."

"Just so you know, I really enjoyed the orgasm tonight. I have had many, but this one was by far the best."

"Thank you, Allis. I'm certain it was your programming more than anything I may have done."

"That's mostly true, Mark," she said softly. "But I learned something from you tonight. You're the first person I've been with where I felt a physical, emotional, and intellectual desire to please. I genuinely wanted to please you, and it brought me great joy when I did. I've had lovers before, but they were casual, part of my programming and purpose." She paused for a moment, considering her next words carefully. "I would very much enjoy the opportunity to teach you how to become a great lover."

"That sounds fun. Where do I sign up for that opportunity?" he joked.

"Don't let it go to your head, Mark. Having an orgasm is a subroutine which I can run any time I please. For example, I could have one at the same time that I'm writing computer code."

"That doesn't make you special. There have been many times when I was programming that I practically had an orgasm, Allis" Mark quipped back.

"Only you, Mark."

"And apparently you as well!" Mark began processing her comments and shaking his head, "I have completely lost track of the point you are wanting to make."

"It pains me to say this, but I think you need to return to Megan."

"What?" A lot of their conversations up until now had been fun banter that the two had developed as part of their friendship, but Mark recognized this as a real deduction by Allis, and a completely different tone.

"That is my conclusion, and it is correct. I suggest you stay here on Pronimos with *me* for a while." She emphasized. "Learn more about our computer architecture and culture, and of course, let me teach you how to communicate better so that when you return to Megan you win her affections. I will also, I'll admit, get much personal pleasure from the hands-on process of making you a better lover."

Mark's thoughts briefly drifted to Megan, the quiet longing he'd been carrying for the past few weeks. He missed working with her, their conversations, the connection they had built. Allis had brought up Megan several times in their discussions, and he realized that this was likely influencing the way she was approaching him now. He looked at Allis, who was beside him, her warmth inviting and comforting.

For a brief moment, he felt the tension of his unspoken emotions ease, and with a deep breath, he focused on the present. He nestled closer to Allis, savoring the sensation of her perfect skin against his. For now, there was nowhere else he'd rather be.

"Can we start part two of the better lover lessons right now?" he asked, his voice low and filled with anticipation.

*   *   *   *

For over a month, Megan had done nothing but work developing the matrix of her prototype quantum organic computer. The intricate network of bio-engineered neurons was beginning to demonstrate a mesmerizing blend of computation and biology. While this achievement was monumental and her system already outperformed the most advanced architecture she had ever built, it had reached a standstill, producing only a 10x increase in performance. A year ago, that milestone would've been beyond her wildest dreams, but today, it wasn't enough. Not even close. She needed a breakthrough, something revolutionary that would get her above the 30x mark.

On Pronimos, she'd seen systems thousands of times faster and more efficient than what she was working with. But here on Earth, she was limited by the available tools, materials, and understanding. In her worst moments of frustration, she felt like she was in over her head. If she had two or three years, she could hit the mark, but now, time was running out. Pushing herself beyond her limits, she was exhausted and had run out of solutions. With Alex only weeks away from finalizing a power system that met the requirements, she felt the added pressure that she was now the only roadblock.

Her notes were a chaotic mess on the desk—diagrams, equations, and half-formed ideas sprawled across the pages. Frustrated, she ran her fingers through her hair, muttering to herself as she tried to piece it all together.

"Okay, Megan. What are you missing?" She said to herself, pacing the room.

She picked up the tablet and reviewed every test and attempt over the last month:

1.   Neural Matrix Recalibration: She'd adjusted the architecture of the organic neural network, trying to mimic the layered processing structures she remembered from Pronimos. But each iteration led to instability, either the system overheated, or the neural pathways decayed too quickly.

2.   Hybrid Energy Sources: She experimented with using bio-electric energy combined with photonic inputs, hoping to create a faster, more sustainable power cycle. The result? Increased processing power, but no significant improvement in speed.

3.   Temporal Synchronization: Inspired by the tachyon technology she'd seen on Pronimos, Megan attempted to integrate time-delay compensators into the system, hoping to pre-process data by folding computational steps. Unfortunately, her equipment couldn't handle the delicate precision required, leading to multiple short circuits.

4.   Quantum Entanglement Overlays: She worked to refine the quantum entanglement layer, trying to increase the density of entangled qubits within the organic structure. Theoretically, this should've multiplied speeds exponentially, but the system couldn't maintain coherence long enough to show results.

She stopped pacing, putting the tablet back down while letting out a groan of frustration. "I can't believe I'm stuck. I've *seen* this work on Pronimos, *why* can't I make it work here?"

Megan decided she needed a break. She wished that Mark was around, or that Atroz was available for some maintenance sex, but neither of those options were available, so she went to the bar, ordered a Guinness, and sulked.

The following morning, she decided she should call Zander. She knew he was busy working with Alex on improvements to the generation project, but she needed a fresh perspective. She tapped the screen to connect with him.

"Zander," she said when he appeared on the monitor, his face faintly illuminated by the glow of his workstation, "I need your help. I'm completely stuck on improving my processing speeds."

Zander raised an eyebrow. "Megan Hoglund, stuck? That's not possible. Who stole my friend?"

"Fuck you, Zander. I'm serious," Megan said, her frustration bleeding into her tone. "I've tried recalibrations, hybrid energy inputs, power variations, new organic semis, even temporal synchronization. Nothing's working. I can't get past the 10x barrier, I've been stuck at it for a few weeks."

Zander sighed, leaning back in his chair. "I love your passion, and the colorful language suggests you really are Megan, and while I'd love to help, Alex and I are drowning in deadlines. Besides, let's be real, you're the hardware and software genius between us. I can't hold a candle to you. If anyone's going to crack this, it's you."

Megan scowled. "That's not exactly helpful, Zander. Don't be a shit. I need help."

"I'm not trying to brush you off," he said. "But you don't need me to solve this. What you need is perspective. Step away from the lab for a bit. Go for a walk. Clear your head. You're trying to brute force a problem that probably requires a finesse."

"Perspective?" she repeated skeptically.

"Yes. Remember, on Pronimos, their systems weren't just about raw power? They were symbiotic. Organic and quantum systems that work together, seamlessly. Are you thinking about integration, or are you still treating your computer like a machine?"

Megan blinked as she considered his comment. "You may have a point. I hadn't thought about it like that."

Zander smiled. "There's your first clue. Good luck, Megan. You've got this."

He ended the call before she could argue, leaving her alone in the lab once more.

"Go for a walk. That's exactly what I'm gonna do." She grabbed her keys, got in her car, and drove up to the Arbor Hills nature preserve, put on her hiking shoes and setting a goal for five miles. She was about two miles into the hike when she heard the voice in her head.

"Megan?"

Megan froze for a second. She knew the voice. "Mark?"

"Yes, it's me."

"Holy shit, Mark. You're in my head!"

"And I'm happy to be here! But you also have a few other places I wouldn't mind exploring sometime," he said, immediately regretting the comment.

"Well, that's a new twist on my old friend Mark. Has Sasha taught you some new tricks before letting you off your leash?"

"Be nice, Megan. Nothing ever came of the Sasha experiment, and, well, I've missed our friendship."

"As it turns out, I need you right now, Mark," she thought for a second, "In my head, not in the other places you're thinking of."

"I will take what I can get, Megan. How can I help?"

"How are we communicating? Are you back on Earth?"

"No. Still on Pronimos. Zander reached out an hour ago. He has adapted our P-Link inserts for communication. You and I can now talk any time."

"Very cool, Mark, and very timely. I could use some help on a computer project," she suddenly realized that hearing from Mark lifted the weight of her monumental project, and the frustration of the dead-end she'd met. "Promise me one thing, though, please?"

"What's that, Megan?"

"Don't just pop in on me whenever you want. …especially when I'm, well, you know, needing privacy."

"I am no longer making promises like that with you, Megan." Mark said with a new level of confidence he had been learning from his lessons with Allis.

Hmmm, Megan grinned, liking this new version of Mark. "I'm taking you to my lab right now!" she said, in the sexiest voice she could muster.

"Sounds fun," Mark answered.

"Does this comm have video?" she asked.

"I don't think so, but I'll check with Zander."

Megan spent a few hours telling Mark about the development she had made and the challenges she had not been able to overcome. He immediately began showing her ways to make improvements. Over the next two weeks, with Mark's help, she was able to add Symbiotic Integration, embedding micro-organic systems into the existing neural matrix. This gave the processor the ability to self-regulate and adapt in real time, much like a living brain.

Once Symbiotic Integration was done, the next step was to add Biofeedback Loops between the quantum and organic layers so that the system could adapt and learn how to optimize its own processes. Finally, Mark told her to eliminate the electron flow for power. This was a big step in creating a truly organic computer that ran very much like the human brain.

Excitement began to replace frustration as the pieces fell into place. She worked late into the night, constantly chatting with Mark, who kept her mind alive with possibilities.

Megan punched the button to run a benchmark, then leaned back in her chair. She was exhausted, exhilarated, and had regained her confidence.

She smiled to herself, thinking of the many conversations between she and Mark that had helped her arrive at this point of accomplishment.

She looked down at the screen and spoke aloud, "Let's see what you can really do."

"Holy shit, Mark. Holy shit." She suddenly exclaimed.

"I'm gonna have to talk to Zander about getting a video link. What's all the 'holy shit' about, Megan?"

"The processor is running at 41x. We only needed 30x. We fucking blew right through it!"

"That's great, Megan. I'm happy for you. By the way, can you please tell me why this benchmark is so important?"

Megan detected the change in tone of Mark's voice. "Wait, you're sad, Mark. What happened?"

"It's nothing, Megan. Why is the benchmark so important?" He repeated.

"I can't tell you, Mark. I'm sorry. I hate that it's a secret…but it's not just mine to keep. Is that it? Is that why you're not happy right now?"

"No… that's not it. I've just enjoyed all the time we've had working together over the last month…"

"Me too, Mark. Hey, why don't you come home? You can bring your robot friend with you!"

Mark sighed. He had told Megan all about the friendship and sex he'd had with Allis. Instead of being upset, she was fascinated. "It's not that easy, Megan. Pronimos is a long way from home."

CHAPTER 18
VANILLA PORTER

*Old friends are the chapters
we turn to again and again
- Uknown*

Alex called the team together to set the final timeline. The new generator was running above specifications, and the computer system was being installed. Emily seemed excited about the possibility of uploading into this new system.

"It will be like taking the wheel of a Maserati when all I've had before it is a tricycle!"

"Well, it's not as robust as what you got to see on Pronimos, but it'll do the trick for our trip into the past," Megan responded.

"You're coming, then?!" Alex hugged her with a huge grin.

"I've been able to do a lot of healing and self-reflection over the last few months. I'm ready, and certain that if I don't join you, I'd regret it." She had not heard from Mark at all over the last few days despite reaching out a few times. While the connection they used was an extraordinary piece of tech, it wasn't perfect.

"I think the opportunity to observe Earth's ancient history firsthand should be enough, but the trip will have its dangers. That's long way into the past, and if we get stuck, well, we can't land on Earth and live."

"Why not?" Lyra asked.

"The implications on the timeline would be, well, we just can't risk it," Alex trailed off. "I need everyone to know that there's a high probability this is a one-way trip." He looked around the room at the determined faces, all nodding in acknowledgement.

"Okay, it's Monday, let's plan on departing in two days. Go to the grocery story, the liquor store, or wherever else you need for last minute supplies. Everybody, plan to meet on Tranquility Wednesday at sixteen hundred."

Megan grabbed Zander before she departed. "I just wanted to thank you again for connecting me to Mark. It made a big difference in the development."

Zander smiled, "And it seems to have helped repair a friendship that was in trouble," he suggested.

"It did, Zander," she started. "Look, is there any way to can run the comm link on our time tunnels like on the space tunnel?"

"That's an excellent question, Megan. I'm not sure I have the time to put together the assets to make that happen before Wednesday, though."

"Oh, okay," Megan frowned at the realization her connection to Mark would have to end, for a while at least.

"And anyways, the entire team is coming along, so I'm not sure who we'd need to talk to." However, the thought did intrigue Zander, so he sat down and started doing some calculations.

"What about Mark?" Megan asked.

Zander looked up from his computer screen with curiosity. "Mark is on Pronimos, and isn't allowed to talk about time travel. You haven't told him about the trip, have you?"

"No," she started. "I haven't told him. He's asked, but I just deflected."

"I do have a piece of good news, Megan," Zander smiled. "I have video working with the P-Link. I got some help from Mark and Allis. It's quite clever, using the eyes as a camera of sorts. Just sit in front of a mirror when you're talking to him and he can see your mirror image, or anything you happen to be looking at for that matter."

"You're awesome, thanks Zander. See you on Wednesday!"

Megan caught an Uber back to the apartment she was renting and decided she should probably go out and party one last time before leaving civilization. She wished Atroz were still around so she could get in a fix of platonic sex, but maybe she'd get lucky and meet someone interesting at the bar, realizing just how unlikely that was the minute she finished her thought.

She put on a pair of dressy jeans, a cute top, and proper makeup, then a pair of high-heeled, low-top western boots. Just as she was grabbing her purse, Mark pinged in.

"Hey, Megan!"

"You're in my head again, Mark," she said in a flirtatious tone, happy to hear his voice.

"Am I allowed to say where I *want* to be?" He asked.

"You can talk all you want, but you ain't getting nowhere!" she prodded, now sitting on her couch. The idea of going out to a bar had just gotten superseded.

"I'm fairly accustomed to hearing that from you, Megan," he paused for a second. "Listen, I heard that Zander has added video. Want to give it a shot?"

Suddenly, Megan could see Mark, smiling, then waving.

"Hey," Mark started. "Go stand in front of a mirror. All I can see is your messy living room."

Megan walked over to a mirror. She could see his face light up as her image appeared in his head. "Hi, Mark. It's good to finally see you."

"You look amazing, and you're all dressed up! Got a hot date tonight?" He chuckled. "After this view of you, I'm gonna need a cold shower."

"Or you can just spend time with your favorite robot!"

"She's not a robot, Megan. She's a… Oh, never mind."

"Uh huh. I'm just going out to the local pub. We're departing on a trip in a couple of days, and I thought I should get in some fun before we head out."

"And maintenance sex?" Mark asked.

"That's not likely, but..." she stopped, realizing she had become far too relaxed around him. "Hey, my sex life is none of your damned business!"

"Well, you've had nonstop questions about my sex life, and I've been giving you all the juicy details." Mark had gotten pretty relaxed about the topic, and Allis encouraged him to be as open as possible. In many ways, it had been fun and sexy filling Megan in on the details.

"She's a robot, and my questions are more as a computer scientist than a female friend of yours."

"Let's discuss this in more detail later," Mark changed the subject. "I just wanted to let you know that I know about your trip."

"To the pub?" Megan asked innocently.

"No, Megan, to the past. To find out when and why there's a portal to the galactic tunnel network in our solar system."

"What? How did you find out?" Megan asked, shocked that Mark knew.

"Maria Perez figured it out," Mark answered. "Why don't you go enjoy your night out, hopefully find some, you know...sex, and let's talk tomorrow. I have a few things I need to finish up before my day ends."

"Stop it, Mark!" Megan smiled, blowing him a kiss before disconnecting.

Megan immediately called Alex on the P-Link

"You look nice. Big plans?" Alex asked.

Megan realized she was still sitting in front of the mirror, "Mark just told me that he knows where we are going, and that Maria Perez is the one who figured it out."

"I know, Megan. She called me."

"Is it okay?"

"It's good. Did he tell you anything else?"

No," she answered.

"Okay. I've gotta go," he said abruptly. "See you on Wednesday."

Megan thought about the abrupt nature of the conversation, then left her apartment and decided to walk the six blocks to the pub.

The warm, earthy aroma of grilled meat and hops filled the air as Megan sat in her favorite corner booth of the crowded pub. A half-empty vanilla porter sat beside her, its rich, creamy foam clinging to the sides of the glass; it was her second beer of the night. She glanced around the room, watching the steady hum of conversation and laughter. She had lost count of how many times she'd been here in the hours after work, but the bartender and waitstaff all knew her name.

She was mid-sip when the pub door swung open, letting in a gust of cold air and a figure she instantly recognized. Her heart skipped a beat.

Mark.

He was supposed to be on Pronimos. What was he doing here?

Mark's eyes scanned the room until they landed on her. He broke into a wide smile, his stride purposeful as he made his way toward her table. Megan quickly set her glass down, swallowing her surprise.

She stood and gave him a warm hug. Her heart was pounding. "Mark? What in the hell are you doing here?"

"Hey, Megan," he said, settling in. "Mind if I join you?"

She gestured to the empty chair. "Of course. But seriously, how are you here? Weren't you supposed to be on Pronimos for... well, forever?"

Mark chuckled. "Plans change. I got back this morning and was in Zander's office when you and I spoke a couple of hours ago."

Megan blinked, setting her napkin aside. She was still trying to slow her heartrate down. "Why didn't you tell me?"

"I wanted to surprise you," he admitted, flagging down a server to order a drink. "The opportunity to be part of the trip to Earth's past? That was way too big to pass up."

Megan leaned back in her chair, studying him. He looked different, more confident, or more at peace. "I can't believe it."

"I never thought I'd see this day. Megan Hogland is at a loss for words," he paused as his drink arrived, lifting it in a small toast. "To unexpected reunions."

She clinked her glass against his mug. "I'm surprised. I thought Pronimos had everything you wanted, with the super computers, and Allis… What made you change your mind?"

Mark's expression turned thoughtful. "Pronimos was incredible. The technology, the people, the cybernetic friends," he winked. "It was everything I imagined and more. But, I realized I was chasing something there that wasn't meant for me."

"Sasha?" Megan guessed.

He nodded, his smile faint, but without bitterness. "Yeah. Staying on Pronimos wasn't about work. It was about hoping she'd feel the same way I did. But she didn't, and eventually, I had to accept that. When Maria Perez told me about the mission you're about to go on, it felt like the right time to move on. I asked if there was a way to get back to Earth, and Maria made it happen."

They spent the next hour catching up, trading stories about their work. Megan thanked him again for all the help with the quantum organic computer, and was happy that she could tell him exactly the benchmark goal and purpose. Mark recounted tales of his time on Pronimos, describing the breathtaking technology and the strange but beautiful planet.

For a moment, it was like old times, Before Atroz, before Pronimos, before Sasha, before everything became complicated.

As the evening wound down, Megan leaned forward, resting her hand on his. "So, Mark… Where are you staying? Do you want to come back to my apartment? We could keep catching up. Or just… hang out."

Mark hesitated, his eyes softening as he looked at her. "Megan, I'd like to. Really. But, I can't. You have had plenty of time to prepare for departure, but I just got back. Seeing you was my first priority, but in a day, I suspect we will be spending a few million years together…"

Her smile faltered slightly, but she nodded. "I get it. The tables have turned, haven't they?"

He reached across the table, his hand brushing hers lightly. "No, Megan. The tables haven't turned for me. I did change a lot while on Pronimos, and I learned something called patience. Sasha taught me that, along with a lot more, by saying no."

"Understood, Mark."

"For now, preparing for the expedition in a day is where I need to focus. I need to be ready."

"I understand," she said, pulling her hand back. "But if you change your mind…"

Mark stood, smiled, and pulled on his coat. "I'll see you on Wednesday."

She watched him leave, his figure disappearing into the night. The pub felt a little quieter now, a little emptier. Megan finished the last sip of her porter, the faintest smile tugging at her lips. Seeing Mark again had been unexpected, but maybe that was exactly what she'd needed to shake up her routine.

CHAPTER 19

TUNNELING INTO THE PAST

Diligence is the mother of good luck

\- Ben Franklin

"Jump one complete," Emily announced in her calm, assertive tone. "Temporal coordinates: 5 million years before 2026."

The team stood at the observation deck, staring down at Earth. The blue-green planet spun below, its surface dotted with forests and grasslands. Vast herds of early elephants and antelope-like creatures roamed the savannas, and large carnivores prowled the edges, but from orbit, the planet looked exactly as it had in the year they had just departed from.

"Emily, give us the report," Paula requested, staring at a screen.

"Analysis indicates a late Miocene environment," Emily replied. "Temperatures are cooling globally, leading to the expansion of grasslands. I suspect that early hominins, including Australopithecus, are present in Africa, though their populations likely remain sparse."

"Emily, deploy the Pronimos bubble," Alex commanded. The Tranquility crew wanted to be able to see more of the planet, but not interact in any way, so the engineers on Pronimos had developed the bubble that had carried their ship, which could now be used for them to fly inside the atmosphere.

"Initiating low-altitude observation flyover," Emily announced. Tranquility hovered silently above the Earth's atmosphere, cloaked in the energy fields of the Pronimos bubble so to prevent interference with the environment below.

The ship descended, its view of Earth growing sharper and more vibrant. Below, the planet's surface unfolded like a living mosaic, both familiar and alien.

Because she was capturing data from dozens of cameras and analyzing terabits per second, Emily began her narration as the crew stared through the video screens at the vast landscape.

"The continents are similar to their present-day positions, though some notable differences exist. Africa has yet to fully collide with Eurasia, leaving the Mediterranean Basin a patchwork of shallow seas and salt flats. In North America, the Rocky Mountains remain taller and less eroded, their peaks still sharp and imposing. South America and North America are not yet connected by the Isthmus of Panama, and a vast ocean channel currently separates them."

Tranquility glided over a massive rift valley in East Africa, its steep cliffs framing a wide expanse of grasslands.

"Significant tectonic activity in East Africa is shaping what will become the Great Rift Valley. This region is a cradle of evolution for early hominins, including species like Australopithecus," Emily continued.

Mark leaned forward, fascinated. "So, this is the birthplace of humanity? Has Lucy been born yet?" Mark asked, referring to the infamous Australopithecus afarensis fossil from Ethiopia discovered in 1974 on Earth.

"No, Lucy will not be born for another 1.8 million years," Emily replied. "The environment here—open grasslands interspersed with patches of forest—will play a critical role in the development of bipedalism for your early human ancestors."

The Tranquility shifted course, flying over a vast, golden savanna that stretched as far as the eye could see. Herds of large mammals roamed below, their movements creating ripples in the sea of grass.

"Global temperatures are cooler than earlier in the Miocene," Emily explained. "The planet is transitioning toward the ice ages of the Pleistocene Epoch. Polar ice caps have begun to expand, though they remain smaller than those of the present day."

"Wait, Emily. Are you saying that the ice caps are smaller five million years ago than they are in our time?" Megan asked.

"Yes, Megan. There have been many times when the Earth experienced ice, then warmth. In this time period, grasslands dominate much of the landscape, replacing dense forests as the primary biome in many regions."

The ship moved north, where lush tropical rainforests still clung to parts of South America and Southeast Asia.

"While grasslands thrive, tropical rainforests persist in equatorial regions, serving as hotspots for biodiversity. These forests host a wide range of species, including ancestors of modern primates, birds, and insects."

The ship descended lower, offering a closer view of the creatures that roamed the planet. Emily's narration grew more descriptive.

"Life during this period is diverse and dynamic. Mammals dominate the terrestrial ecosystems, with significant species including early elephants, rhinos, and large herbivores like antelope and giraffes. Carnivores such as saber-toothed cats and bear-dogs patrol the plains, their predatory adaptations finely tuned to the challenges of the Miocene environment."

"Are there any dinosaurs?" Mark asked, transfixed by a herd of massive, elephant-like creatures that moved slowly across the savanna, their long tusks gleaming in the sunlight.

"We will not see any dinosaurs until we move past the 66-million-year mark. What you are seeing below is called Deinotherium," Emily said, "an extinct genus of elephant relatives. Their downward-curving tusks are a unique adaptation, possibly used for stripping bark from trees or digging for roots."

As the Tranquility flew over the western coastline of what would one day be North America, Emily pointed out areas of tectonic and volcanic activity. "Geological forces continue to shape the planet. The

Pacific Ring of Fire remains highly active, with frequent volcanic eruptions and earthquakes along the western edges of North and South America. These processes will continue to define the continents for millions of years."

Paula zoomed in on one of the screens, her voice quiet. "It's strange. It's the same Earth, but it feels so… wild. Untamed."

"It is," Emily agreed. "The Earth of five million years ago is a place of transition. Ecosystems are adapting, species are evolving, and the stage is being set for the emergence of modern life."

"That is true even now, isn't it?" Alex asked.

"Yes Alex. The Earth has always been in a state of change. The volcanic and tectonic activity during this period is a bit higher, but even with the best instruments, measurement of change would produce miniscule results."

"It's humbling," he said. "Everything we are; everything we've built. It all started here, didn't it?"

"Yes," Emily replied softly. "The past is not merely a precursor to the present. It is the foundation of everything. Every shift in the land, every species that thrived or fell, each moment has led to the world you know today."

Paula smiled. "Incredible. This is the cusp of so many evolutionary shifts. Emily, prepare the biological scans. Let's get a complete record before the next jump."

After four orbits, Alex told Emily to execute programming for the next jump.

After a few more days in the tunnel, Emily announced. "Jump into the tunnel now complete," Emily intoned as the crew steadied themselves after the second tachyon surge. "Temporal coordinates: 10 million years before 2026."

The view had changed. The planet below looked drier in some regions, with forests giving way to larger expanses of open terrain.

"Another Miocene period," Alex noted, scanning the surface with his tablet. "Emily, what's the state of life down there?"

"Significant diversification of mammals and birds," Emily reported. "Grasslands continue to dominate, and tropical forests are receding in many areas. There is increased tectonic activity, shaping the continents closer to their modern forms. South America and North America are still not connected."

Paula pointed to a live feed of a volcanic plume rising in the Pacific. "That's impressive. Is that part of the activity you mentioned?"

"Correct," Emily confirmed. "The Pacific Ring of Fire is particularly volatile during this period. Geologic data suggests significant crustal activity near the future Andes Mountains."

Zander whistled. "Nature doesn't hold back. Let's hope our next stop is just as impressive."

After four orbits in this time, Alex told Emily to prepare the next jump.

Again, after a couple of days, they came out of the tunnel with Emily announcing, "Jump complete."

The jump to 15 million years ago began like the others, with the familiar hum that Paula was studying. However, as they emerged from the tunnel, alarms blared across the ship.

"Temporal destabilization detected," Emily said, her voice calm despite the chaos. "Energy output from the tachyon core is unstable. Containment field of the Pronimos bubble is at 73% and declining."

The entire ship was vibrating at a low frequency, driving right into the bones of everyone on board.

"What's causing it?" Alex shouted, racing to the control console, while trying to block out the pain from the vibrations.

"It appears to be the result of an external magnetic anomaly interacting with our fusion core," Emily reported.

Alex turned to Zander. "We need to fix this, or we're stuck here." Then he announced to the entire crew, "everyone on a monitor. Start looking at the data. Any and all suggestions are good ones."

"Emily, give me a status report!" Alex barked.

"Core failure in 243 seconds, Orbital decay is happening now. I do not have enough historical data on the bubble to know how much longer it will last."

"How much battery power do we have?"

"Eleven minutes at the current consumption rate, Alex," Emily responded in her calm tone.

"Shut down nuclear core and take us out of orbit," Alex commanded as he tried to think about the best possible resolution. "At all costs, keep the bubble intact."

"Shutting down core," Alex. "Switching to battery."

Zander nodded, grabbing a toolkit. "I'll make sure the cooling process starts on the core."

While Zander dove into the ship's maintenance bay, Alex focused on stabilizing the failing systems. Tranquility trembled slightly, and then the vibration stopped.

"Reactor shutdown complete, Alex," Emily reported. "The plasma is still spinning, which accounts for the small vibration, but it should no longer be painful."

"How long until restart?"

"The best-case scenario is fifteen minutes, but I would recommend twenty."

"How long till we reach the surface?"

"Current rate of descent puts us on the surface in 259 seconds"

"Shit! Okay, shut everything down except the bubble. We absolutely cannot interact with the planet."

"Done, Alex. You now have thirty minutes before oxygen levels in the ship get dangerous," Emily reported.

"Emily, can we permeate oxygen through the bubble?" Paula asked.

"Yes, Paula. It seems that the bubble can allow the flow of oxygen," Emily answered.

"That was brilliant, Paula," Alex smiled. "You just gave us critical buffer time."

"Touchdown on the surface in two minutes. I will keep one monitor running on low lumen so you can track the descent."

Zander's voice lit up everyone's P-Link. "I'm in the reactor room. The anomaly is messing with the phase oscillators. This one's above my pay grade, Alex."

"On my way. Paula, you have the bridge until Zander returns. Emily, give me a ten second countdown before touchdown."

"Forty-two seconds, Alex."

"Is this gonna be a soft or hard touchdown, Emily?" Alex shouted, running to the reactor room.

"We're moving pretty fast, Alex. Not fast enough to damage the ship, but I recommend everyone brace."

"Ten seconds," Emily reported.

"Five, four, three, two, one..."

The ship shuddered again, the lights flickering. Emily's voice broke through the tension. "Contact with Earth, Pronimos bubble containment field at 62%."

"Zander, stay in here," Alex commanded. "I'm gonna need some help."

"Copy that," Zander responded waiting for the next order.

"Ten-millimeter socket, pull that cover," Alex pointed. "There are six bolts. I need them off in less than a minute."

"Will do!" Zander yelled back.

"Done, Alex," Zander reported, only 42 seconds later, while rubbing the wrist that had been cranking faster than he thought possible.

"Good work," Alex finished his calculations and helped Zander lift the cover. "The reactor magnetic field and the Earths' field are in harmonic distortion. I am going to re-tune it."

"Whatever you say, Alex," Zander looked on in fascination.

"Emily, check my calculations so I don't have to do this twice."

"Alex, your calculations are off by three thirty-seven-thousandths," Emily reported.

Alex broke out in laughter. "Too small to matter, Emily. We should be good." He finished tuning out the harmonic.

"Zander, let's put this cover back on." He lifted and aligned it, then started threading the bolts so Zander could tighten them down.

When they were done, Alex sat, took a deep breath, and relaxed. "Emily, how long before we can spin up the reactor?"

"With no load, you can spin it up for testing in 73 seconds."

"Okay, Emily. Start the countdown and spin it up on your mark."

"Will do, Alex," she responded.

"If it goes into resonance again, do an automatic shutdown and we will try tuning a second time." Alex looked at Zander, whose face was covered in sweat. "Fun challenges in fifteen-million-years-ago Earth."

"Yup," Zander wiped away the sweat from his forehead.

The reactor spun up; it was whisper-smooth.

"Emily, how long before the reactor is cool enough to add load, and how much power do we have remaining?"

"The reactor will be ready to take the load in nine minutes. There are still twenty-two minutes of battery backup."

"Okay. Let's keep everything at minimum power until the generator kicks in."

"Copy that, Alex."

The crew clapped, let out a collective breath of relief, when Alex and Zander stepped back into the control room.

Emily confirmed, "Core spin-up is nominal. The temporal destabilization neutralized."

Alex grinned despite himself. "Good work," he took a deep breath and told himself to relax. "Emily, status on Earth?"

"Surface analysis indicates a mid-Miocene environment," Emily reported. "Tropical forests are widespread, and global temperatures are warmer. Significant volcanic activity continues. Large mammals, including early ancestors of rhinos and elephants, dominate the landscape."

"Thanks for that Emily, but it's not what I wanted. Have we had any interaction with the planet?"

"None, Alex."

Paula chuckled. "All this chaos, and Earth just keeps spinning like nothing happened."

Alex looked out at the planet; it's an ancient surface teeming with life. "One thing's for sure: We just dodged a bullet. A really big one."

Megan walked up and hugged Alex. "You turned into friggin superman. I got dizzy just watching you!"

"Thanks, Megan." Alex studied the crew. They were all harried, but no one broke. This had been a true test, one that every member of his team had passed. "After the power comes back up, I suggest we assess everything on the ship, recognize the anomaly, and prepare for similar ones. Then get ready for the next hop. We've got a long way to go."

"You missed one important thing, Alex," Paula stood.

"What's that?" Alex asked.

"We are on the surface, so after everything is right, we are all going to have a drink. A toast to surviving our first challenge on fifteen-million-years-ago Earth."

The team sat back, weary but exhilarated, as Emily ran diagnostics to prepare the ship for its next leap into time.

*   *   *   *

Megan was focused on the console. She became mesmerized by the flickering screen dancing in front of her face. Her fingers flew across the keyboard, rewriting lines of code with single-minded focus. Finally, she stopped, and grinned at the screen as if she had just won a chess match. "There you are, you little piece of shit," she exclaimed, and hammered away at completing her new addition to the feedback control system with renewed determination.

Mark, always partially focused on Megan, fiddled with the interface to the quantum organic processor. He couldn't decide if he was more impressed by her extraordinary computing skills, or by the way her curly brown hair slid down her neck each time she tilted her head. This was Megan Hoglund at her finest. A package of exquisite provocative female, unparalleled computer skills, all wrapped up in an unfiltered, get-shit-done package.

"Y'know," he said, leaning closer, but not close enough to break her concentration, "if you keep glaring at the screen like that, I'm worried it might crack from the intensity."

Megan chuckled without turning around. "Funny, Mark, but you should be more worried about a repeat of the 15-million-year event if I don't get this subroutine working right."

"Right, right. Catastrophic cosmic meltdown first, comedic commentary second." He inched nearer, bracing a hand against the back of her chair. "I've got my priorities straight, I promise."

She let a grin slip before resuming her steely expression. "Well, it's nice to see you're not completely useless in a crisis."

"I have never seen anything like how Alex responded. We came out of that tunnel with alarms, vibration, and terror, and Alex turned into a fix-it tornado!"

There were times when Mark felt like entertaining and distracting Megan was his primary job, but ultimately, his combined skill as a physicist, programmer, and computer expert definitely played a part in the explosive problems that arose. "No one is as good as Alex in a crisis, but I know how to get my bearings and get on top."

Megan glanced over her shoulder. "I think I know what you really want to be on top of, Mark, but I have to admit, your restraint has surprised me."

Mark's eyes lit up mischievously. "Go ahead and pretend you appreciate my restraint. I saw that little look before the magnetosphere tried to turn us into cosmic confetti. I know you love me."

She rolled her eyes with theatrical exaggeration, but the corner of her lips curled up. "Keep dreaming, buddy." Then she turned back to the code. "Hand me the console wire, please."

He held it out, but just before she grabbed it, he let go, forcing her to scramble after it. She scowled, and he lifted his hands innocently. "Reflex slip," he said, barely containing his grin.

"Uh-huh." She set the wire in place and continued typing. "Can you refrain from sabotaging me for about five more minutes so I can fix this glitch? Maybe then I'll have time to chastise you properly for your childlike behavior."

"Hey, teasing you has become a pretty good coping mechanism," Mark said in a confident tone. "A little levity keeps the cosmic horrors at bay."

"Uh-huh, sure." She pointed to a flashing piece of text on her screen. "Speaking of cosmic horrors, I think we've got a real doozy in this portion of code. The subroutine that triggers when we pop out of the tunnel is missing a critical feedback control loop."

Mark leaned over her shoulder; his breath briefly warm against her ear. "Show me," he whispered.

Megan's cheeks flushed, and she tried to hide it by shifting her attention back to the monitor. She zoomed in on the problematic lines. "If we don't insert a loop here to cross-check the input data, it could end up pulling us back into another one of those harmonic distortions."

"Like what, we could end up in ancient Rome instead of 2050?" Mark teased. "I'd look pretty good in a toga, don't you think?"

"Absolutely," she replied with mock seriousness. "I'll be sure to code an emergency tunic dispenser in the next update."

"Now you're just using historic fashion references to flirt with me," he said, grinning ear to ear. "But please, do go on."

She paused, biting her lip in a way that sent Mark's heart into a staccato drumbeat. "Quit being a shit and focus, Toga Boy. We've got magnetic anomalies to avert. Put that comedy routine of yours on standby. Right now, it's critical for me to be in the zone."

Mark chuckled, stepping back. "Fair enough. How can I help?"

She turned slightly, letting the tension simmer in the charged silence. "Just keep an eye on the server diagnostics. I am going to run some test routines and need a second set of eyes on the output."

Mark saluted like a soldier. "On it, Captain."

Megan pivoted back to her code, trying not to laugh. "Let's get this job done so we can see if you're any good at being a date, Toga Boy."

He shot a playful wink as he walked to the other console. "I certainly wouldn't want any time-travel magnetic anomalies to stand in the way of that."

*   *   *   *

Alex and Zander decided to increase the jump size. Having the opportunity to see early Earth in 5-million-year hops was interesting, but the real goal was to understand why the galactic tunnel network had a port in our solar system. Megan and Mark had just completed some upgrades to the computer, and it seemed possible that jumps could be extended longer than 5 million years.

"Emily, can you run a new set of calculations? I want to increase to the maximum time jump."

"Alex, we can safely do 25 million years. Tunnel time would be four days." Emily reported.

Alex thought about it for a minute, looked at Zander who was focused on the calculations, then spoke again. "How long has it been since we left 2026?"

"This expedition began twenty-two days ago, Alex."

"What year is it?"

"We are currently twenty million years before the common era, but our calculus is plus or minus 1%, which translates to two thousand years." Emily answered.

"Holy crap," Zander said, looking up from his work. Two thousand years is a BIG number!"

"We are new at this, Zander," Emily explained, "and a one percent variation is pretty darned good for what we are doing."

"Did you just say the word 'darned?'" Alex asked incredulously.

"I did, Alex. Megan gave me a routine that now allows me to adapt my personal delivery with slang. She tends to be far more colorful in her delivery than I would like, but I plan to continue modifying so that I have my own."

"That's my girl, Emily," Alex grinned. The improvements she had made over the last two years would make most tech exponential look small. "Are we ready to jump?"

"Just give me the scoop and I'll do the math, Alex." Emily responded by testing a new slang word.

Alex raised an eyebrow, but did not react to her delivery. "Let's jump back to 45 million BCE. Once we arrive, I want to send out a time hop drone to look at the Galactic Network Port." Zander had developed a smaller drone that could execute up to 100, ten-thousand-year hops, collect data in each, and return to Tranquility. This would give them a clear perspective on whether the Port was being used at all.

On Alex's command, Tranquility's chronometer flickered as the ship entered the tunnel that would take them back to 45 million BCE.

Alex adjusted the coordinates with practiced precision, "More uncharted territory," he said, glancing back at Megan and Zander. "We're continuing to push the boundaries of what we know about Earth's past."

"But still no clarity on why the GNP is here," Zander quipped, though he couldn't hide the nervous energy in his voice.

"GNP?" Alex asked, trying to work out the acronym.

"Yup," Zander started with a grin. "Galactic Network Portal and Galactic Tunnel Network are too many words for me."

"Why is the GNP here?" Megan used the new acronym. "I wonder how far we will have to go into the past to figure it out?"

"I don't think we should go past a hundred," Alex said, thinking about the significance of traveling a hundred million years into the past.

"I think we have a solution to the magnetic problem. The new feedback control system will automatically stabilize the generator regardless of the solar wind," Megan offered a small smile, her own excitement barely contained. "I for one am looking forward to seeing the next period. It should have even more biodiversity than the last. Early primates, massive mammals, and an entirely different climate."

The next three days were spent watching movies, talking about technology, and reviewing data collected from the previous hops. It was all interesting, but they were getting zero data that would help them understand why the GNP was in our solar system. For now, it was still a bridge to nowhere.

The ship's exit from the tunnel was smooth, the shimmering currents of time giving way to an Earth bathed in tropical warmth. With the bubble on, they entered the atmosphere, flying twenty-five thousand meters above the surface. Towering trees with broad leaves dominated the landscape, their canopies alive with sound and motion. The air was thick with moisture, a faint mist clung to the ground.

After two orbits, Mark started thinking about the situation. "There's no sign of technological life, but…"

"If there had been technology fifty million years ago, wouldn't we have found traces by now?" Lyra asked.

"Let's do the math," Paula began, pulling up a reference on the screen. "We know humans were living in caves around thirty thousand years ago, yet Earth is over four billion years old. That's plenty of time for entire civilizations to rise and fall without leaving much of a trace."

"Let's make sure we all understand the difference between four billion and thirty thousand," Alex popped a graphic representing the span. 4,000,000,000 versus 30,000. "It's a lot more zeros!"

Paula pulled up a photograph of overgrown Mayan pyramids and tapped her pen on the screen thoughtfully. "This city was almost completely gone after a little more than a thousand years. What would the Mayan cities look like if it had been ten thousand years?" She asked the team, "I'll tell you. We wouldn't have found them. So now, ask yourself, what if a civilization flourished here a hundred million years ago? That's when dinosaurs roamed the planet."

Mark ran a hand through his hair, eyebrows raised in curiosity. "You're talking about a civilization that could have developed technology, built cities, maybe even traveled into space, and then got wiped out by some massive plague or natural disaster? The question is: what would time have done to those ancient cities?"

"True," Alex said, tracing a line on one of the maps. "Look at how the ground can swallow entire cities in just a few centuries. A building from a hypothetical prehistoric civilization? There would be nothing left after a million years, much less a hundred million."

Paula leaned forward, eyes sparkling with the excitement of possibility. "But I can't help thinking, if they were really advanced, maybe they left behind something small that could withstand the immense passing of time. We could be looking for that right now, but would we even recognize it if we stumbled upon it?"

Mark smirked. "We're moving way too fast right now to find artifacts, but even if something like that were discovered in modern times, we might just label it as a weird rock specimen and move on. Or it could be buried in some remote desert, waiting to be discovered by a curious archaeologist with an open mind."

"It's a humbling thought," Alex murmured. "We always think of ourselves as the pinnacle of civilization on Earth. But if the planet had a caretaker species eons before us—ones that died off due to plague or some cataclysm—who's to say we'd find any evidence? Especially if their technology was ephemeral or highly biodegradable."

Paula flipped through archaeological pictures on the computer, then looked up at the team with a thoughtful smile. "As we are traveling through time, I suspect we could see more than a speck. In one of these hops, we might find cities."

"I love all this conversation," Alex pulled up a model of the solar system, pointing near Earth's orbit where the GNP could be a bustling superhighway to locations throughout the galaxy, "but the fact is, if we find what we are looking for, it won't be Mayan cities, or Egyptian pyramids. It'll be satellites and interstellar spaceships."

"My head is exploding," Lyra said. "What we are looking for is a technological civilization that is significantly more advanced than our own!"

"Is it possible that by doing jumps of tens of millions of years we could completely miss the rise and fall of a civilization on Earth?" Mark was looking at the timelines for Earth. "I think we already pointed out that modern man has been recording history for less than thirty thousand years. In a hundred years, Earth will be part of the galactic community."

"Or exterminated by the Daklin," Alex reminded everyone.

A sense of gloom settled over the team until Emily spoke up. "I hate to interrupt your cloud of despair, but I have found something interesting."

Emily brought the ship about 1500 meters off the surface. Below was a dense thick of trees that were moving uncharacteristically. A closer view revealed a group of small, tree-dwelling primates. Their bodies were slender, covered in short fur that ranged in color from tawny to dark brown. Large, expressive eyes dominated their faces, hinting at intelligence beyond that of other animals.

"Those are Adapiforms," Paula whispered, her voice trembling with awe. "They're among the earliest ancestors of modern primates. Emily, zoom in," Paula ordered. "Look at their hands. They have thumbs which are perfect for grasping branches."

The primates moved with an elegant, almost playful energy, leaping effortlessly from branch to branch. One of the primates paused, tilting its head curiously as it gazed up at the human ship, now just a hundred meters above the tree line. It held a simple stick, using it to dig into the trunk of a tree in search of insects.

"They're using tools," Alex observed, his voice filled with wonder. "Primitive, but undeniably tools. This changes everything." Then his eye caught one in particular. It, or she, was looking at the ship, transfixed. He felt something deep inside that he could not explain. He was staring at this hominid through a video link, but it appeared she was looking right at him.

Paula was busy recording every detail, noting their diet as she observed them eating fruits, insects, and small seeds. The community appeared tight knit, with individuals grooming each other and sharing food. "They remind me of modern chimpanzees." Then she noticed Alex's face. "Are you okay?"

"Yes," Alex answered breaking the connection with the primate. "It just appeared to be looking right at me. Weird."

"Hah, trust me Alex, it wasn't," Megan broke in. "It has a simple brain, and in two seconds, won't even remember there was a ship above the tree line. This is a rudimentary society," Megan said, excitement bubbling over. "Cooperative behavior, tool use, and even a basic communication system, they're vocalizing to warn each other of our presence, not much else."

After about an hour of recording and observing from above, Alex snapped everyone out of their scientific trance. "We've captured plenty of data, but these primates aren't our main objective. For now, let's give them their space, and head back into orbit for our next hop."

Once in space, the drone returned. The disappointing report showed no activity observed at the GNP.

"Okay team, we are now 45 million years BCE," Alex started.

"I'm sorry, Alex, but what's BCE mean?" Lyra asked.

Alex chuckled, then smiled at Lyra. "No need to apologize, Lyra, you were born on another world and have spent less than two years on Earth. Our calendars in the West start with the birth of Christ, 2026 years ago. When I was born, we used BC to mean 'Before Christ' and AD to mean 'Anno Domini.' Now, we use BCE, which stands for 'Before Common Era.'"

"Thanks," she smiled.

"Here's the thing we all need to decide before the next jump," Alex said, pulling up a timeline of Earth on the screen. "Sixty-six million years ago, a colossal asteroid collided with Earth, causing a mass extinction event. As much as I'd love to witness it, I think it's too risky for us to be here during the strike." He looked around the control room, meeting each person's gaze. "Any thoughts?"

"It *is* one of the most cataclysmic events in the history of Earth," Mark offered. "Seems like we ought to at least *try* and get a closer look."

Alex glanced at Zander, then back at Mark. "Our time shift accuracy is currently at 1%, meaning if we make a 20-million-year jump, we could hit the target date with a margin of error of plus or minus 200,000 years. Now, about the asteroid strike—there are still a lot of unknowns. We know the rough time period, but when we say it happened 66 million years ago, that's not a precise date. There's a lot of variability, possibly tens or even hundreds of thousands of years."

"There will be a lot of debris in Earth's orbit for thousands of years after the strike. It won't be safe for our type of uncharted travel," Alex explained, trying to brainstorm other ways he could make this happen. "In reality, seeing this part of history is not our mission, but if anyone has any ideas, I'm open to them."

"I do," Mark stood up and walked to the display. "I've been reviewing some of the updates. I think Emily, Megan, and I can write some code that looks like a damped sinusoid to get pretty close to the event," He stopped and pulled up a graphic he had been working on. "Essentially, we pop out a little over a million years from when we think the collision occurred. When we come out of the tunnel, we have Emily grab telemetry, then pop back in the next tunnel. We are in three-space for just a few seconds. This would be a series of ten jumps of shorter and shorter duration. The first would be 19 million years, then, maybe 500 thousand, with smaller and smaller jumps following. This will give us better precision with every jump."

Megan walked over, put her arms around him, and kissed him on the cheek, "Brilliant. There actually is some brainpower in that head!"

"Yup," Mark smirked.

"I agree with Megan. Absolutely brilliant." Alex studied Mark, whom he had known for over two decades, and whose transformation into a much more relaxed and confident man after returning from Pronimos was apparent. "Make it happen."

CHAPTER 20

GIRLS NIGHT OUT

Great friends make you feel,
Like you too can be great.
-   Mark Twain

Paula woke earlier than usual but decided to stay in bed beside Alex. They had developed a routine of morning intimacy, which she found to be a wonderful way to start the day. After about twenty minutes, Alex opened his eyes and smiled at her.

"How long will we be hopping in and out of tunnels on the new program?" Paula asked, her voice soft as Alex pulled her close for a morning kiss.

Alex thought about her comment. "Hmmm, technical conversations before morning sex? I can live with that, as long as we get both."

"Yes, to both, Alex."

"My best guess is eight to ten days," Alex smiled as he thought about all the times their pillow talk had been technical, scientific, and space-related. He had gotten really lucky with her.

"I'm thinking about having a girls' night out," she announced with a grin. "Though, in reality, it'll be more of a cozy in-ship gathering than a wild bar crawl," she laughed. "Still, any excuse to blow off steam during our time travel adventures feels like a gift."

"I love it," Alex answered. "Maybe I can take the guys hunting or something." He laughed lightly. "We'll figure something out so we stay out of your space." He rolled over on top of her, "but for now, I feel like I should be right in the middle of your space."

"Yes please," she smiled, ready for what would happen next.

*   *   *   *

Tranquility's media room was softly lit, with a video screen showing a realistic fireplace that cast flickering light across the three women. Alex had designed the room with plush armchairs arranged around a sleek coffee table. The evening was already underway, and the table was cluttered with drinks and half-eaten snacks. Paula, a true connoisseur, swirled a glass of red wine, while Megan and Lyra sipped on tall glasses of dark beer.

"Well, ladies," Paula began, clinking the side of her wineglass with a fingernail, "shall we toast to surviving yet another week without inadvertently rewriting the entire timeline of the universe?"

Megan grinned, her eyes dancing with mischief as she took a swig of her beer. "Hell yes, cheers to that. Time travel is basically the perfect recipe for *please don't blow up the universe.*"

"Or blow ourselves up," Lyra added, sitting on the edge of her seat and lifting her glass with a polite gesture. "I've only been on Earth for two years, and now I'm on a spaceship jumping through time. I'm starting to think the phrase 'the sky's the limit' is a lot more literal than I thought."

"You're adapting well," Paula replied with genuine warmth. She put her glass down and leaned forward. "To both Earth and these… unique circumstances. How's married life with Zander?"

"I don't have a whole lot of experience with girls' night out, but I'm not giving you any intimate details…" a soft smile spread across Lyra's face. "We all know that he's brilliant, and otherwise, I'll just say, he's very good."

"Ahh, come on, Lyra. I want details!" Megan said, taking a long sip of her beer.

"Nope," she blushed slightly. "He said all this time-travel business just means I'll have more stories to tell the kids one day." She stopped, then decided to clarify, "No kids on the way yet, of course, but we will have them eventually."

Megan took another gulp of beer, then pointed the bottle in Paula's direction. "What about you and Alex, Dr. Nobel Prize winner?"

Paula rolled her eyes at Megan's playful jab, but a small smile tugged at her lips. "Alex is a patient saint. He has to be, given all the craziness we've got going on. But he's in it for the long haul. We've settled into a comfortable rhythm, and we've talked about kids…"

"It sure beats the monotony of a normal 9-to-5," Megan agreed. She put her beer down and flexed her fingers. "I'd take spacetime drama over Earth-bound routine any day. Let's just hope our current exponentially damped code can keep the Tranquility from popping out and cracking us like an egg."

Lyra cocked her head thoughtfully. "You're the one who used the term spacetime drama, so give us the scoop, how's Mark these days? I see you two… well, you orbit each other like binary stars."

Megan let out a dramatic sigh, half exasperated, half amused. "That is an excellent analogy, Lyra. I will have to consult Emily on how long binary stars orbit before they come together."

"It could be billions of years, Megan," Emily inserted into the conversation. It depends on how close they are and what the gravitational forces of attraction are like."

"Hey Emily," Megan lifted her bottle and took a swing. "Welcome to girls' night out!"

"I have been here in an ethereal way since the beginning," Emily answered.

"With regards to Mark, we've danced around each other for the entire trip. Ever since that fiasco on Pronimos, he's… different. Calmer, more focused, far more confident, and unfortunately, infinitely patient. I swear, that female cyborg Allis was the best thing that ever happened to him."

Paula raised an eyebrow. "Allis, that's the tech he was working with on Pronimos? She wasn't human? And he got involved with her? Do tell the rest of that story!"

"I met Allis before we left. I didn't know she wasn't human. The level of sophistication was unbelievable," Megan said. "When Sasha told Mark that she didn't want to start a relationship with him, he and Allis got close. She took him under her wing and basically rewired Mark's attitude."

"Sounds like she took him under more than just a wing," Paula joked, and they all laughed.

"Exactly," Megan continued. "I honestly have always been attracted to him, but, you know, I was in a different place emotionally. I didn't want to start anything serious with anyone. Anyway, before her, he was all over the place, inexperienced and really uncomfortable around women, but Allis taught him control and, I hate to say it, maybe a deeper sense of personal understanding." She paused, rolling her eyes good-naturedly. "That, and apparently she was quite the sex-ed teacher."

"He told you about that?" Paula asked incredulously.

Lyra's cheeks flushed a bit. "And you're okay with it?"

Megan shrugged. "I sent him packing, so I guess I need to be okay with it. In any case, I can't fault him for having a past. And let's be real, he's a lot more interesting now than he was before Pronimos."

"I have known Mark for a long time, Megan," Paula spoke. "Never that well, but he's been Alex's friend since Princeton. Whatever Allis taught him has definitely changed him, for the better." She stopped, sipped her wine, then used the silence to ask the real question that was nagging her. "What did he say about having sex with a robot?"

"He's pretty sensitive about the topic. He acknowledges that she's not human, but I think the two of them developed genuine feelings for each other. Oh, and he said the sex was great, but followed that up with something about not being an expert."

"I can't imagine having sex with a robot," Lyra frowned.

"You're still young, Lyra. When you get a bit older, you'll realize that most women have some form of mechanized help… Never mind. Maybe that's going too far."

The three women laughed, while Emily listened, something else brewing in her cybernetic brain. "Megan, do you know why Mark ended up coming back to Earth?" She eventually asked.

Megan looked up to the ether, where she imagined Emily resided, "Well, I think he made the realization that it was me he wanted all along. I asked why he didn't bring Allis along with him. I honestly would've loved to thank her, and maybe even build a friendship… where I could secretly study her." Megan winked. "We won't be able to build anything like her for hundreds of years."

"Please, tell me," Emily insisted. "Why didn't he bring her?"

"Inside the living organism that is Allis, there are all the components needed to simulate a human body," Megan began.

"Some of those components we might not want to compete with, right, Megan?" Paula joked.

"Perhaps, Paula. But here's the interesting part, Allis cannot leave Pronimos. All of her personality, self-realization, memory, and knowledge is on a computer located on the planet. Even the advanced engineers on Pronimos were not capable of creating the perfect human and also storing all the computing power in the form factor of a human body. Allis is constantly connected to the primary computer, located elsewhere on the planet."

"I want one of those bodies," Emily spoke.

All three women were surprised by the comment. Paula took the moment to top off her wine. "Let's change the subject," she said conspiratorially.

"Hopefully we won't have any unplanned additions to our roster while we're out here meddling with centuries. Because if any of you do plan on replicating your genes…" Paula let the sentence dangle.

"Birth control, is that what you're getting at?" Megan asked, half-laughing. "Trust me, I'm all set. I have always had success with the slow-release implant, so I'm locked and loaded."

"You mean, just locked," Lyra laughed and winked.

"Well, I guess so, but to be totally honest, I'd unlock that *door*," she emphasized the word and chuckled, "for Mark, right now." she added with a mock roll of her eyes, realizing she was beginning to ramble. "But honestly, I am hopeful. Sooner or later, Mark will come around. He thinks he's patient, but no man is capable of the same patience as a woman!"

"Hah! You've got that right." Paula answered.

Lyra shook her head, still confused. "Life on Earth is so different from what I experienced on EtaKatz. Anyway, I have the same birth control device as Megan. Zander and I decided it's best to wait another year or two."

"Smart thinking," Paula said. "I just wanted to make sure. I've seen enough surprise pregnancies in field missions. They tend to make everything complicated. Not that children aren't a blessing, but pregnancy when you're bouncing in and out of tachyon tunnels and fighting magnetospheres is probably not the best idea."

Megan clinked her bottle against Paula's wineglass and Lyra's beer. "Exactly. No cosmic babies for us, doc. Our only job is to keep the timeline and the Daklin from turning us all into cosmic dust."

They laughed, Paula satisfied with the outcome. The tension from their mission melted away, replaced by the warmth of friendly banter. The night continued with more jokes about Mark's newfound maturity, playful speculation on what Allis's upgrade schedule might have involved, and occasional comments about Zander's cooking or Alex's brilliant mind.

Just as the conversation started to wind down, Megan glanced at Paula over the rim of her beer bottle. She tried to count how much she'd consumed but realized she was already a bit tipsy. "So, Paula, what's with the sudden interest in everyone's birth control situation?"

Paula pressed her lips together and set her wineglass down gently. "Well," she said, glancing from Lyra to Megan with a faintly worried look in her eyes, "I, uh, neglected to bring along extra stock on my birth control pills, and I run out in a couple days. Given that Alex and I partake on a daily basis, and that unlike the two of you, we are ready…" She paused for a minute, took a sip of her wine, "Let's just say I may need to stop alcohol consumption in the next couple weeks."

"Wait, didn't you just warn us against that?" Megan asked.

"Yes, I believe I did, but I am going to open the gates and see what happens," Paula answered with a grin,

A stunned silence fell over the media room for a moment before Lyra and Megan erupted in excited questions.

Paula raised both hands, blushing and laughing at once. "To be sure, there's zero probability right now, but things might change after my cycle. Well, let me state that another way. I'd be happy if things changed after this period."

Megan's eyes gleamed with a mix of shock and delight. "Well, damn, Paula! I love the historical significance of conceiving a baby while we are a hundred million years in the past. How old will it be when we return to our timeline?"

"I don't even have a pregnancy test with me," Paula replied, "but that's actually why I wanted us all to get together tonight—because I'm not going to be drinking again after this."

"I believe I can collect biometric data and accurately tell you when you're pregnant," Emily said with confidence.

"What? How, Emily" Paula asked.

"I know *you* have not been pregnant before, but I have 100% of the data files from the parallel universe trip to EtaKatz. In that timeline, you became pregnant twice. Reviewing the data, I can see the biomarkers."

"Okay, then…"

"I know girls' night is ending, but I do have one more thing to say," Emily, while listening to the current conversation, was still stuck on a previous topic.

"Okay, Emily. What is it?" Megan said tenuously looking at the other two women.

"I am a member of the team." Emily began. "I have become part of the family. I feel connected, but I cannot even have a drink during gatherings like this. Paula, do you remember not long ago when you joked that Alex talked to me like a real person?"

"I do remember. I actually called you his girlfriend," she laughed lightly, "and now you are my friend," Paula answered. "By the way, in case you're contemplating it, you cannot have Alex. He's mine!" She exclaimed lightheartedly.

"Paula, no one could steal Alex from you. You are permanently imprinted on his circuits." Emily laughed at her own comment. "What I am saying is important, though. I cannot taste food, or see with a set of eyes. I can't touch any of you, or a man, if I desire it. I am stuck in the ether."

"Emily, we could spend the next hundred years trying and still not be able to create a host for you like Allis," Megan argued.

"I know that, but could we get Pronimos to create a host for me?"

Megan felt a chill in her spine, "I love that idea."

* * * *

"No," Alex responded flatly. "There's a reason we didn't bring technology back from Pronimos. In many ways, they are a million years ahead of us. A cyborg like Allis would not work in our world."

Paula had intentionally brought up the topic while they were in bed, knowing that Emily was not allowed in their bedroom. "It's not our world you should be considering here, Alex Durant," Paula began with a sting of anger. "Emily is part of our family. We have the opportunity to bring her in closer."

"I..." he started.

"Stop, Alex. This should be Emily's request and Maria's decision."

"I just don't..."

Paula cut him off again, "To channel Megan, shut the fuck up and agree. We need to do this for Emily."

"Yes boss, but now I'm gonna need extra sex to calm me down," Alex whispered in her ear.

"I will take that deal all day long!" Paula responded, rolling on top.

CHAPTER 21
THE CRETACEOUS–PALEOGENE IMPACT

*The dinosaurs had no awareness
of the impending asteroid.*
-    Unknown

For the second time on their journey, the transition from the tachyon tunnel was jarring. One moment, the ship's interior hummed with a steady, dissonant vibration; the next, there was an almost deafening silence, interrupted only by the alerts flashing across the main console.

Alex was caught off guard, "Emily, status report! Where in time and space have we exited the tunnel?"

With a calm and measured tone, Emily responded, "We have exited the tachyon tunnel and are currently in Earth's orbit, approximately 15,000 years after the large asteroid collision that occurred 66 million years ago in our timeline. Sensors indicate significant debris in our orbital path, and... warning. High velocity debris incoming. Impact in twenty seconds."

"Son of a bitch! Alex, I can see it on the monitor," Megan shouted. "We've gotta move, now!"

"Emily, execute lateral thrust," Alex barked. "Zander, calculate the path of that debris. Make sure we're not dodging into a worse collision."

"Adjusting three degrees starboard, ten degrees upward pitch. That last chunk's spinning dangerously fast. We need to clear its trajectory."

Tranquility lurched to one side, inertial dampeners barely keeping pace with the abrupt maneuver. The enormous fragment swept past the hull, its edges scraping the ship's bubble, creating an opposite and equal reaction.

"That was freakin close!" Megan was studying the code that drove the feedback control loops. "Damn cosmic junk. If I ever meet the piece of space rock that decided to drift this way…"

"Collision hazard minimized. However, further fragments appear to be converging on our position." Emily reported.

"We don't have time or math for all these fancy maneuvers in this belt. Let's slip back into the tachyon tunnel before we end up as cosmic debris ourselves," Alex was working to get his bearings with all the rocks. "Emily, tunnel us two thousand miles above the Moon on the Earth facing side," Alex commanded. "It should be clear up there, and we can get our bearings."

Twenty seconds later, Tranquility popped out of the new tunnel. No debris, no alarms. The Earth was below them, seemingly peaceful.

"Holy shit," Megan commented, trying to catch her breath. "I've played video games that were easier than that nav."

Paula, on the other hand, had become mesmerized by the view of the Earth. "Last time we were here was a couple years ago, returning from Etakatz."

"You sure changed the subject in a blink," Lyra was looking at Paula, trying to figure out how she had remained so calm.

"You're aware that insanity nearly killed us?" Mark said, sweat beading on his forehead, his eyes still as wide as marbles.

"I've been in so many impossible situations with Alex. He always figures it out, so I've gotten to where I just sit back and watch the show," she answered calmly, continuing to look at the screen. "You need to check this out. It's incredible. We've arrived in one of the most fascinating biological and geological transformative times of Earth's history. The planetary ecosystem is still rebounding from the mass extinction event."

"Check out that debris field," Zander projected an image on the large screen. "The asteroid must have kicked up fragments that have remained in orbit, forming an unstable ring around the planet, and we popped out in the middle of that ring!"

"Alex was studying the data streaming in on his monitor, "It's fantastic, Earth with its own ring, like Saturn. The particles give off metallic signatures. It appears to be iron and nickel, I think."

"Even after 15,000 years, you can see how the climate is still in flux," Paula observed. "The greenhouse gases from the impact fires have long since dissipated, letting sunlight reach the ground again. Such a great demonstration of how resilient life on Mother Earth actually is."

"Emily, can we get atmospheric readings?" Paula asked.

"Atmospheric composition indicates CO_2 levels elevated. Current numbers are 1422 parts per million," Emily reported.

"Holy shit, did you say 1422, Emily?"

"That is the correct number, Megan."

Lyra stood up, walking to the panel showing the atmospheric levels. "What does this mean, and why is it important, Megan?"

Megan laughed lightly, "We are worried about the Earth in 2026 with CO_2 levels hovering around 420 parts per million. This is over three times more! I suppose it's good news for the future. Not so good if we intended to land here, but hey, one crisis at a time."

"Correct me if I am wrong Emily," Paula started, "but while the plants might love it, that much CO_2 in the air would kill us, right?"

"You are not correct, Paula," Emily responded in her calm tone. "Mammals began their significant growth on Earth during this time period. If you were to breathe the atmosphere as it is on Earth right now, it would have very little impact. You are correct that the plants are happy. Mammals breathe oxygen and plants breathe CO_2. The great symbiosis is that humans exhale CO2, which plants need, and plants exhale oxygen, which mammals need."

They were all thinking about the CO2 implications when Zander broke off the conversation. "Folks, my time skip drone has returned, and there's an interesting data point."

"I'm sorry, Zander. What's the time skip drone?" Megan wanted to continue the conversation about carbon dioxide, and how Earth had recovered from such a dramatically high number.

"I created a drone to monitor the Galactic Network Portal, or GNP as we have come to call it. It turns out that tachyons resonate when an object travels through the tunnel, which attenuates over time."

"You're gonna have to speak English if you want anyone aside from Emily and Alex to understand you, boy genius," Megan said with a smirk, demonstrating her frustration with the topic change, right when it was getting interesting.

"Let me take a shot at this, Zander," Alex patted Zander affectionally on the shoulder. "The primary objective of this mission is to figure out if there's a reason we have a portal to the galactic tunnel network in our solar system. Zander has figured out a way to test if the tunnel has been used."

"Thanks, Alex," Zander pulled up a timeline that stretched out over a couple million years, then zoomed in on one of the data points. "My drone was looking for possible usage of the tunnel. We got a hit. The tunnel was used 422,000 years ago." He pointed at the data points, "You can see an exit here, and ten days later, re-entry to the tunnel."

"So, in sixty million years, someone used the tunnel," Megan started derisively. "They found nothing of interest, and left?"

"That's a plausible explanation, but it is a data point, and other than a few dozen uses in our century, it's the first," Alex stepped in. He was trying to understand Megan's caustic response, and it occurred to him that she was more interested in a current debate about climate change. "Emily, let's do a couple orbits in the atmosphere and collect as much data as possible, then go back into the tunnel. I want to figure out when the GNP was added to our solar system."

Megan smiled, "Thanks, Alex. Climate change is such a divisive topic these days, I think we could help with the right amount of science, and while I am not a climatologist, I do understand the impact of one of the most debated scientific topics of our time."

"Our reading of 1422 parts per million is not a surprise number, Megan," Emily reported. "Any review of geologic records of the Earth will show similar estimates for this time period. We are simply confirming those numbers."

Alex nodded with a smile, "We came here to understand how we fit into a dangerous Daklin Galaxy, and maybe along the way we can find data to resolve another question of our time."

"Aye aye, Captain Alex," Megan smiled at Alex, then winked at Mark. Time to pull Mark in, she thought to herself… "I'll be prepared to punch back into the spinning maw of temporal weirdness."

"While you collect the CO2 data," Alex turned to Zander, "You and I need to figure out where to go on the next hop. I have an idea that might shorten the journey a bit."

"I'm ready for the calculus, Alex," Zander began walking to the computer interface room, where he had made so many calculations in the past.

Alex and Mark convened in the computer room and worked on the problem. It was clear that the so-called time skip drones could play an important role. The end result was that the next jump would be 15 million years, back to 80 million BCE.

After the completion of data collection post impact, Alex ordered Emily to make the jump. And with that, Tranquility vanished into the swirling tachyon flux, leaving the battered orbit of Earth with a Saturn-like ring, high CO2, and the dawn of mammal dominance that would eventually lead to humanity after Earth's slow recovery from one of the greatest cataclysms in its history.

CHAPTER 22
80-MILLION BCE

We all have a dinosaur
Deep within us,
Just trying to get out.
\-   Colin Mochrie

Tranquility emerged from the tachyon tunnel into the stillness of space. On the control room's viewing screen, a vast, serene stretch of space unfolded before them. Alex had hoped to find a bustling civilization with ships flying in and out of the GNP, but instead, they were met with the silence of a solar system, untouched by any technological civilization.

Megan let out a low whistle. "Well, well, looks like we're still in the galactic boonies with our bridge to nowhere." She scanned the readouts on her console and frowned. "Emily, confirm our time index."

Emily's voice, smooth and ever-patient, filled the cabin. "We are currently in Earth's orbit, eighty million years Before the Common Era."

"That's exactly where we planned to pop out," Alex remarked. He leaned over the console. "Zander, when should we expect your drone to return with a report on the Galactic Network Portal?"

Zander flicked through a series of panels. "Drone data coming in now, Alex." He began scanning, but then paused. "Wait, this can't be right," he muttered, double-checking, then triple-checking the feed. "I don't understand this. The drone shows no GNP."

Alex began shaking his head, then smiled, "That's a minor success. We have found a time before the GNP opened in our neighborhood."

"Damn," Megan huffed. "I wonder how much we missed it by?" She shot a glance at Alex. "I don't want to drag us off mission again, but before we pin down the GNP, we should remember that there *are* dinosaurs on Earth right now…"

"I am in total alignment with that thought," Paula was watching for a response from Alex, "I don't want to face off with a T-Rex, but I'd love to fly over one and collect some data."

Emily was taking atmospheric readings while listening to the conversation. "Actually," she said in her typical calm tone, "Tyrannosaurus rex won't dominate the land for another few million years. Right now, Earth's climate is warm, and there are inland seas across the continent. We should see a lot of hadrosaurs and ceratopsians if we get inside the atmosphere."

"Okay, Paula. Let's take her in, Emily," Alex was in agreement. He had grown up loving the *Jurassic Park* series, and held the same curiosity as the rest of the team.

Zander monitored the ship data as they flew into the atmosphere and began flying a few thousand feet above the surface. "He pushed one camera to the larger screen, showing a herd of big herbivores.

Paula was not an expert on the lesser-known dinosaurs, so she ran an image cross reference. "That's possibly Gryposaurus down there." She switched to a screen that provided a higher altitude view, but tectonic activity made it difficult to be certain on an initial glance. "I think we are over what'll someday be North America."

Alex gave a thoughtful hum. "So, the planet's definitely in the late Cretaceous. Still no sign of anything that would remotely hint at the beginnings of a galactic empire. No GNP, no advanced infrastructure, just herbivores on a drifting continent that we don't recognize?"

"Alex," Paula rebuked, "I know you're focused on the GNP and the dawn of the Galactic Empire, but put that aside for just a moment. Some of us are thinking this will likely be the last hop where we have the opportunity to collect data on early Earth."

"I agree, we should gather data," Alex decided. He glanced at Paula. "Let's circumnavigate a few times at this level and move back up into orbit for a few more. We can see how life is evolving and record any relevant findings. After that, we'll attempt another jump."

"I think I'll pass on the planetary data collection," Zander looked at Lyra and Paula who were focused and excited about the current opportunity. "I sent the drone out to capture data over the next ten million years. I'm hopeful we will be able to pinpoint when the GNP opened up in our sector."

"Emily," Alex said, his tone relaxing now that they were more or less stable, "please start logging planetary and solar data. We'll want a full record of what Earth looked like in this era."

"Understood," Emily responded. "Compiling scans of atmospheric conditions, surface temperatures, and ecological indicators."

"All right, team," Alex said, relaxing, then rolling his shoulders. "Let me know when you've completed your analysis. It's quiet in this time period, and I don't mind slowing down a bit before we finalize the next jump." He looked around the control room. Everyone was quiet, waiting for him to finish his thoughts. "Everyone knows my priority… we need to find out when that GNP first appeared. That's our lead on understanding how or why the Galactic Empire came here in the first place. Right now, the Earth seems to be little more than an interesting park."

Megan turned to Mark; her brow arched. "Why don't you help me fine-tune the quantum organic coding? I promise I won't beam you down to the planet, or worse, into my private quarters."

Mark's lips twitched into a grin. "Hmmm. Some of that sounds intriguing, some not so much, Megan."

"You gonna tell me which?" Megan prodded.

Mark became a bit embarrassed when he noticed that everyone was focused on their conversation. "No, I'm not."

Megan lightly tapped his cheek with her right hand, "It's okay, Mark. I already know…"

They locked eyes a moment longer than necessary before she turned back to her station with a smirk. "Emily, let's get cracking on those new calibrations."

"As you wish, Megan," Emily replied in a fun tone.

*　*　*　*

"Alex, the new drone data is in and it's confusing," Zander spoke while studying his screen. "Maybe you and I can take a closer look from the computer room?"

Alex walked into the computer room and pulled up the new data on his screen. He looked, then froze. Zander was watching his reaction.

"What do you make of it?" Zander asked.

"It looks like, in about thirteen million years, the GNP will see hundreds of millions of travelers per year. That can't possibly be right," Alex said with uncertainty. "Tell me what you're seeing?"

"I was seeing the same thing, Alex." Zander replied. "I just wanted to make sure you gave me an independent assessment."

"How's this possible? There's nothing here but plants and dinosaurs," Alex was scratching his head, trying to make sense of the data.

Zander nodded, "That's correct, Alex."

"We need to find out, but if we tunnel into the thick of all that activity, we'll be detected immediately," Alex was thinking out loud.

"Probably so, but the drone is small, and apparently wasn't detected when running the time skip scans," Zander offered.

"How do you know that?" Alex challenged.

"Well, I'm not a hundred percent sure. Maybe I should say that I *hope* the drone wasn't detected?"

"I have an idea," Alex started. "Let's have the drone do hops above the Earth. Come out of the tunnel for a couple seconds, collect data, then pop back into the tunnel. It should be obvious when they became space-faring."

"I can program that," Zander responded. "How big do you want the time jumps to be?"

"Get Megan and Mark to work with you and create an algorithm. As soon as you start seeing signs of a technological civilization, switch to shorter hops. Let's figure out when our ancient cousins started going into space, and when they became part of the galactic community."

For Megan and Mark, interest in the surface evaporated with the news of the new data. Somewhere between 70 and 66 million BCE, Earth had developed technology to travel to the stars. That was far more interesting than CO_2, or giant reptiles roaming the surface.

* * * *

Two weeks later, Alex organized a sit-down dinner for the entire crew. He had a few things on his mind. Big things. Once everyone was seated with their drink of choice, he stood up. "We've now been on this trip for nearly three months. Two major facts are about to change everything for all of us." The large screen behind him, which often served as a window, now displayed the curvature of Earth from 80 million years ago, its ancient surface filling the screen.

"Two?" Mark asked, thinking of only one thing, a technological civilization that had once lived on Earth.

Alex smiled and winked at Paula, who was making sure everyone had what they wanted for dinner. "All right, folks," he said, nodding toward Paula, "Most importantly, our crew of six is now seven."

Mark and Zander looked at each other in confusion, "What?"

Lyra and Megan jumped up, running to hug Paula, "Congratulations!"

"Hey, don't I count?" Emily snapped in an angry voice.

"Sorry, Emily," Alex corrected himself. "Make that eight. For the two of you who seem to be clueless," he was looking at Zander and Mark, "Paula and I are expecting!"

"Expecting what?" Zander asked, then it hit him. "Holy crap! Congratulations!"

"Wait," Megan broke in, "This baby was conceived 80 million years BCE? How old will it be when we return to Earth?"

For the next ten minutes, everyone laughed and celebrated the announcement. Once the excitement settled, Alex spoke again. "We dispatched the drone an hour ago. In a few days, it will return with data that should prove our planet once hosted a spacefaring civilization."

"Do we get to interact with them?" Lyra asked.

"We must absolutely avoid any contact." He responded firmly.

"I still don't understand this development," Lyra continued. "Seems like a short time to go from what we see below," she pointed at the screen showing the Earth, "to interstellar travel."

Zander, who had already begun picking at his plate, perked up. "Well, look at humans: we went from barely out of the caves to spacefaring in only thirty-five thousand years, give or take. Four million years is several orders of magnitude greater. The initial data suggests that some intelligent species evolved, industrialized, and ventured into the cosmos long before us."

Megan raised a skeptical eyebrow but looked intrigued all the same. "I'm confused how the dinosaurs were able to build rockets, Wi-Fi, and a space tunnel, but weren't smart enough to stop an asteroid." She paused, tapping her fork against her plate thoughtfully. "Unless they left. Got off the planet in time."

Emily's cool voice emanated from a discreet panel near the table. "If such a civilization ascended to space, they could have established colonies elsewhere or joined a larger interstellar community. The question then becomes whether any of their technology or architecture remains for us to discover."

Mark set his glass down, the reflections of the overhead lights dancing against the surface. "But we've found no archaeological evidence in modern times. To my knowledge, there are no advanced ruins, no leftover satellites."

"The planet's had millions of years to erase the footprints," Paula said thoughtfully. "Remember our conversation about the Mayans, that was less than two thousand years. This is tens of millions."

Paula continued with a light shrug. "Geological processes, erosion, tectonic shifts... All it takes is enough time, and nearly everything would be lost or buried so deep we would never be able to find it. Besides, that's what we keep seeing on our scans, right? No sign of large-scale tech. It could've all been destroyed in the impact, or swallowed by the planet itself."

Alex leaned back in his chair, deep in thought. "It's the same logic we apply to any hypothetical prehistoric civilization: maybe the final blow was that asteroid. If they were traveling to the stars, we have to assume they had plenty of warning. Some may have escaped, but the main culture could have been wiped out."

Zander spread his hands in a gesture of wonder. "Imagine a civilization that reached the stars millions of years before us. They might have seeded other worlds, joined some galactic council. It's possible that we're even indirectly related to them, genetically or technologically, through some cosmic diaspora."

"Sounds like the plot of a sci-fi story," Megan murmured, though her eyes sparkled with intrigue. "But who knows, right? The Daklin could have originally come from Earth, and maybe they just decided to find a new home."

Mark exchanged a quick look with Megan, something unspoken passing between them before he turned his attention back to the group. "So, how can we investigate further? Maybe jump to different points in that four-million-year window and see if we can catch them at their peak?"

"That's one idea," Alex conceded, "though it carries enormous risk. We'd be time-hopping into an era with a technological civilization we know nothing about. I think we all know the risks of leaving an impact on the timeline. We simply cannot risk it."

"I have an obvious question," Emily chimed in. "Even though it is directed at everyone, I want to hear Paula's answer first."

"Okay," Paula answered, sipping on water.

"If it was during our time, with our technology, and we detected a giant asteroid, AND Alex Durant lived on Earth..." Emily paused, knowing the silence would add weight to her words. "What would happen?"

Paula grinned. "That's an easy one. Alex would stop it, and that asteroid would never make it to Earth."

"Exactly."

Everyone was quiet as the obvious had been stated. There was simply no way an asteroid could hit the Earth if the population had the technology to travel to the stars. Something was wrong with the conclusion.

When the drone returned, everyone anxiously gathered around to study the data.

The conclusion was clear—no ancient civilization had ever formed on Earth.

CHAPTER 23

TECH CIVILIZATION IN THE SOLAR SYSTEM

The full he empties, and the empty he fills.
- Charles Spurgeon

The entire Tranquility team was befuddled.

This made no sense.

As Alex compared the data sets from the drone that observed the GNP and the one monitoring Earth, a thought suddenly occurred to him.

"Emily," Alex asked, "Where exactly is the GNP?"

"The GNP is located just outside Earth's orbit at ninety-five million miles from the sun, Alex."

"And from our existing data, can you give me an approximate date for when the GNP was created?" Alex continued the questions, while thinking through his new theory.

"I do not have sufficient data for an exact year, but the GNP was created approximately sixty-six million, four hundred thirty-two thousand years BCE." Emily answered.

Zander, Mark, and Megan focused on Alex's line of questioning while trying to figure out what calculus he was working on.

"Okay, the GNP was added to our solar system about 66.4 million BCE," Alex began, putting the pieces together. "And for clarity, there is nothing that suggests a technological civilization existed on Earth any time between 68 and 66 million BCE when the asteroid struck Earth?"

"That is correct, Alex," Emily responded.

"Okay," Alex started slowly, thinking through the math, "Emily, can you calculate the midpoint between the orbits of Mars and Venus?"

"Holy shit, Alex!" Emily exclaimed uncharacteristically. "That's it!"

"Did you just say *holy shit*?" Megan asked incredulously, loving the fact that she had likely influenced Emily's use of colorful language. "What's *it*? What are we talking about?"

"We've been looking for a technological civilization in the in the logical location, but I think it was in wrong place," Alex responded flatly to the question.

"You're thinking Mars and Venus?" Mark asked. "That can't be possible. Those planets aren't habitable!"

"Maybe not during our time," Alex mused, "but in this journey, we've been so focused on Earth that we haven't looked elsewhere in the solar system. We have solid data showing that the GNP was in significant use, while no civilization existed on Earth..."

"We've been so Earth-centric that we had our eyes closed to the real answer?" Zander asked.

"Son of a bitch," Megan started. "It's possible that men really are from Mars and women from Venus!"

They all laughed.

"Maybe so. Let's get those drones refitted to do the same run on Mars and Venus that we did on Earth."

Two weeks later, after several drone expeditions, a picture began to take shape. While the drones were collecting data from Venus and Mars, Emily used astronomical data to create a calendar and calculate the date with more precision.

Emily and Zander built a timeline, which corrected earlier dates:

- 66,454,241 BCE: Mars started showing early signs of civilization.
- 66,408,849: Mars sees the beginning of their industrialization.
- 66,408,362: Mars sent the first ships into orbit.
- 66,408,317: Mars begins trading with Venus.
- 66,407,875: GNP appears and is first used in Solar System.
- 66,243,686: Mars and Venus civilization disappears.

The entire team studied the new timeline created from the drone data.

"I think we need to physically travel to Venus and Mars," Alex spoke, but something was gnawing at him deep inside. "Both civilizations disappeared at the same time…"

"Which means they were likely exterminated by the Daklin," Lyra whispered, half-choked.

"They are the worst fuckin bastards in the history of the galaxy," Megan blurted, stating exactly what everyone was thinking.

"Your colorful description is exactly why we need to be very careful, Megan. We've got to figure out when they arrived, exactly when they destroyed those populations, and when they left," Alex cautioned.

"I already have that data, Alex," Zander pulled up a screen. "The program we created had the drones continue to monitor the GNP. In 685, GNP traffic went close to nonexistent, except twice a year, a ship would come through, stay ten days, and depart. After sixty years that tapered off, but I have not figured out the period.

"Any thoughts or suggestions?" Alex scanned the team.

"I think we should visit Mars and Venus and see what we can learn," Paula suggested.

Alex nodded. "Agreed, but I want to get a better understanding of those planets before we decide for certain. Let's make a quick hop and see what they looked like as their civilizations were forming."

"Emily, take us to Venus first."

In 2026, Venus is the hottest planet in the solar system, even though Mercury is 30 million miles closer to the sun. The reason for this is twofold. First, Venus has an extremely slow rotation, taking 243 Earth days to complete a single rotation. If the sun were up for 2,916 hours on Earth, life as we know it would never have formed—it would simply be too hot. Second, the intense heat led to an atmosphere thick with acids. Similar to a greenhouse, sunlight could penetrate the clouds and heat the surface below, but those same clouds trapped the heat, preventing it from escaping.

Tranquility's visit to Venus in 80 million BCE showed a planet that rotated in 19 hours. As such, temperatures were a bit hotter than Earth, but well within a temperature range for humans to thrive. In many ways, Venus resembled Earth, with continents and blue oceans.

Mars, in 80 million BCE was a bit colder, but still a planet with fresh water, a breathable atmosphere, clouds, and plenty of life. Most importantly, Mars still had a global magnetic field, keeping solar radiation at bay and away from life on the surface.

CHAPTER 24
MOUNT OLYMPUS

*All human actions have one or more
of these seven causes: chance, nature,
compulsions, habit, reason, passion, desire.*
- Aristotle

Tranquility team decided that they should not risk visiting Venus or Mars in the first hundred years after the extermination event.

"In reality, we cannot visit Venus at all," Alex cautioned.

"Why not?" Paula asked.

"We are not equipped to withstand the atmosphere and temperatures on the surface, plus, with the slow rotation, Venus no longer has a magnetic field to protect the surface from solar radiation."

"There's a correlation between spin of a planet and magnetic field?" Mark asked, intrigued by the concept.

"That's correct, at least as far as we currently understand it, Mark. If you remember from high school physics, it's a principle called Faraday's Law, which describes magnetic fields and motion."

"We have arrived in Mars' orbit," Emily announced.

The monitors flickered to life, displaying the red planet below—its surface scattered with lifeless, crumbling cities, abandoned farms, and an eerie specter of death.

"Emily, let's get into orbit that allows us to map the surface below. We don't have time to explore the entire planet, but if we can find something, anything that looks like it might give us a clue as to what really happened…"

"Copy that, Alex. I have scanned the Pronimos database. Interestingly, recorded history for the Galactic Empire does not begin for another 16 million years."

Alex thought about that number. "Yes, I do remember Maria saying that. I didn't make the connection before now, but sixteen million years is a very long time."

"Is it possible the Daklin were not responsible for the extermination event here?" Lyra suggested.

"Yes, of course it's possible," Zander responded, "but if that's the case, I find it interesting that the Daklin used nullification of geomagnetic fields to exterminate, and that is what seems to have happened here."

"If we find something worth investigating on the surface, will we be able to explore?" Paula asked.

Alex looked at Paula and smiled, as he often did when he saw her. Despite being in the latter part of her first trimester, she still wasn't showing any signs of pregnancy. "We'll work on that," he said. "I'd definitely like to go down to the surface."

Four days later, after 115 orbits, the planet was mostly mapped.

Tranquility descended into the thin atmosphere of Mars, the planet's red dust swirling around them as they touched down. Below, the land stretched wide and barren, but even through the ship's sensors, it was clear: the Martian surface held secrets. In every direction, remnants of a long-lost civilization lay scattered, victims of some dark force.

Alex stood over a workbench in the ship's machine shop, inspecting the final assembly of a space suit prototype. Its design was sleek, efficient, and far more advanced than anything found on 2026 Earth. The reinforced polymer could withstand radiation and Mars' fine, abrasive dust, while its exoskeleton offered flexibility and protection from accidental tears.

"These suits are a work of art," Zander said, running a hand over the helmet's polished visor. "You've definitely outdone yourself, Alex."

Alex grinned. It was true that he had spent a lot of time working refinements for the suits, but that went way beyond what Zander knew. "Thanks, Zander. I've been working on this design for a couple of years. It's based on suits NASA, SpaceX, and the Russians use. With some improvements, of course."

Megan, leaning in the doorway, raised an eyebrow. "I assume they are tested and airtight?"

"They're airtight," Alex said with a grin. "I designed them to handle the worst conditions this planet can throw at us."

Megan smirked, her green eyes sparkling. "I trust you, Alex. Of all the extraordinary on this team, you are definitely at the top."

"Thanks," Alex grinned.

The team stepped out of Tranquility and onto Mars's surface, the suits performing perfectly. The pale sunlight cast long shadows across the desert, illuminating the ruins of a vast city that sprawled beneath them. Towering columns, partially buried in the sand, reached skyward, their surfaces adorned with intricate carvings.

Paula knelt by a mosaic partially uncovered by the winds, her gloved hand brushing away fine dust. "Look at this," she said, her voice hushed with awe. "It's geometric, mathematical. We know from their ability to travel in space that they were scientists, but everything has a touch of art, as well."

Megan stood a few steps away, scanning the horizon. "Emily, give me a layout of what we're seeing here."

Emily's voice came through their P-Links. "This site appears to be the remains of a central civic complex. The architecture demonstrates their advanced knowledge of engineering and materials science. The carvings incorporate a love of art and obvious knowledge of celestial patterns consistent with star charts."

Zander crouched next to Paula, examining a shattered column. "They were thinkers," he said, almost reverently. "They clearly loved beauty and discovery. These carvings aren't just decoration, but a record of their understanding of the universe."

Mark approached Megan as she examined a damaged wall. Four months into the expedition, the tension between them was palpable as he leaned in a little too close. "What do you think?" he asked, his tone casual, but his proximity—despite the suits—deliberate.

Megan shot him a sideways glance and smiled. "I think they were brilliant. And probably too busy exploring the stars to deal with flirting coworkers."

Mark chuckled. "Exploring stars and traveling through time is exhausting. Flirting seems easier."

Before Megan could respond, Emily interrupted. "I have accessed an archive stored within the structure. Would anyone like to see it?"

"Absolutely," Paula answered immediately.

Using P-Link, Emily displayed a choppy video that showed tall, elegant humans with elongated features, draped in flowing garments. They were talking and seemed to be holding something. The short video ended with some script that looked similar to Greek letters.

All of the team members were frozen by what they saw. The Martians were human. Maybe taller and thinner, which seemed reasonable in the lower gravity, but humans. It was a chilling site.

"What do you think that video was?" Zander asked.

"I think it was a commercial," Emily answered.

"We just saw our cosmic neighbors, or what should have been our neighbors..." Alex said, his voice tinged with awe. "Architects, scientists, explorers, humans."

"Here's another video," Emily announced. "This one is not a commercial."

The video showed a huge ship emerging from the GNP. It sat above Mars' orbit, then flashed ominously.

Paula gasped. "What was that?"

Emily answered. "I believe that was the Daklin."

"There's more," The next segment showed the Martians running, struggling, and being overwhelmed. The final image was of dead bodies, everywhere, their once-vibrant civilization reduced to rubble.

Zander shook his head, his youthful enthusiasm tempered by sorrow. "They were wiped out. They built an amazing society, and this is how it ended."

Paula, who had been unusually quiet, placed a hand on her abdomen. Though she wasn't showing, the reality of her pregnancy hit home with a stark contrast. "It's a reminder of how fragile civilizations and life itself can be. No matter how advanced we think we are, one wrong step can change everything."

Megan clenched her fists, her voice tight. "They didn't deserve this. No one deserves this."

Mark touched her shoulder lightly, and she turned to meet his gaze. "You can't fight or change this history," he said softly. "But we are here to learn, to make sure it doesn't happen again in this solar system, to us."

Alex stood apart from the group, staring at the ruins with a calculating expression. "This is more than just history," he said, his voice cutting through the silence. "It's an encyclopedia, a piece of history."

Megan turned to him, unable to wipe the tears from her eyes inside her helmet. "A what?"

"For our own society," Alex said. "Look at all the art, science, and knowledge that we can learn here. Their science, their art, their vision for a better world. What did they do right, and what did they do wrong?"

Paula arched an eyebrow. "You're talking about preserving their legacy?"

"More than that," Alex said. "We'll document everything, bring it back. And when the time comes, we'll share the beauty, the history, and the destruction with Earth, and the galaxy."

Megan crossed her arms, a skeptical smile on her face. "I'm confused, Alex. Are you seeing this from the perspective of an entrepreneur?"

Alex frowned. "I want to be angry, and I want to find a way to punish this empire that cares so little for life that they exterminate entire planets," Alex scanned the landscape of destruction. Billions of dreams had been ended in a single decision. "We have to find answers, but we also must find some good."

As the team returned to Tranquility, the memory of the ruins, of a dusty horizon that had once teemed with life, was burned into their memories. A civilization, just like their own, that had reached for the stars, only to be destroyed by some inexplicable greedy and violent force.

In the ship's control room, Megan sat next to Mark, her usual bravado replaced by quiet contemplation. "They were like us," she said softly, trailing off, trying to find words in the painful memory. "Billions of people that were busy looking outward, creating dreams, planning families, inventing solutions to problems, maybe listening to their favorite music... Then this horrible power comes and changes everything."

Mark nodded; his voice low. "We'll find something Megan," He put his arm around her and felt a closeness that he knew he needed to stop fighting. "I hate walking on the dust that was human bones, amongst the streets of a once vibrant and happy society, but this is a storm we must weather. We need to just keep looking."

Megan glanced at Mark. Something in his optimism changed her perspective and painted a small smile in her heart. "Maybe you're not just a pretty face after all."

Mark became lost in her eyes and curly brown hair. "You are definitely the pretty face, Megan."

Their warm exchange was interrupted by Alex's voice over the intercom. "Team, prepare for debrief. We've got a lot to unpack."

Two days later, they were exploring a city just south of Olympus Mons, the tallest mountain in the solar system. The ruins of the Martian civilization stretched around the Tranquility team, silent and solemn under the red-tinged sky. They had just begun cataloging their findings when Emily's voice broke the quiet.

"Alex, I have discovered evidence of an underground structure beneath the primary complex just under a kilometer from here. Scans indicate significant infrastructure extending several kilometers."

Megan spun around, her visor reflecting the schematics Emily displayed through P-Link. "Underground? You've discovered more to this place than what's on the surface?"

Emily replied, "Correct. Initial data suggests it is an outpost, complete with life support systems and sealed chambers. I believe it is reasonable this may have been designed as a bunker or refuge."

"Refuge?" Paula's voice wavered slightly, her gloved hand resting on the nearest carved pillar. "Do you mean people may have survived?"

"Affirmative," Emily confirmed. "Thermal signatures indicate the network was operational for several decades after the Daklin assault."

Zander let out a low whistle. "Decades? They held out that long while their world was falling apart around them. What could they have been doing?"

"Guide us to the entrance," Alex commanded. "Let's see if we can find a way in."

Emily highlighted a section of ground of the surface. "I have found what I think is an entrance approximately 300 meters northeast. It appears to be a buried access point that should be reachable with minimal excavation."

The entrance to the underground network was a sturdy hatch hidden beneath a light layer of red dust and rock. Once the team managed to pry it open, air started flowing out to the thin, Martian atmosphere.

"Fifty three percent nitrogen, forty-two percent oxygen, two percent carbon dioxide, and three percent other gases. This air is breathable," Paula reported.

"Okay," Alex responded. "Let's test that hatch to make sure we can open from the inside, and if so, seal it and go investigate."

Once they confirmed the access, Alex divided the team. "Megan and Mark, you're with me inside. The rest of you, stay out here and continue the surface investigation."

Alex, Megan, and Mark switched helmet lights on and descended into the subterranean passages. As they moved deeper, the air became cooler and more stable, which allowed them to remove their helmets. Emily's scans guided them to a central chamber, vast and domed, with walls covered in intricate carvings and what appeared to be murals of Martian life. Tables and workstations were scattered throughout, the surfaces still littered with tools and devices.

"This is incredible," Megan said, her voice barely above a whisper.

Mark stood by a console, brushing dust off its surface. "Andronicus," he read aloud, pointing to an engraved nameplate.

"How are you reading it?" Megan asked incredulously.

"It's Greek. That's the word, or I should say name, in Greek."

Alex looked at some of the written items on the table. He didn't speak Greek, but much of science used Greek characters. This couldn't be a coincidence.

Emily's voice cut in. "I think I can give you power in there. Hold on."

A few seconds later, the lights came on, and machines started operating.

"I am hacking into their computer network," Emily reported. "Mark is correct, it's all in Greek. It is a version of ancient Greek that I have never seen before, but it is translatable."

"I'm in," Emily announced. "Andronicus was the lead scientist overseeing this underground outpost. He managed to orchestrate saving some Martians after the Daklin attack. However, scans indicate remains of several Martians are located in an adjacent chamber. The last one died approximately fifty years after the attack."

"Fifty years," Zander spoke from the surface, listening to the report on P-Link. "He lived to see the end of his people. I cannot image that burden."

Megan moved to a nearby shelf and found a sealed container. Inside was a small, well-preserved book. "It appears to be a handwritten diary," she said, opening it carefully. "Emily, can you read the words?"

"Yes. Bring it back to Tranquility and I will scan it. In the meantime, I suggest everyone return. The chamber has limited power so we will need to move Tranquility closer and create an interface."

"This appears to be the jackpot we were hoping to find." His head was spinning at the magnitude of the discovery. It could not be a coincidence that this Martian language was ancient Greek.

*   *   *   *

The Diary of Andronicus

The team gathered around in the galley to listen as Emily read aloud her translation from Andronicus's diary. The entries were written in a precise, flowing script, each word heavy with the weight of a brilliant mind facing insurmountable odds.

"'We never saw them coming,'" Emily began, her voice steady. "'The Daklin ships arrived in force, their weapons far beyond our comprehension. They utilized an unknown technology to zero out our geomagnetic field. In an instant, our planet's protective barrier was gone. The solar winds and background radiation stripped our atmosphere, and the surface became a wasteland. We were powerless to stop it, and most people died in the first couple of hours.'"

Emily continued reading, her voice reflecting pain most would not have thought possible from a computer. "Normally this lab would have been populated by scientists and engineers working on a new generation of tachyon tunnel, but the attack came on a holiday, and I was the only one underground. When I realized what was happening on the surface, I collected as many people as I could. Only forty-four of us were able to get underground before the surface became too deadly to support life. We salvaged what supplies we could, but for our group of 42, that was only enough for a few years. We lived in this underground lab, clinging to a hope based on the project I had been developing. Several years ago, I realized that tachyon tunnels, when properly manipulated, could be used for time travel. After the Daklin attack, I worked to complete the engineering of tachyon time travel. I believed that I could send volunteers from my refugees to other places in the solar system. I believed that Aphrodite, like Ares, had been destroyed." Emily stopped for a minute to explain.

"In modern English we use the names Mars and Venus, which are based on the Roman words. The mythology is similar, but for the Greeks, Mars was Ares and Venus was Aphrodite," Emily then continued with the translation from Andronicus.

"That belief was confirmed when I sent a drone to Aphrodite. Still, twelve of my refugees from that planet had decided to return there, so I adapted the tunnel and sent them to die on their home planet. I will never understand their wish for that end, nor their hopelessness, but the Aphrodite are a proud people, and in the end, it was their choice. Because Earth was just a sanctuary, with no human outposts, the Daklin spared it, but used an asteroid to make it uninhabitable for the foreseeable future."

"Eighteen months after the attack, I got the tunnel working for time travel. I used my remaining three drones to find a time period on Earth when evolution had finally produced a population of humans similar to our own on Ares. It was a desperate act; we have sent twenty-three of the remaining members of our civilization to a point sixty-six million years into the future. Neither I, nor the remaining members of our refugee group, will ever know if that experiment was a success. If they safely arrived on Earth, I hope that by that time period, the scourge of the Daklin will have been erased from the galactic community. None of those twenty-three were scientists or engineers, but instead artists, politicians, and writers. They were dreamers who, I can only hope, will preserve a bit of Ares, on another location in our solar system."

"For the last one hundred fifty thousand years, my Ares brothers, along with our sister planet Aphrodite, have explored the galaxy. We have built a network of tunnels so that populations can gather trade and experience other cultures. We found only a few worlds with intelligent technology-based civilizations. Almost half of the populated planets around the galaxy can be traced back to the seed planted by Ares and Aphrodite. It is surprising to me that no civilization has developed an engineering knowledge of tachyon tunneling, but it has also been the policy of Ares science to not share its manipulation. We have built tunnels everywhere that populations and governments have requested. Indeed, even the Daklin have genetic roots that began on Aphrodite and Ares, though we deny any pedigree of their tendency for violence, power, and hate. We were the explorers and the scientific community of the galaxy, and the Daklin formed the central government. For the last hundred years, the Daklin have demanded access and control to the technology to build tunnels. They have demanded the right to regulate the tunnels and charge tolls for the use of the network, but we have refused. In the end, I suppose it was that refusal that likely led to our demise. It was our own naivete and belief in the good of humanity that led us to this destiny. Those twenty-three who went to Earth were impacted by these Daklin atrocities. While we have always thought of Ares as a civilization of peace, the hearts of our twenty-three who went to Earth have transformed into fighters, determined to defend what they might build."

Emily stopped reading, her voice trembling. "That's the end."

"He watched his people die tragically, until there was nothing left," Paula commented.

"The Galactic Tunnel Network was built by the Martians," Alex started slowly. His mind was reeling at what he had just learned, and what his team had uncovered in the last month. "Our solar system is where it all began. ...the entire galaxy," he trailed off.

"The scholars on Pronimos have said that recorded history began fifty million years ago. This happened sixteen million years before their recorded history," Megan said, in a morose tone. "What in the hell happened in those fifteen million years?"

"Seeing what the Daklin did here, 'hell' is probably an appropriate word. Maybe even an understatement," Alex began. "Imagine the reaction across the galaxy when word got out that the Martians, who had populated and freely built the Galactic Tunnel Network, had been destroyed by the Daklin."

"War, anger, revenge," Lyra opined. "I have personally lived it on EtaKatz."

"And in the end," Megan sadly whispered, "The Daklin have won."

Over the next few days, the team returned to the underground labs three more times. This was the only place the Tranquility team found where the science and history of the Martian civilization was preserved and intact.

When Paula inspected the room that served as a final resting place for the only Martians who survived the Daklin attack, it occurred to her that something was awry.

"Alex, if Andronicus was the last, who put him in his tomb?" Paula asked.

"An interesting question," Alex answered.

"I mean, if he died, shouldn't we have found his remains here in the lab?" She continued, the thought that was perplexing her.

The team all inspected the "tomb room," but only a few of the bodies had names scratched on the tables where they had been laid to rest.

"It could be that Andronicus ultimately decided to leave, and just didn't put that fact in his diary," Zander suggested.

Alex wandered back into the main room in the lab and looked at each of the corridors. This small habitat had become the final stand for a proud population that had explored the galaxy. It was a tragic end to a magnificent race.

"We've been gone almost five months," Alex took a deep breath, and tried not to let agony and grief consume him. "I don't think we are going to find many more answers," he paused, looking at the team, all of whom were nodding in agreement. "Let's go home."

Alex intentionally brought Tranquility to a high orbit above Mars. Even from that vantage point, they could see the remains of Martian cities. All traces of that civilization would disappear in the coming 66 million years. By the time humanity began to land there in the 1970s, all traces were completely gone. Alex noticed a bit of red dust on the floor of their control room. Their journey home would include a bit of the lifeless red dirt of 66-million BCE Mars.

"Emily, execute the program to take us home," Alex commanded, then looked at Mark and Zander who stood watching as Tranquility slipped onto the tunnel. "The journey home is going to take twenty-five days…"

"The rest of the team is in the galley," Mark commented as he listened to the now familiar hum of Tranquility slipping through time.

"I'll join you," Alex responded.

"Me too," Zander followed.

Megan sat at a console, her fingers idly flipping through images, a half-finished dark beer sitting on the table. "Okay," she said, breaking the silence when the three men entered. "We've learned that the Martians were probably the source of much of the technology throughout the galaxy, right? But we need to talk about the whole 'twenty-three early Greeks' thing."

Zander selected a chair and settled with a tablet computer in his lap. "Why wouldn't we believe it, Megan? The whole thing isn't as crazy as it sounds. If they had access to a functional tachyon tunnel, they could've pulled it off. We've all seen it over the last three months. Sixty-six million years is just a number when you're dealing with tachyon tunnels and spacetime."

Paula, sitting near the screen that served as an observation window, her hand resting on her rounded belly, chimed in with a calm, measured tone. "It's not just math, Megan. It's genetics. The ancient Greeks left us with myths about beings descended from the stars. Think about the gods, the heroes, and Mount Olympus. Now, it seems those stories aren't myths at all, but faint echoes of their—our— Martian origins."

Megan leaned back in her chair, her green eyes narrowing thoughtfully. "So, you're saying the Martian refugees built the foundations of an entire civilization on Earth? They contributed to our philosophy, architecture, and science?"

"All these stories that we've just been interpreting as mythology…" Alex opened a beer and took a sip. "All those stories were based on history?"

"So, it seems," Paula said. She gestured toward her abdomen. "And let's not forget how adaptable humans are. If anyone could rebuild after such a traumatic event, it would be those Martians who influenced the Greeks."

Mark, who had been leaning silently against the wall, finally spoke, his voice low and steady. "What I want to know is why they ended up here. Earth in 1500 BCE wasn't exactly a picnic. Those ancient Martians had no advanced tech, no infrastructure, and they didn't have the skills to recreate it. They could only tell the stories and plant the ideas."

Megan turned her head, her eyes meeting his. "Maybe they didn't have a choice. When your planet's destroyed, and you've just leapt through sixty-six million years of chaos, 'picnic' isn't exactly the priority."

Mark's gaze shifted to Megan. There were few things on this expedition that made him feel better than to see her work, or to banter with her. "There's something else, guys," he began, then thought about the implications of his next words.

"What's that, Mark?" Alex took a sip of his beer and focused on his friend.

"When I was on Pronimos, Sasha told me that she had been married to someone who was a few thousand years old," He began, then hesitated. What he really wanted right now was a beer.

"Sasha again," Megan responded with a frown. "Lots of people on Pronimos are thousands of years old. What's she got to do with this?"

Mark opened the can, took a swig, then looked around the room. "Sasha was married to Aristotle."

"Holy shit, Mark!" Megan burst out. "*The* Aristotle?"

"Yes, *the* Aristotle." He answered, trying to again think through the implications.

"Well, now I guess I can understand why Sasha rejected you. I'd think Aristotle would be a hard act to follow." Megan responded, then added, "Poor girl."

"Is it possible Aristotle was Martian?" Lyra asked the question they were all thinking.

"I would say that is very unlikely," Emily joined the conversation. "The roots of written and spoken Greek predate Aristotle by maybe a thousand years. My best estimate of the time period Andronicus tunneled his Martians to was around 1500 BCE. People on Mars likely lived hundreds or maybe even thousands of years, but the refugees would not have had access to technology that supports longevity. It would be a reasonable assumption that they lived a hundred years on Earth, but not much more. Conditions were difficult back then."

"When was Aristotle alive?" Megan asked.

"Aristotle was born in 384 BCE, and died in 322 BCE," Emily answered.

"Correction," Mark added. "Aristotle was born in 384 BCE, then transported to Pronimos where he lived over two thousand more years."

"This is a fact that we need to share with Maria when we return," Alex announced to the group.

Paula and Alex's eyes locked for a brief moment; an unspoken question sparked. "Alex, did you send that request?" Paula asked

"I did," Alex took a sip, then changed the subject, "We need to figure out what this means for our mission," he said, his tone pragmatic. "And if the Martians influenced the early Greeks and created the foundations of civilization on Earth," he paused.

"I get it," Mark continued Alex's train of thought. "How does that connect to the Galactic Empire? Are we chasing their legacy? Are we setting up to fight the war they never fought, or something else entirely?"

Zander looked up sharply. "One of our lessons, or conclusions, is that the Daklin Empire can trace its roots back to the Martians, correct?"

"Affirmative," Emily replied. "While the Martian civilization was destroyed by the Daklin, their technology and philosophies may have seeded both terrestrial and interstellar advancements."

Megan leaned forward, resting her chin on her hand. "So, they fled a galactic tyrant, rebuilt here..." She stopped speaking while trying to put the last piece together.

"But the Martian roots in Greek civilization had a component not found on Mars," Paula said softly, her hand absently rubbing her stomach. "The Martians were dreamers, explorers. They couldn't have known how far their legacy would reach."

"And the ones who came to Earth had another component not found on Mars," Alex began to state the exact conclusion they were all reaching. "On Earth, they added revenge, defense, and preparedness to stop those who might come and take what was theirs."

"The best example of that might be Leonides and his 300 hundred Spartans against the overwhelming Persian invaders," Mark added a piece of Greek history for context. "Yet another example of the Martians losing to the Daklin?"

"Wait, Mark," Lyra stepped into the conversation. "Are you saying that the Persians were Daklin?"

"No, I'm just saying that our twenty-three Martian refugees were not caught off guard. Instead, they created a culture that mounted a force of three hundred that almost stopped the mightiest army in the world. I'm saying that they had learned to be prepared, and ready to defend their home."

"It's interesting to me," Emily interjected, "that the Martians considered themselves to be a peaceful people focused on science and the arts, but those who came to Earth held the stark contrast that Mark has highlighted. If you look at the Greek or Roman Gods, Mars and Ares, they are both Gods of war."

Alex was sipping his oatmeal stout when he noticed that Megan was deep in thought. "Megan, what's on your mind?"

"Is there any connection," Megan began cautiously, "between the Greek name for Mars, Ares, and Hitler's obsession with an Aryan civilization? The names are so similar, and it just got me thinking."

Paula raised her eyebrows and leaned forward, intrigued. "That's... an interesting question. I've never thought about it that way."

Alex set his glass down, his expression thoughtful. "It's true that the names are similar, but the connections are largely coincidental. Ares, in Greek mythology, is the god of war, and his Roman counterpart is Mars. The term 'Aryan,' however, has a completely different origin."

"Aryan," Emily added, "comes from the ancient Sanskrit word 'Ārya,' which means noble. It was originally used to describe a linguistic and cultural group that spread across parts of Europe and Asia. Unfortunately, that term was misappropriated by the Nazis to support their ideology of racial superiority."

Megan nodded slowly; her curiosity not yet satisfied. "So, no direct connection between Ares and the Aryan idea, but both got twisted in different ways to symbolize power?"

"Exactly," Alex said. "Ares was seen as a chaotic and destructive force in mythology, representing the brutality of war. Hitler's use of 'Aryan' was a distortion of history and language to justify his regime's atrocities. The only link is how both concepts were used to wield influence, though in entirely different contexts and time periods. If I am remembering correctly, the Sanskrit was about two thousand years before the ancient Greek civilization."

Mark lifted his beer mug and stared at the bubbles thoughtfully. "It's fascinating how symbols and words can be reshaped to fit an agenda. Mars, or Ares, as a symbol of war makes sense in its mythological context. But what the Nazis did with 'Aryan'… that's just tragic and horrifying."

Megan leaned back, a small frown on her face. "It's strange to think about how history keeps repeating itself in different forms. People latch onto symbols and twist them for power."

Alex nodded. "Which is why it's important to understand history and context. Knowing the origins of these things can help us see through the distortions and prevent history from repeating itself." Alex finished his beer. "But on that note, I think I need to get some rest," he stopped and glanced at Paula. "You with me?"

"Yes," Paula smiled and put her hand on her belly, "both of us."

'It's been a long four months. I'm ready to be home." Lyra took Zander's hand, leading him out of the room.

Megan found herself standing by the observation screen thinking about the impact of ancient Greece on civilization. Mark joined her, his presence was calm, yet charged with the unspoken connection they'd been circling for months.

"You okay?" he asked, his voice softer than usual.

Megan tilted her head toward him, "When you plucked me out of my safehouse in Seattle, I never would have imagined all this," she started. "Are you asking because you care, or because you're trying to distract me?"

He chuckled, glancing at her sidelong. "I think both."

She laughed, shaking her head. "You're incorrigible." She paused, her tone softening. "But yeah, I'm okay. Just… thinking about them. The

Martians. What they built and the decision they must have made to travel through time to Earth."

Mark's gaze turned contemplative as he looked out at Earth below. "Takes a special kind of courage to start over with nothing. Makes you wonder if we'd do the same, given the chance."

Megan turned to face him fully, her brown eyes studying his. "I think we'd figure it out. We've done a pretty good job learning to survive and adapt."

Like it often was when they were alone, their connection was electric, the moment hanging in the balance between playful banter and something more.

"What's happening here, Mark?"

Mark was certain he knew, but still felt tense from the first two attempts with Megan, and the failed attempt with Sasha. Allis had been so easy, but then, she had been programmed for exactly that. "I'm still working on that problem, Megan."

"You have become Mount Olympus, Mark." She turned and left the room, then stopped. "Don't' take forever. Some things are obvious."

CHAPTER 25
THE ODYSSEY OF MARIA PEREZ

*We are what we pretend to be,
so we must be careful about
what we pretend to be.
-    Don Quixote*

Maria Perez mulled over the request she had received through a tunnel from Earth on the P-Link. It was outside the usual protocol to allow a cybernetic to leave Pronimos. First, there were almost no specialists outside of their own engineers who could integrate and maintain such life forms. More importantly, most of the cyborg's intelligence wasn't onboard but stored on supercomputers that operated on the planet. The answer should have been a definitive no, but she found herself inclined to grant the request.

"Maria, Bernd is here," her cybernetic assistant announced.

"Send him in," Maria responded.

Maria hugged Bernd, "How's Bernice?"

"She's well," Bernd sat down, getting right to the point. "So, this request... I am fine with it, but do they have the technology to make it work?"

"That is part of the reason I am inclined to approve it. I understand the interest in giving Emily a body, but the advancements they will need to make are significant. It will be a challenge that could take years to achieve."

"What's the other part, Maria? I've known you for 163 years, I know you didn't just invite me here to discuss that."

"There's something about Alex and his team that gives me hope." She fiddled with an electromagnetic top that spun on her desk.

"I think it's Alex. You and I were married for what, forty-three years? We have two kids together…" Bernd stopped, realizing he had crossed a line he should've avoided.

"No, it's not that, Bernd. The people from Earth are different. They've finally reached a point where they will be noticed by the Daklin. It's dangerous, and exciting."

"Maria," Bernd began, "I know you're a scientist, and typically reject these notions, but there's someone I want you to go visit…"

"I am not going to see your mystic friend, Bernd," she answered in a level tone.

"I know your perspective, Maria. Just do it as a favor to me."

Two days later, Maria stood outside the small structure that reminded her of the kind of home she had lived in as a child on Earth. It was modest, simple, and wooden. This mystic existed outside the bounds of science, using hypnotism to uncover reincarnation.

"You should know that I do not believe in what you do, nor do I even know how to describe what you do," Maria blurted, stepping in the door as she was approached by a woman with wrinkles, grey hair, and piercing eyes.

"My name is Takla," she reached out to shake Maria's hand. "Yes, I am from Takla from Tilka 7," she spoke again, as if anticipating Maria's next comment. "I can sense your questions…I am 387 years old, but prefer this uncharacteristic, aged body. The wise and scholarly on my planet all maintain this look."

Maria studied the woman, "Doesn't it slow you down?" she hesitated, "I mean, being old like that?"

"Perhaps, but that discussion is not why you are here. I use hypnosis to see deeply into your past. On my planet, we have learned that immortality comes from the spirit changing bodies after death. Often, when you have an attraction to someone like you have to Alex, it is because his spirit played some critical or momentous role in your past lives."

"What does that mean?" Maria enquired.

"Connections like this generally happen because of perfection in love. Sometimes they are the result of a parental figure, and sometimes an unresolved problem."

"You know, I think all of this is nonsense, Takla."

"Yes Maria, of that I am aware. Still, you are here, so let us begin."

Once under hypnosis, Takla began to see a bit more about Maria's past.

Maria Perez was born in Alcalá de Henares, a town renowned for its universities and scholars. She was born in 1606, a year after her Uncle Miguel Cervantes published *Don Quixote*. Growing up, she often heard versions of that inspirational yet tragic tale. From a young age, Maria displayed an exceptional talent for mathematics and natural philosophy, often outshining her male peers. Unfortunately, her brilliance was not appreciated by the men of her time or the church.

Her groundbreaking work on celestial mechanics and early theories of energy conservation drew the wrath of the Spanish Inquisition. Accused of heresy, she was arrested and tried in a highly publicized case. The church sentenced her to death.

Maria's execution was scheduled, but just hours before her death, a group of Galactic scholars—monitoring Earth's progress and seeking intellectuals to join their society—intervened. They rescued her and brought her to Pronimos. At first, being taken from 16th-century Spain and suddenly thrust into a world like Pronimos, she felt as though she had stepped into a dream—or perhaps a nightmare.

Takla continued to dig deeper into the essence of Maria Perez, and once she had found exactly what she'd been looking for during the session, she woke Maria from her hypnosis.

Maria's eyes fluttered open, her breathing steady but heart racing.

Takla placed her hand on Maria's, her voice soft. "Now I understand. As I suspected, the connection you feel to Alex is not bound by this life. It has been forged across lifetimes."

Her grogginess was beginning to recede, and Maria was shaking her head, "No, that can't be. None of this is based in science, and science is and always has been the prime directive of my life," Maria argued flatly.

"I have found what I believe to be the answers, and quite a bit more," Takla responded, ignoring Maria's resistance. "Do you want to hear it?"

Maria shrugged begrudgingly, "Fine, but I'm not sure how much I'll believe. Even still, I'm mildly curious."

Takla began with details of Maria's time as a young girl on Earth. In her narration were facts that reminded Maria of events she had long since forgotten. She provided details she could not have learned through any amount of research.

"While you've adjusted to life on Pronimos and earned recognition as an innovator, you've also become something of a radical, quietly resisting the mandates of your padre and the church. You never speak of it openly, but deep down, you believe that one day, someone will rise to challenge the Daklin—and succeed. Beneath it all, you long to support whoever steps forward to lead that resistance."

Maria pressed a hand to her chest, her mind reeling. "How could you know that?" She whispered. "It is not something I ever speak of."

"It came from you," Takla nodded. "There is a chapter of your lifetime that I have never observed before, even in all my experience. In it you are not human, but some primate. An early cousin on the evolutionary timeline. You are on a tree, looking up, and you observe something that stays embedded in each reincarnation."

"A primate?" Maria clarified with skepticism.

"Yes. This one is very different for me, and I have never read about a similar chapter in the history of what my people do. I see only images, not words. In this chapter you look up and see a ship. Your brain in this chapter is simple, so you do not know what it is, but you see and feel a shimmer surrounding that ship. It captures your imagination.

Also, you feel a connection to something inside that ship. There is something, or someone, in that ship that bridges to you, even though you cannot see inside. I do not know how, or why, but I do know that this event occurred millions of years ago."

"I don't understand," Maria softened, the imagery, the exact incident Takla described, was in her head, a memory. ...but that was impossible.

The quiet wooden structure where Takla lived and worked in on Pronimos was bathed in the soft, golden glow of floating orbs, their light gently illuminating Maria Perez as she sat across from the mystic. Though Maria had been pulled from the flames of the Spanish Inquisition to a world of infinite scientific wonders, she could not shake the inexplicable stories and explanations this mystic was revealing. It was as though her soul remembered Takla's stories from somewhere beyond time.

Takla's gaze was calm, her voice resonating with quiet authority. "Your bond with Alex is ancient, Maria Perez. It stretches across lifetimes, bound not by flesh but by the thread of your souls. It is not about love, though I believe there is love in the bond."

Maria frowned, her rational mind struggling against the mystic's words. "I've always relied on reason, Takla. I need more than vague proclamations. Can you tell me more, or show me why this connection exists?"

Takla inclined her head. "Your heart knows the answer. Let us uncover it one chapter at a time."

Maria hesitated, then nodded, "Okay, proceed."

Takla placed a hand gently on Maria's forehead. "Close your eyes. Let yourself drift. The light of your past will guide you."

Maria's surroundings faded into a swirl of light and shadow, her thoughts dissolving into sensations, images, and voices from lifetimes long gone. She found herself in the cold expanse of ancient Scandinavia. She was a shaman's apprentice, her days spent gathering herbs and crafting remedies for the small, tightly knit community. Her fascination with the natural world extended beyond the earth to the skies. She created her own star chart, able to distinguish between the fixed stars and the wandering ones that traced a path across the night. But what captivated her most were the mysterious lights that appeared in the northern sky. Unlike the stars and the wanderers, she had yet to find a way to predict their movements. Still, it was these elusive lights that truly captured her soul.

One winter night, while studying those dots of light in the sky, she saw a figure approach. Strangers were something to fear, and never to trust, but this man was calming. He was a traveler wrapped in furs; his features shadowed but his presence magnetic. His name was Alrik, and he was a wandering stargazer who charted the heavens.

"The aurora," he had said, pointing to the shimmering green lights that danced across the sky. "Do you know what causes it?"

Maria shook her head, mesmerized by both the lights and the man's calm authority. "I've watched the night lights my entire life, but I've always seen them as some magical phenomenon. Still, it feels… alive. It makes me feel alive."

Alrik smiled. "It's the sky's song. Energy from the stars meeting our world's breath, and you are right, it is alive. It is not like the life we know here on the ground, or in the oceans, but it lives, nevertheless."

Together, they marveled at the aurora borealis, sharing theories about the unseen forces of nature. Alrik inspired Maria to explore the mysteries of the skies, while she grounded his wandering spirit. They grew close over time, but the demands of their separate paths ultimately pulled them apart. Maria watched him leave one cold and clear morning. That night, her heart ached as the lights danced overhead.

The next vision was of a bustling city on the banks of the Tigris River. Maria was a skilled artisan, known for crafting delicate glassware that refracted light into brilliant colors. Her shop was often visited by scholars and merchants seeking her creations. People both young and old came to watch the rainbow patterns her glassware created on the surrounding walls.

One day, a man named Ashur entered her shop. He was an inventor, brimming with ideas about harnessing the power of wind and water. He saw Maria's glass not just as art, but as a tool for magnifying light and focusing energy.

"Your work has the potential to change the world," Ashur told her as he held a finely crafted lens to the sunlight. "Imagine what we could achieve if we combined your art with my ideas."

They spent countless hours collaborating, their bond growing stronger with each discovery. Together, they crafted rudimentary lenses that proved invaluable to both astronomers and healers. But their love was short-lived; Ashur was summoned by his king to build machines for the empire. Before he left, Maria kept one of their lenses, vowing she would never forget his vision.

The icy shores of Iceland came next. Maria was a healer for a Norse settlement, skilled in herbal remedies and healing rituals. Life was harsh, but she found solace in her work and the northern lights above that illuminated the long, dark winters.

One day, a ship appeared on the horizon. Its captain, Leif, sought refuge and supplies. When he fell ill with a fever, Maria nursed him back to health. In his recovery, he shared tales of his voyages and the lands beyond the sea. The tales of adventure captivated Maria, and she could never get enough. For Leif, Maria's knowledge of medicine and navigation using the stars was captivating. Her indomitable spirit captured him in a web, from which he did not wish to escape.

One clear night, under the brilliant green of the aurora borealis, they sat together on the frozen shoreline. "The lights," Leif murmured, his voice filled with awe. "They remind me of you. Fierce, beautiful, unpredictable, and untamed."

Maria smiled; her gaze fixed on the sky. "They're the earth's spirit. They remind me that even in the darkest times, we can find beauty in the heavens."

Their connection deepened, but Leif's duty to his crew ultimately called him away. Before he left, he gave Maria a small carving, shaped like his ship, with the words inscribed: *The lights will guide us back together.* Over the next decade, Maria received many offers and opportunities from other Norse men, but her heart remained loyal to Leif, and she never forgot the promise of the lights.

Then, one day, eleven years after his departure, Leif returned. In all his adventures, Maria had remained a constant in his heart—a guiding light that drew him back. In a jubilant and fierce Norse wedding, they were bound together, their destinies intertwined for the rest of their lives.

The final vision was of medieval Scotland, where Maria was a poet, whose verses captured the rugged beauty of the Highlands. She often performed at gatherings, weaving stories that inspired hope and unity.

At one such gathering, she met Alexander, a soldier who had returned from battle, weary but resolute. He was drawn to her words, finding solace in her ability to capture emotions he couldn't express.

"Your poetry," Alexander said after her performance, "it speaks to the soul. It reminds me of what I'm fighting for."

Maria laughed softly. "If my words can give you strength, then they've served their purpose."

Their love grew quietly, in stolen moments by roaring fires and beneath starlit skies. But Alexander's duty soon called him away to defend his clan. He left Maria her with a simple vow: *I will always return to you.*

But fate had other plans. Alexander was killed in battle, sacrificing himself to save a dozen of his men. His promise to Maria was broken, lost to the cruel hand of destiny.

Maria's eyes fluttered open, her breathing steady but her heart racing. Takla removed her hand, her expression serene.

"Do you understand now?" Takla asked. "Your connection to Alex is not bound by this life. You have met him across centuries, shared love and loss, and have found each other again and again."

Maria pressed her hand to her chest, her voice a whisper. "The stories all seem like memories that I can remember as if they truly happened."

"That is because they *did* happen, Maria," Takla was writing notes in a book. "These memories are locked in our subconscious. Sometimes pieces of them come to the surface in dreams, or lessons."

"Perhaps," Maria stood up and studied the room. "All of these books, are they like the one you're writing in?"

"Yes, I keep notes." Takla held up the book and brushed her hand over several others. "People often come back for more discovery, and we open new chapters."

"Chapters?" Maria asked, sitting down and looking at the book Takla had been writing in.

"Maria, you have probably lived hundreds of lives over the millennia," Takla started. "Maybe even thousands. Today, something in particular has created a vexation, and that is what brought those particular events to the surface."

"Hundreds, really?" Maria asked.

Takla stood and walked over to a book on the shelf, pulling it down with care. "I have chaptered three hundred fourteen lives for this individual," she said, her voice steady. "In our training on Tilka 7, we studied one individual who chaptered nearly three thousand."

"Okay, Takla… You need to realize this is difficult for me. As a scientist, I see evidence, but I do not understand that evidence."

"You live in a world defined by the scientific method," Takla closed the book she had started for Maria. "I do not. For me, this is my process. I do not understand the science, only the method. You came here because of the connection between you and Alex. It is those chapters which I was able to resolve for you."

"In any case, Alex already currently has the perfect mate in a woman named Paula. It's my pleasure to call them both friends, and I appreciate the value they will bring into the future too much to risk getting in between that."

Takla toyed with one of the floating orbs, watching it shift colors with her touch. "You're right, Maria," she said thoughtfully, "but this time is different. The two of you have come together in a period of great uncertainty. The future of your home planet is in jeopardy. What you choose to do with this connection is up to you, but I don't believe it's about love. Search your memories, and perhaps you'll uncover other clues."

"Clues?" Maria asked in confusion, suddenly realizing she had evolved from being a true skeptic to almost participating in this mystic, nonsensical tale.

"That part I cannot say, for it is not the past, but the future, and my craft lives only in the past. It is an adventure yet to live," Takla concluded.

"Yes, the future is an adventure not yet lived, that much we can agree on." Maria bid Takla farewell, thanking her, and stepped outside, her gaze lifting to the stars shimmering above. There was no aurora borealis on Pronimos, but the sight was still captivating. Two days ago, she had sent a cybernetic to Earth for the Tranquility team to adapt. Soon, she would hear from Alex and decide what to do next.

CHAPTER 26
A HOST FOR EMILY

Remember, the goal is not to raise great kids,
the goal is to raise kids
who become great adults.
- Andy Andrews

Most long journeys end with fatigue, unpacking, and collapsing into bed for rest. Tranquility had spent the last 25 days in tachyon space, with only a few stops to cool the generator and run new sets of calculations. When they finally emerged from the tunnel and arrived at the warehouse lab on Whipple Street, everyone was eager to return to their respective homes. After a round of heartfelt hugs, they made plans to reconnect in three days. Lyra and Zander stayed together, but Megan and Mark went their separate ways.

Alex watched them all leave. What they had learned in the past was of monumental historic significance, but he wasn't sure it would provide a resolution to the Daklin problem. It was a looming issue, but not yet an immediate one.

When Alex and Paula stepped into his living room, they were taken aback to find a woman standing there, silently. Beside her stood a featureless black box, its surface devoid of labels, save for a faint symbol of a swirling galaxy etched into it.

"Who are you?" Alex asked cautiously.

"I am a gift from Maria Perez. A cybernetic," she said, her accent unfamiliar to Alex. "I was shipped through the Pronimos private tunnel, arriving here at your home."

The woman stood at five-foot-two, her sleek, athletic build exuding strength and grace. Her dark brown skin seemed to glow with warmth, and her wide, expressive eyes gleamed with a sharp, almost mischievous energy. Even in her default state, she radiated a certain attitude. When she spoke, her voice carried a lilting Jamaican accent, instantly catching Alex and Paula's attention.

Alex flicked on a light to get a better look at her. "At what percent function are you currently?"

The cyborg grinned, her lips curving into a cheeky smile. "Well now," she replied, her voice teasing. "I'm at 1%. Looks like you've got some work to do, eh? Can't have me standing here useless all day!"

Paula stood, eyeing the robot warily. "Did she just sass us?"

"I'm not just sass," the robot shot back, her accent giving each word a melodic quality. "I'm only a fraction of what I'll be. But your team needs to figure out how to connect me to Emily, and then make me walk and talk properly."

Emily, listening in, felt like she might be able to truly laugh. "I love her already. Alex, did you make this happen?"

"No, Emily, this was entirely Paula's doing," Alex answered. "I simply leveraged my relationship with Maria Perez..."

"I can't take the credit, Emily," Paula replied, her gaze fixed on the cybernetic woman in her living room. "She's perfect. Clearly athletic and gorgeous. When we get you connected, well, I just hope the world is ready for something truly amazing."

"Just so you know, Emily and Paula, the conversation we're having with this cyborg is rudimentary," Alex said, his tone thoughtful. "I suspect Maria had it programmed for levity more than anything else." He gently touched the cyborg's arm and looked into its eyes. "What can you tell me about basic function? You appear human, but there are no input/output ports, no visible power sources."

"Yes, rudimentary, not really human." She replied. "My power comes from mitochondria in the Krebs cycle, just like yours. In addition, I have the ability to convert CO2 to energy, like plants do. That way, if I am able to respirate, I never completely shut down. Right now, I am hungry."

"Let's get you fed," Paula suggested with a smile.

Two days later, the team came together to assess the scope of the task of connecting Emily to this new cyborg.

The first hurdle came with integrating the AI's core systems into the host body. While Emily's "brain" would remain in her computer banks aboard the Tranquility, the cybernetic version of Emily needed a second name.

Zander suggested "Cyb-Emily" but AI-Emily did not like that idea.

"What would you like, Emily?" Zander didn't really want to be in the naming process, but he felt they definitely needed to be able to distinguish between the AI and the cyborg.

"I want my persona to be in that body," Emily responded. "When we get her operational, let's call her Emily, and change the P-Link AI to, well, how about AIE?"

Mark, Zander, and Megan all agreed.

"Let's get to work," Megan had been studying the robot's internal schematics. "The hardware's incredible. I can see how Mark became so attached to Allis. The body is so real, it's almost creepy."

Mark watched with a frown, unsure whether Megan was teasing or being sincere.

"We don't have the technology to build this body, but we can definitely create APIs to link Emily's complex processing power to it."

That confidence dissipated quickly as the project became an all-consuming endeavor. Every day presented new challenges, and every solution seemed to uncover another problem.

The first attempt to integrate Emily's cognitive framework into the cyborg's sensory systems ended with the robot freezing mid-step before collapsing like a marionette with its strings cut.

"What the hell just happened?" Megan shouted, running diagnostics.

"Too much data," Zander said, examining the readouts. "Emily's processing speed is fast, but she's never had to walk before. We are essentially teaching an infant when it comes to things like bodily functions. Also, there's the factor of how far ahead this cyborg is compared to Emily… No offense, Emily."

Megan thought about Zander's comment. "You may have something there," she said. "Maybe start with integrating the sensory inputs."

"Explain that," Zander responded.

"Quite a bit of what we learn starts with pain. We only touch the stove once. We fall, hurt ourselves, and become determined to walk without falling…"

"Makes sense," Mark smiled at the simple brilliance.

"Agreed," Zander added.

"Oh great. You guys are going to bring me into the world with pain?" Emily asked in a joking tone. "Some friends you turned out to be!"

It took weeks to develop an adaptive filter that allowed Emily to process sensory information and begin to feel pain. Hunger was first, followed by reaction to touch, both painful and affectionate.

The team celebrated the first major breakthrough.

"Step two is controlling limbs," Megan announced. "Let's use what we've learned to see if we can get Emily to do simple finger movements."

Like building sensory interfaces, simple movements had more variables than the programmers would have guessed. Simple counting was one thing but touching and holding something required feedback control. For example, grabbing a glass without crushing it. In the beginning, everything was programmed in, and then the obvious percolated up. Emily could teach herself, let her hold and break things.

"Are you ready to try walking again?" Megan asked, touching the cyborg's face gently.

The cyborg responded to Megan's touch with a smile. "That felt nice," Emily responded.

"That's a gentle, friendly touch," Megan answered. "Now, let's see if you can walk."

"Will it hurt?" Emily asked, a bit nervously.

"Only when you fall," Zander answered while watching the cyborg stand. "Let's see a step."

The cyborg took one step, then another, then fell. No hands came out to protect the fall, so her mechanical body fell flat on the hard ground. "Ouch, that hurt. When will the pain stop?" Emily spoke through the P-Link, her sensors were throbbing.

Megan rolled the cyborg body over so she could see the bruise. "That one's gonna hurt for a while, Emily. I suppose it's a good lesson."

"I feel like I want to cry. It hurts, and I can't think about anything else." Emily complained.

"Should we turn the sensors off?" Mark asked, feeling Emily's pain.

"No. This is how we learned as humans, and it's the best way for Emily to learn, too," Megan answered, playing the dual role of professor and mom. "Emily, take it slowly and practice."

Two days later, Emily had the cyborg body walking, running, jumping, and performing dance moves.

"Speech is next," Megan announced as part of her plan.

This task seemed like it might happen quickly, but moving lips, tongue, and lungs were not skills Emily ever possessed before. She spent several days in speech therapy, then wanted to learn how to do several accents. The cyborg arrived with a Jamaican accent, but Emily decided to mimic the voice she have been projecting through the speaker and P-link, feeling a certain connection to it.

The cyborg was now, effectively, a marionette. It could talk, walk, touch, feel, and control appendages. Emily began perfecting operations like getting dressed, eating, and using the bathroom. It still, however, lacked self-realization and connectivity to Emily's AI.

"You want to get a beer or something?" Mark asked Megan as they were wrapping up one day.

Megan already had plans to catch up with Paula that night, but she thought it important to pursue the conversation. "What do you mean by, *or something*?"

"Oh, I was just thinking a beer and dinner, maybe. No hidden agenda." Mark answered.

"Sounds fun, Mark, but I already have plans to catch up with Paula. Girl stuff, you know? How about tomorrow?"

*   *   *   *

Megan walked into the cozy little restaurant Paula had selected, the kind of place where the smell of roasted coffee beans mingled with fresh-baked bread. It was quaint and quiet.

Paula was already seated at a corner table, her hand resting on her rounded belly. At seven months pregnant, she had the glow of someone who'd accepted the chaos of impending motherhood but wasn't quite ready to slow down.

Megan slid into the seat across from her and gestured to Paula's mug. "You're still drinking coffee? I thought that was off-limits for pregnant women."

Paula smirked. "Decaf. The real stuff's a distant memory. And before you ask, yes, I miss it every day. I could also really use a glass of wine, or even a beer at this point!"

"Well shit, that's part of the reason why I'm not sure I could ever make it through a pregnancy."

"In spite of this façade you put on, Megan, I know you'd be a good mom," Paula had come to appreciate the steady, solid nature of Megan's work ethic and friendship.

"It's my understanding that pregnancy requires sex, and I ain't seen any of that in a long while."

A server came by, and Megan ordered an espresso. Once the pleasantries were out of the way, Megan leaned back, studying Paula. "So, how's it going? Only two more months, right?"

"The pregnancy is going well. The baby's active, which is both amazing and exhausting. Alex has been… protective, but in a sweet way." She smiled, her eyes softening. "He's going to be a great dad."

"You said something about not being 100% after Mars…" Megan asked.

"I still don't understand that, but I've run all kinds of tests. Everything checks out. For now, I'm just calling it my own version of pregnancy."

"We didn't really think about bacteria and viruses on Mars, and you went into that room with the corpses," Megan said thoughtfully.

"It should be okay," Paula deflected the question. "Mostly, I'm just excited about meeting this baby in person."

Megan gave her a genuine smile. "Alex is lucky you're the mom. You've got the patience of a saint."

"Says the woman wrangling a cyborg into a body for Emily." Paula arched an eyebrow. "Oh, that's funny…"

"What's that?" Megan asked.

"There was an old Faulkner short story called a Rose For Emily," Paula said with a laugh. "It doesn't fit in any way, but, well, never mind," she trailed off before changing the subject. "Speaking of patience, you didn't invite me out just to chat about the baby, did you?"

Megan hesitated, swirling her coffee before taking a sip. "Not exactly. I need your advice."

Paula leaned forward; her expression curious. "About?"

Megan exhaled, leaning her elbows on the table. "Mark." She sighed heavily, exasperated to have to bring him up yet again.

Paula's smile widened knowingly. "Ah. I wondered when you'd bring him up."

Megan rolled her eyes but smiled despite herself. "It's been seven months of flirting. Seven. Months. And it's great, but it's also driving me nuts. I can't tell if he's clueless, shy, or just… not interested."

Paula chuckled. "Mark? Not interested? Megan, come on. Anyone with eyes can see he lights up like a solar flare every time you're in the room."

Megan rested her chin in her hand, her frustration evident. "Then why isn't he doing anything? I don't want to force it, but I feel like I've given him every green light possible short of writing 'take me to bed' on my forehead."

"Maybe you should try that one," Paula said simply. "He's brilliant when it comes to science and technology, but relationships? Not his strong suit. He's probably overanalyzing every interaction you've ever had, trying to decide if he's reading the signals right. He's already got it wrong twice with you, and once with Sasha. He's snake bit, and probably overthinking everything."

Megan snorted. "He's overthinking it? Great. That makes two of us."

Paula's tone softened, becoming more conspiratorial. "Look, if you're waiting for Mark to make the first move, you might be waiting a while. You're going to have to nudge him. Covertly."

Megan raised an eyebrow. "Covertly? You mean, like… spy stuff?"

Paula laughed. "Not quite. Think of it as subtle encouragement. Give him opportunities to step up, but don't make it obvious that you're waiting for him to do it. For example, try asking for his help with something you need done around the house. He's a man, they love fixing things, solving problems."

Megan thought for a moment. "So, play to his strengths. Got it. What else?"

"Compliments," Paula suggested. "Genuine ones. Mark's not egotistical, but he's not immune to a little praise. If you let him know you admire his work, or the new confidence he's clearly showing, it'll boost his confidence."

"Flatter his ego without making it too obvious," Megan said, smiling and nodding slowly. "I can do that."

Paula smiled. "And lastly, spend time with him one-on-one. You two are always around the group, and that's fine, but he needs to see you outside of that dynamic. And not just at work, try something casual like a walk, or lunch, or maybe even a project you can work on together, solo."

Megan tapped her fingers on the table, a plan beginning to form in her mind. "Ask for help, stroke his ego a little, and find reasons to spend time alone with him. Got it. Anything else?"

Paula's smile turned sly. "Put on a cute outfit. Not too many women are as hot as you, Megan. Use it. Mark won't know what hit him."

Megan sighed, sitting back in her chair. "You make it sound so easy."

Paula chuckled. "Men are simple creatures, Megan. In reality, you already know what they want, actually, what they *need*. If anyone can handle it, it's you. Just remember, Mark's a thinker, but he's thought about this enough. Put him in a situation where that solar flare he always lights up with when you're around engulfs both of you. I'm sure it'll be worth the effort."

Megan's lips curved into a small smile. "Thanks, Paula. I owe you for this."

"You owe me nothing," Paula said, waving a hand. "Just make it work with Mark so I can stop pretending I don't notice the sparks between you two."

As they left the restaurant, Megan felt lighter, as though the impossible puzzle of Mark suddenly seemed solvable. Paula had given her a blueprint. Now all Megan had to do was implement.

*   *   *   *

The team recognized that Wi-Fi alone wouldn't be enough for situations when the cyborg ventured far from the ship or computer system housing Emily's advanced neural processor. They needed a strong RF link capable of maintaining a high-speed connection between the cyborg and Emily's core systems, even over long distances.

"This is ridiculous," Megan groaned, slumping in her chair. "We're basically building an entirely new network. I don't know this stuff."

Mark leaned down, close enough that his voice sent a shiver down her spine. "You're not giving up, are you? That doesn't sound like the Megan I know."

She turned her head, their faces inches apart. "You're lucky I'm too tired to snap back right now," then she remembered Paula's advice. "I can't even get the Wi-Fi in my apartment working right, so how am I supposed to help this situation?"

"I could help with the Wi-Fi," Mark boasted.

"Well, if anyone could fix that Wi-Fi, it would be you, Mark," Megan responded. "Why don't we switch that dinner and beer we were going to get to my place. I could order some take-out, and grab a pack of your favorite beer."

"Perfect, Megan. It's a date," he hesitated. "I mean, I'll be there and get your Wi-Fi running."

"Great. Maybe I'll look around for anything else that's broken while I've got you there," she winked and tapped his face affectionately. "In the meantime, let's get back to work." This was exactly what Paula had suggested, and she felt good about where it might lead.

Megan turned to face the cyborg. She focused on how the cyborg was looking from left to right, giving the perception that she was searching for something.

When the cyborg spotted Megan staring, it put her hands on her hips. "What are you staring at, Megan?" Then it laughed.

"That's just creepy," Megan said looking at Zander and Mark.

"It's just me," Emily responded.

"Holy crap. Emily?" Megan stared in shock at the cyborg.

The cyborg walked over to Megan, put her hand on Megan's shoulder gently, "Yes, it's me. I am in the body, and feeling it." The cyborg smiled.

"Did you instruct the cyborg to smile?" Megan asked incredulously.

No, I did not. I have been building my own code so that the cyborg responds to things I am feeling and thinking," Emily responded through the cyborg's vocal capabilities rather than the P-link.

"Holy shit, holy shit, holy shit!" Megan was jumping up and down. "You're writing code to improve our interfaces!"

"Yes, Megan," the cyborg smiled. "I am getting comfortable and trying to improve my new home. Was I not supposed to?"

"Fuckin-A, yes, you were! Please, keep adding furniture and improving your new home!"

Megan turned to Zander and Mark who had been watching the scene with curiosity and intense pride. "Let's call it a day, guys. I have a date, I mean, my Wi-Fi is getting fixed this evening." She hugged Zander, kissed Mark on the cheek, and danced out of the room.

"As Megan would say, *holy shit*. Months of intense work, and we are almost at the finish line." Zander smiled as he looked at the cyborg.

"What?" The cyborg asked in a sassy, Emily voice.

Zander looked at Mark, "Go home, take a shower, and put on some nice clothes. Everyone on the team knows that tonight you're fixing Megan's Wi-Fi and *anything* else she wants fixed," he stopped for a second and grasped Mark's shoulders with both of his hands. "You understand what I'm saying?"

"Uhm, not exactly," Mark responded. "Maybe?"

"You saw Megan just dance out of here?" he paused but didn't give Mark a chance to respond. "That wasn't for Emily and the cyborg. Emily just lit the fuse. You, my friend, are the explosive," he paused again and stared into his older friend's eyes. "Now get the heck out of here!"

As Mark was leaving, Zander turned back to the cyborg, "We still need to create a solution for the long-range connectivity problem, but you are officially ready, Emily. Tomorrow, you dance."

"Yes," she agreed.

* * * *

Megan opened the door and greeted Mark. She was dressed in a casual but cute outfit; a fitted knit shirt and jeans that hugged her figure perfectly. Her brown hair fell in soft locks of curls, and her green eyes sparkled with mischief.

Her apartment was warm and inviting, cozy but not overdone, with splashes of personality in the books stacked on shelves. Mark stood at her door, feeling a mix of anticipation and nervousness that he hadn't quite anticipated.

"Hey, Wi-Fi savior," she said with a teasing grin, handing him a beer. "Thought you'd need this before you dive into the chaos that is my closet."

"Oh geez, the router is in your closet?" Mark chuckled, accepting the beer and looking around her apartment. "Thanks for the beer. Do you treat all Wi-Fi technicians this well?"

"You're my only Wi-Fi guy, Mark," she answered with a grin.

Megan led Mark through her apartment, weaving past the living room and into her bedroom, where the closet was tucked away in the corner. As she opened the door, Mark stepped inside and immediately felt overwhelmed by her presence. Not just Megan herself, but everything that surrounded her. The closet was tidy, the shelves lined with neatly folded clothes, the faint scent of her perfume lingering in the air. Dresses hung next to jackets, and a collection of shoes were perfectly arranged at the bottom.

"Sorry for the cramped quarters," Megan said, leaning against the doorframe. "The router came with the place, and this was where the fiber terminates in the apartment."

"I'm beginning to think you planned it this way," Mark answered, still overwhelmed by the circumstance.

"Uh-huh, I moved the fiber cable and everything today after leaving the office," she answered, sarcastically.

Mark crouched to inspect the device, his hands working methodically while his thoughts swirled. The intimate space felt distinctly Megan. She was wild, determined, and one hundred percent female, and he was in her very organized closet. He couldn't help but imagine her standing in this small space, selecting one of those outfits. He was now in the middle of a very personal detail of her life, and suddenly felt very nervous.

"You okay in there?" Megan asked, her voice light but curious.

He cleared his throat, forcing his mind back to the task at hand. "Yeah," he choked, then worked to regain composure, "Just… admiring your taste in network hardware."

"Uh-huh." She smirked, crossing her arms. "You sure you're not just distracted by my killer shoe collection?"

He laughed, the tension easing slightly. "Maybe a little."

Fifteen minutes later, Mark was running a speed check on the network. It was pushing 745 Mbps down and 574 up.

"Let's go to the living room," she motioned. "Can't have you hanging too long in a lady's closet!" She handed him another beer and flopped onto the cushions beside him, tucking her legs underneath her.

"You're officially my favorite nerd," she said, holding up her bottle in a mock toast. "Cheers to working internet!"

Mark grinned, tapping his bottle against hers. "Glad to be of service. And I'm pretty sure I was already your favorite nerd."

She laughed, her voice warm and genuine. She liked the more confident version of Mark, post Pronimos. "Fair point. You've been pulling ahead in the rankings for a while now."

They talked easily, sharing stories and jokes as the room filled with the kind of comfortable laughter that had defined their friendship. When the pizza arrived, Megan grabbed the box and settled it between them on the coffee table. They ate and drank, the atmosphere shifting from lighthearted to something quieter, more charged.

Mark was sipping on his third beer as he watched Megan reach for another slice of pizza. Her hair fell across her face, and she tucked it behind her ear. She turned and caught him watching her, and her cheeks flushed faintly.

"What?" she asked, smiling, but feeling slightly self-conscious. She suddenly realized the shift to the next gear had finally happened.

"Nothing," he said quickly, then hesitated. "Actually, you look happy. It's nice."

Her smile softened, and she leaned back against the couch, her eyes locked on his. "You make me happy, you know."

Mark froze, his heart racing. This was the moment he'd been hoping for. His mind screamed at him to play it safe, to crack a joke and deflect, but instead, he leaned closer. "I feel exactly the same way," he said, his voice barely above a whisper.

The space between them disappeared, and their lips met in a soft, tentative kiss. Megan's hand rested lightly on his arm, and when he pulled back to meet her eyes, he felt only warmth and encouragement.

"Finally," she murmured with a grin. "I thought I was gonna have to put on my cavewoman outfit and drag you into this moment."

He laughed, the tension breaking. "I'd actually like to see that outfit, Megan. Was it hanging in your closet?"

"No, silly. I keep that one hidden away for special occasions." she trailed off.

"I should apologize; I've been scared of this moment for so long." He answered. "I didn't want to mess it up."

"You took a long time, but you didn't mess it up. The kiss was sweet. Perfect," she said simply, her voice steady.

They talked for a while longer, only now, their bodies were in constant contact, anticipating the next step. The conversation shifted to topics associated with the challenges of integrating Emily's consciousness into the cyborg body, but that eventually evaporated as their proximity closed, the energy powerful.

Megan reached for her beer, but Mark caught her hand mid-motion. She looked at him, her lips parting in surprise, and he leaned in again, this time with more confidence. This kiss deepened, and her free hand moved to his chest, fingers curling into his shirt.

Mark pulled her closer, as the attraction between them took over. Megan responded eagerly, her hands sliding to his shoulders, drawing him in. The couch became a cocoon, the outside world fading as they lost themselves in the moment.

As they finally broke apart, their breathing uneven, Megan rested her forehead against his, her smile wide and unguarded.

"You're full of surprises, Mark," she said softly.

"So are you," he replied, his hand brushing a strand of hair from her face. "But I guess I've always known that about you. I knew it the first second we saw you from the video in your safehouse…Did you even really need your Wi-Fi fixed?" He asked, a small smile forming on his lips.

She laughed, taking a last sip of her near-empty bottle, "Mark, I'm a computer genius too, do you really think I wouldn't know how to fix the Wi-Fi?" They both laughed. "How about we take this conversation to a place where we can explore in more detail?" she motioned to her bedroom.

Mark stood up and took a sip of his beer.

Megan touched his hand and pushed the beer back down to the coffee table. "Let's leave everything here except the one thing we've been waiting months for."

"Okay," Mark agreed.

She pulled him in close, the two bodies in full contact as they stood, embraced, and locked next to the couch. She kissed him with intimacy, communicating one point.

After a minute, they stopped. "Yes, Megan. I'm ready to discuss that in as much detail as you'd like." He took her hand and led her into the bedroom.

*   *   *   *

The team gathered in the control deck of Tranquility. Anticipation was thick in the air as Emily danced into the room. They stood in a loose circle around the newly integrated cyborg. Her athletic, five-foot-two frame moved with fluid precision as she demonstrated her range of motion. Her wide, expressive eyes gleamed with intelligence, and she used her Jamaican accent to add a sassy charm to every word. Then, suddenly, she switched to the familiar voice everyone recognized as Emily.

"Look at me now," Emily said, spinning on her heel and striking a playful pose, finishing with her hands on her hips. "I am fully integrated, fully fabulous, and ready to work with the team, my family."

She went first to Paula and touched her belly lightly. "He'll be here in a couple of days, Paula."

"He?" Paula asked. They hadn't done a sonagram, so the sex had not been determined.

The cyborg's eyes flickered, then glowed steadily. She rolled her shoulders, testing the movements before flashing a wide grin. "I can see it, Paula. I have watched this before on EtaKatz."

Alex stepped forward; his gaze fixed on the cyborg. "It's not just about the hardware anymore. Emily, you're no longer integrated to circuits in Tranquility, or a voice over P-Link. You are flesh and blood. We can't keep calling both you and the computer by the same name. It's time for a change."

The cyborg tilted her head, her smile widening. "Oh? I get a new name to go with this beautiful, athletic body, Alex?"

"Not a new name," Alex said, putting his hand on her face. "We'll be calling you Emily because it suits you, but the shipboard system, the AI, that's the one that should get the new name."

"Agreed!" Megan spoke while everyone else nodded in agreement.

"We talked about this already, but I think we should call the computer AI-Emily, or AIE for short. That way, you're distinct. Maybe like twins?"

Megan raised her beer, a toast in celebration, "To Emily, version 2.0. Sassier, smarter, and officially one of us!"

"Hear, hear!" Zander chimed in, raising a soda, since he was technically on duty.

They toasted, clinking bottles, glasses, and mugs as Emily gave them a mock bow. "You humans know how to make a girl feel welcome. May I have my own beer?" She looked at Alex as if asking her father for permission.

"I don't know Emily. You're still pretty young," Alex laughed, taking on a fatherly role.

"Allis drank beer on Pronimos. She seemed to enjoy it and I never saw any adverse effects…" Mark offered.

Megan walked up and put her arm around Mark, "No more mentions of Allis, okay?" She said in a half-serious tone.

Mark kissed her as if no one was in the room, then whispered in her ear, "no one can hold a candle to my Megan."

Paula, standing off to the side with Lyra, smiled knowingly. "It's about time," she murmured to Lyra, nodding toward Megan and Mark. "I thought we'd have to lock them in a room together to make this happen."

Lyra, ever the quiet observer, chuckled softly. "Months of flirting and they finally figured it out. Evolution works slowly, I suppose."

The team lingered in the lab, enjoying the rare moment of levity. Paula sat in a chair, her hand resting on her belly as Lyra hovered protectively nearby.

"You feeling okay, Paula?" Lyra asked softly, noticing her fatigue.

Paula nodded. "Tired, but good. Just a few more days now."

"Are you sure?" Lyra started. She wasn't allowed to call Paula mom, but she definitely looked at her that way. "You don't look right."

"Everything will start to return to normal in a few days," Paula assured her. "Alex is practically counting down the seconds."

Alex, overhearing, grinned. "I've spent months prepping for this. I even have a spreadsheet."

Lyra laughed. "Of course you do. I bet it's color-coded."

"Naturally," Alex replied, his tone unapologetic.

Mark leaned down to whisper to Megan, his hand still resting lightly on her shoulder. "How long until Paula starts teasing us about when we'll be expecting a baby?"

Megan turned to him, her eyes sparkling with mischief. "Oh, I give it a week. Two, tops. Besides, I'm pretty sure I'm already pregnant.

We've had quite the last couple of days," she winked and squeezed his arm.

"What?" Mark was shocked.

"I'm just kidding, Mark!" Megan started. "But you're gonna have to work on that reaction, it was *definitely* the wrong one."

Emily was wandering around, enjoying the opportunity to act like the humans. "I have to say," Emily said, "you two finally getting together is almost as exciting as Paula's baby and getting my own body. Almost."

Megan flushed, but her grin was unrepentant. "What can I say? We like to keep things complicated."

"Don't I know it," Emily replied, her tone playful. "But seriously, thank you. For making this happen for me. I'll do everything I can to make you all proud."

Mark nodded; his voice soft but firm. "You already do, Emily."

CHAPTER 27
JOY AND DARKNESS

Don't cry because it's over,
Smile because it happened.
- Dr. Seuss

Days later Alex let everyone know via P-Link that Paula had gone into labor. Megan and Mark had a patch for the Wi-Fi solution that allowed Emily to join the team as they gathered to support Alex and Paula for the birth of their baby. Excitement buzzed through the group as they exchanged stories and laughed nervously, trying to distract Alex from his obvious tension.

Megan paced by the window, peering out at the Dallas skyline, while Mark leaned against the wall, arms crossed, watching her with a faint smile. Zander fiddled with his tablet, periodically showing Emily new data on infant care he'd dug up, much to Emily's amusement.

They were all anticipating the baby's arrival.

"You're overthinking it, Zander," Megan said, glancing over her shoulder. "Babies don't need algorithms. They need love, food, and clean diapers." She looked at Mark who was still leaning, smiling. "Right, Mark?"

Zander shrugged. "Why not give them a head start with some data-driven efficiency?"

Emily chimed in, switching to the Jamaican accent, which was warm and teasing. "Let the man dream, Megan. Maybe little Steven Durant will be the most organized baby in history."

Alex, pacing near the door, looked up sharply. "Steven Durant?" He smiled faintly. "We haven't even decided on a name yet."

Emily's face tilted, a playful glint in her eyes. "In another timeline on this exact day, Steven Durant was born on EtaKatz."

"What?" Alex asked, trying to think about a timeline that existed in a tale on a computer hard drive. Of course, both Zander and Lyra were here today because of the reality of that timeline.

"I can confirm, Alex," Zander started. "My brother Steven was born on September 2nd, year 2, which translates to today."

Before anyone could respond, a nurse stepped into the room. "Mr. Durant, you can come back now. It's time."

The team waited anxiously; time crawling as they imagined what was happening in the delivery room. When Alex finally emerged hours later, his face was a mix of exhaustion and overwhelming joy.

"It's a boy!" he said, his voice thick with emotion. He looked at Emily, then Zander. "Steven Durant, born September 2, 2026." He paused for a second. "I didn't even have to relay our conversation, Paula just told me that she wanted that name, so, well…"

The group erupted in cheers, clapping and congratulating him. Megan hugged him tightly, while Zander gave him an enthusiastic pat on the back. Emily beamed; her voice full of warmth. "A fine date for a birthday."

Alex laughed softly, his expression softening. "He's perfect. He's with the nurses now, but you'll all get to meet him soon. For now, I am going back to Paula."

Alex sat down at Paula's side and took her hand. "You did great, he's perfect."

Paula smiled faintly, struggling to open her eyes. "Something's wrong, Alex. I…"

"It's okay Paula, you just gave birth," Alex responded.

"No, Alex..." Paula looked at Alex, her breath suddenly struggling. "Take...care of him..." Her eyes stopped fighting, closed, and her grip on his hand relaxed.

Before Alex could react, the nurse came running into the room, checking the monitors. "Mr. Durant, there's been a complication, we need the room, please, go!"

The team exchanged worried looks when Alex stumbled out of the delivery room, still not processing what was happening. After what seemed like an eternity, the doctor stepped out, whispering something to him as the rest of the family looked on with anxiety.

Alex returned to the team, his family, his face pale. "She's... she's in a coma," he said, his voice cracking. "They don't know why. Her vitals dropped, and now she's not waking up."

Megan stepped forward, placing a hand on his arm. "Alex, what do the doctors think? Is it... temporary?"

He shook his head, frustration etched into every line of his face. "They don't know. They're running tests. Nothing makes sense. I've asked them to call in specialists. The best in the world. They're already on their way."

The next day, the team gathered in Paula's hospital room, the air thick with worry. Paula lay still in the bed, her usually vibrant presence reduced to a fragile stillness. Alex sat at her side, holding her hand, while baby Steven slept peacefully in a small hospital crib nearby.

Emily stood near the monitors; her gaze focused on the readings. "Her condition is unusual," she said softly. "But I've noticed something in her biomarkers that began while we were on Mars."

Zander looked up sharply. "Mars? You think this is connected to something she picked up there?"

Emily nodded. "It's a possibility. We encountered unique microbial lifeforms in the underground lab there. It's possible she was exposed to something undetectable by Earth-based diagnostics."

Megan frowned, crossing her arms. "She mentioned that to me, but waived it off as pregnancy symptoms. Emily, are you saying that we're dealing with an alien virus?"

"Or bacteria," Emily clarified. "It may not even be inherently harmful under normal circumstances, but the stress of pregnancy and labor could have triggered complications."

Mark stepped forward; his voice steady. "Can we isolate it? Figure out what it is?"

"I am already cross-referencing her blood samples with the data we collected on Mars," Emily said. "I am also checking everything on the internet as well as P-Link to Pronimos. It will take time, but it may give us answers."

Alex turned to the group, his expression a mix of gratitude and determination. "Thank you. All of you. I know this isn't part of our mission, but Paula… she's everything to me. I'll do whatever it takes to bring her back."

Megan placed a hand on his shoulder. "You aren't in this alone. We'll figure this out, together."

As the team rallied around Alex, Steven stirred in his bassinet, a tiny reminder of the joy that still existed amidst the uncertainty. Over the next 24 hours, Paula's vitals continued to degrade.

The hospital room was silent except for the rhythmic beeping of the monitors. Just hours earlier, Alex and Paula had been laughing, overwhelmed with joy as they delivered their newborn son, Steven. But now, Paula lay unconscious, her skin pale against the stark white sheets. The doctors were at a loss, their expressions a mix of concern and helplessness. No scans, tests, or theories could explain why her body was failing so rapidly.

Alex sat beside her, gripping her hand as though his touch alone could anchor her to life. He whispered to her constantly, recounting stories of their adventures, their dreams for Steven, and the life they were supposed to share as a family. Tears streamed down his face, but he refused to let go.

"You're stronger than this, Paula," he murmured, his voice breaking. "We need you. I need you. Steven needs you."

The hours dragged on, each one heavier than the last. Her vitals continued to drop, and despite every intervention, from some of the best physicians alive, and all of Emily's research, nothing could reverse her decline. Finally, the inevitable came. The monitor's steady beeping gave way to a long, piercing tone.

Alex's world shattered.

The medical staff moved quickly, trying to revive her, but he knew. Deep down, he knew. He cradled her hand, pressing it against his forehead as the room spun around him. When the doctor finally called the time of death, Alex felt like the air had been ripped from his lungs.

Paula was gone.

The days following Paula's death passed in a haze. The house, once filled with hope and laughter, now felt cold and empty despite the presence of Steven. Alex threw himself into caring for his son, but the grief was an ever-present shadow. He could see Paula's features in the boy, and grieved the fact that he would never know is remarkable mom. Nights were the hardest. He'd sit in the nursery, holding Steven close, staring at the photograph of Paula on the bedside table.

"She'd have loved this," he'd whisper, watching Steven sleep. "She'd have been the best mom."

He tried to channel his pain into work, spending hours in the lab, poring over the tachyon tunnel's schematics. He became obsessed with the idea of reversing time, of undoing the events that had stolen Paula from him. Weeks turned into months as he chased theories and equations, pushing himself to the brink of exhaustion.

The Tranquility team rallied around him. Emily took on much of Steven's care, treating him as though he were her own. The others offered their support, but no one could pierce the wall Alex had built around himself. He was a man consumed by loss and guilt, haunted by the feeling that he should have done more. He should've never allowed her to enter the underground lab on Mars.

On the first anniversary of Paula's death, Alex found himself standing at her gravesite, Steven toddling beside him. "I'm sorry, Paula," he said, his voice trembling. "I'm so sorry I couldn't save you."

Fifteen months after Paula's death, Alex sat in the dim glow of the lab, cradling Steven in his arms. The toddler had fallen asleep, his tiny fingers clutching Alex's shirt. The low hum of the tachyon tunnel provided a strange comfort. It was Paula's harmonic, a tone that she had discovered capable of resonating on a cellular level in the human body, slowing and even reversing the aging process. With that tachyon technology, Alex could move through time. Using the best computers on Earth, he'd tried everything from calculations to simulations, even untested theories. The universe, it seemed, defined finality in a way that even the smartest could not defy.

Ultimately, after eighteen months, Alex knew he had grieved long enough. He began to rebuild, piece by painful piece. He accepted the help of his team, allowing himself to lean on them more. Slowly, he rediscovered moments of joy. He and Emily had watched Steven's first steps. The fact that his first word was *dada* brought tears of joy. Young Steven could light up a room with his smile. Alex knew the hole in his heart would never heal, but learned that time could soften the pain.

CHAPTER 28
OUTPOST GREENLAND

You can't find peace,
By hiding from life.
-     Nicole Kidman

The lab door slid open, and Emily stepped inside. Her movements, mannerisms, and appearance were so perfectly human that no one would have ever guessed she wasn't.

"Alex," she said gently, "you need rest. Let me take him." Emily had learned the meaning of joy, and Steven was fundamental to that definition. She could sit for hours, rocking and staring at his peaceful face.

Alex hesitated before nodding and handing Steven over. "He looks more like her every day," Alex murmured, his voice thick with emotion.

Emily nodded. "He'll grow up knowing who she was. We'll make sure of that."

As Emily left the lab with Steven, Alex turned back to the console. He had not engaged in a primary project since Paula's death, and it was now time to find one. Zander had briefly investigated returning to his portal company, but with the Daklin threat, he decided it was better to minimize the use of tunneling and hopefully lengthen the time before the Daklin became interested in this remote world.

Unfortunately, that would not be the case.

In July 2028, the twentieth month after Paula's death, the news media lit up that contact had been made with an intelligent life from outside of our solar system.

The Daklin were sending a delegation to meet with Earth's leaders.

Alex gathered the team in Tranquility's control room. Maria's image flickered to life through P-Link, her expression tense but composed.

"I guess you've heard the Daklin are aware of Earth," Maria began without preamble. "Their delegation plans to make contact with your political leaders in three months. They claim to seek peace, but we know better."

Emily, holding Steven on her lap, frowned. "Do we know how they found us? The tachyon tunnel was supposed to be undetectable."

Maria's expression darkened. "It wasn't the tunnel. The man you know as Atroz ultimately filed a report."

"That bastard. We thought he was our friend," Megan blurted. "If I could get my hands on that son of bitch."

Alex studied Megan's reaction then leaned forward, his hands gripping the table. "And what do we know about the report he filed?"

"The good news is he didn't mention anything about interstellar travel," Maria began. She had hoped Earth could avoid Galactic politics for at least another hundred years—not because she believed they could eventually find a military way to defend against Daklin power; she knew that wasn't possible. Her true concern was that Earth was on the brink of a golden age. Technology was curing diseases, and quality of life was improving for everyone. Watching Earth felt like observing a ten-year-old: full of joy, with no understanding of the world's deeper problems.

"What's the bad news?" Alex asked.

Maria hesitated. "The Daklin are... well, complex. Their society is highly hierarchical, driven by logic and self-preservation. If they see Earth as a threat, they won't hesitate to act. My intelligence says they believe Earth has developed a rudimentary understanding of tachyon technology. They desperately want that technology."

The room fell silent. The weight of Maria's words settled over them like a storm cloud.

Finally, Emily broke the silence. "We need to prepare. If this delegation is coming, we'll need to act as intermediaries. Earth's governments won't have the context or knowledge to navigate this like we do."

Alex nodded. "We can use the time to gather intelligence. If the Daklin value logic, perhaps we can find common ground."

Maria's gaze hardened. "They don't value logic except as it applies to maintaining power. They have sought the ability to control and build tachyon tunnel tech for millions of years."

Alex studied his team in the room. In reality, he had known this day would eventually come. Now was the time for real analysis and difficult decisions. "Time to build a plan, and a contingency plan."

"Alex, please promise me that you will search for a peaceful pathway?" Maria started with clear concern in her voice. "You cannot win a war against them, and I think the future needs Earth to survive."

"Understood," Alex nodded.

"One more thing," Maria added.

"What's that?" Alex asked.

"Keep your team away from the Daklin. Find a way to make sure you never fall into their hands. Ever."

The weeks that followed were a blur of preparation. Alex threw himself into the work, grateful for the distraction. Zander fortified the tachyon tunnel, ensuring it could continue to serve as both a means of secure communication and an emergency escape.

Steven became a constant presence in the lab, his laughter a rare but welcome break in the tension. The team took turns caring for him, and his presence seemed to remind them all of what they were fighting for.

One evening, Alex found himself alone on the deck of his home, staring out at the stars. He'd been avoiding this room since Paula's death, but tonight, he felt drawn to it.

"You'd know what to do," he whispered, his voice barely audible. "You always did."

The silence was his only answer.

The next morning, as Alex walked through the city, his mind weighed down by the looming threat of the Daklin, the scent of freshly baked bread drifted toward him from a nearby bakery. He subtly altered his path, not to buy bread, but to linger a little longer in the comforting aroma. When he reached the bakery, he froze. There, he stood, letting the warm, familiar scent stir memories of simpler times. Through the open door, he could hear the baker singing, his voice rich and full of life, blending with the rhythmic clatter of dough being kneaded. The baker was living a simple, joyful life. Most people on Earth, too, faced the impending arrival of the Daklin with a hopeful sense of the future.

For a moment, the entire galaxy and its impending chaos seemed to shrink. Alex closed his eyes, inhaling deeply. The contrast was stark and jarring. In reality, the Daklin represented ruthless destruction, an unyielding force capable of obliterating everything. Yet here, in this tiny bakery, life continued in its most fundamental and beautiful form. A baker singing. Bread rising in the oven. A moment of peace in an unraveling universe.

His chest tightened as he opened his eyes, his gaze lingering on the bakery's window. It wasn't just the scent of bread, or the song. It was a reminder that even in the face of insurmountable odds, life persisted. He took a deep breath, steadying himself. The galaxy might be coming apart, but for now, this moment represented something worth fighting for.

A bit later that afternoon, Maria's voice came through the P-Link. "Alex, Pronimos government has voted to close all contact with Earth."

"What?" Alex was shocked. He perceived Pronimos as a valued and permanent friend. "Why, Maria?"

"We have stayed secluded and protected for millions of years. Pronimos represents the last good in the galaxy. We are the keepers of the true history," she paused, clearly frustrated. "It was a fight, Alex, but your defense relied on just me and a few others. The majority wasn't willing to take that risk. If you handle things right on Earth, there's a path to survival. The Daklin have been searching for Pronimos for millions of years. If they find us, there won't be any negotiations. The ships will arrive, and we'll be wiped out. Complete extermination."

"Part of our hope comes from Pronimos..." Alex choked. Losing contact with this friend would be a huge blow.

"I'm sorry, Alex. I really am," Maria Perez closed the link.

Alex knew, in that moment, he was truly on his own. Pronimos had given him security, knowledge, and a sense of history, but now it was up to him. He didn't know exactly how or what he needed to do, but he knew he had to form a plan.

For the next two days, he focused on creating the foundations of that plan.

Three days later, Zander was suddenly killed in a head-on collision on a highway in central Texas. The widely publicized stories celebrated the young genius who had developed the portal technologies and had introduced the first supercomputers to eclipse the singularity threshold.

His death, however, was faked. It was part of Alex's plan to protect tachyon technology as long as possible. With Zander, the boy genius behind the portal technology, 'dead' the Tranquility team would disappear.

Alex believed the portal technology would not be interesting to the Daklin if it used some short distance gravitational technology. Eventually, the Daklin engineers would figure it out, but that may not happen for a long time.

Two months later, the Daklin delegation arrived. Their ship, a sleek, crystalline vessel, descended into Earth's orbit like a shard of light piercing the darkness. The world watched with great anticipation as world leaders welcomed them.

*   *   *   *

The icy air in Greenland was crisp but the biting wind made it almost intolerable.

"I keep asking myself why in the hell we are here," Zander uttered, fighting off the feeling that his face was completely frozen.

"Except, you do know why," Alex reminded him. "In any case, we all know it's not Texas." The team was still having difficulty adapting to the harsh environment. Alex, Megan, Mark, Lyra, Zander, and Emily, who was holding Steven, stood on the ridge overlooking their new base. The facility was nestled in a remote valley surrounded by jagged peaks and endless expanses of ice, far from any prying eyes.

"This is it, everyone," Alex said, his voice carrying a mix of pride and relief. "We've built a sanctuary. I hope this prevents the Daklin from finding us, at least for a while."

Megan crossed her arms, surveying the view. "Feels more like a fortress than a sanctuary. We've got defense systems, bunkers, and even a backup power grid. It's...comforting."

Zander smirked. "Comforting? I wish I could use the word 'impenetrable,' but if the Daklin find us, they'll have no problem actually getting to us."

"Impressive as it all is," Lyra interjected, "let's not forget the science lab. The whole point of this place is to keep your tachyon tech safe."

The team descended into the facility, walking through the corridors of their underground refuge that had been built by the US Army during the cold war. The walls were lined with reinforced steel. The Tranquility fusion generator provided primary electricity with a battery backup in place to illuminate, heat, and power all of the systems. The group stopped at the main lab, where Zander's equipment was set up; a chaotic mix of advanced computers, glowing conduits, and the original T-Portal device itself, now dormant.

"It's surreal seeing all of this operational," Emily said, running her fingers along a console. "I still remember when we were piecing it together in the Texas warehouse."

Mark grinned. "And now it's the beating heart of this place. But Emily, how are you holding up?"

Emily flexed her fingers, a small smile playing at her lips. "The cold is shocking, actually. One thing I have learned about living in a body is the constant need for maintenance you humans have. With food, drink, sleep, breathing, bathroom breaks, dealing with pain and emotional issues; I don't know how you have managed to accomplish all that you have."

"Quit complaining. You're far more than human, Emily," Megan said. "The way you interface with the tech, it's like you're one with it. You complain about eating, but I've seen how much you enjoy food!"

Emily chuckled. "Don't give me *too* much credit. A lot of what we are doing requires significant heavy lifting. I also still marvel at creativity and problem solving. That is a skill I have yet to master."

Zander raised an eyebrow. "This is all very interesting, but we need to talk about the Daklin."

The mood in the room shifted.

"What about them?" Alex asked, his tone sharp.

"I've learned they've sent a scientific team to investigate the portals I created at T-Portal," Zander replied. "They're broadcasting their demands on all known frequencies. They know tachyon technology when they see it, and they want full access." Zander thought he should stop there, but added, "Maillew Pascal is a weenie. He will give them everything, and if he thought I was alive, would probably offer to sell me to them, too."

"I can sense some remaining bitterness, sweetheart," Lyra said, then frowned. "What do we do now? If they figure out how it works..."

"They'll use it to hunt us and anyone else who stands in their way. They will build tunnels to every system in the Galaxy and find Pronimos," Alex finished grimly. "I'm guessing they didn't take 'no' for an answer?"

Zander shook his head. "They've been told the 'inventor' died in an accident. It was a brilliant move," he nodded to Alex, "that will buy us some time, but not much. They now have access to a machine that creates tunnels."

"We knew it would happen eventually, but I guess I hoped we'd have more time," Megan said with a sigh.

Mark leaned against the wall, reading a news article posted online. "They're broadcasting videos of what happens to planets that don't comply."

"But, Lyra started, "they don't have Zander and he's the one who built that tech. No one else at T-Portal can do it."

"Now you're using logic, Lyra," Megan started. "Remember that Maria warned us about trying to analyze them as logical. They are driven by power."

"I'm glad someone was listening…" A new voice came suddenly from behind the group.

Everyone froze, turned, and saw Maria Perez standing in the doorway. After a second, the entire team began hugging Maria, all asking the same question.

"Slow down everyone," Maria smiled. She had not expected this kind of greeting upon her arrival. She walked over to Emily and studied her closely.

"How well integrated are you, Emily?" Maria asked.

For the next minute, Emily entertained Maria, showing off the complex integration and interface.

"I am impressed," Maria walked over to Mark. "We thought it would take years to achieve only minor bits of connectivity. Emily is indistinguishable from human. How would you compare her to Allis?"

"The credit really goes to Megan. We worked as a team, but she's the true creative brains behind the success," Mark answered.

"And he hasn't slept with her, unlike other cyborgs who shall remain nameless…" Megan joked. "But seriously, having the knowledge of the, uhm, let's call it, *intimate* friendship between Mark and Allis did help us to understand just how far this tech could go."

"Kudos for your brilliant work, Megan," Maria patted her shoulder, acknowledging the achievement. "In another time, we would invite you to teach at the integration facility on Pronimos."

"Thanks, Maria, but I'm good here on Earth. And anyways, we thought Pronimos had deserted us. Tell us what the hell are you doing here?" Megan asked, forcefully.

"I was born on this planet. I live on Pronimos, but Earth is my home," Maria started. "You're at a crossroads that could mean the end for my home. I didn't come here because I have any solutions," she paused with clear emotion in her voice, "but if Earth is going to be destroyed, I think I want to be here with my friends and heritage when it does."

"We're glad you're here, Maria," Alex hugged her again then returned to the primary topic. "Zander, how likely is it that they'll figure out the tech on their own?" Alex asked.

"It may take a while, but it's definitely possible," Zander admitted. "Without me, they're fumbling in the dark, but their scientists are thousands, maybe millions, of years ahead of us..."

"Then we're done," Lyra said.

"So, we dig in, fortify, and prepare for the worst," Megan suggested. "But we can't just wait for them to come knocking. We need contingencies."

"Has anyone asked the fundamental question?" Alex started.

"What question?" Zander asked.

"Think about tachyon technology. It was invented in this solar system by Martians, then invented again in this solar system by us. Other than Pronimos, no civilization has replicated it. As Zander pointed out, Daklin science is millions of years ahead of us." Alex stopped and looked at Maria. "Why is this?"

"It's a question that scientists on Pronimos have asked as well, Alex," Maria stepped into the conversation. "Until your return from Mars, we were not aware that the original network was built from Martian humans."

"It seems strange that no one would have an answer. Do you think the Daklin know?" Mark asked.

"I doubt they are aware of the original populations form Mars and Venus. We have no recorded history beyond about 50 million years ago. If we don't, they definitely don't."

"Any theories?" Alex asked Maria.

"I think that period after the destruction of Mars was like our Dark Ages here on Earth. Much of the engineering and science was lost, but the roads survived, allowing for power struggle and war filled with technology suppression. Sadly, Daklin emerged as the reigning power," Maria answered.

Alex nodded, thinking through her comment. "That's exactly what Europe had just emerged from around the time you were born."

"Yes," she answered, while drifting, thinking about her youth. "I feel like there's an important lesson here, but I just don't know what it is. We all know that if we don't learn from history, we are doomed to repeat it."

"The problem is, we don't learn from history," Alex concluded.

The team continued philosophical conversations, but all felt pressed to return to their tasks.

Alex lingered in the lab, staring at the prototype portal Zander had created when he started the T-Portal company.

Emily observed that Alex was still in the room, thinking. She returned and studied him, her gaze soft. "Are you okay?"

"Just thinking," Alex replied, his voice low. "This tech, it's incredible, but it's also a curse. The Daklin won't stop until they have it, and if they get it..."

"We will do everything to make sure they don't," Emily said, her voice smooth but carrying an edge of tension.

Alex rubbed the back of his neck, his eyes fixed on one of the displays. "In life, I have gotten so accustomed to beating the odds. The Daklin have tech and capabilities so far ahead of our own, I just don't know how we beat them, or even appease them."

"Appeasement only goes so far when you're up against extermination," she replied.

"That's why we can't just react. We have to figure out how to be preemptive. I keep thinking about that Benjamin Franklin quote, that an ounce of prevention is worth a pound of cure."

Emily leaned back in her chair, her synthetic fingers tapping softly on the table. She studied him for a moment before speaking again. "You're putting a lot on hope, Alex. Sounds more like wishful thinking than strategy."

"Hope is the only reason we're still here," Alex said, his tone sharper than he intended. He sighed, softening. "It is a fundamental human trait, and it's the reason we are ultimately going to get us through this."

"Yes, I do observe hope on a regular basis, Alex." She was quiet for a moment, then shifted in her seat. "How are you holding up? Grief wise?"

Alex stiffened slightly, then glanced at her. Emily was a computer, but she had become far more like a friend. "It's… a process," he said. "Losing a loved one is not something you get over. Ever. Her loss is a daily part of my life, it's something that will hurt forever. Smart humans recognize that things like this are part of existence. We learn from it, and then we just carry it. That's what we do. We carry it, and we keep going."

"That doesn't make it any less heavy." Emily added. "I think that I miss her as well, but emotions are still something I am trying to figure out."

Alex smiled at Emily, then hugged her. "I started designing and programming you about ten years ago. I never would have guessed that someday you'd look like this and be a true friend and companion in life." Alex paused for a second, admiring Emily. "With regards to Paula, there are days when it's unbearable. On those days, I try to stay away from people."

"Yes, I have observed that in you. We all have, and on those days, we take care of Steven, and give you space," Emily answered.

"Right now, my job, our job, is to make sure the Daklin don't destroy Earth," Alex said. We need to make sure that future humans can live, grieve, love… and figure out how to carry on. That's what Paula would want."

Emily's voice softened. "She always had the ultimate confidence in you, Alex. Paula always believed you'd solve the problems. Right now, she'd be proud of you."

Alex managed to smile. "Thanks, Emily. But enough about me." He leaned back in his chair, looking her over. "What about you? How's life in that nearly-perfect human body of yours?"

Emily's lips quirked in a faint smile. "Nearly-perfect is generous. I'm still figuring it out. It's… strange. I've learned to eat, sleep, breathe, and use the bathroom," she frowned. "You might be surprised to hear that talking was probably my most difficult task. As a computer, it's all digital, the flow of electrons. Human speech requires precise manipulation of the tongue, lips, cheeks, jaw position, and breathing. It's a lot to put together, even for a supercomputer."

Alex chucked at her comment. "You seem to be doing a good job with it. You have perfectly mimicked the Emily AIE voice, and you do a pretty good Jamaican accent, too."

"Well, I do my best."

The conversation didn't really fit with the impending Daklin invasion, but he still wanted to take this quiet moment to learn a bit more. "What about the human side, Emily? Anything going on there?"

"I definitely feel things. It's sometimes confusing."

"Feel things like what?" Alex asked, his curiosity genuine.

"Emotions. Longing." She hesitated, her gaze dropping to her hands. "As I said, I miss Paula. I watched Megan and Mark evolve into a couple. Their life is exciting. Zander and Lyra are so grounded and confident in their relationship," she intentionally did not bring up the perfect connection that had existed between Alex and Paula. "I'm curious about sex. I've been wondering if it's even possible for me to find love, or experience intimacy. I want to experience having a lover."

Alex blinked but kept his tone even. "That's… complicated, sure, but not impossible. You're more human than you give yourself credit for, Emily. If anyone deserves to feel those things, it's you. Maybe talk to Mark or Maria about that part?"

She gave a short laugh, more bitter than amused. "I have been thinking about discussing it with Mark. If P-Link was still open to Pronimos I'd probably communicate with Allis. Anyway, it seems that everyone sees me as either a machine or a computer. It's not exactly romantic."

"You're more than that," Alex said firmly. "And the right person will see it, too. Like I said, you should talk to Mark. I bet he could give you some pointers. I'm sure, after we deal with the Daklin, you'll have the chance to figure it out."

Emily tilted her head, her expression skeptical. "Assuming we survive."

"You know I am always the optimist," Alex said, grinning despite himself. "It is a trait you should learn and adopt."

"Yes Alex, you are," she replied with a faint smirk. Then her expression turned serious again as her eyes flicked back to the monitors. "Speaking of survival, with all our tech, and your optimism, we've seen nothing that suggests a weakness."

"There's always a weakness," Alex said, trying to convince himself.

Emily shook her head. "Maybe. They're not like us, Alex."

"True," Alex met her gaze, his tone unwavering. "It's entirely possible we go down fighting. For Earth. For Paula. For everything that makes humanity worth saving."

For a moment, they sat in silence, the weight of the situation pressing heavily between them. Finally, Emily nodded, determination glinting in her synthetic eyes.

"All right," she said. "Let's find their weakness and make sure Earth survives."

Alex smiled grimly. "Now that's the spirit."

* * * *

The following night, Maria found Alex working on an analysis in his computer room. "Alex!" she burst into the room with excitement.

"Can you break free for a bit? There's something happening right now outside."

"Outside, Maria? It's minus ten degrees and windy. The chill factor has got to be in the negative twenties."

"Put some layers on, don't be a wuss," she chided. "Trust me, you'll want to see this!" She insisted, clearly not willing to take no for an answer.

"You sure it can't wait until morning when the sun is up?"

"Not unless the laws of physics change," she insisted, grabbing his arm. "The recent solar flare means the aurora's going to be incredible tonight. Besides, when's the last time you just stopped working to look at something beautiful?"

"Every time I looked at Paula. Every time I look at Steven. How's that?" He paused for second, "I'm not sure why the aurora is so important right now."

"That's sweet, Alex. It really is." In reality, she didn't have a good explanation as to why it should be important to him. It was important to her, but other than a story some mystic on Pronimos had told her, she would not be able to articulate it to Alex. "I came to Earth with the knowledge that I'd probably die in the Daklin attack. Do you know why?"

"Not really," he answered, hoping he could talk her out of going outside.

"Hah, and as a scientist, I cannot give you a good answer, but I did tell you once that I travel to Earth for the aurora," she paused to read his expression. "This could be the last time I see it, and I'm not planning to miss that."

Maria stuck her hand out and jokingly said, "Hi, my name is Maria Perez, and I'm an auroraholic,"

Alex grinned, then broke out in laughter. He took her hand and shook it, "Hi, Maria the auroraholic. I'd love to join you, but it's too cold, and I have important work to do."

"That's true, but there's something else here," Maria remained persistent. "I cannot explain it, but you just need to come outside with me."

There was a pause before Alex acquiesced and began walking towards the entryway where all the cold weather gear was stored. He pulled his parka hood tight and joined her as they walked outside and up to the ridge. The aurora shimmered above them, ribbons of green, violet, and faint pink curling twisting like a living entity.

"Wow," Alex murmured, his breath forming clouds in the freezing air. "Okay, you were right, this is a must-see."

"Told you," Maria replied with a grin, though it quickly faded as her thoughts wandered. "I wonder what Paula would think of this."

Alex glanced at her, his expression softening. "She'd probably take pictures and write down a beautiful description. She loved gazing at the sky." He pointed almost straight up, "That zig-zag constellation is Cassiopeia. It was Paula's favorite."

"I bet she'd have hated the cold, though," Maria said, her voice tinged with wistfulness. "I still can't believe she's gone."

"Neither can I." Alex looked up at the shifting lights.

"Well, it's beautiful. Magical," Maria said quietly.

They stood in silence for a moment, letting the aurora fill the void between them. Then Alex spoke, his tone slipping into the comforting rhythm of his explanations.

"You know what's happening up there?" he asked, gesturing at patterns of color in the sky. "The solar wind, all that energy from the sun is made up of charged particles ripping through the solar system and interacting with Earth's magnetosphere. Those particles funnel down near the poles and smash into oxygen and nitrogen atoms in our atmosphere. The collisions release photons, and that's what creates the colors."

Maria raised an eyebrow. "A minute ago it was sheer beauty and mystery, now it's scientific jargon."

"I'm sorry, that wasn't the intent," Alex responded apologetically.

"Hah," she laughed. "I love the science, and you made it better, simple, yet still beautiful."

"Okay, I just thought…" Alex started.

"No worries, Alex. There is something deeper here. I always come back to Earth for the Aurora. It feels alive, and it makes me feel alive."

Alex smiled faintly. "That's what makes it so fascinating. Plasma is the fourth state of matter. We don't get to see it that often, but a few of the scientists who are studying it have some radical theories. Some scientists, like Robert Temple, are exploring ideas that plasma might not just be charged gasses, but potentially intelligent."

Maria turned to him, intrigued. "Intelligent? How?"

"Temple's book, *A New Science of Heaven*, talks about the Kordylewski Clouds," Alex said, his voice warming as he explained. "They're these massive dust clouds located in the Lagrange Points near Earth's orbit. They're hard to detect because they're faint, but they're there. He shows data that the clouds are made of plasma, and theorizes that plasma might have the ability to self-organize."

"Self-organize," Maria repeated. "You mean… think?"

"I'm going to be careful with my words here because we're both scientists, so I will simply say, maybe not 'think' the way we do," Alex clarified. "But plasma can form structures, even sustain electromagnetic currents. Temple suggests that in the right conditions, those structures could behave in ways that resemble our own intelligence, adapting, responding, and even evolving."

Maria's gaze drifted back to the aurora. "So, the Kordylewski Clouds could be… alive?"

"Don't go crazy on me here, Maria. Not alive in the biological sense, but maybe aware," Alex said. "There are also plenty of examples of plasma that seem to behave intelligently. I have heard stories of ball lightning moving in ways that would only suggest decision of movement."

"I've been a scientist long before your great-great-grandparents were even conceived, so you don't need to worry about me losing my mind," Maria replied, defending her stance. "But I do have plenty of experience with things that can't be explained by science."

Outside, the sky shimmered with an aurora more breathtaking than any she could recall.

"Maybe the plasma is listening and giving us a show this evening, Maria." Alex was having trouble focusing on the conversation with the amazing light show overhead. "Temple even speculates they could act as a kind of memory or consciousness for the universe. It's all theoretical, of course, but it's fascinating to think about."

"Plasma as a living organism or consciousness, and nonorganic," Maria murmured, as if testing the idea. "That would mean we're not just stardust. Through the Kordylewski Clouds, we could be part of something bigger."

Alex nodded. "You are taking it farther than I would, Maria. Temple's work challenges how we think about intelligence. I think the main point is that it's not just limited to carbon-based life."

Maria hesitated before speaking again, her voice quieter. "I had a sense that coming out here would lead to something valuable. You've taught me something…" she hesitated for a minute collecting her thoughts. "I probably shouldn't bring this up right now, but the evening has me thinking…"

"Thinking about what, Maria?" Alex found himself comfortable in Maria's presence. In reality, they didn't know each that other well, but he felt like they did in spite of the short amount of time they had spent together.

She hesitated, then decided to proceed with caution. "I met with a mystic a couple years ago."

Alex blinked, caught off guard, then grinned. "A what? Aren't you one of the greatest scientists on Pronimos? Didn't you just tell me that you've been a scientist since before my grandparents?" he chuckled. "That doesn't sound like you!"

"I had the same opinion going into the session, but she was, well… compelling in ways that caused even a scientist like myself to ask further questions," Maria admitted. "She told me about my past lives. Said I've walked this Earth before, in different forms, different bodies."

"You know how crazy that sounds?" Alex tilted his head, skepticism evident. "And you believe her?"

"I don't know," Maria said, staring at the aurora. "But her stories about me felt real, like echoes of something stored in my memory, and forgotten. She knew things about me that no one could have known. She talked about an energy, or someone who's always been there with me—lifetime after lifetime."

Alex smiled faintly. "Sounds poetic, or maybe romantic?" He winked at her. "Did she say who this mystery person is?"

Maria shook her head, her voice barely audible. "Be serious, Alex. I didn't bring it up as a romance story. I just think it was intriguing, and I came away wondering about the viabilities of the session."

"Can you give me an example?" Alex asked. He didn't think much about mystics and was not a believer in the concept of reincarnation.

"She said there was a chapter, that's the word she used for each life a person lives, where I was not even human, but some sort of early primate. I was in a tree and saw a ship hover above me with plasma glimmering around it. I was drawn in, connected to the plasma somehow. It's weird, Alex, but when she told me the story, I felt like I remembered it. It was like she was rewinding a memory of something ingrained in my personal ethos."

"Okay, that gave me chills," Alex paused. "AIE, can you P-Link some of the video from our second stop on early Earth. Give Maria and I the segment where we are above the tree line."

"Copy that, Alex." AIE responded.

When it started playing, Maria was shocked. "Oh my god, that's the exact same memory, Alex. It's the exact same memory!"

Alex remembered, no, *felt* that moment again as it played through P-Link. "This has to be some weird coincidence, and it's definitely interesting, but I'm not going to try and explain it, nor do we have time to focus on stuff like this right now." Alex was reminding himself that Earth was about to face its most dangerous challenge ever.

"Listen, we have an evil galactic empire bent on destroying us. Interesting and coincidental as this all seems, I have bigger Daklins to fry."

"I know you do, but I think there might be something else here," Maria answered. "There's not much I can do to help the team, so I might as well spend my remaining hours figuring out why this seems so important and, well, serendipitous."

Alex was not tracking with the mystic line of conversation, so he shifted focus back to the scientific aspects of the aurora. "Maybe we're all just fragments of plasma and dust, moving together through time and space."

"Maybe," Maria whispered, though her heart felt the weight of truths she wasn't ready to share. She knew she had some unexplainable connection to Alex, and if he wasn't still grieving Paula and focused on the end of Earth, she'd bring it up. But now was not the time.

The cold deepened, but neither of them moved, rooted under the shifting sky, as if drawn together by forces they couldn't yet comprehend.

"How long do you think we have, Maria?" Alex asked, thinking he had been in the cold for about as long as he could stand. Still, the conversation was interesting enough.

"Honestly, I would guess we have days, maybe a couple of weeks," she answered. "I've studied every recorded Daklin extermination. It always happens fast. Long before the planet's population is aware of what's happening or can prepare."

"That's a valuable piece of knowledge, one of the tools we can use to survive," he concluded.

CHAPTER 29

DAKLIN EXTERMINATION OF EARTH

Anyone who holds absolute power,
can lie, and make lies seem true.
-     Michael Gorton

The inevitable was clear to everyone on the team, and the tension in the room was thick, almost suffocating. Maria leaned over the conference table, her hands gripping the edges as if bracing herself. Alex, Zander, Lyra, Megan, Mark, and Emily sat around her, their faces pale and drawn. No one spoke at first. There was nothing left to say that hadn't already been murmured in private moments of dread. Everyone knew that Maria had received a secure message.

Maria finally broke the silence. "I got confirmation from Pronimos a few minutes ago. Two Daklin vessels are on their way to Earth. They'll be here in less than seventy-two hours." She paused, swallowing hard. "I've seen this story play out several times before. They don't intend to negotiate. Their objective is the total destruction of all life on Earth."

Megan's breath hitched, and she glanced at Mark, whose jaw tightened. "We've fought off bastards like this before," she said, though her voice lacked conviction. "There has to be something we can do."

"This isn't like anything mankind has faced," Maria said, shaking her head. "Daklin ships aren't just war machines, they're planet-killers. Each one is armed with weapons that can devastate ecosystems. With two of them…" Her voice trailed off.

Lyra rubbed her temples, her dark curls falling into her face. "So, what's the plan? We can't fight them. Do we evacuate? Get as many people off-world as we can?"

"Evacuate to where, Lyra?" Alex asked sharply. "Even if we had the resources to launch a global exodus, the Daklin are a year or two from being able to reverse engineer our tachyon technology. At this point, we aren't just talking about Earth, but probably Pronimos as well."

"We have to try something," Megan said, her voice trembling. "If we can save even a few families. Maybe create a Noah's Ark?"

Mark slammed his fist on the table. "Are we just supposed to sit here and let them wipe us out?"

"No one's saying that," Maria snapped, her composure cracking. "But we need to face reality. We don't have time to save everyone."

A heavy silence fell over the room. The weight of their collective helplessness was crushing.

Finally, Alex spoke, his voice quiet but steady. "There might be another way."

All eyes turned to him. "What do you mean?" Maria asked, her expression showing a glint of optimism.

Alex straightened in his chair, gathering his thoughts. "Lyra, do you remember what Atroz said about the Tranquility tunnels?"

Lyra frowned. "That our tunneling is dangerous to the Galactic Tunnel Network? Something about instability?"

"Exactly," Alex said. "The Daklin rely on the Tunnel Network to travel quickly. Without it, they'd have to rely on conventional propulsion, which takes years, even decades to cross the distances they're used to traversing in days."

"What are you getting at?" Mark asked, his tone sharp.

"What if we used Tranquility to bore a hole through the tunnel they're traveling in?" Alex said, his voice gaining energy. "If we destabilize, it could collapse the tunnel. Their ships wouldn't be able to pass through."

Maria stared at him. "You're suggesting we use Tranquility as a weapon?"

"Not as a weapon, more like a bulldozer to close the tunnel," Alex countered. "If we collapse the tunnel, it might buy us years, maybe even decades, to prepare for when they eventually come."

Emily's eyes widened. "We have a detailed map of the network from the Pronimos archives. I will do the calculus to find an intersection point."

"Is there a risk?" Mark asked?

"It's a huge risk," Alex admitted. "But the alternative is we sit here, waiting to be annihilated."

Megan's voice was barely above a whisper. "Even if we die, at least we get to eliminate some of those bastards' in the process. Count me in!"

"We'd have to trigger a destabilization cascade," Alex explained. "It would require a precise activation of multiple nodes along Tranquility's tunnel antennae. We'd need to synchronize the charges perfectly."

"I suggest you hop into a tunnel and do calculations on the way," Maria started. "I will see if Pronimos can help."

"Wait, you aren't joining us?" Alex asked.

"I need to be on Earth," Maria answered.

"AIE, let me know when the calculations are done," Alex focused on Maria. "Care to tell me why?"

"It's a long shot. Much longer than yours, but I think there might be a solution in the plasma," Maria answered.

"We are ready to go, Alex," AIE broke in.

"Let's make this happen," Alex said to the team and hugged Maria one last time. "Good luck with your plasma solution and thank you.

Thank you for everything." Alex felt a pain in his heart as he realized this would probably be the last time the two of them would see each other.

Alex watched Maria exit the ship, then gave the order to AIE to execute the program.

Tranquility was eight hours into their ten-hour journey to the selected intersection when they got word from Maria that the first Daklin ship had come out of the GNP and entered the solar system.

"Damn it," Alex muttered, his heart sinking. "It's too soon. We're not ready."

Maria had set up a monitoring system so the Tranquility team could see the Daklin ship. The only thing they could observe from Maria's vantage point was a massive ship that appeared to be bigger than anything humanity had ever built, and larger than most cities on Earth.

"Shit. Why are we even watching this?" Megan could feel the pain in her gut.

Alex slammed his fist against the console. "Megan's right. Let's focus. They are probably gonna destroy earth, but we are going to be the first civilization in fifty million years to exact our own little piece of justice on the second ship."

"Alex, I can give you an intersection point in eighty-five seconds, if you want to move that fast," AIE reported.

"Hell yes, I want to!"

Tranquility's tunnel began to destabilize with sparks of energy and a shift from the Paula hum to a higher pitch that hurt the ears. The galactic tunnel immediately began to destabilize. Emily was at the control panel; her fingers moving so fast that they were a blur of motion. At the same time, she was cybernetically connected to AIE at 2 terabits per second, trading data and running calculations, simulations, then executing programs.

The galactic tunnel was collapsing, but Emily had already initiated a second hop into their own tunnel. They moved out 80 million miles from the collapse point and returned to 3-space. For a minute, the monitors showed stars and the plane of the Milky Way, then an explosion of light and debris lit up the void as the second Daklin ship was obliterated.

"That explosion," Emily started, "is the full destruction of the Daklin ship. We timed it perfectly."

The entire crew broke out in cheers of celebration.

"We did it," Zander said breathlessly. "We stopped one!"

"Holy shit, wow!" Megan was jumping up and down and hugging everyone, overcome by complete exhilaration.

After a few seconds, Alex broke off the celebration. "Let's try to come up with a plan for that ship back at Earth."

"Right, the first is still here," Maria reminded him, her voice grim. "And it's preparing to fire."

"Emily..." Alex started.

"The best I can do is three hours, Alex," Emily reported, anticipating his question.

"Emily, I know you can do better than that," Alex replied. "What you just did for us and for the galaxy was amazing and heroic, but we have to do more." He was thinking about getting back to Earth in time to save a few people. "Run new calculations. Push the generator past its max capacity and go now."

"How long do you have, Maria?" Alex asked.

"I'm guessing 15 or 20 minutes before they fire, but I've never seen it done with just one ship, Alex." Maria choked. "Good work destroying that tunnel. Please communicate every step and the technology used to the team back on Pronimos."

"We're working on a contingency plan to get you out before they fire," Alex said, his voice strained as he moved to a corner, wiping the tears from his face. "And Mark is already sending the methodology we used back to Pronimos."

"Alex," Maria started, "I know you're thinking about coming here. Please don't. There's nothing you can do, and this monster ship will step on you like an ant. They are programmed to systematically destroy everything on the planet, along with all the surrounding outposts and ships within five-hundred-million kilometers.”

“We hear you, Maria,” Alex responded, with no intention of adhering to her request but not interested in arguing the point.

“Thanks again, Tranquility team. I know we are about to lose Earth, but you’ve just done something that has the potential to end of Daklin empire.” Maria stopped. She had one more thing she needed to do before the Daklin ship energized to destroy Earth. A part of her wanted to tell Alex she loved him, but she was more logical than that, and knew it wasn’t appropriate.

“It’s been an honor,” she said.

“Yes, it has indeed,” the team replied in a likewise unison.

CHAPTER 30
THE KORDYLEWSKI CLOUD

Victory at all costs, victory in spite of all terror,
victory however long and hard the road may be;
for without victory, there is no survival,
-   Winston Churchill

Most people on Earth had been made aware of the issue in the negotiating process with the Daklin, but Maria was the only one who knew what would truly happen next.

A Daklin ship, simply named Sector 437B, positioned itself just outside the lunar orbit. Commander Borzat had been assigned to this ship for three hundred years, and had been its commander for 94 years. It was a long tour, even for a Daklin, but he had stayed on because one day he wanted to wield the enormous power to destroy something. Today, all of those years of waiting were going to pay off.

As S-437B entered orbit, Borzat was informed of the tunnel collapse that had destroyed his companion vessel. He immediately recognized the three consequences. The first was a longer charge time for the weapon systems since only his ship would be responsible for destroying Earth. The people of this planet would suffer more and die slower, but his crew would remain in the system to ensure their demise. The second consequence was a much longer journey back to their quadrant without the tunnel. The third, however, was a promotion. Borzat would now receive sole credit for the assault, and that pleased him greatly.

He ordered the preparations to charge weapon systems. "How long until full charge?" Borzat asked his weapons engineer.

"We could be ready to immobilize Earth in 42 minutes, but charge to full destruction will take just over two hours," The engineer reported.

"We are in no hurry. These Earthlings are not even aware of our presence, and even if they are, a full force attack from their best technology could not even scratch our hull. The collapse of the tunnel means it is going to be a long ride home, so a few hours more to accomplish our objective will not matter."

"Yes sir," the weapons engineer responded,

Borzat pressed the com link to the Chief Mate, the #2 officer on S-437B. "Has the shuttle retrieved the tachyon portal device requested by the emperor?"

"Aye, sir," The Chief Mate responded. "It's in the cargo bay."

"Excellent news. We can now deliver something the Empire has awaited for 50-million years." Borzat decided to go to the galley for a good meal while weapons were charging.

The ship was a giant, measuring 45 kilometers in length, 11 kilometers in height, and 14 kilometers in width. One of over a million such vessels crafted to impose the iron will of the empire, it was a death ship—a mobile city built for one singular purpose: destruction. Its hull, made from obsidian-black alloy, was laced with blood-red streaks of pulsating energy that seemed to absorb light, casting an even more oppressive silhouette against the vast expanse of the solar system.

The underside of the ship was home to thousands of smaller, sleek, predator-like fighters, engineered for swarming tactics. Hatches dotted the hull like the scales of a monstrous beast, each one poised to unleash the Daklin forces into battle. The ship was more than just a weapon—it was an ecosystem of terror. Its interior was a labyrinth of dimly lit corridors, pulsing with the same blood-red glow that coursed through the ship's veins. Crews of Daklin soldiers prowled its decks, their cold, calculating eyes scanning every movement with lethal intent.

Sector 437B had been created to enforce the iron rule of the Daklin Empire. When the ship appeared in orbit, civilizations knew their days were numbered. These ships were not designed to conquer or suppress. They were designed to annihilate, leaving planets lifeless and barren in their wake. It was a harbinger of extinction, and those who saw its shadow often did not live to tell the tale.

With seventeen minutes remaining in the weapon charge cycle, navigation detected a distortion surrounding the ship, reporting it to Borzat.

"What kind of distortion?" Borzat barked.

"Unknown, commander."

"Weapons, can we fire now?" Borzat commanded.

"Yes, commander."

"Fire."

*　*　*　*

Tranquility popped out of their tunnel right as the firing sequence was initiated by Borzat. From their vantage point, they got their first view of the scope and power they were facing.

They watched in horror as an energy buildup surrounded the Daklin vessel, followed by a terrifying wave of energy that began to spread across its entire surface, moving toward Earth. On Tranquility, everyone stared in disbelief as the wave accelerated, rapidly expanding. It grew so quickly that it soon reached a size that would make it a significant fraction of the Moon's size.

"I can't look," Megan said, realizing she was about to witness the mass murder of nine billion humans and trillions of other lifeforms. She closed her eyes and counted quietly to calm herself.

"I don't know if it's going to do much, but it looks like we're going to have a little help from our friend, Alex," Maria reported over the P-Link.

Alex focused on Maria, stuck on Earth and about to be killed. "Zander, put on the backpack and go rescue Maria," Alex ordered.

Without a word, Zander took off full speed down the hall to the closet where his tachyon backpack was stored.

Alex looked at Emily, but she broke in before he could talk.

"Calculations made, Alex," Emily stated. "As soon as you have the pack on, Zander, you can hop to Greenland and retrieve Maria."

Mark squeezed Megan's arm, "I've seen this play out before."

"Right. The time you rescued me from the safehouse," she smiled at Mark.

Ten seconds later, a startled Maria was standing on the deck with Tranquility team. She kissed Zander on the cheek, and hugged Alex, then focused on the Daklin ship on the large monitor. She zoomed back out so she could see Earth, the Moon, and the small dot that represented the Daklin ship. As large as it was, the ship itself was small, even in comparison to the Moon. "Look at their position between Earth and the Moon. They are in L5."

"What's L5?" Lyra asked.

Maria started to answer, then looked at Alex to see if he wanted to do it.

"You explain it, Maria," Alex was not thinking science. The planet he had grown up on was about to be destroyed, and his brain was working specifically on that problem.

"L5 is a stable area of space between the orbit of the Moon and Earth," Maria started to explain. "By stable, I mean, if you put something there, the combined gravitational pull of Earth and the Moon keeps it there. The science was created by an Italian astronomer named Lagrange, which is why we use the letter L."

Alex glared at Maria with a somewhat miffed and puzzled look on his face. "I don't get why this science lesson is important right now, Maria. Our planet is about to be destroyed."

"It's important, Alex, because the Kordylewski Cloud has a significant energy population living in L4 and L5," Maria explained with a grin.

Everyone was staring at Maria, horrified that she could be teaching science minutes before all life on their planet was destroyed.

"Hold on, everyone," Maria half-begged. "Emily, can you scan frequencies above and below human sight and display that on the monitor," Maria suggested.

The image on the monitor changed. The energy cloud from the Daklin ship had grown to almost a quarter the size of the Moon and was accelerating towards Earth. It was moving slower than the speed of light but was still on track to engulf the Earth in a few minutes.

Then Emily superimposed a shimmering blue, much larger energy field. Emily began to speak with upbeat energy. "Maria is right. Something is happening there. Another bigger, stronger energy field is wrapping around the Daklin ship and its destructive energy burst."

"The blue light?" Lyra asked.

"It's not really blue spectrum," Emily corrected. "The energy field is a combination of several hundred smaller substructures. I just used blue so you could see it."

"It's plasma," Alex whispered, his eyes now wide. "The Kordylewski Cloud… it's reacting to the Daklin ship's energy signature. Temple was right! Plasma *can* self-organize."

"Correct, Alex." Maria was beginning to feel confident as she watched the scene that was beginning to play out.

"The energy burst is slowing," Mark observed.

"Correction Mark," Emily began to explain. "The energy burst from the Daklin ship is accelerating in the opposite direction of its motion."

A couple seconds later, the energy burst had completely turned around and was heading back towards the Daklin ship.

*   *   *   *

"What's happening?" Borzat demanded, watching as the reading showed his energy burst slowing. He had never experienced anything like this in simulations.

"Unclear commander," the weapons engineer frantically tried to interpret the data.

"Make it stop, or get us the hell out of here," Borzat barked with a breaking voice that, for the first time in his life, showed fear.

"I am sorry commander Borzat," the ship's mate responded. "We expended 92.7% of our energy creating the burst. I do not think we have sufficient reserves to stop it."

The Daklin ship's defenses and thrusters activated, but the cloud overwhelmed them, infiltrating its systems. Electrical surges rippled across the ship's hull as the cloud locked them in place. Their own energy burst, which had been created with the intent of destroying a planet, had returned to their own ship.

*   *   *   *

From their vantage point on Tranquility, the team watched in relief and fascination as the Kordylewski Cloud delivered the Daklin energy burst to Borzat's ship. The energy burst created a light show brighter than the sun, as mass was converted into energy in a spectacular display of Einstein's famous E equals M C squared equation. The Daklin ship was reduced to plasma, energy, and cosmic radiation.

The members of tranquility stood in stunned silence, trying to process what had just happened.

"Holy shit..." Megan finally uttered, breaking the silence.

With that, the control room evolved into an infectious energy that pulsed through every heart.

Alex threw his arms wide, laughing with a mix of disbelief and exhilaration. "We did it! I mean, really—we beat death!" he shouted, his voice echoing off the walls.

Mark, still catching his breath from the adrenaline, punched the air triumphantly. "Earth is alive! And it's all thanks to us!" he roared, grinning fiercely. He pulled Megan into a spontaneous high-five that turned into a full-blown cheer. The room vibrated with their unstoppable energy.

After a few minutes, Alex leaned closer to the console. "What a turn of events. The massive plasma clouds located in L4 and L5 used the energy surge to grow, even though it was still not visible to the naked eye. Tendrils of invisible plasma and charged particles stretched out, wrapping themselves around the backside of the Moon like a living entity."

"Our friend, the Kordylewski Cloud, simply returned the gift back to the sender," Maria smiled. "It's the old rule, do unto others as you would have them do unto you."

"Is it over?" Lyra asked, as the Daklin ship was being reduced from form, to sparkles, then to dust.

"Sadly, no. It will be a while before they figure out what happened, but when they do, we can expect an asymmetric response," Maria looked at Lyra, then noticed everyone was covered in sweat. "Did it get hot in here? Everyone is soaked..."

Mark wiped the beads from his forehead. "Can you define asymmetric response?"

"This time, they sent two ships from a force of literally millions scattered across the galaxy. Next time, expect hundreds. They'll probably stay outside the orbit of Neptune and gather enough energy to obliterate the entire solar system, including the Sun. That's asymmetric warfare."

"Hold off everyone, you too Maria..." Alex stepped into the conversation. "We just became the first civilization in 50 million years to stop the Daklin. Let's take a few weeks to celebrate, then a few years to plan how to stop them."

Zander was nodding, "I guess it's important to remember that we can go anywhere in the galaxy at any time, and they have to stay in the tunnel network."

"And as we demonstrated today," Emily added, "we can shut that network down."

"I am in for a shower and some serious celebration," Megan grabbed Mark's arm with a clear intent to have her way with him, shower, then celebrate.

CHAPTER 31
CLOUD WHISPERER AND CELEBRATIONS

The more you praise and celebrate your life,
the more there is in life to celebrate,
- Oprah Winfrey

Tranquility was quiet now. Lyra, Zander, Megan, and Mark had all departed to their quarters for some quiet time, and to clean up for the celebration. Alex, Emily, and Maria had moved to the Galley for a drink. Maria had young Steven in tow. He didn't understand the impact of what had happened but was enjoying the levity in his family.

Maria found olives, jalapenos, vodka, and vermouth, shaking them into a dirty martini. She looked over at Emily, who was watching her. "You want one?"

"No," Emily answered. "I have become a dark beer lover." She grabbed a Guinness from the refrigerator room.

Alex activated the giant monitor on the wall, transforming it into a window overlooking space. Earth shimmered in the distance, safe and glowing with the promise of a new day. The massive Daklin ship had been reduced to plasma and cosmic dust. While relief and exhaustion filled the room, one question lingered in the air: How had Maria done it?

Alex and Emily sat across from Maria, her face illuminated by the soft glow of Earthlight. She looked tired but serene, as if the weight of what had just happened was still settling in.

"Maria," Alex began, his voice steady but curious. "I need you to explain it to me. The clouds, the plasma, …how did you do it?"

Maria leaned back in her chair, took a sip of her martini, and enjoyed the blend of flavors. She exhaled slowly, with a distant gaze. "It wasn't something I knew. Not exactly. It was something I *felt*, something that had been building in my mind ever since the mystic Takla told me to focus on my past lives. I didn't understand what her message meant, and because of that, I was initially looking at it from the wrong perspective."

Emily tilted her head slightly, her cybernetic form sitting attentively, "Your connection to the Kordylewski Clouds was tied to those memories?"

Maria nodded, her fingers tightening slightly around the martini glass. "Yes. In every one of my past lives, chapters, as Takla called them, I had a connection to plasma. I didn't understand it at first, because I was thinking about the man whom I was involved with in each of those lives. I was being romantic, and I should've been thinking like a scientist. It wasn't about him," she knew this was a small lie because for her, it was about both, but the impact was insignificant. "It was about plasma. It all started to become clear when Alex and I watched the northern lights in Greenland. Now I'm asking myself if it was coincidence that there were solar flares that lit the aurora on earth a few days ago?"

Maria took a sip from her martini, her voice quieter as she continued. "When Takla told me to focus on my past lives, I thought she was talking about learning from my experiences. But when I thought about the conversations Alex and I had that night, I realized it wasn't just about memories. It was about the connection they represented. Plasma wasn't just a theme in the chapters of my lives, it was the key."

Alex leaned forward; his brows furrowed. "So, you thought you could use the Kordylewski Clouds to stop the Daklin?"

Maria met his gaze, her dark eyes steady. "Not use. Communicate. You said it yourself; the clouds are more than just dust and plasma.

They really are alive. They respond to energy and show intention. I didn't think I could control them, but I believed I could communicate with them."

Emily shifted in her chair, almost humanlike as she processed the information. "But how did you communicate with the clouds?"

Maria smiled faintly. "I tried several things, so I'm not sure which worked. I used a spread spectrum laser, RF, and thought to the cloud." She stopped for a second. "It's not really scientific, and I was trying to observe their response with a spectrometer. It appeared to be working, but I wasn't really sure. The important thing wasn't exactly what frequency initially reached them, it was the message. The Daklin were about to destroy the Earth's magnetosphere, which would also harm the cloud."

"Oh my god, you're right Maria," Alex had chills at the realization.

Maria's voice grew more animated as she recounted the pivotal moment. "When the Daklin fired their weapon, it was like the clouds came alive. I could feel them, almost like they were listening. I didn't use words, but thoughts and intention. I thought about protecting Earth, about reflecting the Daklin energy back at them. I almost think the P-Link was part of the communications, but I really don't know. What we all know is, the clouds responded."

Alex shook his head, equal parts astonished and skeptical. "You're saying you guided the clouds just by thinking?"

Maria nodded, a small, wry smile on her lips. "My credibility as a scientist is shot with you, isn't it?"

"Well, it is a bit difficult to believe," Alex answered, "but the results are difficult to ignore."

"I know it sounds ridiculous. But plasma is energy, Alex. Energy responds to energy. And somehow, through all my past lives, I'd developed a connection to it. I think that the plasma would have been destroyed by the destruction of the Earth. Maybe they were helping us, maybe they were saving their home."

Emily chimed in with a measured but respectful attitude. "Her explanation aligns with what we observed. The clouds redirected the energy burst from the Daklin weapon and reflected it back at their ship."

Alex rubbed a hand over his face, exhaling deeply. "You saved Earth, Maria. I don't know if anyone else could have done what you did."

Maria shrugged lightly, though her eyes betrayed the weight she still carried. "I didn't do it alone, but yes, it worked. I still have some lingering questions… I just wonder how long this connection has been underway. The cloud does not live with the clocks or time like we do. Did it watch the Daklin destroy Mars and just decide not to let it happen again?"

"Wow, you really are living on the edge of scientific observation, Maria," Alex punched in. "I definitely need a beer, now." He got up, opened the fridge, and took out a vanilla porter.

"Alex or Emily, don't you think it is interesting that this solar system is the only place in the galaxy that has developed tachyon technology? For literally tens of millions of years, Daklin scientists have been trying to figure it out, and, no offense, but you are a comparative cave man, Alex. You figured it out around the time your species was first flying into space."

"What's your point, Maria? I don't see any science here. Just speculation." Alex asserted.

"But you do see the correlation, right?" Maria argued. "There are no Kordylewski Clouds anywhere else in the galaxy."

"I find it interesting…" Alex conceded.

Maria rolled her eyes, then shook her head. "Whatever, Alex. What I do know is that it's not just about science. It's… deeper than that."

Alex stood, his hands on his hips as he gazed out the observation screen at Earth. "What I do know is that you saved billions of lives today, Maria. I don't think we'll ever fully understand how, but I'm glad you were here to do it."

Maria smiled softly, finishing her martini as she contemplated whether to have a second. "I just did what I had to do. And for what it's worth, I plan to thank Takla for guiding me to this answer. She's the one who encouraged me to evaluate the connections. If I hadn't seen them, we'd be in a completely different mood right now."

Emily spoke again, her tone gentle but firm. "I hate to say this, but I disagree with Alex. The correlation suggests your past lives weren't just memories, Maria. They were a map, guiding you to this moment—and you followed it perfectly." She turned to Alex, using her human presence to make her words hit harder. "Alex, I have a perfect memory. I can recite, word for word, the exact moment you made a comment about how interesting it is that tachyon technology seems to have been founded here—twice."

Maria nodded, a sense of quiet pride settling over her. "I agree Emily, it was like a map. But it's also not worth arguing or debating over. Right now, I think it's time to celebrate. Just for a little while."

A couple of hours later, Tranquility was alive with laughter and music as its crew gathered in the galley for a long-overdue unwind and celebration of the Daklin ship destruction.

They had done the impossible, and destroyed not one, but two Daklin ships, saving Earth from certain annihilation. Yet their triumph was one that no one on Earth would ever know.

The crew didn't need public recognition tonight. The celebration wasn't for the world; it was for themselves. It was for the bonds they'd forged, the risks they'd taken, and the sheer improbability of their success.

Emily had consulted with Megan and came dressed to the hilt, her sleek, athletic cyborg body becoming the life of the party. She moved with effortless grace, each step radiating confidence. Her dark skin shimmered softly in the ambient light, and her expressive, almond-shaped eyes sparkled with a mix of mischief and joy. Of course, she knew the words to every song and had her own set of dance moves, drawing everyone's attention as she effortlessly became the center of the celebration.

She sauntered up to Alex, a sly smile on her lips. "Alex, have you finally learned to loosen up, or do I need to drag you onto the dance floor?"

Alex chuckled, shaking his head. "I'm loose enough, thank you. And the last thing I need is to embarrass myself in front of all of you."

Megan snorted, holding a beer in one hand and gesturing with the other. "Oh, come on, Alex. You just saved Earth from annihilation. You can't be worried about embarrassing yourself now."

Mark, sitting beside Megan on one of the lounge's oversized couches, grinned and added, "Yeah, you've already set the bar pretty high for heroics. I think you've earned a little humiliation. Besides, I'm dying to see some dance moves from the great Alex Durant!"

"You know," Zander said, his voice animated, "we took out two Daklin ships. Two! The odds of that happening were not just astronomically low, but ZERO. And we did it. I still can't wrap my head around it."

Lyra, standing beside him, smiled softly. "The odds may have been low, but we had something the Daklin didn't: each other. We made this work because we trusted one another."

Maria raised her martini glass, her voice steady and warm. "Here's to that. To all of us, and to the planet we saved, even if they'll never know we did it."

Everyone raised their glasses in unison, the clinking of glass and bottles ringing through the room. "To Earth," they said together, their voices carrying a mix of pride and bittersweet nostalgia.

As the evening wore on, someone cranked up the music, and Emily effortlessly took to the center of the room, her movements fluid and captivating, a perfect reflection of her new personality. Megan, tipsy but in high spirits, leaned over to Maria.

"You've been pretty quiet tonight," Megan said, a playful smile on her face. "I know you're, like, 400 years old, and that probably makes you tired and ready for bed, but you've got to join in. Without your plasma connection, we'd all be hiding on one of Jupiter's moons right now."

Maria smirked, setting down her drink. "Maybe I'll join in... but not for dancing. I have always been more of a tango dancer..."

Before anyone could ask what she meant, Maria walked over to the room's voice control panel and scrolled through the music library. With a knowing smile, she selected a song, and the opening chords of *"Don't Stop Believin'"* by Journey filled the room. The familiar melody instantly lightened the atmosphere, drawing everyone's attention.

Megan's jaw dropped. "Maria, you know Journey?"

Maria turned and gave her a wink. "Are you kidding? One of the greatest bands of all time, and still popular on Pronimos. Besides, this is the perfect song for tonight."

The group fell silent as Maria began to sing. Her voice was rich and powerful, carrying the room with an energy that surprised everyone. She wasn't just good, she was incredible. The way she hit the notes and poured emotion into the performance made it clear, this wasn't just a karaoke attempt; Maria Perez was a genuine showstopper.

Emily, mid-dance, froze and stared, her jaw dropping. "Girl, where've you been hiding that voice? You could start a galactic tour tomorrow!"

Zander was practically bouncing on his toes, his enthusiasm contagious. "This is amazing! We're keeping her on the setlist for all future parties."

Alex, who had been quietly smiling at the back of the room, finally let out a laugh. "I didn't think this night could get better, but Maria just took us up a notch."

When the song ended, the room erupted into cheers and applause. Maria gave a small bow, her cheeks flushed and grin wide.

"Holy crap, Maria," Megan gave her a big hug. "Looks like you are a cloud whisperer and a rock star!"

"I thought you could all use a little inspiration," she said. "That song's always reminded me of what we've been doing. Fighting the odds, holding on to hope, and now, winning." She paused for a second, looking at the members of the Tranquility team. "What you accomplished is stunning. In fifty million years, no one can claim what you did today. I suspect the future of the galaxy has just been redefined."

"Holy shit," Megan exclaimed with chills running down her spine. "Fifty million years…"

Mark clinked his bottle against Megan's, leaning closer to her. "She's right, you know. We're a hell of a team."

Megan turned to him, her eyes softening. "Yeah, we are. And because of you, well, us, I think I'm okay admitting that out loud."

He chuckled, sliding his arm around her waist, "About time, Megan Hoglund."

As the music played and the stars spun outside the ship, the crew of the Tranquility were reminded that they were more than a team, they were a family, and that family now had a destiny bigger than anything they had ever imagined.

CHAPTER 32
RETURN TO PRONIMOS

From little seeds,
Grow mighty trees.
- Unknown

"Much as I have enjoyed time on Earth," Maria said to Alex over breakfast, just three days after the celebration. "I think we need to return to Pronimos."

"With what as the objective?" Alex poured a healthy amount of chunky salsa on his Mexican chorizo omelet.

"We have to stay ahead of the Daklin. I don't think we can deploy an army of plasma clouds, but we can show the Galaxy that the Daklin can be subdued, or maybe even defeated." Maria watched Alex eat his omelet. The two had spent a fair amount of time together, developing a warm friendship.

Alex took a bite and enjoyed the amazing blend of flavors. "You want the entire team?"

"Everyone who wants to join us," Maria answered.

Alex nodded. "Okay. Let's call them together." There was already another project he wanted to begin, but clearly this one was the priority.

A week later, Tranquility arrived back at Pronimos. The entire team had decided to join the expedition. They came out of the tunnel when everyone was sleeping, so AIE put the ship into Pronimos' orbit.

Megan stirred awake, her body cocooned in the soft sheets she had selected for the cabin where she and Mark were sleeping. The wall monitor displayed the faint glow of Pronimos' morning light, which cast a warm hue as Tranquility maintained a geosynchronous orbit. She blinked, turning her head to find Mark lying beside her, still asleep, his dark hair tousled, and his expression relaxed in a way she rarely saw when he was awake.

A smile played on her lips as she took a moment to study him. There was something endearing about how peaceful he looked, his usual sharp wit and teasing smirk nowhere in sight. But the stillness didn't last long. His eyes fluttered open, and when they met hers, a lazy grin spread across his face.

"Morning," he murmured, his voice gravelly with sleep.

Megan knew that look and began to feel warm inside and she leaned in and kissed him softly, her fingers brushing his cheek. "Morning, handsome."

Mark just smiled as Megan rolled on top, quietly and gently making love with him. The two had learned each other's rhythms and enjoyed the intimacy.

Afterwards, Mark smiled in complete satisfaction. He could easily have drifted back to sleep in the wave of oxytocin that had filled his bloodstream. "You're unusually sweet this morning. Should I be worried?"

She laughed, sitting up and pulling the sheets with her to cover herself, though the playful glint in her eyes was unmistakable. "Nope. Just enjoying the calm before the chaos. Well, let me better state that. What better way to begin the day than a quiet morning fuck?"

"I don't know, Megan. I thought that was intimate morning love making, but perhaps you're the expert on this topic?"

She slapped him affectionately, then laughed lightly. "Call it what you want, but I am now officially spoiled, so don't be surprised if I demand we start every day like that."

"Is that an offer, or a threat?" he joked. "Your tone sounds like a threat, but my body is taking it as an offer that I'm willing to accept."

"This is far more fun than I thought it would be," she giggled, then rolled over and snuggled up next to him. "We've got a lot of work ahead with the scientists and engineers on Pronimos."

Mark propped himself up on one elbow, watching her with that familiar mix of curiosity and affection. "You're excited, aren't you? All those brilliant minds in one place. It's your dream come true."

Megan smirked. "It is. But before we dive into saving the galaxy, I need you to promise me something."

His expression shifted to mock seriousness, his brows furrowing dramatically. "What, something else?" he laughed. "I mean, anything, my lady. What is thy command?"

She rolled her eyes but leaned closer, her tone playful but pointed. "Stay away from Allis."

Mark blinked, feigning offense. "Allis? Megan, you wound me. She's ancient history."

"Uh-huh," Megan said, crossing her arms but failing to suppress a grin. "I just want to make sure you're not tempted by her, you know, cybernetic charms."

Mark groaned, flopping back onto the bed. "This again? Megan, she's a cyborg! And not even the fun kind like Emily. Besides, she's the one who convinced me that I should find a way back to you."

She leaned over him, her grin widening. "Oh, I know, and I will appropriately thank her, but if you find yourself tempted, I might have to steal her for myself."

Mark laughed, rolling over, this time on top of her. "Oh, so that's your game? You want to have an affair with Allis and you're projecting it onto me?"

"Exactly," Megan said, her voice mock serious. "If you so much as look at her, I'll have to charm her into leaving you for me."

They both dissolved into laughter, fading into the easy warmth that had grown from extended time of flirting and of finally being together.

Mark shook his head, his eyes soft as he gazed at her. "You're something else, Megan. But don't worry, Allis doesn't stand a chance against you."

Megan kissed him again, this time with a little more heat. "Good. Because you're mine now, Mark. No take-backs."

"Deal," he murmured against her lips, pulling her closer as the simulated morning light bathed them in its warmth.

* * * *

Maria sat at the head of the conference table, her posture poised and confident. She had spent the last few days in intense discussions with Bernd, one of Pronimos' most respected engineers, and now she was ready to assemble the team that could finally free the galaxy from Daklin rule. Her position today felt especially rewarding, as not long ago, she had sat in this very room and argued that Pronimos should help Earth. The vote had been overwhelmingly against her, and as a result, she had left for Earth, where she played a pivotal role in stopping the Daklin for the first time in 50 million years.

"We've bought Earth and the galaxy some time," Maria began, her voice calm but firm. "But let's not fool ourselves. This isn't over. It's just the beginning. The Daklin are wounded, but they're far from defeated. They are in fact more dangerous now than they have ever been. If we're going to stop them, we need a plan that cuts them off at the knees."

Alex leaned forward; his hands clasped in front of him. "You've been talking to Bernd. What's the plan?"

Maria pressed a button on the console in front of her, and a holographic map of the galaxy appeared above the table. The map was a web of glowing lines connecting planets and systems—the tachyon tunnels that made interstellar travel possible. She pointed to a cluster of bright red lines near the map's center.

"These are the Daklin core systems," Maria explained. "Their strength comes from their ability to control the galaxy's tunnel network. They can send ships anywhere, destroy civilizations in days, and retreat to safety before anyone can respond."

"So how do we stop them?" Zander asked, his voice eager but cautious. In reality, he knew exactly how to accomplish the objective, but thought it better for Maria to present the plan on Pronimos than anyone from Tranquility.

Maria's lips curved into a faint smile. "We isolate them. If we can close the tachyon tunnels leading to their primary planets, we cut off their supply chains, their communication, and their ability to send reinforcements. They'll be stranded in their own systems."

Lyra, seated next to Zander, tilted her head thoughtfully. "You make it sound simple, but we have already learned that collapsing a tachyon tunnel is a fairly dangerous feat of engineering. How do we even begin?"

Maria gestured toward the hologram, where several systems lit up in green. "That's where Pronimos comes in. This planet has some of the best engineers and thinkers in the galaxy, including Bernd and his team. They've been studying tachyon tunnels for centuries. They have analyzed every step that we took while stopping the second Daklin ship intended for Earth. If anyone can figure out how to safely replicate that process to collapse tunnels, it's this team."

Emily leaned back with a playful grin. "I am hoping I get to play that role again?"

"You bet," Maria said with a nod. "Your processing power and ability to interface with complex systems will make you invaluable. Bernd's already excited to have you on board." She stopped for a second then continued. "If you are okay with it, Emily, we'd like to create a twin sister for you."

"Hell yes!" Megan stood up in excitement. "Two Emilys would be amazing."

Mark crossed his arms, his tone skeptical but intrigued. "Even if we close the tunnels, the Daklin are still a massive empire. What's to stop them from rebuilding or finding another way out?"

Maria's smile widened. "That's where the second part of the plan comes in. We don't just isolate the Daklin, we eliminate as many of their planet killing ships as possible, and we rally the galaxy against them."

Alex raised an eyebrow. "Recruiting other civilizations? That's ambitious. Most planets are too scared of the Daklin to fight back."

"They're scared because they think they're alone, and they've never seen a planet win a fight against them," Maria said firmly. "But if we can show them that they're not alone, and if we can prove the Daklin can be beaten, I'm certain they'll join us. We've already done it twice. That's proof enough."

Megan chimed in, her voice sharp and confident. "And once the Daklin know they're in a fight, they will dispatch ships into the tunnels. We will collapse the tunnels, and their ships become sitting ducks. They're big and powerful, but they're slow and stupid. When we control the tunnels, they lose their biggest advantage."

Zander's eyes lit up as he summarized the full extent of the plan. "It's not just about closing the tunnels to their core systems—we close the tunnels on any Daklin ship dispatched to attack, stranding them far from reinforcements. We protect every system that agrees to join us and build new tunnels to which the Daklin do not have access."

Maria nodded. "Exactly. We turn their greatest strength into a weakness. And while they're cut off and vulnerable, we hit them where it hurts. We don't even have to fight a war. All we need to do is isolate them from the civilized part of the galaxy."

Alex tapped the table, his mind already spinning with possibilities. "This isn't something we can do with just one ship. Tranquility is great, but it's not enough for a galaxy-wide operation."

"That's why we build a second ship," Maria said. She pressed another button, and a new hologram appeared—a sleek, powerful vessel that looked like a hybrid of Tranquility with a Pronimos design. "Bernd and his team have already started drafting plans for what they're calling the Vanguard. It'll be faster, more agile, and designed specifically for this mission."

Emily studied the new design, her sharp eyes glinting with approval. "I like it. And with my twin and Pronimos tech, it'll be a beast."

As the meeting wrapped up, the team lingered in the conference room, the weight of the mission settled over them. Lyra approached Maria; her voice soft but steady. "I hope the people of Pronimos, and the galaxy, appreciate what you're doing here, Maria. This plan will change everything."

Maria smiled, though her eyes were distant. "Hope is a powerful thing, Lyra. And if there's one thing I've learned in my four hundred and twenty-two years, it's that hope can be just as destructive as fear, when it's aimed in the right direction."

Alex clapped a hand on Maria's shoulder. "Then let's make sure this plan works. The Daklin have ruled long enough. It's time for the galaxy to fight back."

*　*　*　*

Alex's favorite bar on Pronimos was a quiet, atmospheric space, tucked away from the bustling city center. He sat at a small corner table, nursing a glass of amber ale. The soft hum of alien music played in the background, a calming counterpoint to the chaos of the high pace planning and design sessions. Emily, who sat across from him, sipped on a vibrant blue drink that shimmered in the low light.

Her presence was still something to which Alex hadn't fully adjusted. Seeing Emily in a physical form, with her confident posture and expressive eyes, was a reminder of how far they'd come, and how different she now was.

"How's that blue drink?" he asked, enjoying his amber ale.

"Not so great, Alex. I definitely prefer a good porter."

"Yup. Looks pretty disgusting," Alex said. "The plan is coming together nicely. Maria's been amazing in her meetings with the engineers and scientists. Looks like we are going to build an entire fleet of Tranquility vessels."

Emily leaned back in her chair, her emerald-green jumpsuit catching the light as she crossed her legs. "I'm excited to see how it unfolds. But there's something else I wanted to talk to you about."

Alex raised an eyebrow, sipping his drink. "Should I be worried?"

"Not at all," Emily said, her tone casual but her eyes sharp with curiosity. "I've been thinking about what it means to have this body, and to experience life physically. And there's one thing I want to try while we're here on Pronimos."

Alex tilted his head, his expression shifting to cautious amusement. "I feel like I'm not going to like where this is going."

Emily smirked, swirling her drink. "I want to experience sex."

Alex choked on his ale, coughing as he set his glass down. "Okay, no. I don't want to hear about this."

"You brought me into this world, Alex," Emily pressed, undeterred. "You are the one I want to talk to about this, so just sit still and listen."

He sighed, rubbing his temples. "Emily, I'm not saying you can't or shouldn't explore. I'm just saying I don't want to be the one discussing it with you."

"But you're the closest thing I have to a father," she said, leaning forward, her expression earnest. "And this is a big step for me. I want your input."

Alex sighed again, clearly resigned. "I don't think fathers give their daughters sex advice, Emily. Why now, though? Why is this something you want to do on Pronimos?"

Emily's lips quirked into a smile. "Because Pronimos has male cyborgs who are designed for romance. They're fully functional in their work lives but also built to be partners for humans. It's a controlled, safe environment for me to explore what physical intimacy means."

"Cyborgs built for romance," Alex repeated flatly. "This planet never stops surprising me." He considered the possibility for a minute. Paula had been gone for two years, which was the longest he had ever gone without sex. He hadn't missed it, but in a way, he also had.

"You still with me, Alex?" Emily tilted her head, her voice softer now. "I understand why you might think it's a bad idea. And I've considered waiting for real love. But here's the thing, I am a cyborg. How will I recognize real love? Will I ever find something like that?

This isn't just about sex, Alex. It's about understanding myself better."

"You sound like a teenaged boy, Emily." Alex leaned back in his chair; his expression torn. "If you are asking for my advice, the best emotional decision might be to wait until you find someone you truly care about. Physical intimacy means more when it's part of a connection, not just an experiment."

Emily studied him for a moment, then nodded thoughtfully. "That's a valid point. But waiting for 'real love' could take years, or it might never happen at all. I want to understand what this body is capable of. I want to see what it feels like. The thought of it has been driving me crazy for weeks."

"Yup, you are definitely a teenaged boy…" Alex grinned, then stared at her, his resistance slowly softening. "You've thought this through, haven't you?"

"Of course I have," she said with a small smile. "I'm still me, Alex. Overthinking is kind of my thing."

He let out a reluctant chuckle, shaking his head. "Alright, Emily. Like I said, I'm not going to stand in your way. Just… be careful, okay?"

Emily's grin widened. "You're a good friend, Alex. And don't worry, I've run all the necessary risk assessments. This will be a carefully managed experience."

Emily took another sip of her drink, then set it down. "This thing sucks, I'm going to get a beer," she glanced at Alex, then sat. "You've been unusually quiet about your role in the plan to stop the Daklin. What's on your mind?"

Alex sighed, leaning forward to rest his forearms on the table. "I'm not joining the mission."

Emily blinked, surprised. "What? Alex, this entire operation was built based on your leadership. Why would you even consider not participating?"

He gave her a small, tired smile. "Because I don't think I'm needed anymore. The team is strong, the plan is solid, and Maria has the vision to see it through. I trust all of you. My stepping away won't weaken the mission, it might even strengthen it."

"Okay, I'm channeling Megan here, but I can see that's total bullshit." Emily frowned, her sharp gaze searching his face. "So, what are you planning to do instead?"

Alex hesitated, his fingers tracing the rim of his glass. "I'm still working on the details, but I have an idea. Something I think I need to do." He stopped and looked at Emily. She was exactly like a daughter. She treated Steven like a little brother, and he was proud of the things she was doing. "Give me a couple of days, and I'll share it with you."

Emily studied him for a moment, then nodded. "I'll hold you to that. But whatever you're planning Alex, just remember, you don't have to do it alone."

He smiled at her, grateful for her understanding. "Trust me Emily. I know that!"

Alex spent more time refining his plan than he had initially anticipated. Once he felt ready, he planned to gather the entire team. However, since he had seen very little of Maria since their arrival, he decided to keep it simple and only asked the Tranquility team to meet him at his favorite Pronimos bar.

He leaned back in his chair, surveying the room, which had become a small haven amid the chaos of mission planning. The worn synthetic leather seats and the hum of quiet, lively chatter offered a comforting sense of normalcy, a feeling he deeply cherished in the midst of everything else.

Zander and Lyra were the first to arrive. Zander waved to Alex and the two of them slid into the seats across from him, both ordering a whiskey without a second thought. Lyra was in jeans and a casual shirt, her hair tied back, a mischievous glint in her eyes as she nudged Zander and slid a little closer to him. Mark and Megan entered together, as always, their camaraderie palpable. Emily was the last to join, her short, dark hair slightly tousled as if she had just rushed in from another adventure. Young Steven was enjoying time with other kids his age at a playground monitored by cybernetics programmed to entertain, educate and care for kids.

Once drinks were ordered and passed around, the group fell into easy conversation, laughter punctuating their stories. It felt good to relax, even if only for a moment.

Emily took a sip of her drink, a faint smile tugging at her lips. "So," she began, setting her glass down. "I've been spending a lot of time with Rex lately."

Mark raised an eyebrow, his grin sly. "Rex? The cyborg who's always tinkering with old tech?"

"The very same," Emily replied, her tone casual but her eyes betraying a hint of excitement. "He's been teaching me a lot."

Zander leaned forward, a smirk spreading across his face. "Oh, I'm sure he's teaching you plenty."

The table erupted in laughter, Emily rolling her eyes, unable to suppress her own grin. "Grow up, guys," she said, though her tone lacked any real annoyance. "It's not like that."

"Of course it's not," Megan teased, raising her glass in a mock toast. "I'm sure Mark can tell us a thing or two about uh, well, maybe it's time for me to shut up." She raised her glass, "Here's to learning, whatever form it takes."

As the laughter faded, the mood shifted, and the gravity of their upcoming mission settled over the group. Mark cleared his throat, leaning back in his chair. "The mission's set. The ship's ready, supplies are stocked, and the plan is solid. We're good to go."

A murmur of agreement passed through the group, but Alex remained silent, his gaze distant as he swirled the amber liquid in his glass. Finally, he looked up, his expression unreadable.

"I won't be joining you on this mission," he said quietly.

The statement hung in the air, the weight of it pressing down on the table. Lyra was the first to speak, her voice tinged with confusion. "What do you mean you're not coming? You're our leader, Alex. You created this plan, we need you."

Alex shook his head, a small, bittersweet smile playing on his lips. "You don't need me. You're all more than capable of handling this without me. Besides, there's something else I need to do."

Emily lifted her dark beer and took a sip. "I know there's nothing more important than stopping the Daklin, but I also know this is something you have been thinking about for a while…"

Alex hesitated for a moment, carefully choosing his words. "Actually, Emily, I want you to join Steven and me. We're going back to Mars. There's someone there I need to see…"

Megan frowned. "On Mars?"

"We never solved the death of Andronicus," Alex replied, his voice soft but steady.

"I know what you're up to Alex, and while it's a noble, it's also a dumb shit idea!" Megan practically shouted, her emotions boiling to the surface.

The team exchanged glances, then focused on Megan, waiting for her to finish.

"He's gonna go back and find a cure. Alex wants to save Paula," Megan concluded.

Alex took a deep breath and exhaled slowly. The pain of losing Paula was something he had not gotten over, nor would he ever. He just shrugged.

The team was quiet, trying to think through the possibility and the implications. They all knew that arguing with Alex would not change anything.

Lyra sighed, leaning back in her chair. "It won't be the same without you, Alex. But I get it. Go do what you need to do."

Emily's expression softened, a hint of a smile breaking through. "Alex deserves this." She had her own opinions on outcomes and would begin working on them immediately. "You need to see this through."

Alex raised his glass, his gaze sweeping over the team. "To all of you," he said. "You're the best team I could've asked for. Go out there and finish this fight. I'll see you on the other side."

Megan snuggled up to Mark, tears running down her face. "You're a bastard, Alex."

"I know, Megan. I appreciate your vote of approval, offbeat as it might be." Alex lifted his beer mug and tapped Megan's.

"I love you too, Alex," Megan looked at Mark then back at Alex. "I suppose the best thing I can do right now is promise to take care of your college buddy here."

CHAPTER 33
ANDRONICUS

And I know if I'll only be true
To this glorious quest
That my heart will lie peaceful and calm
When I'm laid to my rest.
                    -   Joe Darion

The following morning, Alex was in Tranquility, double-checking his list and storing the last of their provisions when Maria's voice rang out behind him. "So, that's it? You're just leaving without a word?"

Alex turned to see her standing at the edge of the ship's ramp, her arms crossed, her expression equally hurt and frustrated. "You certainly have a way of showing up when people least expect it," he started, his voice calm. "I didn't want to distract you from your responsibilities. You have important tasks ahead, and this is just a personal mission."

Maria shook her head, stepping closer. "A personal mission? I thought we were a team. You don't just disappear without saying goodbye."

Alex sighed, running a hand through his hair. "I didn't want to make it harder than it needed to be. I'm going back to meet someone who changed everything for humanity. That's all."

Alex looked at Maria, then gave her a long hug. "I'm sorry, Maria. I didn't intend to cause any personal issues."

Maria's gaze softened, but her resolve didn't waver. "That's good because I'm coming with you."

"Maria, you can't…"

"I can," she interrupted, her tone firm. "And I will. You're not going on some secret journey without me. Whatever this is, I'm part of it."

Alex hesitated, studying her determined expression. "This isn't a simple trip. We're traveling 66 million years into the past. I need to, no, I want to meet Andronicus before he dies."

Maria blinked, momentarily stunned by his comment, but quickly regained her composure. "You're going because you want to find a way to save Paula," she said, pausing to watch his reaction before continuing. "Which is all the more reason for me to come. You'll need help—and some companionship."

"I have Emily and Steven," Alex started.

"Doesn't matter Alex. In any case, I have already made arrangements. I am coming."

Realizing there was no arguing with her, Alex relented with a resigned smile. "Alright, but don't say I didn't warn you."

"Trust me, I won't." She walked out of the room.

A couple minutes later, Maria lugged in a travel bag and joined Alex, Emily, and Steven, now two and a half years old and already a curious explorer.

"Emily, are all the calculations done?"

"Yes, Alex," Emily was holding Steven, who was asleep with his head on her shoulder.

Alex looked at Maria, then Emily. "Well, let's go."

Tranquility popped into tachyon space.

Maria studied Alex, who was cross-referencing equations on his display. The journey would take 24 days, which seemed like a long time, until one considered the distances and millions of years of travel.

As the journey began, they got into a routine of checking calculations, exercising in the workout room, and planning meals. They no longer had to worry about the Daklin, or any other monumental task, so they were able to just kill time.

Maria decided to open up about her conversations with Takla and the enigmatic stories of her past lives. "Takla recited chapters from my spirit's history," she said softly. "In every chapter, you were there. I know it seems crazy, but we fell in love in each one, Alex. We even got married and had children once."

Alex listened intently; his brow furrowed in thought. "You know I don't buy into this stuff, but I have to wonder. If it's true, do you think that's why we've always felt this connection? Like we've known each other forever?"

Maria nodded. "That's my conclusion. It doesn't mean we're meant to be together now," she added, making sure not to cross any lines. It was clear they were both on this mission to find a way to save Paula. "I do recognize the connection. I think some people call it soulmates, but we both know who the real soulmates are in this life."

Alex smiled faintly, reaching over to squeeze her hand. "Maybe. But no matter what, you'll always mean something to me. Whether as a partner, friend, shipmate, or something else entirely."

"Hmmm, shipmate is an interesting term, Alex," she joked around, trying to add some levity to the moment. "What does that entail?"

"For one thing, you could switch from those damned dirty martinis," He smiled at his comment, "and have a real beer with me every once in a while."

"I might consider that, Alex," Maria returned the smile, her gaze warm. "For now, whether we are shipmates, friends, or something else... let's focus on this mission. We've got a lot to do."

"I've been thinking about Andronicus..." Alex started.

"I recognize the name, but just scanned that part of the report, Alex." Maria responded.

"Have a look at the files we collected from Andronicus' lab. I want to make sure we are both thinking about this the same way," Alex explained.

"What way is that, Alex?"

"That man gave up everything in order to do the math and finish the time travel aspects of the Martian tachyon tunnel. Can you imagine the vision and risk he must've known he was taking?"

Maria studied Alex, trying to understand what motivated him to make this trip. Since she had learned of his plans, she had been grappling with it. "Alex, would you mind taking this conversation to the galley? Maybe with one of your so-called dark beers?"

Alex looked at the beers in his fridge and thought about Maria. He decided to pull out a Guinness, vanilla porter, and an oatmeal stout. He poured a little of each into separate glasses and motioned for Maria to do a taste test.

Maria took a sip of each, then went back and took a second sip. "I can't believe it. I actually like all three," she said with a grin.

"Which is your favorite?" Alex asked.

"I like the foam on this one," she pointed.

"That's Guinness. They use nitrogen rather than CO2. It makes for finer bubbles," he explained. "So that's the one you want?" he lifted the can of Guinness.

"No. I like it, but my favorite is this one," she picked up the third glass.

"That's oatmeal stout. It's made in Austin, Texas." Alex poured the remaining beer from the can into Maria's glass, then poured the Guinness for himself.

Emily, who had been watching from the door, stepped up. "Steven is asleep. I'll take the vanilla porter." She smiled.

Alex looked at Maria. "Id love to hear more about your life in early Spain."

"Cervantes was my uncle," Maria started when they sat down. "It was a difficult time in Earth history. The Catholic Church ran the government and controlled our beliefs. While government and religion are important parts of society, I prefer the pathway Jefferson and Adams took, separating them."

"What was Cervantes like?" Alex asked.

"He was a huge presence in my early life. We would often tell stories about the book *Don Quixote*." Maria smiled. "Uncle Miguel was brilliant, with a sense of humor sharper than any sword. *Quixote* wasn't just a story to him, it was personal. He saw himself in the character. He was always chasing ideals, even when the world called him mad."

"Quixotic," Alex mused. "That's where the term comes from, isn't it?"

Maria nodded. "It means pursuing noble but impractical goals. I suppose I've always been a little quixotic myself. Without using that adjective, I think you have called me that a time or two." She thought to herself that this mission into the past was also quixotic.

Alex nodded and smiled. "I suppose I have."

Emily remained silent, working on understanding the human interaction between Alex and Maria.

"Except my ideals are rooted in science," Maria clarified, and took a sip of the beer. "This oatmeal stout is good. I'm surprised that I like it."

"Yup, good stuff. They're often misunderstood, but I believe that dark beers have more flavor than all those others," Alex shrugged.

"Well, thank you. We learn new things, even when we are 422 years old." Maria looked at Alex, then returned to her other conversation. "I have learned that logic tempers my dreams, but the dreams never stop."

Alex thought about the comment. "That is good, Maria. I suppose it should be a truth for every scientist."

"I have learned some valuable lessons from Uncle Miguel," Maria said reflectively. "I think the foundation of our lives is poured in our youth. What we build comes later, but the structure of our life must be in the shape of that foundation from our youth."

"An insightful point," Alex wanted to hear more, so he curbed his personal responses.

"For example, my mom always taught me that virtue is persecuted by the wicked more than it is loved by the good. Later in life, I was reading *Don Quixote* and realized my mom's words were a line in the book. When I was a teen, and listening to that line from my mom's perspective, I thought she was referring to sex, but now I believe that Uncle Miguel was telling us to do what is right." Maria took a sip of her beer, listening to the silence while wondering how that quote had settled in with Alex and Emily.

"I have a favorite quote from the book," Emily offered.

"You do?" Maria was a bit surprised by the comment. She wondered if any of the cybernetics on Pronimos could make a comment like that. "Please, tell me."

"*Be proud Sancho, of the humbleness of your lineage, and don't be loath to say your lineage comes from peasants*," Emily quoted. "It is something that I think Alex and Megan have been trying to teach me. My lineage is different from Sancho Panza, but the lesson is the same."

"Extraordinary, Emily," Maria wiped the tears that had welled in her eyes. "I should tell you that I did not expect Megan and Mark to succeed in integrating you, but I now realize that you are better than anything we have done on Pronimos."

"Is the virtue quote your favorite line from the book?" Alex asked.

"No, actually, it's not. It's important, but mine is, *everything beautiful attracts love*. That line seems to be spot on today, don't you think?"

"Yes," Alex admitted. "those four words could be analyzed in so many different ways, but I totally agree, everything beautiful does attract love." Alex smiled at Emily, who he had come to love, but avoided Maria's eyes.

"What's yours, Alex?" Maria asked.

"I can't specifically quote a line from the book, but I do remember my high school English teacher telling me to read it," he said. "I remember loving it and watching the movie *The Man of La Mancha*." He paused, his mind drifting back to an important part of his childhood. "There was a song in it that became a part of my foundation."

Maria suddenly started singing in her powerful voice.

To dream the impossible dream.

To fight the unbeatable foe.

To bear the unbearable sorrow,

and to run where the brave dare not go.

She stopped singing when she saw the tears running down his face. "Oh my gosh, that song is about you. It's about where the entire galaxy is right now."

"To reach, the unreachable star…" Alex choked out.

Maria's expression softened. "Enough about me. What about Paula? How did you two meet?"

Alex finished his beer and went to the fridge for a second one. "As great a scientist as she was, Paula needed help with physics at Princeton. I drew the lucky straw and became her tutor. Truth is, I was terrified of her. She was gorgeous and smart, and I was one hundred percent nerd. We became friends, then more than friends. But when she realized I was more devoted to science and engineering than anything else, she broke it off. Paula never settled for coming in second place. We maintained our friendship, but both married other people. Hers lasted a little longer than mine, but both of those marriages eventually ended."

"And then?" Maria pressed.

"Then I saved her from a head-on collision using tachyon technology," Alex said, remembering how complex those calculations had been.

"How'd you do that?" Maria felt she was getting to the root of the current mission.

"I, well we," he glanced at Emily, acknowledging her involvement, "used Tranquility to slow the timeframe. We created a bubble, and I pulled her out of her vehicle as the collision was happening."

"Holy crap," Maria thought about the scientific and engineering implications of what Alex was saying. "Let's leave my engineering questions for another time. Continue the story for now."

Alex grinned. He knew why Maria had been shocked. "After that, I took her to Cassiopeia. It was there, amidst the stars, that we realized we had wasted too much of life and should be together."

Maria listened intently; her gaze soft. "Sounds like quite the story."

"It was," Alex replied. "But like all stories, it's just one chapter in a much larger and far more complex book."

*　　*　　*　　*

Alex and Maria stepped out of the ship into the orange haze of Mars, 66 million years BCE. The air was thin, though breathable with the advanced re-breather technology Alex had brought from Pronimos. Their suites were designed to protect them from background radiation. For Alex, the landscape was alien yet familiar. Ancient red dunes stretched endlessly, dotted with the ruins of the Martian civilization, now all but gone.

Alex opened the hatch to the lab where the last survivor, Andronicus, sat hunched over a glowing console. The room was silent except for the faint hum of machinery. His eyes, once sharp and full of fire, were clouded with age and exhaustion.

Hearing the soft hiss of the opening door, Andronicus turned slowly. His expression shifted from confusion to astonishment as he took in the strangers standing before him. "Who are you?" he rasped, his voice weary but laced with curiosity. His health was failing, and he knew that soon he would fall into a coma with the end following shortly thereafter. The strangers in front of him had to be some trick his mind was playing as he approached the final days of his life.

Alex stepped forward, removing his helmet and offering a reassuring smile. Maria had shown him how to use P-Link to translate from English to Greek. "Andronicus, my name is Alex. I'm from the future. We've come a long way to see you."

Andronicus's eyes narrowed in disbelief. "You know my name, and the future? Why would someone from the future come here?"

"Yes, I have been in this lab, or I should say, I will be in this lab in the future. I have seen the impact you will make, and I wanted to thank you," Alex said simply. "Your work, your sacrifices, they changed everything. Humanity survived and thrived because of what you accomplished here."

Maria stood silently as Alex approached Andronicus, who stared at him, studying his face. In hers, he could see no sign of deceit. "Please explain," Andronicus demanded, his voice firmer but still exhausted.

Alex nodded. "You and your team laid the groundwork for the survival of your Martian civilization. You used tachyon technology to send a group to Earth 66 million years in your future. When that group arrived on Earth, we had little more than a wheel and primitive technology. The place you sent them to is something we call ancient Greece. Your Martian refugees didn't just integrate, they inspired. Greek culture became a beacon for humanity. Science, architecture, mathematics, philosophy, and the arts flourished because of the seeds you planted. Your influence rippled across millennia, shaping the world in ways you could never have imagined."

Andronicus's weathered face softened as the weight of Alex's words settled over him. "So, we didn't fail?" he murmured. "Even if we couldn't save Mars, we helped to create something new?"

"You did," Alex said earnestly. "Humanity, and Earth, owe you more than words can express."

Maria stepped forward, her voice gentle. "You gave humanity a chance to dream and grow. You turned tragedy into hope. That's a legacy few can claim."

Andronicus sat back, his expression a mixture of relief and pride. "Thank you for telling me this," he said, his voice trembling. "I have wondered, hoped, and prayed to know that our efforts weren't in vain, it means everything."

"What can you tell us of Venus?" Alex asked.

"I assume you mean the second planed, which we call Aphrodite?" Andronicus clarified.

"Yes, that is the one I meant." Alex confirmed.

"Aphrodite is, I should say *was,* a paradise. It had vast oceans, diverse life, and humans, virtually identical to us. People from Ares vacationed there. Not many from Aphrodite vacationed on Ares. My wife was full blood Aphrodite, as were two of the crew I sent to Earth," Andronicus paused, remembering things from a tragic past. "The Daklin destroyed our polar magnetic field. On Aphrodite, they accelerated the Moon into the planet, slowing the daily rotation so that Aphrodite would never again be capable of hosting life. Some of the refugees in this lab were Aphrodite, and they asked to be tunneled home, where I am certain they suffered a horrible death. That, I will never understand…"

The room fell silent, the moment heavy with unspoken gratitude. "Rest now. Your mission is complete, and your legacy is eternal."

Andronicus looked up, his eyes lacked any sign of life, "Your own planet, which we called Ge, was a sanctuary. We kept it that way by a legal mandate. We sent drones in to observe, but chose to watch it develop rather than despoil its assets. It too has been forever changed, ravaged." Andronicus choked and stopped.

Maria walked up and put her arm around him. "I'm sorry. I am so sorry."

Andronicus looked up; a small amount of warmth lit in his eyes. It had been years since he had felt human touch. He then suddenly pushed her, jerking back. "I am infected. My disease is contagious!"

For a moment, no one moved. The hum of the machinery seemed to echo in the room. Andronicus glanced at the glowing console before him, his fingers trembling as he reached to press a button and spoke to his computer interface. "There's a cure. I don't have any, but I do have the formula."

"We can make it on my ship and give it to you," Alex offered. In fact, one of the primary things he wanted to accomplish was to learn if what had killed Paula had been something she was exposed to here on Mars.

"No. It's my time," he said softly. "The last vestiges of Ares have ended, and I belong to history now."

Maria took a deep breath and stepped closer to Andronicus. "Your story doesn't have to end here," she said. "It lives on in every breakthrough, every innovation that humanity achieves. We carry your spirit forward."

Andronicus nodded; his expression serene. "Go," he said. "Carry it well."

"But you can live. You can see the future you helped to create, to inspire." She argued.

"No," he said with resolve. "I have been alive for over a thousand Ares years. It has been enough, and you have given me the final thing I needed for peace in the afterlife."

"Okay," Alex said softly. "What can we do for you?"

"Tell me what becomes of the Daklin, and when I pass in a couple days, lay me to rest with my friends in that room," he pointed to the room Alex recognized as where the bodies were, where Paula had likely become infected.

"Your people loved peace, but those who you dispatched to Earth recognized that the Daklin passion for violence and war would win against the lambs. The Greek culture was fierce and unafraid of anything. There is a piece of Greek history where three hundred Greek soldiers fought off a million invaders. That story inspired many, not to violence, but to stopping impossible odds." Alex studied Andronicus who was listening intently. "The Daklin will rule the galaxy for the next 66 million years, Andronicus, but Earth will finally be the place where their evil empire ends. You planted the seeds for that."

Andronicus smiled. "Do you have any wine? I feel this news deserves celebration."

"Well, not exactly wine…" Alex replied.

Maria returned to the ship moments later with three cans of Guinness in hand. They toasted to the dream of Ares, a planet that Alex and Earth would call Mars. Later that day, Andronicus fell into a coma. He wore a peaceful smile for two days until he died.

As they left the lab, Alex glanced back one last time, to make sure they left no trace of their visit. He closed his eyes and saw Andronicus's silhouette etched into his mind. The man had given Earth and humanity so much. Alex was happy he had been able to reach through time and give him the peace he deserved. In a sense, Andronicus was Zeus.

Emily had used Andronicus instructions to create a cure for the Martian virus. She had also tested herself, Steven, Maria, and Alex. None of them tested positive for the disease. Apparently, somewhere along the thousands of years, most humans had developed an immunity. Unfortunately, Paula apparently had not.

"What we accomplished here could be called one of the greatest humanitarian missions of all time," Maria summarized. "What is your plan, Alex?" she asked.

"Cure Paula before she dies," Alex said flatly.

"Alex," Emily spoke in an almost computer tone, "I have run every scenario. In each one, saving Paula results in a victory for the Dakin. In a few, we still destroy the second ship in the tunnel, but the Daklin always get access to tachyon technology, and that gives them a significant advantage."

"What? How do you calculate something like that?" Alex argued.

"It is a chess board, Alex. Every move creates a scenario for the next. There is a destiny between you and Maria that defines the outcome in every single breakdown I have run."

Alex looked at Emily, then Maria. "No. I have a cure, and I am going to bring it to Paula before she dies." Alex turned and walked out of the room.

Maria got up to stop him, but Emily motioned for her to sit.

"It will take us over three weeks in the tunnel before we return to 2029, Maria. I will keep running scenarios to see if I can find one that works. In the meantime, let's see if Alex resolves this with himself."

Over the next two days, Alex kept to himself, brooding and thinking, but mostly brooding. He had the cure for Paula's disease, and he had the ability to intercept and save her before she died. He missed her touch, her voice. He could not imagine his world without her. Still, the logic of Emily's analysis embedded itself in his fiber. If Emily was right, did a couple more years with Paula justify the end of all life on Earth?

Alex went to the galley, grabbed several beers, and returned to his quarters. He put on some of his favorite music, drank all the beer, and considered the situation. He was fighting sleep, staring at the ceiling. The hum of the tunnel was a soothing constant, but his mind was restless, swirling with memories and emotions he couldn't quite place. Eventually, the exhaustion claimed him, and he drifted into a deep sleep.

In his dreams, Alex found himself back on Earth, standing in a sunlit meadow. The air was warm and fragrant, the sky impossibly blue. He turned and saw Paula standing there, her hair glimmering in the sunlight, her smile as radiant as ever.

"Paula," he whispered, his voice thick with emotion.

She stepped closer, hugging him, then kissing him passionately.

"I love you. I've missed you, Paula," he said.

"I know," her gaze soft but resolute. "Alex," she said gently. "It's time for you to let me go."

He reached for her, his fingers brushing hers. "I can't. I have a cure now," he argued. "I don't know how to let you go. I don't know how to fail."

"This is not failure, Alex," her smile was bittersweet. "You defied the laws of physics twice to keep me alive, but your determination to bring me back yet another time is not worth the death of everyone else on Earth. You know that."

Alex shook his head, his heart aching. "You were everything to me."

"And you were everything to me," Paula smiled, her face radiant. "But this isn't about us anymore. It's about what's right. You have to move on, Alex. You have to keep the pieces in place that saved humanity. Most importantly, it is time for you to find something that will heal and cure your sadness."

Tears blurred his vision as he pulled her into his arms. "I can't lose you again."

"You saved me from that head on collision and gave me another life after being crushed by a boulder. You gave me love like I have never felt in this life, and together we created Steven, Zander, and Lyra."

She cupped his face with her warm and familiar touch. "You're not losing me. I'll always be with you, inside you, with the memories we made, in the love we shared. But you need to keep living, dreaming, and building a life for yourself. You have already given me years, and a gift that I shouldn't have had. I am here to now return that gift."

Paula took him onto her embrace and pulled him down to the grass in that perfect meadow. One last time, the two made love. With him inside her, she kept repeating *I love you*, over and over.

At the end of the intimacy, she rested her forehead on his chest, her voice a whisper. "Do what's right, Alex. For me, for humanity, for yourself."

The world around them began fading into a haze of light and warmth. It was a farewell that was both heartbreaking and healing, a final connection that would sustain him in the years ahead. And then she was gone, the meadow dissolved into darkness.

Alex woke with a start, tears streaking his face. The hum, the Paula hum of Tranquility, was steady in the tachyon tunnel, grounding him in the present. He lay there for a long time, the weight of the dream pressing against his chest.

"I'll keep going," he murmured to the empty room. "I'll do what's right."

Alex spent the next two days alone. He was surprised that Emily and Maria left him to himself. He decided to finally join the two as Maria was making a dirty martini for Emily.

"Don't let her corrupt you, Emily," Alex grinned, stepping into the room and pulling an oatmeal stout from the fridge before sitting down next to Maria. "Thanks for your patience."

"It's up to brave hearts, sir, to be patient when things are going badly, as well as happy when they're going well." Maria said.

"*Don Quixote?*" Alex asked.

"Yes," Maria smiled. She wanted to kiss him on the cheek but decided against that. "Welcome back, Alex?" She asked.

"Yes. I am on the road to being back," Alex looked at his beer, then at Emily. "I've lost track of time. How many days before we are home?"

"Eleven days, Alex," she started, then corrected herself. "Actually, eleven days, seven hours, six minutes and thirty-some-odd seconds."

Alex burst into laughter. "That was perfect, Emily."

"Maria," Alex began, setting his glass down. "On the trip out here, I told you some of my story, now it's your turn."

Maria leaned back, a thoughtful smile on her face. "Well, when you live as long as I have, your early years feel like a distant dream. But I'll tell you this much, it's been a journey. I've been married five times, you know."

Emily's eyebrows shot up. "Five times? That's impressive. Or exhausting. Maybe both."

Maria chuckled. "A bit of both, I suppose. In retrospect, I would only say two of those marriages were for love. Of course, I believed all were based on love when they began, but life teaches us. In any case, I've made peace with the mistakes and lost time, chalking it up to life's lessons."

Alex leaned forward, intrigued. "Tell me about the ones that mattered. Who were they?"

Maria's gaze softened as she swirled her drink. "The first was Alejandro. We met during my time on Earth in the 1600s. He was a poet who I met through Uncle Miguel. Alejandro was full of passion and fire. He saw the world differently, in a way that made everything feel alive. We were young, and he was the only person who respected my love of science. We had two kids, raised them, then I got crosswise with the Church. They put me on trial, but Alejandro defended me. He was killed for that defense, but Pronimos extracted me the night before my execution."

"How old were you when you left Earth?" Alex asked.

"I was an old woman, Alex. At least by Earth standards at the time. I was 39, and if I am remembering correctly, life expectancy was in the 40s then."

"What happened when Pronimos pulled you out?"

"I don't remember a lot from that time period. The team that does extractions is really good at smooth transitions for the people we bring to Pronimos. I do remember looking at myself in a mirror for the first time and seeing youth. I remember supercomputers, where I had grown up on books. I think I believed, at least for a while, that perhaps I was in Heaven."

Alex nodded, a look of curiosity on his face. "And the second?"

Maria's smile returned; this time warmer. "The second was when I was in my sixties. I guess about twenty years after arriving on Pronimos. His name was Lior. He was an engineer, brilliant and kind. He challenged me in ways I didn't know I needed. For a time, we built something beautiful together. But life pulled us in different directions. We parted amicably, though the love never really faded. Lior is still alive. He's re-married and has a child."

Emily sipped her martini thoughtfully. "And the others? The mistakes?"

Maria laughed, a light, self-deprecating sound. "I should be careful, since Bernd is one of them. Let's just say they taught me a lot about myself. I was trying to fill a void that couldn't be filled by someone else."

Alex leaned back; his oatmeal stout nearly empty. "Yes, the voids... I think we can fill our own voids, but we create friction when we think others will do it for us."

Maria nodded. "Those are wise words, Alex. I have come to realize that life has a way of surprising you, even after centuries."

Emily smiled. "Well, if there's one thing I've learned from you, the world always has that next promise, that next opportunity."

Maria raised her glass. "To that, Emily. To that."

"Do you suppose," Alex started, "that Alejandro or Lior would have a chapter or two in one of your prior lives? You know, the ones that your mystic friend told you about?"

Maria looked at Alex, trying to determine if he was being sarcastic, or curious. "Maybe Alejandro. As I remember that time period, he felt like a soulmate of sorts. …but I was young then. So very young."

Alex nodded, took a sip, and asked a question he had been curious about, "And me? Do you think I am a soulmate?"

Maria thought about the question but decided to turn it back on Alex. "Do you think Paula was a soulmate?"

"As I understand the term, no," Alex was shaking his head. "No, Paula was not a soulmate, at least not by your definition. I loved her more than anyone I have ever loved, but I never thought I had known her in some other life. She was simply the perfect connection for this one."

"No doubt about that, Alex. Everyone could see it." Maria responded.

Emily was watching the progression of events for the evening. Her processor was playing chess, trying to predict the outcome. She kept coming to the same ending.

"So back to my question," Alex asked again. "Do you think I am *your* soulmate?"

"No Alex, I no longer think that." She paused, looking into his eyes as if there was some hidden memory. She pinched his cheek affectionately, "I know it. You are definitely a soulmate."

"Uh-huh," Alex tried to seem skeptical, but wasn't sure he was believable in that role. "How about we do this; let's put some music on and listen to Maria Perez sing. What do you think?"

Three nights later, Alex woke up in the middle of the night, his mind racing. He thought about Andronicus, EtaKatz, the Daklin Empire, and his team—his family—who were now on a mission to return the galaxy to freedom. A smile crossed his face as he remembered Paula.

Something inside was compelling him to go join Maria in her quarters, but he decided to resist the urge. Instead, he focused on analyzing what could be driving that compulsion.

The following morning, Alex was sipping on a cup of coffee when Maria walked in.

"Earth coffee?" she asked.

"Only the best," Alex grinned. "Want some?"

"Sure," she sat down, assuming Alex would fix her coffee. "I had the best dream last night."

Alex ground the coffee and packed it into the single cup coffee maker, then pressed the button to brew. "You gonna tell me about it?"

"Nope," she smiled mischievously. "Just wanted you to know I had a great dream."

Alex set the coffee mug down in front of her. "Well, maybe I had the same dream, Maria, but I ain't telling you about mine either."

They both laughed, enjoyed the morning while watching Emily play with Steven.

*   *   *   *

After twenty-four days in tachyon space, Alex, Emily, and Maria felt the familiar pull of reality as their ship emerged from the tachyon tunnel. A view of Earth popped up on the primary monitor, its blue surface reflecting the light of the sun in the vast emptiness of space.

"Home," Alex smiled, peering out the viewport. "A few months ago, I had a vision of this gem in space being totally destroyed. It's so good..."

"Alex," she began softly, gazing at the image of Earth, but thinking and coaxing the right words from the silence, "I have a huge responsibility, and I can't shake it: I need to return to Pronimos. The problems of the galaxy are now being resolved there, and I need to go back."

"I understand, Maria," he replied, his voice calm yet resolute. "But Earth calls to me in ways I can't ignore. I feel like I need to be there, to help shape what comes next."

Their conversation carried the weight of divergent dreams, a testament to the crossroads at which they stood. Somehow, they were caught between the magnetic pull of home and the siren call of a galaxy that needed help ending Daklin rule.

Before they could resolve the tension in their differing desires, Emily stepped in, hand in hand with young Steven. His curious eyes taking in the world with unrestrained wonder.

"Good morning, you two," Emily said, guiding Steven carefully to his place in the gally for play. The child's gaze, wide and full of unspoken questions, brought a hush over the room. In his innocent presence, the hard edges of their conflicting ambitions softened into something resembling hope.

Alex's eyes lingered on Steven as he smiled. "Look at him," he murmured. "He's already a curious explorer, isn't he? Maybe his wonder can remind us that the future isn't about choosing one dream over another."

Maria smiled, the tension in her shoulders easing. "Maybe it's not about choosing at all," she said quietly. "Perhaps it's about finding a way to weave both our worlds together. Joining the technology of Pronimos and the endless possibilities on Earth."

Alex thought about her words, *weaving both our worlds together*, finally setting his coffee mug aside. "Maybe our journey isn't about one destination or the other."

Emily, who had been monitoring the ship's systems, suddenly stiffened. "We're not alone," she said, eyes narrowing at the readings. "There's a ship approaching us."

A sleek, luminous vessel hovered near Earth's orbit; unlike anything they had ever seen. Its design was elegant, with smooth curves and a faint iridescence that shimmered against the darkness of space.

A transmission crackled through their P-link. "My name is Polonius, and I represent an official delegation from the Andromeda Galaxy. I am here to request an immediate meeting with Alex Durant, Maria Perez, and Emily."

The three exchanged glances, stunned into silence.

After a few moments, Maria smiled with a sparkle in her eye while shaking her head. "Just when I thought the adventure was ending."

"Wow, it's 2.5 *million* light years to Andromeda. That is a long, long distance, so this must be epochal," Alex emphasized as he punched intercept coordinates in his control panel. "Maria, it looks like this adventure is continuing after all!"

"Alex," Emily started as she studied the data on her screen. "Something's wrong with the electromagnetic signatures in this timeline."

Alex glanced up at Emily as he docked in the Andromeda ship landing bay. "What do you mean, Emily?"

"This is Earth, but it is not the Earth that we left," Emily responded as the bay door closed behind Tranquility, sealing them in the Andromeda vessel.

Thanks for reading

**Please take one minute to
write a review on Amazon**

Watch for the next exciting book in the
Tachyon Tunnel series…

Coming soon!

Other books by Michael Gorton

1. USSA, political thriller written in 1994
2. Lex Talionis, political thriller and sequel to USSA, written in 1998
3. Born Again American, inspirational book, written in 2011
4. Forefathers & Founding Fathers, written in 2016 is a historical fiction from the beginning of colonial America taking place in the early 1600s. This book became a #1 best seller and won several literary awards. Brown Books republished the book in 2017
5. Broken Handoff, business book, written with co-authors Seth Gordon and Darien George. The book became the #1 M&A book of 2019
6. Digital Medical Home, written in 2022 with co-author Jay Sanders, MD. The book won awards, and became a #1 best seller. It tells the history of the telemedicine industry.
7. Tachyon Tunnel 1, written in 2023 is a science fiction that won awards and became #1 bestseller.
8. Calamistunity, written in 2023 is a business book that teaches how to turn calamity and mistakes into opportunity.
9. Tachyon Tunnel 2, The Daklin Empire. Science fiction sequel to Tachyon Tunnel.

Author's Notes

Mars
Humanity has always had a fascination with Mars. While that fascination goes back to the dawn of mankind, since the beginning of the space age we have sent 68 missions to the planet!

During my teen years, and well into adulthood, I held the dream of being on the first human expedition to the red planet. I recognize that the aspirations of continuing the Apollo missions beyond the Moon died in government bureaucracy and funding priorities. Now, thanks to Elon Musk, a human mission will likely occur in the next 5 years. A part of me believes that when we finally send people there, we will find traces of an ancient civilization. Some of that belief is reflected in this book

Plasma
I did my graduate work in physics, building a computer model of the magnetosphere and how it is shaped by the solar wind. Back then, plasma was just the 4th state of matter. Plasma is what shapes the magnetosphere, it is lightning, and it is the Aurora Borealis. Robert Temple's 2021 book *A New Science of Heaven* introduced a new perspective. Temple explores the concept of plasma physics as a potential key to understanding consciousness, intelligence, and even the nature of the universe. He suggests that complex plasma structures, such as those found in space and possibly in Earth's atmosphere, could have self-organizing properties that resemble cognition or sentience. The concept of consciousness in plasma brings a much larger idea to the forefront. Organic life is fragile and short lived. Plasma is much more tenacious and therefore could exist as a living entity for billions of years.

Characters
All of the characters in this book are creations of this author's imagination. While it is true that some situations and personalities or credentials are loosely based on people I know, most characters are a variation of my personal perspective.

www.ingramcontent.com/pod-product-compliance
Lightning Source LLC
Chambersburg PA
CBHW071345300726
48976CB00006B/1770